Praise for Charles de Lint's previous work:

"A brilliant imagination . . . de Lint takes you where you've never been before."

—Ottawa Magazine

"One of the most original fantasy writers currently working."

—Booklist

"A rare ability to awaken in the reader a sense of knowledge and wonder."

*—R*A*V*E Reviews*

"A masterful portrayer of the supernatural . . . knows his folklore inside and out. Writers this good don't come along that often."

—Fantasy Review

"He shows that, far from being escapism, contemporary fantasy literature can be the deep mythic literature of our time."

—The Magazine of Fantasy & Science Fiction

Tor books by Charles de Lint

Dreams Underfoot
The Fair at Emain Macha
Into the Green
The Little Country
Moonheart
Spiritwalk
Svaha

SVAHA

Cover art by Sam Rakeland

A Tor Book
Published by Tom Doherty Associates, Inc.
175 Fifth Avenue
New York, N.Y. 10010

Tor® is a registered trademark of Tom Doherty Associates, Inc.

ISBN: 0-812-53409-3

First Tor edition: November 1994

Printed in the United States of America

0 9 8 7 6 5 4 3 2 1

this one's for Ron Nance
(Sam says hi)

Acknowledgments

I'd like to thank the following for the loan of their expertise and their enthusiasm (hastening to add that any mistakes are my own): Lynn (Moonwolf) Bedrock, Charles R. Saunders, Midori Snyder, Rodger Turner, and, as always (because the books would be so much less without her input), my wife, MaryAnn.

svaha—Amerindian; the time between seeing the lightning and hearing the thunder; a waiting for promises to be fulfilled

All men should strive to learn before they die
What they are running from, and to, and why.
—James Thurber

He who is sleeping,
the Spirit, I bring him,
a kinsman.
—*Medé* song fragment

The last time the Indian Nations rode to war, their warriors were dressed in the suits of lawyers. They took the war to the World Court and this time they won, reclaiming vast tracts of the old tribal lands. When they withdrew into those Enclaves, they sealed themselves away from the Outer Lands with technologies none had imagined they possessed.

This time the Nations would not allow the treaties to be broken.

—From the foreword of *A History of the Native Enclaves* by Satomi Ko (Shigaku Publishing Discs, 2094)

One

~ 1 ~

Rattle and drum.

It was beautiful music. Deer hoof rattles and cedar-shelled water drums. The clatter of bird quills against the skins of the hoop band drums. Speaking to the *animiki*, the grandfather thunders. The voices of the People raised in song.

"Midewewigun, n'gaganoodumaugonaun," they sang. The drums speak for us.

In the clear night skies, the *animiki* rumbled. Giwitawei-dang, the scout thunder that goes all around the sky. Andjibnes, the renewer of power.

"Mino-dae aeshowishinaung," the People sang. *"Tchi mino-inaudiziwinaungaen."* Fill our spirits with good; up-right then may be our lives.

The underpinning rhythm of the drums spoke to the feet of the dancers, to the shaking rattles in their hands, the stamping of their heels. A Parting Dance. Alone in the center, one man sat, his water drum speaking under the palms of his hands.

"N'midewewigunim, manitouwiyauwih," he sang. Upon my drum bestow the mystery.

"K'neekaunissinaun, ani-maudjauh," the People replied. Our brother, he is leaving.

Not to walk the Path of Souls, but to walk in the Outer Lands.

"K'neekaunissinaun, zunugut ae-nummook." Our brother, difficult is the road.

Alone he drummed by the post of a living green tree that had been cut and then erected in the center of the glade. A great fire burned beside it.

"K'neekaunissinaun, kego binuh-kummeekaen," the People sang. Our brother, do not stumble.

They sang to him, of the path he would take, as though he had died, as though he would never return during this turn of the world's wheel. In some ways, it was true, for to walk the Outer Lands meant one could not return, whether one lived or one died. To the tribe, it would be as though he died. So they sang to him and let their drums speak to the thunders, asking the grandfathers to bestow their medicine on him to give him strength on his journey.

He acknowledged the gift. *"Kikinowautchi-beedaudae,"* he sang. It shall be written.

Then he set his water drum aside and rose to dance. He offered his hand to the oldest of the women present. Maudji-Geezhigquae—Moving Sky Woman. His uncle's mother. In conducting her to the dance, through the joining of the hands of young and old, he sought to gain endurance from her long life. It was also the hand of man espousing that of woman, the giver of life.

Other women then rose and danced. Old men joined, followed finally by the very young. The water drums continued to speak. The *animiki* replied. The bird quills on the hoop band drums and the rattles in the hands of the dancers added a high counterpoint rhythm.

Now they represented a *madjimadzuin*, a moving line, an earthly Milky Way connecting those who have gone before with those who follow. The old singers often told of the

Milky Way stars that rode the skies at night, how they were a part of an enormous bucket-handle that held the earth in place. If ever it broke, the world would come to an end. So it was with the chain of *madjimadzuin*. When it broke, a clan ended.

The People danced that *madjimadzuin* now to assure their departing brother that the tribe would continue, that it would hold a place for him. They would meet again in the west, across the river that separates Epanggishimuk, the Land of Souls, from the world of the living. They would meet again in that spirit realm joined only to this world by *meekun-naug*, the Path of Souls.

He would be reborn from Epanggishimuk, into the tribe once more. The *madjimadzuin* would remain unbroken.

Later he stood in the Lodge of Medicine with a *medé* of his totem, Manitouwaub—Sees Like a Spirit. The *medés*' computers hummed around them, but no other sound carried in the broad room. He glanced at the wall mural depicting Negik—the otter totem, first patron of the Medewewin. The bright primary colours of the mural relaxed the tension in his shoulders. He let his gaze travel left from Negik to where his own totem gazed back at him from a corner of the mural, Makinak—the turtle. He inclined his head slightly, then bore his knapsack from the Lodge, Manitouwaub walking at his side, neither of them speaking as they travelled to the borders of the Enclave. There they were met by their chief, Zhawano-Geezhig—Blue Sky.

The borders of the Enclave rose misty before them, an opaque gaseous wall that stood as high as the eye could see, and higher. It had no true physical shape as might be measured by the eye, yet it was a more effective wall than any other barrier yet devised by men, in or out of the Enclaves. Manitouwaub took his spirit pipe from his bandolier and the three men shared its sacred smoke.

"Saemauh waussaeyaukaugae," Zhawano-Geezhig said to him. Tobacco will clear the cloud.

He nodded, understanding. Even in the Outer World, the *manitou* would be with him.

Manitouwaub gave him the pipe which he stowed away in his knapsack.

"Tci-manaudjimikooyaun, n'd'aupinumoon," he said to the *medé.* I am honoured to receive your gift.

Manitouwaub spoke no word, merely embraced him. All words between them had been spoken before. The time for instruction had passed. Now was a time for ritual only, to evoke the sacred medicine of the *manitou* for his task.

He turned then. An engineer appeared at his elbow to show him the way through the barrier—a door-shaped greyness that appeared in the opaque mists, controlled by a miniaturized instrument that the engineer held in his hand. Just as he was passing through, he heard Zhawano-Geezhig say softly, *"Auzhigo n'waubumauh gawissaet."* Already I see him fall. Then he was through the barrier, stepping from the clean night air of the Enclave of the People into the poisoned world of the Outer Lands.

Later still, he stood on the roof of a deserted tenement building, looking not at the endless sprawl of the Toronto-Quebec Corridor that ran for a hundred klicks like a river of broken buildings and streets from the southwest to the northeast, nor at the smog-yellow skies that hid the stars and bright light of the moon above him, but back along the path he had taken, back to where the pale mist of the Enclave's borders rose ghostlike at the edge of the corridor where the northward march of the ruined structures ended.

I will remember, he thought. Though I never return, I will remember.

He was Gahzee Animiki-Waewidum of the Turtle totem whose home had once been the Anishnabeg/Huron Enclave of Kawarthas—Place of Bright Waters and Happy Lands. No matter where he fared, or what the people of these Outer Lands did to him, that could never be taken away.

In the days to come, memory might comfort. But not now. What was lost was still too fresh. Loneliness cut too deeply. The reality of the Outer Lands was too intense, all around him.

Thunder sounded in the distance. Bodreudang, the approaching thunder. A storm was coming. Not the clean rain of the Enclave, but the acid rain of the Outer Lands. Still it was good to hear one of the grandfathers in this place, good to know that *manitou* still walked its hills and valleys where only the ruins of buildings and the buckling concrete of forgotten streets grew now.

Suddenly he smiled, then threw back his head and laughed. He was still Gahzee Animiki-Waewidum—Swift Speaks With Thunder. No longer simply a *medé* of the People, but their *animkwan* now as well. A dog-scout for his tribe in the Outer Lands. He could go forth doleful, with his head hanging, like a wolf with its tail between its legs, or he could go as one of the People, cheerful in adversity, accepting the challenge for what it was.

"*Inaendaugwut,*" he murmured. It is permitted, meaning that while events were caused by forces outside of a man, the exercise of personal talents and prerogatives were predicted by a man himself. This was not exile into which he fared. Rather the *manitou* had steered him into an opportunity to grow in spirit and in accordance with the world.

Shouldering his pack, he made his way back down the treacherous steps of the building's inner stairwell and began his journey, heading northeast along the TOPQ Corridor. When the rains finally came, he ducked into the shelter of a nearby building, miles distant from where he had first heard the thunder. Legs crossed, he sat in its doorway and watched the acidic rains hiss and splatter on the stones outside the door.

~ 2 ~

Kaoru Okabe watched as her partner packed a small travelling kitbag and shook her head. That was Lisa, always taking everything to extremes.

"Lighten up," she said, leaning back on their lumpy futon which was folded up to make a couch. She played with the channel control on her com-link's vid as she spoke, switching bands, looking for something worth watching. "What's the worst he's gonna do? Dock you a few credits? For that you're hitting the street?"

Lisa Bone shot her a quick hard look, then resumed her packing. In the light of their lamp—scavenged from a dump months ago, its solar batteries already fading three hours after nightfall—her eyes gleamed like pale blue sapphires, lids painted with a rainbow design. Her black hair was cropped ragged and short, held away from a gamine's angular hollow-cheeked face with a length of grey and orange checkered cloth. Standing out starkly against her pale skin—red as cut strawberries on brow, cheeks, and chin—were the dark messenger stripe tattoos that saw her safely through the no-man's-land of the squats.

"Adder told me to get it back, or it'd be got back," she said as she carefully folded an antique T-shirt and placed it in her kit. It was a gift from her grandmother, made of genuine cotton and worth a small fortune. "Out of my skin," she added.

"Adder's just making you sweat. If the chinas nabbed the package, what can you do? It's not like he's got no insurance."

Lisa looked up again, the fear plain in her eyes. She started to speak, then shook her head.

Kaoru sat up with an abrupt motion. The silver bells braided in her black hair—which marked her as a fiberdisc dealer as surely as Lisa's tattooed stripes told the world she was a messenger—jingled sharply.

"Lisa," she said slowly. "What aren't you telling me?"

"You don't want to know," Lisa replied.

"Screw that. We're partners and—"

"Our partnership's dissolved, Kay. If I were you, I'd start packing. I told you, someone's going to be here looking for me, real soon now. If I'm not here, they just might settle for you."

Kaoru crossed the floor and caught Lisa's arm. "*What* aren't you telling me?" she repeated.

"Goro-san," Lisa said, her voice toneless. "Turns out the package was his. Adder says Goro wants to know, if the chinas jumped me, then how come I'm still living? He thinks I sold it to one of the tongs, or stashed it to sell later."

Under its mulatto shade, Kaoru's face went white. "Goro-san," she repeated dully.

The name hung in the stale air around them. Shigehero Goro was the *oyabun* of the local yakuza's Goro Clan.

Their squat was on the third floor of a deserted warehouse, just within sight of the tall gleaming spires of Trenton Megaplex. In the Plex the citizens had as much light as they wanted; patrolled streets, real apartments with data infeeds, positions with one of the Kaisha, the corporations that ran the Plex. In the squats outside the Plex's towers, the chinas and rats scrabbled for a living, relying on bootlegged vid links or mainlining fiberdiscs for their entertainment. They were marginals, hoping to buy into citizenship; barred from the towers, but forced to squat on their doorsteps, looking for handouts and slagwork—anything to turn a credit.

The Kaisha had their own security, but inside and outside the Plex the real powers were the warring tongs and triads, and the yakuza of Shigehero Goro. Close-knit organizations that no sane person would cross.

"You . . . you could sell yourself to him," Kaoru said when she finally found her voice. "Put in a little geisha time in one of his meat bars. . . ."

Lisa shook her head. Sure it was a way to get into the Plex, but it was a dead end. All it cost you was your soul.

"He's not having any part of me," she said.

She went around to her various stashes in the squat, retrieving her small store of possessions. Hard credits, because Goro would have killed her Bankcard by now. A plastic Steeljack fléchette auto-pistol, still encoded to the dead security drone that she'd stolen it from, complete with three spare clips of its small fléchettes. Plastic-wrapped concentrated food bars. A two-month supply of vaccine tablets. Another pill container, this one filled with water-purifying tablets.

"Where will you go?" Kaoru asked.

"I dunno. Up the Corridor—maybe to Kings."

"That's more than a hundred and fifty klicks. You're never going to make it on foot."

Lisa was all too aware of the dead lands that lay between the two Plexes. Klick upon endless klicks of abandoned city blocks—the badlands of the Corridor that separated the Plexes. And when you thought of what inhabited those wastes . . .

"I don't have any choice."

She closed up her kitbag and swung it to her back. It was heavy. One week out beyond the squats she was going to wish it was twice as heavy because she was going to need every bit of what was in there and more. She looked around the squat. It wasn't much, but it was better than most had. A lamp and a heater, both outdated, but the solar batteries still sucked up enough juice to run them a few hours into the night. A few plastic-coated pictures on the wall. Her favorite was the one of Jammy Jim, heartthrob of the rats once, faded now from popularity, but still the one vidjammer she'd take into her bed. The futon she and Kaoru shared. Some pillows. Not much, but it was more than she was going to have in the days to come. And Kaoru . . .

"Come with me," she said. "When they show up here . . ."

Kaoru shook her head. "I can't. It's suicide. You ever hear of anybody surviving the hike? I've seen rats go out with twice your equipment and—"

"The only reason we don't hear about them is because they made it and they didn't bother to send a transmission back."

"Lisa—"

"I met a guy in the Market just last week who hiked up from the Osh Plex."

"I can't, Lisa."

"I can't stay."

"What's he going to do?" Kaoru tried again. "It's not like—"

"I'm *desperate*," Lisa said and left it at that.

She picked up her personal com and hooked it to her belt. Like every messenger, she'd immediately torn out the chips that would let Adder use it to pinpoint her position in the squats, replacing them with bootlegged ones that let her catch OTA casts—over the air broadcasts from the Plex's entertainment channels. Once she was out of the squats, it'd be useless as a com-link—too far for Adder's range—but she'd still be able to pick up the OTA casts for twenty klicks or better.

Shrugging into her jacket—a synthetic leather number with a built-in hood specially designed to withstand the acidic rains—she turned to Kaoru, looking for something to say. You didn't just throw away ten months of a partnership without saying something, but her mind was empty and all she could visualize was Goro's yaks—

The metal firedoor leading from their squat out into the third floor of the warehouse reverberated with a sudden pounding. They both stared at the grey metal. Kaoru took a step towards it.

"Kay, don't."

"It's too late," Kaoru said. "Don't you see that now, Lisa? We can't get away."

She went to the door and worked free the metal holding bar just as a new thunder of pounding shook it. When she stepped back, the door was flung open and she was facing three of Shigehero Goro's augmented yakuza. Some yakuza had exoskeletons to heighten their already finely tuned reflexes and musculature; most had been genetically tailored from birth or had internal implants.

These three were clean-shaven, dressed in long grey kevlar overcoats and grey bodysuits. She could almost feel the hot breath of the dragons tattooed on their backs. The black plastic of automatic Steeljacks filled their hands.

"Are you Lisa Bone?" the foremost asked. He spoke in the patois of the squats—a mixture of French, English, and Asian languages—but on his lips the patois held a clipped accent.

Kaoru shook her head numbly. "N-no . . ." she said and turned to where Lisa was standing, but the room was bare.

Lisa was gone. The ragged flap of tuiron cloth at the window was still moving. She'd left through the window. Down the fire escape. Was there another yak waiting for her down there? Kaoru wondered.

"Where can we find her?" she was asked as she turned back to the intruders.

"I . . . I don't know . . ."

The foremost yak regarded her steadily. His metallic eyes unnerved her—although she knew they were just infrared contacts that allowed him to see in the dark. She wanted to blink, pull her gaze away, but couldn't move. When he finally looked away, releasing her gaze, she let out a breath she hadn't been aware of holding. Then the Steeljack in his hand spat and there was a hole in her stomach, the small fléchette exploding. . . .

She reached out a hand towards the yaks, but they were no longer concerned with her. As she dropped to her knees, they stepped past her and began to tear apart the squat. The burning pain in her stomach spread. She held a hand to the wound, drew it away, and stared at her own blood with an uncomprehending expression.

I . . . I should have . . . run with you . . . Lisa . . . she thought as she fell face forward and the last of her life fled.

There were two yaks waiting in the alley behind the warehouse when Lisa crawled out the window onto the fire escape, but she hadn't been planning on going down anyway. The fire escape was too obvious. A born paranoid, she had yet another escape route prepared. She went up onto the roof, moving cat-quick, charged with adrenaline and fear.

When she reached the lip of the roof, she hauled herself up, then peered back down into the alley. No alarm. The yaks were still standing down there, one leaning up against the side of the other building behind the warehouse, eyeing its back door, his partner standing beside their black and chrome Usaijin three-wheelers, speaking into a com-link. The sound of the scooters rose up to the roof, a whisper-soft sound as their Stirling engines idled. Crawling back from the edge, Lisa rose lightly to her feet and ran across the roof.

If she'd been clever, she would have had her stolen Steeljack encoded to herself long ago. With the smart circuits in its handgrip adjusted to her palm, she wouldn't be facing Goro's men empty-handed. If she'd been really clever, she would have done that and been carrying the Steeljack when making her last delivery. The chinas would have thought twice about jumping her then.

The chinas.

She wasn't even that sure that they'd been genuine. Her messengers' stripes should have given her safe passage through their territory—the chinas needed messengers too. No, someone had known what was in that package—how much it meant to Goro, perhaps, or its actual value—and thought the risk worth taking. That meant inside information. Something the chinas wouldn't have. But one of the tongs might.

Not the triads—they were almost respectable now, still as racially pure as Goro's yakuza, and unlikely to start a new war. But the tongs . . . they had evolved into a mix of various Asiatic peoples whose one goal was to take down the triads and yakuza, replacing them with their own organizations. One of their groups could have hired the chinas. Easily.

She'd been through it all before, ever since she'd been set upon, the package stolen. Thinking about it just gave her a headache—the center of pain emanating from the blue-black bruise on her temple where she'd been hit when she was knocked down and her satchel snatched. It was time to stop thinking about it. Even if she figured it all out, there was nothing she could do about it. A rat didn't go waltzing into the headquarters of one of the tongs, demanding recompense. Didn't go crying to anyone. Who'd listen?

As she neared the far side of the roof, she speeded up and launched herself across the ten-foot gap between the buildings. The old futon she'd salvaged and dragged up to the other roof broke the force of her fall, though it left her a little breathless. No time for weakness. Not with yaks on her ass. On her feet, she set off again, across another roof, another gap between buildings, another rotting futon breaking her fall.

This roof had a door leading down into its darkened interior. She took the steps in the stairwell two at a time, hand trailing along the rusted banister for balance. She was almost blind in the dark, but she'd run this escape route more than once. Just for practice. A born paranoid all right.

When she reached the ground floor, she eschewed the front and back doors, making her exit through a side window, runners greased, window sliding open silently. Out of the building, she stood absolutely still, listening, testing the air for sound, watching for movement, every sense alert.

Stars and moon were something one only saw on the vids; the smoggy skies were too thick with carbon particles to let their light cut through the night's shadows. But there was a dull glow coming off the towers of the Plex. Enough to see by. The streets appeared empty. Nothing in sight. Nothing stirring. No sixth sense prescient *feel* of being watched.

Too bad she didn't have her own wheels—the salvaged twelve-speed she used on deliveries belonged to Adder and she only had the use of it. Rats didn't own much. If they did, they'd be living in the Plex.

She gave it a few more moments, then sped for the far side of the street where she vanished, swallowed by the shadows of the squats.

It was time to find the Ragman.

~ 3 ~

Phillip Yip stared at his desktop display, an irritated frown creasing his smooth almond skin.

He was a small compact man who ignored the current trend towards snug bodysuits in favour of baggy rose tuiron trousers and a grey shirt. A plastic ID badge was affixed to the right breast of his shirt by a velcro tab. Its digitally encoded information bar contained his retina, voice, and palm prints, as well as pertinent personal information. His name and rank appeared above the bar in standard script and ideographs. Above that was a photo of a smiling neatly attired security officer in his dark green Ho Anzen uniform that bore little resemblance to the picture Yip presented at the moment—slouched in his chair, clothing rumpled, dark eyes darker still with a combination of frustration and anger.

Leaning forward, he overrode the voice-activating mechanism of his system by working the keyboard. Fingers tapping the keys, he called up the data a second time, hoping for a mistake, but the program dove into the laser-based information storage system and enthusiastically filled the screen with the same data, cursor smugly pulsing at the end of the body of print.

"Don't you ever get tired of that manual keyboard?"

Yip looked up to see Huan Som smiling in the doorway to his cubicle. His partner was nattily dressed in a pale blue bodysuit and a new dark jacket, the latter hiding some of the overweight shape that his bodysuit merely accentuated. His black hair was cut within a quarter-inch of his pate, round face beaming under its receding hairline. They'd been partners for close to five years now. In the mostly Nipponjin security firm, the few Sino and Indochinese usually worked together, in and out of the office complex.

"I get tired of voices yapping constantly in my ear," Yip replied. "Even my own."

Huan shook his head. "You just can't stand to sit idle when you could be moving—even if it's just your fingers."

Yip shrugged. There was no gain in denying the truth.

"Are you ready to go?" Huan added as he came into the cubicle.

Their shift had been over for fifteen minutes. Huan had tickets for the first theatrical showing of Shinoda's *Angry Love*, based on Gaho Ota's best-selling litdisc of the same title. It was a multigenerational romance set in Chinese Mongolia during the Food Riots of 2053. Apparently the period costumes were superb. It started at twenty-one hundred, which left them just enough time for a relaxing dinner before the show. But only if they left now.

Yip sighed, glancing back at the screen. Huan wasn't going to like this any more than he did, though not necessarily for the same reasons.

There was just enough space in the small box of a room for Yip's desk and two chairs. Huan removed a foodbar wrapper from the empty chair and tossed it into the mouth of the disposal unit on the wall beside the desk. Settling down in the chair, he carefully adjusted the folds of his new jacket. Up close, it proved to be an intricate weave of blue and purple threads. A Bijin design, Yip realized. Worth about three days' salary.

Huan caught him looking at the jacket and grinned. "If I didn't need to wrap this elegant body in only the best," he said, fingering the silk-smooth material, "I could afford to get married."

"Who'd put up with you?"

"You do."

"My fiber's too coarse."

Laughing, Huan shook his head. "You're married to your job, that's the problem. What are you working on now?"

Yip's gaze went to the screen, then back to his partner. "How do we arrest a computer?" he asked.

Huan's eyebrows arched quizzically.

"It's an old DMC in Sector Five. Its energy-conserving

circuits got fouled up and it decided that the best way to save a few credits would be to ice up a couple of floors."

Huan went pale. Most of the old Decision-Making Computers had been replaced by Artifical Intelligence systems, both for convenience and for situations just like this. The older the DMCs got, the less they could sustain their work loads. There'd been a few small problems before, most of which were still in litigation as no one would take responsibility for the errors. The Kaisha running the sectors placed the blame on the Megaplex, since the Megaplex controlled maintenance; the Megaplex argued that since the DMCs were in the various Kaisha's holdings, the responsibility was theirs. It was an old argument, made worse in the present situation due to the data Yip had coaxed from records storage.

"Casualties?" Huan asked.

"We got off lucky. It was during an off-shift, so there were just skeleton crews working. Fifty-five bodies. Plus three crashed systems, with all records irretrievably lost."

"Lucky?" Huan's tone spoke volumes.

Yip nodded. "If they'd been on-shift, we'd be talking in the neighbourhood of five hundred dead."

"*Chiksho!*" Huan breathed. The curse lingered between them, then Huan asked, "Whose systems crashed?"

"This is where it gets worse. One was Combank, an affiliate of Ininzi/Bell Northern. Imagine what that's going to do for IBN's honour, on top of last week's hearings."

Ininzi/Bell Northern and its affiliates made up the major corporation in the Trenton Megaplex—a conglomerate that squeaked by with 52.1 percent of the Megaplex's holdings. Charges of system crashings had recently been leveled against them, backed with enough hard evidence to go into litigation. Bringing them to court were Shiken Sciences and Exxon Technics, with 9.3 and 17.6 percent in Megaplex holdings respectively.

Last week, the hearings saw an IBN manager testifying that he'd been ordered by his board to investigate the viability of crashing Exxon's systems, thereby allowing IBN to pick up Exxon's biochip laboratories at rock bottom prices. Hotly denied by IBN's lawyers, who subsequently proved that the witness had enough of a grudge against the company to make up any story, it still wasn't enough for IBN to regain its current lost face. Today's disaster, when picked up by the media, could be all too easily construed as IBN's attempt to show that they were the victims of system crashing as well.

"I can't imagine the Megaplex without IBN in control," Huan said. "If this gets out . . ."

Yip nodded grimly. "The other two systems belonged to Guwa Publishing and Fax Vid—both of which are listed as sub-companies of Shiken."

"I don't follow . . ."

"It gets worse. Although they're a part of the Shiken group, their main shareholder is Oitsuku Holdings, which is apparently owned by one Fumiko Hirose."

Understanding dawned on Huan. "The Goro clan's lawyer. So it's the tongs that are to blame, not IBN."

"The tongs or the triads. They both want what Goro's rumoured to have—Enclave Technology."

Huan nodded. "A priceless commodity."

It had been whispered for weeks that Goro had acquired a disabled Enclave flyer and was now beginning to bring the technology into the yakuza-owned tech labs. Because his own people were being so closely watched, he was moving it through the squats, using non-citizen messengers unaffiliated with any underworld connections. The first shipment was due to be moved any day. It might already have been shipped and be in the Megaplex at this moment.

"There's nothing we can do about the Claver technology," Yip said, "but when IBN discovers Shiken's connection with the yaks . . ."

"It'll mean war," Huan said. He wiped his sweating brow with the back of his hand. "Not just skirmishes, but an all-out war."

"And the decision we have to make is, do we speak to

our own supervisors, or do we go directly to IBN and try to forestall it?"

"Go to IBN . . . Have you gone mad? Takahata will have our hides."

Yip sighed. Tomiji Takahata, the owner of Ho Anzen Securities, was not known for his leniency, that was true. But there was more at stake here than corporate loyalty.

"Think for a moment, Som," he said. "Who will Takahata side with? IBN, already partially in disgrace and riddled with *gaijin*, or the yakuza who are at least Nipponjin?"

"Goro is a criminal!"

"But he is Nipponjin."

"He . . ." Huan met Yip's steady gaze and rubbed his temples. "It's too confusing."

Yip nodded. "I work for Takahata," he said, "but my loyalty lies with the Megaplex. And you?"

"This makes my head hurt," Huan said.

"Where do you stand, Som?"

"Why bother asking? With you, of course. What do we do?"

Yip stared at the screen. "If this information becomes unsecured, IBN will have no other choice but to attack Goro—it's that or lose even more face. But if we can keep it secure, they might listen to reason."

"A war will serve no one," Huan said. "Surely they will see the sanity in that?"

"When," Yip asked tiredly, "has sanity ever mattered in a situation like this?"

Yip's fingers moved on the keyboard and his system dutifully erased all the pertinent data it had stored. But that data still existed in the master storage, there for anyone to call up as would be done all too soon—by the media as well as other investigators.

"There is another solution," he added. "We can try talking to Goro, or at least his lawyer. There might still be time for them to erase their connection with Oitsuku Holdings."

"Now I know you're mad," Huan said.

Two

~1~

Gahzee roasted the rabbit that had been caught in the snare he'd set the night before. He sat on his haunches in front of the small, almost smokeless fire, his back to the wall of a deserted workers' barracks, and studied the surrounding terrain while he waited. When the rabbit was cooked, he ate it slowly, then buried his fire and the rabbit skin. The bones and guts he left on the cracked stoop of the barracks for the scavengers.

Two days into the Corridor, he'd spied more wildlife than he'd expected. Gulls and crows. Rabbits, squirrels, mice, and rats. The only large life-forms were the coyotes he spotted from time to time, solitary grey shapes that kept their distance. One had been following him for the past day and he'd taken to thinking of it by the name of the great uncle *manitou* Nanabozho. A trickster.

Like the tribes, the coyote had used its natural wiles to survive all the changes since the white men first came. The coyote people had suffered at the hands of the whites as the tribes had, their numbers decimated, simply because they didn't fit into the whites' false views of the structured order of the world. But they hadn't suffered the reservations and broken treaties, the lies and the false hope found in a whiskey bottle. They hadn't known the despair that made so many young braves see no other solution to the emptiness of their lives except suicide.

It took playing the white man's game, using his own strengths against him, for the tribes to finally win back their respect, their lands, their harmony with the *manitou*, their rightful place as the guardians of Mother Earth. Playing the white man's game, but remembering the medicines of the People.

A sweat lodge vision changed everything.

It came to Daniel Hollow Horn, the Lakota musician whose *madjimadzuin* led in an unbroken line back to John Hollow Horn, who had performed a medicine sun dance at Manderson in 1929 in defiance of the Indian agency, pierced his skin and performed the dance for the sake of the sacred lands of the Black Hills. After the love affair North America held with the musics of England, Jamaica, then Africa, in the early 1990s the music industry finally turned to that of America's own Native Peoples for the source of a new sound, and Daniel Hollow Horn was there.

In a time of megahits and superstars, Hollow Horn's music surpassed the sales of any previous artist in the history of the industry. It was rock 'n' roll, it was tribal medicine music, it was a new sound that was imitated but never reproduced with the same fevered intensity that took Hollow Horn straight to the top of the charts. At one time he had an unprecedented five CD singles in *Billboard*'s top twenty at the same time, including the number one and number three spots. Hit followed hit, the money rolled in, and he used it to breathe life into his vision.

He sent young men and women of the People to the white man's universities, a few at first, then in ever-increasing numbers, as the phenomenon of Native rock continued in quantum leaps and bounds, his financial worth skyrocketing with it. What began with only reluctant support from the tribal elders of the various Nations, was soon embraced wholeheartedly as the results began to appear.

By the late 1990s, the first science graduates were working in laboratories funded by Hollow Horn, seeking to make real the physical aspects of the Lakota's sweat lodge vision. Native lawyers took their grievances to World Courts that had been set up to mediate the madness in South America, the Middle East, and Indochina. While the world powers continued their puppet wars and blustering, the Native Nations were taking back their own.

When New York and Los Angeles were destroyed by terrorist warheads, the tribes had won back their lands and the first barriers were raised, forming the Lakota Enclave in the Black Hills and the Navajo/Hopi Enclave in the American Southwest. By the time Europe was suffering the chaos of the Food Riots, while the United States and Russia had fallen in a limited nuclear exchange, the Japanese claimed Canada, and the Chinese much of Russia and the States, there were twelve Enclaves in North America, two in South America, two in Australia, one in Africa, and the Soyot Enclave in Siberia. And the tribes had their first two space stations in orbit with skyhooks connecting them to the Lakota and Haida Enclaves. A decade later they added a third space station, connected by skyhook to the Wadi Enclave in Australia.

The tribes withdrew completely from the Outer Lands. Radiation and the escalating greenhouse effect were unable to penetrate the Enclave barriers. The west coast of the United States and Florida were under water. The southwestern deserts and Canadian prairies had become jungles. The massive TOPQ Corridor—overgrown brainchild of the Japanese that vied only with a similar industrial complex in China—had fallen from producing fully one-half of the world's technological needs to be a deserted warren of abandoned factory complexes, warehouses, living quarters, and commercial properties hundreds of kilometers long. Only a handful of Megaplexes survived.

Though they could do nothing to prevent the nations of the world from killing themselves and the land, the tribes could still wait. Wait for the time when they could cleanse all of Mother Earth. They had learned patience. They had finally won their first battle after a century and a half of poverty and a constant undermining of their self-esteem. They could wait a little longer. In their Enclaves, safe from the madness of the Outer Lands, each with its monument to their greatest hero, Daniel Hollow Horn, they could wait forever.

When the sun rose, it was only a brighter smudge behind the overhanging build-up of carbon dioxide that choked the sky. The silence was vast, disturbed twice a day by the rumble of the subway, speeding between the Megaplexes in its underground vacuum tunnels with a sound like the voices of the grandfather thunders. Gahzee could already feel a tightening in his chest from the unclean air, despite the immunity boosters he had taken before he left the Enclave.

How do they live in this world they made? he asked himself as he continued through the TOPQ ruins. With no songbirds, only scavengers. No rich greens of meadow grass and forest, only these sickly growths that played at being tree and shrub. Save for Nanabozho and his coyote brothers, no deer or other large mammals, only rodents and bugs.

How do they live? He would find out. For having left the Enclave, there was no return for him. No tribe now, save the tribe he made for himself.

"Hey, Nanabozho!" he called to the coyote who was still trailing him, hoping for more handouts. He could tell it was the same one by its odd eye colouring—the right one was brown, the other a steely blue-grey. *"Ni'tckiwe Myeengun."* Wolf's brother. "Shall we be a tribe—you and I?"

The coyote ducked away behind some rubble at the sound of his voice. Gahzee laughed quietly. Run and be wise, he thought. You've learned that much in these dead lands. But you'll be back. We'll be friends, you and I, before this journey is done. A tribe of two.

And that night, Nanabozho did return. Gahzee was working on the longbow that would be his primary weapon in the Outer Lands, for the Enclave allowed none of its technology beyond its barriers except for the biochip com-link implanted behind his left ear—the one physical thread still connecting him with what he had left behind. The coyote wolfed down the offering of meat that Gahzee had put out for him, well away from the small campfire but still in its light, then lay down and watched Gahzee work on his bow.

"I could have brought a bow," Gahzee said conversationally, smiling as the coyote's ears pricked up at the sound of his voice, "but I knew there'd be many nights when my hands would be looking for work. And what of my arrows, you ask? See? I have fletches and tips that need only the straight shafts that I've yet to find. Have you seen such wood in this place, brother?"

The coyote was still there when Gahzee rolled himself in his blanket to sleep, and though he was gone in the morning, he rejoined the *medé* in time for a noon handout which Gahzee laid on a stone a few yards closer than the food had been the night before.

"A tribe of two," Gahzee said softly.

His fingers itched to touch the thick grey pelt, but he forbore any movement until they were both done with their meals and it was time to travel once more.

~ 2 ~

The doorman at the Ch'ing-jen Fan eyed Lisa's striped messenger tattoos and slowly shook his head as she approached.

"Nobody's got nothing to send, little sister. Better take a hike, *tung ma*?"

Lisa understood. He was a big, pureblood white with long yellow hair and grey-blue eyes, and he liked to think that what he was doing meant something, even if it was just watching the door of a rat's nest like the Ch'ing-jen Fan. His bare chest was overhung with cheap medallions—the centerpiece being a dried ear that he'd supposedly cut off a yak—but full of machismo though he might be, it still wouldn't be that smart to argue with the antique shotgun lying across his knees. What was an antique in the Plex, was a source of power in the squats.

"The Ragman," she said, adding in Mandarin, *"Wo hen hsiang chien t'a."* I want to see him.

"You got a name?" he asked, also switching from patois.

Lisa flipped him a hard credit.

The doorman caught it easily. He let the smooth coin run up and down his knuckles with a practiced motion, then made it disappear into a pocket of his vest. *"Ch'ien Hsiao-chieh, ma?"* he asked. Little Miss Credit, eh?

Come on, asshole, Lisa thought, but she hid her impatience behind masked features and merely shrugged.

He held her gaze until she broke eye contact, then grinned. "Go ahead," he told her, waving her through.

"Hsieh-hsieh," Lisa said with a quick bob of her head. Thanks. I'd like to see you eat my shit, she added to herself as she stepped by him.

She hated kowtowing to assholes who let the smallest taste of power turn them into tin gods. But this was a tong bar, the Ragman had an office in back, and he'd be gambling in here for hours. If she wanted to get hold of him and be on her way before dawn, she didn't really have a whole lot of choice.

The Ch'ing-jen Fan was a squats equivalent of a yak meat bar in the Plex. All it took to get in was hard credits, and you'd better be prepared to leave some behind unless you had some real strongarms in tow, or the kind of luck that operated beyond the tables, because the tongs didn't like to see their money leaving.

This time of night, the place was packed, the air thick with clouds of opiate and Tabaccanin smoke. There were chinas and tongs at the long gambling tables playing *mah-jong* and *pachinko*. A dim vid flickered in one corner, pumping out a bootlegged Plex channel. Tinny music blared from the speakers that had nothing to do with the movie on the vid, where a couple of leather boys were beating on a mulatto made up to look like an Enclave *dojin no*, complete with red body armour and a feathered war bonnet. On a small dance floor a few couples were going through the motions, grinding their hips against each other, a flickering solar lantern strobing over their slow moving bodies.

Along one wall was a long narrow bench where wireheads were popping fiberdiscs into their temple-noded interfaces. Tarted-up geishas, male and female, were serving drinks. They looked more like they'd stepped out of a porn vid than a yak meat bar in their shimmery bodysilvers that left their breasts and genitalia bare. The silvery tinkle of disc dealers' bells cut across the music as she stepped into the room, but she motioned the sudden approaching crowd of them away. One of them spat on the floor at her feet, but she was already turning to the tables, looking for the Ragman. He wasn't hard to spot.

There was only one Ragman in the squats. He was sitting with some chinas and a fat mulatto, his midnight black skin gleaming in the flickering lights from the dance floor. The sides of his head were shaven, but he had a mohawk swatch of knotty dreadlocks that ran down the center of his skull, falling to either side of his head and down to the small of his back like fat brown snakes. When he looked up, sensing Lisa's gaze on him, he flashed her a white-toothed grin that was so broad it seemed to split his face.

"Business or pleasure, darling?" he called out to her.

"Business."

The Ragman gave the other players a shrug. "Sorry, girls. Duty calls and all that shit, *ma*?"

When one of the chinas started to protest, the Ragman's strongarm pushed himself away from the wall where he'd been standing and stood behind the Ragman, his arms folded across his massive chest, his gaze nailing the china to his seat. The Ragman had found J.D. wandering out past the squats, out of his head and repeating over and over again, "Jah's dead, mon, Jah's dead," whereupon the Ragman christened him J.D. and took him in. The only voice the big strongarm would listen to was that of the man who'd pulled him up from the gutters and given him a sense of place in the world again.

"Let's go into my office," the Ragman said, ushering Lisa towards the back of the bar where various rooms were for hire. J.D. followed like an enormous shadow, loosed from its moorings to come floating across the room behind them.

"I hate to lose you, darling," the Ragman said.

His office was a wizard's nest of electric, solar, and computer equipment, a hedge of wires and machinery that took up one entire wall of shelves and spilled out across a worktable, the Ragman's desk, and all over the floor. The Ragman sat behind his desk, his face flickering in the light from the screen of his tabletop console screen. Lisa perched across from him on the edge of a crate that was padded with a cushion. After closing the door behind them, J.D. had taken up his usual stance against it, arms crossed across his chest. Lisa could almost feel the weight of his gaze on her back.

"I've got no choice," Lisa said. "I've gotta run, or my ass is grass."

"There's always a choice."

Lisa shook her head. "You don't understand. Goro's yaks are already out gunning for me. And *don't* talk to me about his meat bars, because—"

"I'd never insult your intelligence, darling. Your good sense sometimes, but never your natural smarts."

"Gimme a break."

The Ragman smiled. "I know you too well, Lisa. I've been keeping an eye on you. You're a cut above the usual rat. You take time to find things out. You're interested in what's going on—and not just in the squats. There's places for people like you."

"Sure. Lying on the street with a yak boot up my butt. Look, I know you like me. The feeling's mutual, okay? But time's running out. All I need from you right now's a couple of maps and—" She started to reach for her pack, but thought better of it when J.D. shifted behind her. She straightened in her seat. "I've got a Steeljack in there that I need encoded."

The Ragman's eyebrows lifted.

"I can pay."

"I don't doubt you, darling." he said. "I just want you to listen to an idea I've had. Can you spare a poor old man just a few more minutes of your time?"

"Old man?"

To laugh, Lisa thought. The Ragman might look around sixty, but he could out-think, out-drink, out-talk, out-gamble, and plain out-do anyone she knew. The only thing he couldn't be was out-pushed. Or out-waited. So if he had something he wanted to say . . .

"Sure," she said with a sigh. "Fire away."

"The Jones Co-Op is always looking for talent," he told her.

Lisa shook her head. "Oh, no. The toms feed on us rats—or didn't you ever notice?"

"That's Plex prop talking in you—crap you picked up off the vids."

"I don't call Black Bobby choking on bricks propaganda," Lisa replied.

Black Bobby had been a junkwalker—a rat who made his living salvaging out beyond the squats. He'd been found two nights ago with a brick stuffed down his throat and the mark of the toms slashed onto his forehead.

"Black Bobby was screwing around," the Ragman said. "Selling shit to the yaks that they had no business knowing."

Lisa regarded him in a new light. While nobody knew exactly who made up the Jones Co-Op, what everyone did know was that they were buying up Plex shares, infiltrating the Kaisha with their own people. Supposedly, they had a revolution brewing—a planned overthrow of the Plex—but their biggest impact in the squats was on the black market where they sold Plex goods to eager consumers who didn't have a hope in hell of buying themselves citizenship, but still wanted a taste of the good life. They also liked to squash rats.

"You're in with them, aren't you?" she said finally.

The Ragman nodded.

"So what's the deal? How come you're always beating on your own people? I mean, you're not called toms 'cause you're such pussycats. It's 'cause you feed on rats."

"I told you—it's Plex prop, that's all. When their leather boys go hunting fun in the squats, we're the ones that take the fall."

"So what do you do? Are you really trying to take down the Plex?"

The Ragman shook his head. "We just want to even things out a bit, that's all. We're like a virus, darling, running through their security, crashing a system here, freeing up some tech for the squats there. Guerrilla tactics."

"Yeah, I always took you for a monkey man."

It was easier to make light of what he was telling her, than to think about what it meant. Because now that she knew, who was to say she could even walk out of this room in one piece without signing up? Why, she wondered, did the shit just get deeper every time she took another step?

"I don't need this," she told him. "Look, help me out with the Steeljack and maps, I'll give you my credits, and then I'm outta here. Long gone. All you'll see is my heels."

The Ragman shook his head. "No threats, darling. If you don't want to sign up, you're free to walk. I trust you to keep your mouth shut."

Lisa thought about J.D.'s bulk, guarding the door behind her. Yeah. Sure. Except this *was* the Ragman, and he'd never put it to her before.

"Why now?" she asked. "Why'd you wait until now to try to recruit me?"

"I told you—I like you, darling. I didn't want you in over your head, except now you've done yourself the favour all on your own. See, this gig could turn sour anytime. We've got the Kaisha on our ass. We've got the triads, the tongs, the yaks . . ."

Lisa laughed. "So what's the bad news?"

The Ragman's features settled into a serious expression. "Word is the package you lost was a chip of Claver data, darling. Think about that shit in Goro's hands. Now think about the Kaisha getting their mitts on it."

"Claver . . ."

The *dojin no* of the Enclaves were supposed to live in utopian splendor behind their barriers. They had tracts of unspoiled land. Clear skies. Skyhooks linking them to orbiting space stations. If the Kaisha got hold of that technology . . .

"They'd cut us right off," she said slowly.

"I told you you weren't stupid. The Jones Co-Op wants that technology, darling. For everyone."

"But what can *I* do to help? I'm just—"

"You saw the chinas that made the snatch. If you can finger them, we can make them talk."

"You're forgetting something real important here," Lisa said. "I'm the one who the yaks want to skin for losing that package. I can't go *anywhere* in the squats without getting my butt shot off."

"No problem. We can suit you up as a swagger girl, darling—mask, ID, all the gear."

The leather boys and swagger girls were kids from the Plex who came slumming in the squats, looking for thrills. The only reason most of them survived to go back to the Plex when their day's fun was over was that if they didn't, the Plex sent out its rent-a-cop drones to stomp rat butts until the rats finally got it through their heads: don't mess with the Plex babies.

With a swagger girl mask and the other gear, Lisa could go anywhere, never mind her striped messenger's tattoos. They'd be hidden under the mask.

"Real ID?"

"True blue, darling. Coded right into the Plex. We'll set you up with a Bankcard, even give you a squat in the Plex if you want."

Wait'll I tell Kay, Lisa thought.

"Time's wasting, darling."

"I'm thinking, I'm thinking."

Though where was the decision, really? Hitting the dead lands, with a fifty-fifty chance of getting burned out or jumped by some mutant freak before she reached the squats of the next Plex, or taking up the highlife? Lisa Bone, spy. Just like Facedancer on the vids. And then she thought of the Ch'ing-jen Fan's doorman—of swaggering up to him, giving him a whack with a buzz-stick maybe, and watching him jump when its small charge goosed him.

"Who's the macho man on the door tonight?" she asked.

The Ragman rolled his eyes. "Night man—guy named McKenna. Donnybrook only works days now."

Lisa'd had a thing going with Donnybrook until she finally got tired of muscles masquerading as brains. But she still liked him.

"Do I get a strongarm?" she asked.

"Anything, darling—but just remember, the highlife only lasts until we run those chinas down. Then it's on to other kinds of work. No free rides with the toms. Are you in?"

"You'll keep the yaks off my back?"

"They're not even going to know you're still alive."

Lisa grinned then and reached a hand across the clutter of the Ragman's desk.

"I'm in," she said.

~ 3 ~

Fumiko Hirose's secretary might look like one of Goro's augmented yaks squeezed into a beige bodysuit a size or two too small, but Hirose . . . Yip stood just inside her office and gazed appreciatively at her as the door hissed shut behind him.

She was the Dragon Lady herself—direct from Maki Nakayama's last action vid. Red geisha stockings hugged the long legs under a slitted dress of black synthsilk. Her shoulders were bare, pale against a dark fall of long hair that was so black it almost seemed to swallow light. Her features were classic—small perfect lips, almond-shaped eyes, high cheekbones.

"Will you have a seat," she asked after a few moments, "or should I send Otsu back in with a camera?"

"*Gomenasai,*" Yip said. Your pardon.

"Please sit."

Yip remained where he stood. "Your secretary—Otsu? —he has access to a scanner?"

Hirose frowned and glanced at the screen set into her disc. "Phillip Yip," she read. "Sino/Nipponjin. Thirty-four years old. Single. Life resident. Officer of Ho Anzen Securities who hold the principal security franchise of Trenton Megaplex. Combank account number 773-52-9. Current balance, 2534.06 credits." She glanced up. "Shall I go on?"

"*Iie, dozo*. Somehow I fail to see—"

"The point? We don't need to have you scanned. We know exactly who you are, *neh*? That you are unarmed. That you carry no live com-link. Even that you . . ." She glanced back at the screen. "Yes. That this visit has not been recorded with your superiors."

"Palm print reader in the outer door?" Yip asked. He'd been curious about the manually operated entrance. When Hirose nodded, he added, "And scanners in the outer room?"

Again Hirose nodded. "I might add, the *oyabun* has no interest in liaisons with your firm, official or unofficial."

Of course, Yip thought. Goro would already have informers in place—as many as he required and each of them undoubtedly much higher up in rank than Yip.

"That's not why I'm here," he said.

"Then perhaps you should explain, *neh*? Please, have a seat."

She leaned back in her own chair, steepling her fingers as she studied him. Through her plastiglass desk, Yip could see the hem riding high on her red-stockinged thigh. She noticed the direction of his gaze and smiled, but made no motion to pull the hem down.

"O-sake wa?" she asked when he was seated, offering him a drink.

"Iie, gomenasai. I would have preferred to speak directly with Goro—for this concerns him—but I must admit that your company is infinitely more pleasing on the eye."

When she smiled again, a moment of warmth touched her cool gaze. "This is refreshing," she said. "A security officer with charm. Are you an exception to the norm, or are they finally giving officers some lessons in social manners?"

Her smile kept the sting from the words.

"I'm off duty," Yip said.

She arched her eyebrows. "Then perhaps we should retire to a restaurant?"

Yip blinked. On the surface, she appeared to be merely flirting, as she did so well for the vid cameras in court while she proceeded to rip her opposition's argument to shreds, but at the same time, she seemed almost serious.

"Regretfully, no," he replied.

"Mata dozo," she said. Another time.

For a long moment she seemed just a woman and he just a man, then Hirose sighed and her business mask slipped across her features.

"Hai," Yip murmured and wondered, what are the chances?

"And you've come today because . . . ?" Hirose asked.

As Yip explained, she watched him from under lidded eyes.

"This is all just speculation, of course," she said when he was done.

"I've wiped the information from my own system," Yip replied, "but it's still there in the public files for anyone to call up. It won't take the media, or a great deal of imagination, to put it together as I already have. The only reason we have any time at all is that the investigation is under my jurisdiction and I can freeze the pertinent system files. But not for long."

Hirose shrugged, not agreeing, but not disagreeing either. "What do you want from me?"

"Drop those companies. Get rid of Goro's connection to them. You're already after IBN in court—who's going to believe that you won't attempt more direct means of attack as well?"

"Bad business."

"*Gomenasai*, but the yakuza have a certain reputation. Surely you can see, that if you don't do something, IBN will have no recourse left but to attack you directly as well?"

"We had nothing to do with the DMC in Sector Five to which you refer."

"It doesn't matter if you did or didn't. It's what IBN will perceive that matters."

"*Hai.*" She leaned forward. "And what do you want out of this, Phillip Yip?"

"Nothing."

Hirose laughed. "I find that unlikely. I can't deny that you have been a help. There are those who would say, why trust a traitor? But I believe you speak the truth and that your advice is sound."

"I am not a traitor," Yip said coldly.

"*Iie?* Would your superiors at Ho Anzen agree with you, do you think?"

"I do this for the good of the Megaplex—which I am honour-bound to protect. If there was to be war between IBN and your people, the whole Megaplex would suffer. In such a case, I put Ho Anzen's contract with the Megaplex above thc company's own concerns."

"So you want nothing? No future consideration?"

Yip rose from his seat. "I have no time for any more of this. Good day, Fumiko Hirose."

Her voice stopped him before he reached the door. "You aren't much of a team player, are you?"

"No," he replied without turning.

"And yet you want nothing for yourself. You do it only for honour—the *giri* that you perceive binding you to the Megaplex as a whole, rather than one corner of it. Some might consider that a surprising and perhaps dangerous attitude for a half-blood."

Yip turned slowly, a flush starting up the back of his neck.

"I mean no insult," Hirose said. Then to diffuse his anger further, she added, "I'm a half-blood myself—my grandmother was Korean."

"Yet you work for the yaks . . . ?"

She shrugged. "I'm as much a Nipponjin as any who claim the blood," she said. "More than most, perhaps. But I don't see the same boundaries between peoples as what you have called 'my people' do, *neh*?"

"And yet Goro retains your services."

"I get results."

Yip smiled. "How could you not? I've yet to meet a sharper wit in such an attractive package."

"*Domo,*" she said. "*Ja mata*. I think I like you."

Yip carried the warmth of her smile all the way across town to his own office. It helped combat the growing sense of disquiet that spread in cold waves from his stomach. For, no matter that it was for the greater good, he had still betrayed his principle employers by going directly to the yaks, rather than taking the matter to the courts as it should have been.

Her smile helped. But not enough.

Dreamtime

The Twisted Hairs were a council of elders, shamans who came from all the tribes to teach the Walk, the path with heart, the path of the wolf. Of all the People, only they travelled without fear through the Outer Lands, entering and leaving the Enclaves at will, for they had such control over their bodies that disease could find no foothold in their flesh. They spoke with the Twenty Count, the *manitou* that Gahzee's tribe knew as Kitche Manitou, the Great Mystery, but who referred to themselves as numerical tones. They were to be found in the center of every Wheel.

In their teachings everything fit on a Wheel. The simplest had fire in the east—the home of the spirit and art; earth in the west—the home of the body and magic; water in the south—home of movement and music; wind in the north—home of the mind and science. On that Wheel, the void lay in the center, a catalyst from which the Twisted Hairs spoke with the voice of the Twenty Count, home of language and math.

Everything fit on a Wheel, and though words changed from tribe to tribe, and names changed, the Wheels never did. On one Medicine Wheel, the Anishnabeg *medé* who bore the name Gahzee Animiki-Waewidum was a Dreamer, placed midway between magic and music, between healing and holding, and the Kachina-hey, the dream teachers, were his mentors.

To speak with them he laid a dreaming crystal under the pillow he made of his jacket. He offered his sacred smoke to the grandfather thunders, then he rolled a spirit bell in the palm of his hand. The bell was a perfect silver sphere, the fairy jingle of its voice speaking to the four quarters, completing another Wheel: Grandfather Sun in the east, crossing the sky to marry Grandmother Moon in the west where they made love. Their first born were the plants in the south who gave the People oxygen and sustenance. Their second born were the animals in the north who realized resonance with all that is.

Smoke and sound. Through them, the will focused its intent.

Lying down, Gahzee interlaced his fingers—his left hand dominant, for his was a warrior's path, that of one who follows his own Walk, rather than that of a soldier who does only what he is told. Shaping a Dreamer's hand sign—his index and little fingers protruding at straight angles from the curved backs of the center fingers—he closed his eyes.

Fire finger, water finger. Through them, and the crystal under his pillowed jacket, the Kachina-hey would speak to him while he dreamed.

The last things he saw, before he closed his own eyes, were the mismatched eyes of Nanabozho who regarded him from where he lay just within the glow of their dying fire. One brown, one blue. It was no surprise to Gahzee that the Kachina-hey who spoke to him that night in the Dreamtime had the same mismatched eyes.

When he woke—

I miss my home, grandfather.

What is it that you miss? Your brothers and sisters? The voice of the land? Or merely your comforts?

I miss it all.

Children pine; a warrior Walks.

The road is hard, grandfather. To have lost all I have known—

Have you changed so much, then? Knowledge fled? Strength turned to water?

Memories prove to have little comfort.

The path with heart is only as difficult as you allow it to be, grandson.

I know. And I will complete it. But what of after?

A warrior's Walk is never done.

I know that, too. But tribeless—

You could learn to twist your hair.

—was all he remembered.

He sat up. What passed for dawn here in the Outer Lands was still hours away. The sky was a dull smudge above him. The fire was dead. They coyote was gone.

Twist my hair? he thought and laughed aloud.

It had only been three nights and two days and already loneliness had him aspiring to wisdoms far beyond his reach. But still. Even a Twisted Hair began as a simple woman or man. Places of wilderness were the testing grounds.

And was there ever such a place that better deserved to be named a wilderness? he asked himself, looking around at the dark bulks of the abandoned buildings that loomed beyond his campsite.

Laughing again, he replaced his dreaming crystal in his *skibdagan*—the soft moosehide medicine bag that hung from his belt by day. Tying its drawstrings tight, he placed it by his jacket and lay down once more. He was asleep in moments, dreaming again, but these were ordinary dreams, as different from the Dreamtime as hearing a tale was from doing the deed.

Three

~1~

Shigehero Goro, the *oyabun* of the Goro Clan, was an enormous man with the physique of a sumo wrestler. In his late fifties, his topknot was still black, as was the small pointed beard on his rounded chin. Fumiko Hirose had never made the mistake others had who had seen him as merely a caricature, an immense clown playing at being a warrior. It was one of the reasons she maintained the respect she did in the male-oriented society of the yakuza.

She watched him now, practicing *kendo* in his dojo with two of his yakuza, straw sandals slapping on the hardwood floor, the dragon tattoo on his back glistening with sweat, the rapid-fire clack of his *shinai* loud in the small room as the two yaks tried to break his defenses with their own split bamboo practice swords. That *kendo*, the way of the sword, had little place in contemporary society where differences were settled in court or on the streets with Steeljacks, meant little to Goro. The training sessions honed his reflexes, physical and mental, and he came from them with his *ki* burning like a cold fire in his eyes.

At that time, Hirose had often thought, any man who did not take Goro seriously was either a brave man or a fool.

She sat on the observers' *zaibaton* near the entrance of the dojo with Goro's second-in-command, Yamamoto Ishimine. *Tatami* mats for meditation, dressing, and bowing in at the beginning of a practice session, ran the lengths of the walls. Ishimine was a small man who wore baggy clothes not as a fashion statement, but to conceal the exoskeleton that augmented his muscles. No daily training for him, but he held his own in the ranks of the yakuza all the same.

"*Sa,*" Goro said when he was finally done. "You have news?"

He looked at Hirose, so she spoke first. "I met with Phillip Yip—did you see it on the monitors?"

"*Hai.*"

"I believe he's telling the truth."

"I still don't trust him, *neh*?"

Hirose shrugged.

"But we will do as he recommended," Goro continued. "*Ja mata,* see that Co-Op terrorists are blamed for the DMC's malfunction. Have Aoki credit this Yip for uncovering the evidence to that effect in the Ho Anzen system and deposit a thousand credits in his Combank account." He raised his brows at the slight frown that touched Hirose's mouth. "Is this a problem?"

"I like him," she said. "And he helped us."

Goro shook his head. "He helped the Megaplex and only incidentally helped us. Do as I've told you and he will be bound to us—in the eyes of the world, even if we can't win him over. But he might prove useful. It took heart to come to us as he did."

"*Hai.*"

"Why don't you see him again?"

It wasn't really a question. Hirose nodded, unable to argue against the cold fire in Goro's eyes. There were times when one could successfully push one's own arguments with him, but this wasn't one of them.

"And you," Goro said, turning to Ishimine.

"The messenger has disappeared," Ishimine said. "Men are searching—for both her and the chinas she claims robbed her—but . . . " He shrugged eloquently. "The squats are what they are. An army could be hiding in there and never be found."

"There *is* an army hiding in there," Goro said. "Co-Op, triads, tongs, chinas, rats—what would you call them if not an army?"

"They have no leader—"

"There you are wrong," Goro said.

It was an old argument. In all the Megaplex it seemed that only Goro was farsighted enough to see exactly what a danger the Co-Op presented. Hirose tended to agree with him.

"I am not pleased," Goro said.

"*Gomenasai,* but we still have the Claver flyer—"

"True. And that chip held everything that was in its computers, *neh*? Without it, we add months, perhaps years, to our work. Time we do not have. Find that girl, Ishimine."

"*Hai.*"

Goro turned back to Hirose. "And cultivate this Phillip Yip, Fumiko. Trouble is coming and we might need a scapegoat. *Ja mata,* the citizens love pinning the blame on their own security officers."

"*Hai,*" she said.

He turned away from them and left by a door on the far side of the dojo which would take him to where an attendant was preparing a steam shower and massage for him. He had dismissed them from his mind, Hirose knew, as surely as though they were already gone. And yet, on an almost cellular level, he would be aware of every move they made until they had left the dojo. A very dangerous man.

"You have only yaks in the field?" she asked Ishimine as they waited for the elevator.

He nodded glumly. "For all the use they're proving to be."

"Why not hire some leather boys to scout around the

squats for you? They can go in places where your yaks would be too obvious, but who'd suspect a leather boy of a complicated thought, little say spying, *neh*?"

Ishimine's face brightened. "*Domo domo,* Fumiko."

She smiled, then stepped into the elevator. When Ishimine joined her, she looked at their reflections in the mirror. Now who is there to tell me how to set Phillip Yip up for the slaughter? she wondered. To set him up and still be able to sleep at night. For she genuinely had liked him. Unfortunately, merely coming into Goro's sphere of influence, he might as well be considered the late Phillip Yip.

With Goro, you were either for him, or you were dead. And she didn't think Yip to be the kind of man to forsake his duty no matter what the threat. In that sense, he and Goro were very much alike, except that Goro's sense of duty wasn't remotely as altruistic as Yip's. Goro's duty was to himself. All else bowed to his will. Sooner or later.

Either that, or it was broken.

~ 2 ~

The collar of Huan Som's tailored bodysuit seemed too tight just now. He sat on the edge of the plush chair and plucked nervously at his jacket while the owner of Ho Anzen Securities and his own section head studied him. The three of them sat in Tomiji Takahata's penthouse in the Tonda District, an opulent *apato* that would take a lifetime of Huan's salary merely to purchase, little say furnish.

Takahata sat at his ease across from Huan, a drink in one hand, half his attention on the porn vid playing in one corner. His kimono, a translucent blue, Huan could only dream of owning. Natural silk, natural dyes. Beside Takahata, Huan's section head looked as out of place in his plain grey bodysuit as Huan felt. But Kimitake Aoki showed no sign of discomfort. He sipped his saki, lean features unreadable.

"And why have you come to us with this information?" Takahata said suddenly.

"P-pardon?"

"What do you want?" Aoki translated.

"Why, nothing, Takahata-san. My loyalty is first to you—to the company. What Phillip does is wrong."

"*Hai,*" Takahata said. "Well, we thank you for your concern, Som. You can go now."

Aoki waited until Huan had fumbled his way out of the penthouse by way of the elevator before laughing.

"You see humour in this?" Takahata asked.

Aoki shrugged. "That one has the soul of a *neijin*," he replied. A toad-eater. A flunky.

"*Hai*. And to think we must give their kind employment."

The Equal Employment Act ensured that no citizen could be denied work, so long as he was qualified and had compatible shares with the company where he sought employment.

"It will change," Aoki said. "*Mata*. Everything does."

"But not always for the better. Imagine Shigehero Goro in control of the Megaplex." Takahata sighed and returned his gaze to the vid. "What do you think of his story?" he added absently.

"It bears looking into. But Yip's a good worker—solid, loyal."

"A company man?"

"A man dedicated to his job."

Takahata looked away from the vid. "That's not necessarily the same thing, *neh?*"

"*Domo*. But a man who would turn in his own partner—how can *he* be trusted?"

"You think he plays a subtler game? Could he have taken the information to Goro himself and is merely sacrificing his partner to keep himself safe? Or has he fabricated the entire thing?"

"*Areya-koreya.*" One thing of another. "It bears investigation. But either way, Huan Som must go. A man who will break one loyalty will break others."

"I don't like the idea of him taking Ho Anzen material with him when he goes. Kokusai would leap at the chance to take our place the next time the franchise comes up for review."

"There are other ways to remove an employee," Aoki said.

Takahata smiled. "See to it, Kimitake."

Aoki remained until Takahata's geisha for that evening arrived. Politely declining his employer's offer to make it a threesome, he found himself a public com-link on the way home. After assuring himself that he had a secure line, he put a call in to Shigehero Goro, his other employer.

Four

~ 1 ~

With the coming of dawn, and the memory of the Dreamtime still moving inside him, Gahzee saw the wastes of the Outer Lands through new eyes. He had come to them from Kawarthas Enclave with loneliness weighing on his heart, seeing their ruined reaches through his new lack of a tribe, through what he had lost. His understanding of them had been coloured by his own past. Now he perceived them for what they were: not simply lands ruined by their present keepers, but also lands abandoned by the People.

If not for the People, all of Mother Earth would wear this shroud. And yet . . . was it proper that any part of her should? Was not the loss of even one small tract of land a cause for shame? Then what of these vast reaches?

"Hey, Nanabozho," he said to the coyote who lay near the dead embers of his campfire.

The coyote regarded him with one eye—the blue eye of the north quarter, the colour of peace.

"What medicines do the *manitou* maintain in this place?" Gahzee asked. "Do they remember the People?"

And if they did, of what did that memory consist? A good thing lost? Or an anger at their abandonment?

The coyote appeared to consider Gahzee's question. A questioning look rode his canine features, but suddenly he stood, both eyes open in the dull morning light, blue and brown, their gaze travelling past the *medé*. For a long moment he held that watchful pose, then he turned and vanished into the rubble.

Gahzee turned slowly, nape hairs prickling. Empty ruins lay spread out before him—the same unrelieved view as enclosed him on all sides. The shells of deserted buildings. The brown vegetation, bled dry of colour. The emptiness. But there was a sense of something else in the air as well. A shift of the wind. A change in the even tempo of the morning air. And then he saw what his new brother had sensed and acted upon. The coyote's genetic makeup kept his reflexes as fine-tuned as a taut bowstring. He survived not so much by standing firm against the current, as flowing with it.

It was too late for Gahzee to follow his brother's example.

Animkwan, was he? Dog-scout for the People in the Outer Lands? The thin smile that touched his lips was self-deprecatory. A child still to earn his name would have been more careful.

The people of the Outer Lands had finally discovered his presence.

First one, then another shuffled from doorways that gaped like ragged maws in the fronts of the buildings. Without Enclave immunity boosters, the elements had ravaged their limbs and features. Their skin was pocked and peeling, with many red and open sores. Some had one leg shorter than the other. Others no legs. Those walked on their arms, weaving back and forth in a rolling forward motion like drunken apes. There was one with a third arm growing from his chest, the limb hanging flacid against the blistered skin. Another with the shriveled remnant of a second head still dangling from its shoulder. Women with patchy bald spots in their dirty hair. Men with bleeding lips and eyes clouded to a milky white. All of them stick-thin, bellies swollen.

Gahzee counted a dozen as he bent and shucked into his jacket. His backpack had been ready for travel. He slung it on with an unwasted motion, judging the slow progress of their approach. If he moved quickly he might still be able to escape without a confrontation, but glancing about, he saw that they were approaching from all sides.

Avoid those who still dwell in the Outer Lands, Manitouwaub had warned him. They listen to voices other than reason.

Now was the time to wish he'd argued longer at the Elder's ruling that no piece of Native technology should leave the Enclave except for the biochip com-link implanted behind his left ear. With just one laser rifle . . . He picked up his unfinished bow, holding it with a two-handed grip.

"Hey," he called softly, then added in their patois which he had studied before leaving the Enclave in preparation for his trip. "What people are you?" It was the closest he could come in their language to asking the first question one of the People asked upon meeting a stranger. *Waenaesh k'dodaem?* What is your totem?

They stopped at the sound of his voice, but made no reply. Perhaps, he thought, his accent was making his words indecipherable.

"Do you have a leader? A spokesman?" he tried, speaking slowly, carefully enunciating every word.

There was new movement in one of the doorways. Shuffling aside, they made way for a young man who walked like an old man. He had a crutch under his left shoulder, his left leg dangling loosely from the knee and dragging in the dust behind him as he came forward. Parts of his scalp hung from his head by tenuous strips of skin. His face was as pocked as mud baked in the sun, red sores set off by blue tattooing. His clear grey eyes were disconcerting, as much for their piercing clarity as for their incongruity in that horror face.

He stopped a half-dozen paces from the *medé*. The others continued their own hesitant approach.

"You are the spokesman of these people?" Gahzee asked. He kept his features calm but he watched for an opening—any opening—to make an escape.

Leaning on his crutch, the man grinned. All around, the others began to bob their heads. The man touched his chest with a closed fist. His shuffling companions pressed closer.

"I am a stranger," Gahzee said. "I did not mean to trespass in your lands."

The leader's eyes grew strange, darkness gathering in their clear depths. He thrust his face towards the *medé*.

"I'll eat your fuckin' heart!" he screamed suddenly.

Gahzee took a quick step back, raising his unfinished bow as a club. Before he could swing it, they were all over him, bearing him to the ground. The stink of their unwashed bodies clogged his nostrils. He shrunk from the contact of their sores against his skin. He fought the press of their clawing hands, but there were simply too many of them.

They tore his pack from his back. They fought each other over its contents. Over the jacket they ripped free. Over the moccasins they pulled from his feet. They bound him with the strips of his own pack and left him lying in the dirt, bruised and choking on dust, while they continued to jabber and argue over his gear. Through their melee, their leader dragged himself closer until he stood over Gahzee. He leaned on his crutch, wheezing heavily.

"Didn't think you fuckers really existed," he said when he finally caught his breath. "But I seen the vids—I know what you Clavers look like. Out looking for blood, was you? Counting coup—that whatcha call it? Didn't think a bunch a' poor fucks like us'd be any problem, didja?"

"I came in—" Gahzee choked on the word "peace" as the man spat in his face.

"You came to fuck us over, Claver—plain and simple. But we gotcha now. You just think about what we're gonna do with you. We'll get us a big fire goin' an roast you good. Get that healthy meat in us. It's gonna clear up a lot of pain.

Medicine you call it—right? The shit that's in you that keeps you clean. Well, it's gonna medicine up a bunch a' poor fucks, Claver. You just think on that."

Gahzee fought the bonds that held him, but whatever else these people knew, they could tie a knot that held. He laid back in the dust to conserve his strength then, his head turned to watch as the leader sent his shuffling people out to gather wood.

There is no death for the People, the Elders taught. Only a change of worlds.

Gahzee understood and believed that. He just hadn't expected it to come so soon.

~ 2 ~

It was like being a whole new person, Lisa thought, when she first admired the effect of the swagger girl gear in a mirror.

The white Kabuki-like mask effectively hid her striped messenger's tattoos, leaving only the sapphire blue of her eyes showing through the eyeslits. Built into the lower part of the mask was a miniature air filter and a speaker grid which gave her voice a slightly mechanical rasp. The purity of the air bothered her at first—the antiseptic taste burning a little in her throat—but she soon got used to it.

The baggy red synthesized leather jacket effectively hid the bulge of the newly encoded Steeljack under her arm, while fitting snug at her waist. Tight black pants of the same material hugged her legs and butt, with the short metallic buzz-stick poking up out of a rear pocket. The yellow boots, steel-toed and flaring at the ankles, were the latest swash style, while the headdress of spiked black feathers added just the right finishing touch.

"I don't take orders real well," she told the Ragman when he tried to dissuade her from showing off the gear to Kaoru. "But don't worry. Donnybrook'll take real good care of me and we'll be hitting those china bars just as soon as Kay gets an eyeful. I promise."

It wasn't until she was out on the streets with Donnybrook in tow that she realized just how effective the get-up was. She'd see people she knew and they never looked twice at her—or if they did, it was just to sneer at the swagger girl, out slumming with a strongarm to keep the big bad rats at bay. But her initial pleasure wore off quickly as the hostile stares continued, block after block. She began to just feel weird behind the mask, breathing the purified air while everyone she passed was sucking back the squat stink.

She passed more than one old rat, holed up in a doorway, wheezing for breath, skin getting splotchy and pocked. Too poor to afford vaccine tablets, they had to make do the best they could. It made her think twice about the toms' purported goal with their Jones Co-Op. A little bit of everything for everybody. It didn't seem quite so altruistic anymore. Not when you thought about it. It was more, why the hell hadn't something been done a long time ago, *before* things got this bad?

She had a tense moment when two yaks passed them on their black and chrome Usaijin scooters, but neither gave the pair of them more than a cursory glance.

"Why aren't you walking up here with me?" she asked Donnybrook when the yaks were gone, "instead of trailing along behind like some Plex drone playing bodyguard?"

"I just like to watch your ass in those leathers, babe."

"This gig's strictly business," she told him, but she was secretly pleased.

She gave a considering look over her shoulder, knowing that all he could see was her expressionless swagger girl mask, brows and lips painted, the rest a blank white. Another good thing about the mask, she thought. Nobody could read what went on behind it.

"Well, you know me," Donnybrook said as he fell into step beside her. "I always like to mix business with pleasure." Then he started to sing softly, "Out on the streets, up in her squat; Lisa Lizard, gets me hot. Nobody knows the pleasure I've known, when Lisa Lizard gives me the Bone."

He was wearing a tight brown bodysuit with a Kevlar vest overtop. Flexing the biceps of one brawny arm, he gave her a sideways glance and a broad wink, a big grin on his face. This time her mask hid a blush. Though he looked like a bodybuilder, Donnybrook was a frustrated vidjammer and was forever holding forth with some godawful verse. But bad though his songs were, he still hadn't given up on getting her back, and Lisa couldn't help liking it just a bit. Not that she'd ever let him know, though.

"Yuk, yuk," she said.

"Hey, you're the one that wanted me up here walking with you," Donnybrook said. "A real swagger girl'd have her strongarm either carrying her around on his shoulders, or tagging along behind—everybody knows that much, Lisa."

She shook her head. "Not Lisa—remember? It's Maki Ota now." And she had the ID and Combank card to prove it, though she hadn't tested either yet. But coming as they did from the Ragman, she wasn't worried. The man had connections.

"Maki Ota, come let's grope-a," Donnybrook said with a laugh.

"Gimme a break."

They continued their bantering up the street until they got close to Lisa and Kaoru's squat. Then both fell silent. The deserted warehouse appeared no different than it ever did, but Lisa still sensed some change in the air. Maybe coming back here hadn't been such a good idea.

"I hope Kay's all right," she murmured.

"I don't see any yaks," Donnybrook said. "They probably split as soon as they found out you weren't around."

"Yeah, but what if they—"

Donnybrook laid a finger against the painted lips of her mask. "You're always thinking too much. Let's just go find out—slow and easy."

The hairs at the nape of Lisa's neck prickled all the way

across the street, but by the time they reached the front door and hadn't been challenged, her pulse was almost back to normal.

"Wait'll she sees this gear," Lisa said, leading the way up the stairs. "She's just gonna die."

And then they were standing in the doorway of her squat, looking down at Kaoru's corpse, and the words Lisa had spoken on the stairs came back to lie in her mouth like cold ashes. Donnybrook took one look at the body, then he was moving into the room, Steeljack in hand. He covered the room with a broad sweep of the weapon, checking every possible hiding place with practiced ease, before he turned back to Lisa.

She was kneeling on the floor beside Kaoru, cradling the dead girl's head in her arms. Behind her mask, her eyes swam with tears.

"Why . . . why did you stay . . . ?" she said, her voice choking with grief.

Donnybrook crouched beside her. Reaching out, he closed Kaoru's eyes. "We've got to go," he said softly.

The masked face turned to him. "Why . . . did they do it?"

"We can't stay here, Lisa. If we don't get—"

He broke off, gaze swinging to the window where Lisa had made her escape. A sixth sense had his gun hand lifting, the Steeljack already spitting fléchettes before the yak was all the way in the window. The yak's augmented muscles brought him in with a blur of motion, but Donnybrook got lucky. His first two shots skidded off the kevlar overcoat. When the third was deflected as well, it went straight up the yak's chest and took off the side of his head. After the speed of his entrance, the yak's body seemed to fall in slow motion, collapsing on the floor with a dull wet thump.

Donnybrook grabbed Lisa's shoulder. "We're out of here," he said, trying to pull her to her feet.

Behind the mask, Lisa swallowed thickly. The brief moment of violence had barely registered. She resisted Donnybrook's grip with a strength that surprised the both of them.

"I'm not leaving her here."

"Lisa, we've got no time to—"

"I'm *not*!"

The blue eyes that glared at him from the mask's eyeslits were cold now, grief pushed back. Donnybrook started to protest, then sighed. He put away his Steeljack and hoisted the corpse in his arms.

"Get your 'jack out," he told her. "First thing that moves, don't fuck around—just shoot it."

He led the way back down the stairs.

The yak had been alone—a rearguard left behind in the unlikely event that Lisa really was stupid enough to return to her squat. They took his Usaijin—Lisa on back, arms around Donnybrook's waist, the corpse balanced on the alcohol tank in front of him—and drove out past the squats into the badlands where they laid Kaoru's body out on the floor of a long-abandoned building and covered it with stones.

They were both sweating heavily by the time the skies dulled into morning, but Lisa wouldn't stop until they'd raised the cairn four feet high. Then she knelt beside it and rested her head on the cold stones, finally letting herself go. She wept alone against the stones while Donnybrook stood awkwardly in the doorway of the building, scanning their surroundings, all too aware of her sorrow but not knowing what he could do to ease it. Some things just cut too deep.

It was a long time before Lisa came to stand beside him in the doorway.

"You going to be okay?" he asked softly.

"No."

He turned from the view outside to look at her. Her eyes were swollen and rimmed almost as red as her tattoos, shoulders sagging, swagger girl mask and feather headdress dangling from one limp hand, the headdress's feathers dragging on the floor. But the hard look had returned to her eyes.

"You're not thinking of doing something crazy," he said, "like taking on the yaks all by yourself?"

She shook her head. "That's a no-win situation."

"Then what are you thinking?"

She put on the mask, straightened it, then tied the headdress in place. She couldn't do anything about the yaks. But the Jones Co-Op might be able to, once they got enough clout. So she'd back the toms all the way and make sure she was riding high in their ranks when the time came that there *was* something she could do.

"Let's go look for those chinas," she said.

When Donnybrook went out to start the Usaijin, she turned to give the cairn a last look. It was one thing taking off into the badlands on her own, knowing that Kaoru was alive and going about her business in the Trenton squats. But knowing she was dead, that she couldn't ever come back and be with her again . . .

And it was her fault. If she hadn't lost that package to the chinas. If she hadn't ducked out the window when the yaks came calling.

Only what would that have served? They'd just both be lying dead in their squat and everything else'd just go on.

"I'm gonna miss you, Kay," she said softly.

Now the mask hid her grief as she went out to join Donnybrook on the stolen yak scooter.

~ 3 ~

It was not shaping up to be a good morning, Yip thought.

After leaving Goro's lawyer, he'd taken the Okuda Line to Sector Five to oversee the shutdown of the problem DMC, then remained on hand while technicians worked until dawn to integrate one of Jiszuki Inc.'s new AIs with the old system. He still had to return later this morning for the final systems check when he would affix the Ho Anzen security seal to the new design.

All night, while he stood around watching the techs work,

he'd tried to keep thoughts of Goro's lawyer at bay, but with little success. Fumiko Hirose's classic features and her impossibly long legs made a constant intrusion. He knew that her simple flirting was only a part of her operating style—he'd seen her work the court prosecutors and judges often enough to be aware of that. Yet like every other male who was on the receiving end of her charm, he couldn't help but think that with him it might be different.

He kept wanting to call her, knowing all the time that he'd just be making a fool of himself. Only what if she really *did* feel something for him?

She's a Dragon Lady, his reason argued with him. Geisha-trained, for all her degrees. Working for Goro, she could be nothing else. Making him desire her, raising the possibility of a liaison between them that would never come about . . . that was what she did best.

Punchy from lack of sleep, he sat in his office cubicle trying not to think of her. It was easier this morning, for there were other things on his mind. His partner was late—not an unusual occurrence with Huan, but he was later than normal today. And then there was the morning news he'd called up on his desktop display.

"EVIDENCE OF CO-OP TERRORISTS DISCOVERED IN SEC-5 DISASTER," the headline screamed. And there, in the body of the report, was his own name as the investigating officer who'd diligently unearthed the terrorist connection.

That was enough to cool his desire for Goro's Dragon Lady of a lawyer. Who else could be responsible for this?

Movement in the doorway lifted his head from the screen to find his section head entering. Kimitake Aoki took the seat across the desk and smiled at Yip.

"Congratulations," he said. "I've just come from Takahata-san's office, *neh?* He's very pleased with your quick resolution of the DMC problem. Good work, Phillip."

Yip nodded absently. He couldn't very well deny his involvement without admitting to what Ho Anzen's owner would consider treasonous behavior for one of his employees.

"*Domo,*" he said. "Just doing my job."

"And doing it well. This is a real breakthrough in the case we're building against the Co-Op. Takahata-san wants you to take it over."

"The investigation of the Co-Op?"

"*Hai.*"

Yip's eyes widened slightly. For a half-blood, it was a great honour. It meant a heavier workload, but it also meant a raise in pay and position.

"I am honoured by his confidence," he said.

"There will be a briefing later this afternoon," Aoki said. "Perhaps you should use the time to study the case file and consider some strategies."

"And the AI installation?"

"See it through, by all means." Aoki rose from the chair, pausing in the doorway. "The meeting will be at sixteen hundred—in Takahata-san's office."

This time Yip managed to keep his surprise from his features. He'd been in the owner's presence only when Takahata spoke to the company as a whole, never in a private session.

"*Ja mata,*" he said. "I'll be there."

He gazed thoughtfully at his desktop display when the section head was gone and quickly read through the remainder of the report. No arrests. That was good. At least no innocents would suffer for what was the responsibility of the triads and Goro's people.

He leaned back in his chair. So he was to take over the Co-Op investigation? Such an important case . . . He saw Goro's hand in this, binding him to the yakuza with favours. The new position, the favourable report.

A sudden thought occurred to him and he called up his Combank account. Why wasn't he surprised at seeing that a deposit of a thousand credits had been made in it last night?

I won't be a part of this, he vowed. I won't be Goro's man inside Ho Anzen, playing the two against each other, currying favours like a dog seeking approval from two separate masters.

But you began it, his reason told him, not allowing him the luxury of maintaining his pride. You went to Goro. For the better good of the Megaplex, perhaps, but you went all the same.

He rubbed at his temples where a headache was threatening. Now he had a reason to see the Dragon Lady again.

He took an Anraku from the drawer of his desk and went down the hall to the toilet for some water with which to take the headache pill. Standing at the sink, he stared at his reflection in the mirror. One pebble was all it took to start an avalanche, he thought. Easy to begin, but how to stop?

From a cubicle behind him he heard the obvious sound of someone snorting frost. The synthetic drug was illegal, but it made a certain sense to Yip that members of the Megaplex's security force would use it. There'd be men wired high on it, even while they arrested other users and brought them in. It made a perfect analogy of what was wrong with society.

Dedication was to self first, then to whatever could forward one's passage to the top of the heap. Wealth and power were the goals. The opposite of wrong was not right, but poor. Like the rats in the squats.

Domo, he thought. Why am I surprised? If history's to be believed, this has always been our way.

The door of the cubicle opened behind him. Shock went through Yip like an electric jolt when he saw that it had been his partner in there icing his nerves with frost. For a long moment he regarded Huan's dilated pupils, the telltale redness under his nostrils, then he turned without a word and returned to his office.

Dreamtime

On another Wheel were Windigo and Misabe.

Though the Twisted Hairs knew that tale, as their knowledge is braided from the collected wisdom of all the tribes, it is the Anishnabeg elders who still tell of the three ways that a person becomes a *windigo.*

One of these is through the visitation of a *windigo manitou*, for Windigo is capable of becoming a guardian spirit. Those who do not reject its teachings, when Windigo reveals itself in a dream or vision, are molded into an image of the creature, acquiring a pathological taste for human flesh.

Another cause is starvation—an enforced fast when there is no food available, causing a person to kill his comrades for sustenance. Unlike the pursuit of visions, when the way of the *windigo* is undertaken voluntarily, this cause does not lead to insanity.

The third occasion is through the sorcery practices of an enemy, when the evil *medé* sends starvation or the *windigo manitou* to the victim he wishes to injure.

The human *windigo* first manifests his insanity through a state of melancholia, becoming very anxious and progressively more inactive. Left untreated, he finally arises from his stupor and grows increasingly violent. Every *windigo* has once been a melancholic, and every melancholic, if allowed to become ill enough, will manifest cannibalistic tendencies.

The *windigo* is itself a Wheel. In winter it can be seen as a giant skeleton of ice. In summer, it melts away, no longer disturbed by hunger. Yet when winter takes its turn on the Wheel, the creature comes to life once more, driven by its maddening hunger and a desire for human flesh.

Medé can help in the early stages of the madness, but once the transformation is complete, it is only when Misabe steps onto the Wheel that harmony can be restored through the death of the monster.

The elders tell of the first *windigo* who let an evil *manitou* possess him in a winter of great hunger. Rising from his sleep, he went forth to hunt with no success until he came to a prosperous village far from his own. He gave a great cry of rage, seeing their good fortune, and all the people of the village were transformed into beavers which he skinned and ate.

The more he ate, the greater he grew in size. Instead of alleviating his hunger, the very act of eating actually fostered a greater hunger. North he went then, into the deeper forests, and wherever he walked, the more game there was. He ate and killed, ate and killed, growing all the time.

At the same time, the hunter Misabe returned from a long journey to find his village devastated, his people slain. Through the guidance of a *medé*, he went into a vision dream where his totem Noka, the bear, appeared to him and showed him what had befallen his people.

With the help of Noka, Misabe made medicine the next day. When he took it, he began to grow until he too was a giant. Following the tracks of Windigo, he finally located the creature on the shores of a far northern bay. Without waiting, Misabe attacked and Windigo, weakened by his immense hunger, was soon slain.

Some elders use the tale as an example of gluttony and restraint, teaching that the *windigo manitou* would enslave anyone too preoccupied with sleep or work or play or drink or any pursuit, but that is another Wheel. On the Wheel that holds both Misabe as well as Windigo, it is not restraint that brings harmony. Rather it is the will's defeat of evil.

Grandfather?

Find Misabe on your own Wheel, grandson.

But they have stolen my medicine.

They have stolen only what exists on the flat surface of their own reality. Look beyond the surface, grandson, to the deeper reality of the People. That which is manifested and that which is manifesting. You must seek now the medicine that lies in your heart.

Do you mean have courage?

It is never that simple. Courage, of itself, is not enough. You must understand your fears and face them. You must walk large as a tree, with your blood quick in you and swift-running. You must use the cleverness of your brother the coyote and the strength of your own heart. That is the medicine of the People and no one can take it from them, grandson, save the weakness of their own wills.

Grandfather?

There was no reply.

Five

~ 1 ~

Gahzee thought he had closed his eyes for only a moment, but when he opened them he saw that enough time had passed for his captors to have built a tall pyre of dead wood and broken furniture in the center of the square. Now they were approaching him. He tested his bonds. They held as firmly as before.

Dreamtime, he thought. How could he have slept so deeply in such straits to take that Walk? That was simple to understand—it hadn't been his doing. Without dream crystals or preparations, the Kachina-hey had drawn him into the Dreamtime, but as was their way, instead of giving him a weapon against his captors, they had left him with only words.

He needed courage and strength, they said. And slyness. Find Misabe on his Wheel.

Hey, but freedom of movement would do more.

His gaze went to his shuffling captors. Their grey-eyed leader stood by the heaped wood, chanting at the sky, his ruined face turned to the heavens. Gahzee couldn't understand the words. Perhaps they were only gibberish. But in them he heard what the leader had told him earlier.

We'll get us a big fire goin' an' roast you good.

His skin crawled as though it could already feel the flames licking at him, skin swelling, blistering.

Get that healthy meat in us.

They were *windigos*. They thought that eating his flesh would be medicine against their sicknesses. But what they suffered from were genetic flaws. Radiation exposure. Ruined lungs from breathing this fouled air. They didn't have the naturally high melanin content of the People to protect them from the ultraviolet rays. The immunity boosters to cleanse the Wheels on which their bodies turned. The safe environment of the Enclaves to protect their genes.

They thought eating his flesh would cure them, but all his meat would do was feed their *windigo* madness.

Courage and strength. Slyness.

Gahzee blinked sweat from his eyes. In the mad features of his captors he saw no weakness he could exploit. It was time for him to die. To change worlds.

He thought of his weapons teacher Oktowanakskam—Floats in Air. *When you enter combat,* Oktowanakskam would say, *you must be ready to die.*

Well and good, Gahzee thought, when a brave stands free to confront his foe. For if he was ready to die, then he moved more freely on the Death Wheel. He could dance to any quarter and drum his victory. But what of when he was tied and bound?

Stoic acceptance of death didn't hold much appeal.

His captors caught him by the arms and dragged him toward the pyre that had now been lit and was sending up a stream of oily smoke to join the already fouled air above. He kept himself stiff, until a few of them began to fight over his clothes. Then he went limp, head lolling, eyes open, pupils turned upward with only the whites showing.

It was his totem who had told him in a vision that while the *manitou* gave men life and could instruct them as the

Kachina-hey did in the Dreamtime, a man could only retain harmony through his own strength and will.

Be ready to die and death will see you as a brother.

See my weakness, his limp body told his captors. *Half-dead already. But this shirt, these leggings . . . surely they are too fine to burn? What medicine lies in their weave and stitch? See my clear dark skin, unblemished by disease. Surely the medicine is very strong.*

With his arms and legs securely bound, the clothing couldn't be removed. His muscles were flaccid; he was obviously helpless. He let them worry at his bonds, rolling in their grip like a dead weight.

Be ready to die.

This time he would remember. He wouldn't attempt to calm them with words again. He wouldn't hesitate in his own defense until they overwhelmed him as they had before.

Even after his bonds were free, he waited. He let them strip his clothing from him while the numbness in his arms and legs began to diminish. They fought over the clothing—their leader screaming himself hoarse over their babble. It was only when they reached for him again—to retie the bonds, to heave him into the pyre that blazed high with the hiss and crackle of its flames—that he flowed up from the ground.

Be ready to die.

There was no wasted motion. The heel of his right hand rose against the nearest chin, driving the head back with a sharp crack that broke the jaw. His left hand chopped across a windpipe. His knee rose into a midsection. He spun once, heel catching a throat, then made himself enough room to leap into a flying kick that brought down two more of his captors.

The sudden violence of his attack made the remainder of his foes draw back, but this time Gahzee was not interested in a peaceful settlement. They had already shown him how they would reply to that.

He went for where they were thickest, a blur of motion

that drove in amongst them with heel or hand, elbow, knee, the side of hand, heel of foot. They scattered, howling with pain and fear. Their leader screamed at them to regroup, that he was only one man, and then Gahzee was in front of him.

He kicked the leader's crutch away. As the man began to fall, Gahzee drove the hardened side of his hand against the nape of the man's neck. As he collapsed in the dirt, Gahzee drifted down beside him on one knee, fingers stiff for the killing blow, Stalking Death lying in his eyes—the sudden death that came upon a man all unawares. It buzzed like a red coal behind Gahzee's eyes, as hot as the pyre. It rumbled like a grandfather thunder in his mind.

The leader stared wide-eyed at the *medé*, knowing his death when he saw it, but Gahzee stayed the killing blow. He let his hand drop and looked away from his enemy. The square was empty except for two dead men and those few who were dragging themselves away on wounded limbs. He let them go. Reaching down, he grabbed the leader's shirt, his fist filling with bunched folds of cloth at the man's throat, and dragged him up into a sitting position.

"You and I will talk now, I think," he said, "and the first thing you will tell me is your name."

"Uh . . . it's Ellis . . ." The fact that he was still alive was only just sinking in.

"Ellis," Gahzee said softly, tasting the name of his enemy's name. It had little resonance.

He rose smoothly to his feet and gathered up his clothing. It was torn in places, but it would suffice. When he came upon Ellis's crutch, he picked it up and offered it to him.

"You have gear that belongs to me," he told the leader. "We will recover it."

"Sh-sure," Ellis said. "Anything you say."

He led the way towards the nearest buildings at his limping pace. Gahzee followed, barefoot in the dirt. He had recovered his medicine bag. After checking that its contents were undisturbed, he retied it to his belt. Along the way to the buildings he collected his compass, his empty pack with its straps torn off, his half-finished bow. Ellis stopped a half-dozen yards from the gaping doorway of the closest structure.

"The gear," Gahzee said.

"It's inside."

Gahzee motioned for him to precede him and followed him in. The *medé* walked a Stalker's Wheel now, a hunter's Walk. His every sense was alert—as they should have been when he was first attacked.

The trick is not simply to acquire the knowledge, Oktowanakskam would say, *but to survive the lessons.*

He could sense the people of this place, in hiding, watching him, but no longer a threat. He had broken that Wheel of theirs, but that didn't mean he could relax.

He paused in the doorway, waiting for his eyes to adjust to the dimmer light, then joined Ellis on the far side of what had once been an enormous foyer. A door there opened into a large room overflowing with what could only be the spoils of their raids. Gahzee smiled when he saw the old twelve-speed bicycle close at hand. It had a black solid frame, fat tires to take it easily over the rough terrain, racks on front and back to carry gear.

"Where did you get that?" he asked, pointing to the bike.

Ellis spat. "Took it off a rat that strayed too far from the squats."

"Squats?"

"It's where the little fucks live—clustered like rats 'round the Plexes, 'stead of livin' the free life we do."

And it's such a good life, Gahzee thought, but he was touched with pity. From satellite photos and tapping into Megaplex vid broadcasts, he knew of the slums that had sprung up around the Megaplexes. Life there was hard, but life for Ellis's people was harder still. Those who lived in the slums still had the chance to buy into the Megaplex. Ellis's people had no chance at all. And even the slums were denied to them. But they still had their pride.

"How far are these squats?" he asked.

"Day—day an' a half." Ellis pointed northeast as he

spoke. He was closer to them than he'd thought, Gahzee realized. He felt the weight of Ellis's gaze upon him.

"The gear," he said.

Ellis called out and an old hag came out of the far door. She was stoop-shouldered, obviously in pain, her greasy hair growing in uneven splotches from her scabbed scalp.

"My wife," Ellis said.

Startled, Gahzee realized that it was disease that had made him think her an old woman. His pity grew stronger, but he didn't lessen his stance on the Stalker's Wheel. Under his watchful eyes she collected the rest of his gear. He packed it away as she brought it to him, tying the pack to the rack behind the seat of the bike he'd spotted when he first came in. Ellis made no comment at his commandeering it.

He wheeled it outside and waited for Ellis to join him.

"You're dead, y'know," Ellis said. He scratched at a sore, his eyes empty of antagonism which gave his words a curiously prophetic quality. "God'll fry you all for what you Clavers done."

"And what have we done?"

Ellis lifted a limp hand that took in the desolation all around them. "Fucked the world."

Gahzee shook his head. "We withdrew from the world—you have only yourselves to thank for what you did with it." He spoke calmly enough, but doubt touched him again. And shame.

Ellis shrugged. "Don't matter now, I guess. Everythin's fucked. But somebody's got to pay."

Looking at him Gahzee thought, somebody already has, but he kept his thoughts, as he had his doubts and sense of shame, to himself.

He swung onto the bike. For a long moment they regarded each other, then Gahzee pedaled away. When he looked back, far down the long block, Ellis was still standing there, just staring at the blazing pyre. A shiver touched Gahzee and he pedaled quickly out of sight. A half-mile from where he'd left Ellis, Nanabozho rejoined him, loping alongside the bike as it bounced over the ruts and holes that were eating away at the roadway.

He heard Oktowanakskam's voice again.

The trick is not simply to acquire the knowledge, but to survive the lessons.

A simple lesson this time: pay attention. Failure to do so resulted in finding oneself on the wrong side of Stalking Death. The hunted, rather than the hunter.

"Hey, brother," he told the coyote. "Next time a little more forewarning would be welcome."

Nanabozho yipped once, then ran quickly ahead. Gahzee had to pedal hard to keep up.

~ 2 ~

"Maki Ota, *nan datte*?" the doorman of the Hama Tanoba said as he ran Lisa's ID through a security check. He was a needle-thin man with a disconcertingly broad face that made him look like a ball on a stick. He had enough Nipponjin blood to work the door, but probably wasn't a yak.

Lisa tapped her deactivated buzz-stick against her thigh, wanting to give him a slap with it, with the buzz thumbed to high, to wipe the leer off his face, but she wasn't stupid enough to think she'd get away with it.

The Hama Tanoba was a yak meat bar on the Strip, the fringe of the squats closest to the Plex where most of the clubs were, and the doorman'd be wired up to a computer-laser system just like the kind the security drones inside the Plex had as part of their riot gear. They wore computer backpacks that also contained a power core, hooked up to a hand-held firing mechanism the size of a small rifle. The only difference between those of the drones and the doorman was that his wouldn't be so bulky.

The computer spat her ID card, the doorman catching it with familiar ease.

"You got a green, sweets," he said, handing it back to her.

"In you go. You need any frost or fibrewire, you come back and see me. Kinky Kyoto's the name—making you happy's my game, *neh?* You have yourself some fun now."

"Domo," Lisa murmured.

She gave Donnybrook a quick look, then swaggered into the interior of the club, leaving him behind on the bench where the other strongarms waited for their charges. The only security the yaks liked inside their meat bars was their own.

Though it was still early, the noise and glare of the place hit her like a slap. Leather boys and swagger girls, chinas and a few rats with the credits to blow, were all partying. Vid screens dominated the walls, playing the latest Yakiman vid at full aural and visual volume. On the slow spin of the dance floor, individuals were swaying on the fast rhythm of the vid, mulitcolored glory lights flashing 3-D holos all around them. Half the tables were empty. Those that were occupied were already overflowing with bottles and drink glasses. The waiters here were naked except for small bird costumes around their genitals that used their penises as bills. The waitresses might as well have been nude as well, with their long cloaks of black streamers that opened strategically with their every movement to show holographed dragon tattoos on their breasts and butts.

At any other time Lisa would have killed to get in here, just for the kick. Tonight all she wanted to do was get the job over with. Finger those chinas and get on to some serious yak-hurting. Kay's death was still a raw pain inside her; a hole that could never be filled again. Nothing seemed to help. Not even seeing Jammy Jim sitting with a couple of swagger girls in a corner. For just about as long as she could remember she'd had the hots for the vidjammer. Now here she was, finally in a position when she could waltz right up to him and give his admirers a little buzz-stick hint to shake their butts away from him, and she couldn't even muster up a smile behind her mask.

She went to the long bar at the far end of the club and ordered an Akari Fizz. Sitting on a stool, with her back against the bar and her legs crossed, sipping the Fizz, she made a careful survey of the room.

"Try a hot wire?"

She turned to see that a leather boy had taken the seat beside her. His temples had burn marks from his fiberdisc nodes and under his synth leather jacket he was wearing a bodysuit with a plasti-crotch. Nothing to be proud of, Lisa thought, as she raised her eyes. From his hand dangled a web of fine wire mesh holding a hot pink fiberdisc chip.

"Guaranteed to fuck your mind."

She thumbed on her buzz-stick and slapped it lightly across his knees. He jumped at the contact.

"Bitch," he muttered and backed away.

She gave the room another slow survey then left the bar, her drink unfinished.

"Leaving so soon?" Kinky Kyoto asked as she collected Donnybrook at the door. "What kind of action you looking for, sweets?"

"Nothing you've got."

"*Ja mata.* You don't know till you . . ." he was saying, but she was out the door before he could finish.

Out on the street she leaned against Donnybrook for a moment, tugging up her mask slightly at the chin to give herself a flash of real squat air. The stink hit her like a line of frost. She was getting too used to the antiseptic filtering system of the mask. It was making her act too much like a real swagger girl would, and she didn't like it.

"How many's that?" she asked wearily.

"Who's counting? You want to call it a day?"

"It's a day," she said, but neither of them smiled at the weak joke. She looked down the street. "Guess the Oku's next."

She led the way down to the next meat bar.

By midnight the meat bars were hopping, but Lisa was beat. She and Donnybrook had gone from one end of the Strip to another, checking out the yak bars, the tong gambling dens, and every kind of club in between, without success. Even taking it easy, she had too much alcohol thinning her blood right now, leaving her a little light-headed. The dope and Tabaccanin smoke was so thick that it was starting to clog up her mask's filters. The taste that came through was still antiseptic, but it was mixed with something not so clean at the same time. It was sort of how you'd expect used ashtrays to taste.

"That's it," she said as they left the Tanaka Tanoba. "I need a break."

"You heading for the squat the Ragman set up for you in the Plex?"

Lisa shook her head. "I don't think I've got the energy to play the game right if one of their drones stops me."

"I got room."

The sexual innuendoes that had marked the beginning of their search had long since been put aside. Donnybrook knew she was hurting and whatever else he might be, he wasn't one to push at a time like this.

"You know what I'd really like? To take that yak's Usaijin and head out into the badlands again. Not to where we . . . you know. Just to get away."

Donnybrook didn't question her. "You got it," he said.

He put his arm around her and steered her out of the Strip to where they'd stashed the scooter on their return from Kaoru's cairn. Lisa leaned gratefully against the solid presence of his shoulder and put her legs on automatic, happy to let him take the lead.

~ 3 ~

"There," the leather boy said. "That's them."

Kanji Yono stepped from the alley beside the Tanaka Tanoba and tracked the pair that the leather boy had pointed out. He gave a brusque nod. A swagger girl and her strongarm. The girl, according to their informant, had been in and out of the clubs all night, sitting at each bar with a drink, watching the crowds, making no moves, then leaving for another. It was possible.

He tossed a pair of hard credits to the leather boy. "*Ugokuna,*" he told him. Get away. He waited until the boy was gone before turning to his partner. "What do you think?"

"It's worth checking out," Masao Sho said.

Yono nodded. "*Ja mata*. Let's see where they go, *neh?*"

This close to the Plex, it was better to be certain that what they had was a rat playing the swagger girl instead of the real thing. *Oyabun* Goro wouldn't appreciate having security drones sniffing around because a pair of his yaks got a little too eager in plain sight of their patrols.

The two big men split up, Yono continuing after the pair on foot, Sho waiting until his partner was almost out of sight before following on a two-man Usaijin scooter. When Yono gave a sudden wave, Sho booted the quiet engine into a higher gear and sped to join his partner.

"They've got themselves a Usai," Yono said as he climbed on back.

"*Chiksho!* Which way did they go?"

Yono pointed down a long corridor of a street, deserted tenements rising like walls, four stories high, on either side. Going that way would take them out of the squats and right into the badlands.

"What are they doing out there?" Sho muttered as he sent the Usaijin down the street.

"What does it matter?" Yono replied, leaning closer to speak. "*Sa*. She's the one we want."

~ 4 ~

When Yip returned to his *apato* from his briefing with Tomiji Takahata and his section head, Kimitake Aoki, he called up a plastican of Tombo beer from the pressurized fridge and collapsed in a chair to drink it. Popping the tab, he took a long swallow and stared moodily out the window.

The seventh-floor apartment was in the Baidai District, the middle-class suburbs of Sector Three. The only difference between this area and that of the lower-class Mazushii District was that the high-rise *apato jutaku* here were separated from each other by squares of Zen rock gardens, giving one some sense of space from one's neighbours. In the Mazushii only narrow lanes disjoined one building from the other, but even there no one complained of overcrowding. Not when the squats was their only other option. No matter where one lived in the Plex, at least one could always hope to move up in the world.

As he was doing now, Yip realized. The thought didn't please him at all.

Everything was changing. Too quickly. And the rewards that were coming his way—a better job, a raise in pay, a sense of greater worth in Ho Anzen's upper ranks . . . He hadn't earned any of it.

He had planned to inform the Combank that he wouldn't accept the yak deposit in his account, but then thought, why bother? The gesture would only be that. A gesture. The fact of the transaction couldn't be altered. It would remain in the Combank's system whether he accepted the credits or not.

What he should do, he thought as he started his second Tombo, was withdraw the deposit into hard credits, then take them down to the squats and hire some rats to make a *kamikaze* run on the *oyabun*. Who knows? They might even get lucky and take him down, though in the long run it wouldn't make any difference.

After years of inter-clan wars, Shigehero Goro's father had consolidated the various yakuza clans of the Trenton Megaplex under one *oyabun*. Upon his death, the younger Goro had continued his father's work, maintaining the yaks' war against the triads and tongs while taking over more and more legitimate businesses. They meant to rule the Megaplex and were slowly succeeding. And now that the Goro Clan had access to some Claver technology, the inevitable would be drawing closer that much sooner.

Yip sighed. The worst thing was that most of the Kaisha

were run by Nipponjin who, while they publicly professed abhorrence at the idea of the yaks ultimately having control of the Megaplex's corporations, privately preferred that to either the tongs or triads gaining dominion. At least the yaks were pure Nipponjin—in some cases, more so than the various Kaisha presidents and owners.

Yip didn't see it that way, but then he was a half-blood himself and part of a younger generation who believed that racism had been as much to blame for the world's troubles as individuals seeking power. Asian people had once been the minority on this continent. Now they were in the majority with, except for the *dojin no* in their Enclaves, the other races mostly relegated to the squats.

Live and let live, was Yip's credo. Rat or citizen, it didn't matter to him. They were all humans.

But he had his exceptions—those who had no respect for the rights of others. Like the yaks. He would be happy to see Shigehero Goro dead. The *oyabun* was a heartless criminal who cared for no one outside his clan. But even if Goro were successfully assassinated, there were a dozen lieutenants eager to take his place. The yakuza were more like a hydra than a dragon in some ways. When you cut off one head, twenty more would rise up to take its place.

And besides, Yip didn't have it in him. Moving against Goro through anything but legal channels would make him no better than the yaks.

Ja mata. Maybe he should just call up the Dragon Lady and spend those credits on a dinner with her in one of the Tonda District's restaurants, where most meals cost the same as about two weeks of his salary. His old salary, he amended.

He finished the Tombo and crumpled its plastican in his fist. Maybe he should just give the credits to Huan and let him burn out his nose on some top quality frost. *Areyakoreya*. One thing or another. What difference did it make?

His com-vid buzzed on his way to fetch another beer. He thumbed it on to find Fumiko Hirose regarding him from its vid-screen.

"Mushi-mushi," he said to her. "Why is it that I'm not surprised?"

"Yip-san?" she asked, obviously puzzled.

He studied her for a moment, but could find no trace of mockery in her features at the use of the honourific.

"Gomenasai," he said. "To what do I owe the pleasure of this call, Hirose-san?"

"Perhaps I simply wished to meet you socially."

Even on a vid-screen, her sensuality made Yip ache. *"Mata dozo,"* he said. Another time. "Though I find it unlikely."

"You're an attractive man."

He shook his head. "Perhaps to some. But not to a woman such as you, *ney?* What is it that you would like from me?"

Even her frown at his rudeness attracted him. Stop it, he told himself. She's a Dragon Lady. A geisha of the Goro clan, nothing more.

"Ja mata," she said. "I wanted to warn you that while the *oyabun* has taken your recommendation, he has also taken an interest in you. This is the reason for your recent promotion and the credits he has transferred to your account."

"Why?"

"He wishes to put you under obligation to him."

"I'm not yakuza, so I feel no obligation. What I want to know is why you are telling me this."

"I told you, Phillip. I like you."

"Domo." And I, you, he thought.

"I thought you should know of Goro-san's intentions," she added. "His interest in you has only begun."

"And am I now under some obligation to you for telling me this?"

Now her frown preceded a real anger. Her eyes flashed, her features became a mask. "I understand your caution, Yip-san, but I thought you a more insightful man than you are proving to be. Consider: In any relationship, a certain amount of faith is required on the part of all parties concerned. *Sumimasen*. I am sorry to have interrupted your evening."

His screen went blank as she broke the connection.

Chiksho! Had he been wrong about her, or was she simply such a consummate actress? He felt like dirt. His heart ached.

A certain amount of faith.

Hai. But how much faith could he give to one who lived in the camp of the enemy?

Walking from the com-vid, he got his third Tombo from the fridge and put away half of the plastican in one long swallow.

A certain amount of faith.

He thought of Huan in the toilet at work, snorting frost in a cubicle. He hadn't spoken a word to his partner for the remainder of the day, and Huan hadn't approached him. How long had Huan been addicted? What had driven him to do it?

Yip had only been angry. Furious. Hurt. But he'd never thought to try to talk to Huan.

Hai, he thought. A little faith. But I will begin closer to home, Fumiko Hirose. I will clean my own house before I consider visiting yours.

If there was even a welcome for him there any more.

He finished the beer, looking out his window at the Zen pattern of the stones in the square below, then put on a jacket and left his *apato*.

Six

~ 1 ~

It was a day, day and a half to the squats outside of the Trenton Megaplex, Ellis had said. But on his commandeered bike, Gahzee had made good time, better than he could have on foot. When he stopped to make camp that night, he could see a dull glow in the northeastern sky. The lights of the Megaplex.

This time Gahzee was careful. He left the bike and his pack where he planned to make camp, and made a sweep of the neighbouring buildings and streets, scouting for any sign of Outlanders such as Ellis and his people. He found none. By the time he returned to his campsite, a drizzle had started up. He retired to the ground floor of the nearest building before the acid rains fell in earnest, hissing and splattering on the cracked and buckling pavement.

Nanabozho joined him in his shelter, keeping his distance when Gahzee lit a fire by the door to warm water for tea, but coming closer as soon as Gahzee broke out some dried beef jerky which he shared with the coyote.

"No hunting for you tonight, brother?" Gahzee asked.

"I'd think a trickster such as yourself could dance between the raindrops."

The coyote cocked his blue eye in the *medé*'s direction.

"But there's no need, is there?" Gahzee continued. "Not when I've already provided for your belly."

He shared some dried apples with his companion then went to work on his bow once more. Nanabozho lay by the fire, staring out into the wet night. When the rain finally let off an hour or so later, the coyote slipped out the door and was gone.

Gahzee immediately laid aside his bow and stepped outside as well, walking a Stalker's Wheel. The rain, for all its acidity, had still cleared the sky somewhat. Not enough to see the stars or Grandmother Moon, but the lights of the Megaplex appeared brighter. There was no sign of the coyote—no sign of anything, animal or man. This time Nanabozho had simply set out on his night's ramble, rather than sensing danger.

Returning to the building, Gahzee climbed its stairs to the roof. There he stood and stared out across the abandoned buildings, shadows lying thick around them, streets winding like pale ribbons between the structures where their routes weren't blocked by debris.

Gahzee had travelled by flyer to both the Nez Ch'ii Enclave of Navajo and the Wadi Enclave in Australia. There the tribes lived a life very different from that of his own People in the eastern woodlands of Kwarthas Enclave. Mother Earth's breasts were burnt and dry in their tribal lands. There were no forests, only deserts and lonely mesas. But there was still life there. Everywhere one turned, there was life. If one knew how to look. But here . . .

This was a land empty of resonance, Gahzee realized. There were people—such as the Outlanders who had captured him and those who lived in or about the Plexes—but they gave nothing back to their Mother. On that Wheel, there was little for their Mother to give in return, so the turn of the Wheel grew smaller and smaller.

The animals that still made the Outer Lands their home

were not enough to restore harmony to these barren wastes. That was why Kitche Manitou had created the People. It was their Walk to bless the land and its children with their care, to speak with voices of drum and sacred smoke to the *manitou*, to weave the harmony between the Wheels that are and the Wheel of the mysteries. The path with heart.

The Outlanders had broken the spirit pipe that Manitou-waub had given him when he left the Enclave. Leaning against a parapet, he took paper and tobacco from his pocket and rolled a cigarette.

"*Saemauh beendae/aeshkaugae,*" he said softly as he lit the cigarette. Tobacco cleanses my heart. "*Saemauh beeni-naendumishkaugae. Saemauh bizaundae/aeshkaugae.*" Tobacco cleanses my mind. Tobacco brings calm.

He smoked slowly, sending the grey wreaths skyward—sacred smoke, sacred breath. When the cigarette was done, he flicked it over the edge of the roof and watched it land in a shower of sparks on the cracked asphalt far below.

Thunder grumbled in the sky, high and distant. Besreudang—the thunder that comes from the highest clouds and marks the end of a storm.

Gahzee looked up and smiled. "I hear you, grandfather," he said.

It was as he was turning away to go back down to his bedroll that he caught a flash of light from the corner of his eye. Something between his camp and the Megaplex. It came again.

He marked its position in his mind, determined to investigate its source in the morning.

He had much to learn of the Outer Lands. He meant to understand its smallest workings, for it would be his home now that the Enclaves were closed to him. But first and foremost he was an *animkwan*—a dog-scout for the People. He could study and learn as he made his way through the TOPQ's barrens, but his primary objective was to find a downed flyer, and discover why an Enclave had suddenly ceased all broadcasting; not only ceased broadcasting, but also no longer replied to the broadcasts sent to it by the other Enclaves.

The fire had died down while he was gone, but he fed it no new fuel. Unrolling his bedroll, he laid it out by the wall near the dying coals. Sleep came quickly.

~ 2 ~

The yaks were about two klicks out of the squats and just planning to close in on their quarry when the thick cloud cover above loosed its first misting spray of acid rain.

"Shit," Kanji Yono muttered and tapped his partner on the back.

Masao Sho was already angling their scooter into the shelter of the nearest building. Neither yak was wearing the proper rain gear. But then neither was the pair they followed. Their quarry would have to wait out the storm as well. The faint hum of the Usaijin's Stirling engine faded as Sho shut it down inside the building. Yono got off the back to stretch his legs.

"Call in our position?" Sho asked, tapping the gridface of the scooter's com-link.

"*Iie*," Yono said, shaking his head. "Now we're *neijin*?"

Sho gave a curt nod, registering his own disdain. Neither of them cared to be considered toad-eating flunkies. One rose in the yak ranks through showing initiative as well as by following the *oyabun's* orders. One didn't rise if he called in every few minutes to ask if he could scratch his ass.

"They can't travel either," Yono said. "Not dressed as they are."

Moving to the door, he looked out through the rain in the direction that their quarry had taken, the infrared sights of his metallic contact lens allowing him to see as clearly as he might in daylight.

"*Hai,*" Sho said.

He sat down by the Usaijin. With his partner taking the

first watch, he brought out a hand-held vid Playman. He inserted a game chip and began a solitary game of *go*, playing against the smart circuits in the chip that simulated the style of a seventeenth-century *go* master. Even with a handicap, he'd yet to win a game with this particular chip.

~ 3 ~

When they first got there, all Lisa did was pace back and forth in the rubble-strewn foyer of the building where they'd taken shelter from the burning acidic rains. She was restless and paid no attention to the singed feathers of her headdress, the pock-marked stains on her jacket and mask. She let mask and headdress drop to the floor, continuing to pace while Donnybrook sat with his back up against a wall and quietly watched her. She finally paused by their stolen Usaijin and started to paw through the scooter's saddlebags.

"Find anything?" Donnybrook asked.

"Just yak shit."

A black cloth face mask. A small metal case of throwing stars. Spare Steeljack clips. A water flask half-filled with saki. Black fingerless gloves.

She tried the latter on, but they were far too big for her. She let them drop to the floor.

"Why don't you sit down?" Donnybrook said. "I'm getting wired just watching you."

Lisa sighed and came over to where he was sitting. She put her back against the wall and slid down until she was on the floor beside him.

"Did you ever get religion?" she asked.

Donnybrook shook his head. "Kinda hard to get into when you're living in the squats."

"Tell me about it."

"So why do you ask?"

"Just thinking," Lisa said.

"Kaoru?"

"Yeah, Kaoru." Her shoulders slumped as she spoke the

name. "She didn't have religion either. Her mom taught her the Buddhist rap—you know, where Sakyamuni says that everything comes around again? But I dunno. I'd like to think she went somewhere better. I'd like to think she wasn't just going to show up in the squats again."

"Maybe she'll get reborn as a Plex baby."

"Fat chance. And who says that's better anyway?"

Donnybrook shrugged. "I figure it's all shit, Lisa. The lights go out and you hit the dark road . . ." His voice trailed off and he laid a hand on her knee. "I wasn't thinking."

" 'Sokay. That's the way I feel, too. Least this way nobody's gonna be dumping on her anymore, right?"

"That's one way of looking at it."

Lisa picked up some loose bits of stonework and began to pitch them against the far wall. "Remember the parties we used to have? It was Kay's idea to hit the badlands that first time. We had that big bonfire and we danced around it, whooping like a bunch of Clavers in a *dojin no* vid. I got so wired on that 'yote button you gave me, I was sure I could see the stars that night."

"I always wanted to try the real shit," Donnybrook said, "but I never had me a Claver connection."

"Don't kid yourself—it's all synth. I don't care what anybody says. Nobody's got access to real peyote. Stuff we're doing probably isn't anything like the real shit. It'd be like the difference between smoking real tobacco and that Tabaccanin we get outta the Plex."

"Real tobacco was supposed to kill you—very slowly."

Lisa shrugged. "Yeah, but when you watch the Clavers smoking it, it's like it's sacred. Like it means something. Not just sucking back a nic' hit, synth or not."

"You're really into the Clavers, aren't you?"

"Nah, I just like the vids, that's all. I know they fucked everything up in the real world. But they're kinda neat, when you *imagine* them, you know?"

"Did you ever want to go into an Enclave?"

"Oh, sure, Who didn't? And these—" she touched the dark red messenger tattoos on her cheek, "—'re just like the warpaint, you know, except they're permanent. But I'd die if I ever ran into one of those suckers in real life. I like my hair—on my head, not on some Claver's belt."

"Did you ever think that maybe it was all bullshit?" Donnybrook asked. "Just another Plex fairy tale?"

"Look around you," Lisa said. "This is what the Clavers left us. It's kinda hard to call this bullshit."

They were quiet for a long spell then, just listening to the hiss and splatter of the rain outside fade and finally stop. Lisa leaned against Donnybrook's shoulder.

"I'm really gonna miss her," she said.

"I know you are."

"I never thought it could hurt so much."

"It never gets any easier," Donnybrook said. "Comes with the territory—that's what the Ragman says every time we lose somebody. We've got the Plex, all squeaky clean, and then the badlands, and they're a different kind of clean. Empty, like a blank screen. And right in the middle, there's the armpit of the world. The squats. And who gives a shit what happens to its rats?"

Lisa nodded. "What do you think of the Ragman?" she asked. "What do you think about him being a tom—running the Co-Op?"

"I've known that for awhile," he said, "so it's like no big surprise for me. And he doesn't run the Co-Op. Everybody in it's got a piece of the action, Lisa. That's the whole point of it."

"So you really think there's a chance they can do something?"

"Don't know. But it's the best shot we've got. The only shot—at least that's the way I see it."

"I guess."

He gave her knee a squeeze and got to his feet. "Looks like the rain's letting up."

Lisa followed him to the door.

"I've got a funny feeling," he said as he looked out. "It's like something's not quite—"

His voice broke off and he started to fall. To Lisa, it was

as though she suddenly shifted to a slo-mo vid. The air grew so thick that his body took forever to tumble to the floor, blood spraying out of his throat like a fountain on half-speed.

A buzz centered in the back of her head. She was drawing out her Steeljack before he struck the floor, before she was even really aware that he'd been shot, that he was dead. The auto-pistol filled her hand, rising up to point at the doorway, her finger squeezing off a round just as a blur of grey motion was filling the space there.

Her fléchette hit the yak square in the face, his features exploding. He was thrown back. His Steeljack dropped from his hand. Lisa stepped forward, moving slow because the air was like molasses and she had to wade her way through it. Her Steeljack was aimed out into the night. The buzz in her head became a shrill whine. She fired, her fléchette pinging against the metal of a yak scooter, throwing off a flare of sparks as it exploded. She started to fire again, but then something struck her at the base of her spine.

She sprawled forward, her third shot going wild, exploding in the air with a bright flash. She started to turn, tried to bring her Steeljack around in time to get off another shot. She knew she didn't have a hope in hell of matching a yak's augmented reflexes, but she had to try.

The second yak was just coming down from his kick. Her back felt like it was broken. Her Steeljack came up to cover him. He landed, but was already moving, to the side, in again. A flashing blur of a foot coming right for her. She tried to track him with the Steeljack, but the boot took it out of her hand with a blow that numbed her entire arm.

She fell, thinking, the bastard's so sure of himself he isn't even using his Steeljack. A callused hand grabbed the material of her jacket around her throat and dragged her up from the ground.

"The package!" he demanded, spittle spraying in her face.

He was cutting off her air. Her spine felt like it was on fire. Her right arm was a numb weight that dangled limply at her side. The buzz in her head was a high-pitched shriek.

His metallic eyes looked robotic, like the sight sensors of a vid death machine. She started to reach for the grip he had on her throat with her left hand, then let that hand fall behind her. Her fingers closed on her buzz-stick. Thumbing it on high, she drove it up into his groin.

She used the toy out of desperation and almost wasn't prepared for the effect it had on the yak. Something to do with its electronics shorted out the yak's nervous system. His augments were implanted—not genetically tailored, she thought dully, everything still running in slo-mo.

A shudder ripped through the yak. He lost his grip and fell on top of her, the buzz-stick pushed farther into his groin, playing more havoc with his augments.

Lisa flexed her numbed right hand. Pins and needles burned up and down her arm. Her temples ached from the whine inside her head.

Work! she told her hand.

It crawled at a snail's pace towards her Steeljack. At full power, the buzz-stick had about ten seconds worth of juice left in it. In moments the yak would be fighting off the disruption of his augments and then she'd be dead meat.

Her fingers fumbled, finally closed around the Steeljack's grip. She brought the pistol up, muzzle pointing at the yak's left temple. Then the juice ran out of the buzz-stick.

"Puking *gaijin*!" the yak cried. "I'll—"

Lisa squeezed off a round.

The yak stiffened above her. As he fell on top of her, the full weight of his suddenly limp body drove the remaining air from her lungs. She clawed at his weight, trying to shift his heavy corpse. There were going to be more of the bastards. But she wasn't going to let them do her in, lying here. She meant to face them on her feet, with her Steeljack in her hand.

The whine between her temples started to go around and around her head like a whirlpool. She managed to shift the yak's body enough so that she could wriggle free. But now there was a huge dark well opening up before her gaze. She way lying on her back, but felt as though she was falling up into that well. Gravity no longer holding her. The ground under her just spitting her up.

Hold on, she told herself. Just hold on. . . .

The Steeljack fell from her hand again. Then the sky swallowed her with blackness.

~ 4 ~

There was no answer when Yip tried the door of his partner's *apato*. He stood in the hallway considering, then returned to the elevator and took it to the roof of the building. It was too late for Huan to be out in the bars, and since he had no current lover, there was only one place he would be at this time of night. For all his fashionable excesses, Huan was serious about meditating, as serious as Yip was for his own T'ai Chi Ch'uan.

Though Huan was a practicing Tendai Buddhist, when he wished to meditate, Yip knew he could invariably be found in the Shinto shrine on the top of his *apato jutaku*. Most buildings in the Megaplex, residences as well as businesses, had such shrines on their roofs.

The elevator let him out into a cubicle from which a door led to the rooftop proper. The stonework and metal girders were pocked and corroded from the acidic rains. The shrine itself was made of natural stone, centrally placed on the roof. It could be approached through two *torii*—god gates made of upright posts, one with a single crossbar, the other with a double. Gulls were roosting on them. They flew off from their perches at Yip's approach.

Huan sat on a stone outside the shrine, legs drawn up under him, eyes closed. He was dressed in a plain grey kimono, his feet bare. He didn't look up at Yip's approach.

Yip settled on his haunches in front of him. The memory of Huan's frost habit lay at the forefront of his thoughts.

"How long has it been?" he asked softly.

Huan's eyes opened slowly. His gaze settled on Yip, but

for a long moment he held to his silence. When he finally spoke, it wasn't in reply to Yip's question.

"I don't understand," he said. "You're the one that betrayed Takahata, yet you receive the promotion."

"That didn't come from Takahata," Yip told him. "It came from Goro. How long have you been taking frost?"

"What does it matter?"

"It matters to me, *neh?* Let me help you, Huan."

"I betrayed you," Huan said. "That's the kind of partner I am. Do you still want to help me?"

"Betrayed me?"

"I went to Aoki and told him what you were doing. He took me to Takahata's penthouse."

Yip's eyes narrowed. They knew? He'd just had a meeting with them this evening to go over the Co-Op case file. There had been saki and polite conversation. Takahata had praised him again for dealing with the terrorist threat so quickly. Aoki had mentioned other of Yip's successes to the owner. Neither had betrayed any knowledge of his visit to Goro's lawyer. What game were they playing with him?

"So you're in Goro's pocket now, are you?" Huan went on. "Then perhaps we're not so different as I thought."

"A gift from Goro—*hai,*" Yip said, "but it's a sword with two points. One that he'll impale himself on."

Huan shook his head. "You won't find it so easy to betray the yaks."

"I don't plan betrayal—I plan justice. This is my job, Huan."

Huan merely laughed. "That's what I always told myself. We justify everything to ourselves, Phillip. I tell myself that I take the frost because it makes me more alert and lets me do my job better. I take bribes because it lets me buy the frost. I do what I can to advance myself, a Thai in this Nipponjin company, even if it means betraying confidences. That is the true way of the world, Phillip. Not *giri*. Obligation is the burden hardest to bear, *neh?* Then why bear it, I ask myself? Do you think Takahata or any owner cares about *giri* except what is due to themselves?"

"And our friendship . . . ?"

"You mean my professed love for you, don't you? The long-standing joke." Huan sighed. "That was partially true—once. It's difficult not to admire, and learn to love, a man so dedicated to his work as you. It was like having Kozo Goh as a partner—do you remember him?"

Yip gave a curt nod. Kozo Goh had been a hardboiled samurai detective on the vids when he was young. The series still ran in syndication in every Megaplex.

"But after a time a man grows tired of walking in Kozo Goh's shadow, *neh?*"

"If you'd spoken to me . . ."

"You'd have done what? Worked less hard to make me look better?"

"No, but—"

"But nothing. I don't blame you. It was my choice to play the part of your *neijin*— my shame. But then this opportunity arrived on my doorstep. How could I pass it up?"

"I can't believe—"

Huan's laughter cut him off. "What you are is naive, Phillip. You truly see the world in black and white and have yet to understand that everything is a weave of uniform grey." He lifted a fold of his kimono. "Like this, *neh?* We are all good and bad, weak and strong, mixed together—all except for you."

"That is the drug speaking in you."

Huan shook his head. "That is the truth speaking in me. Perhaps I need frost to function in my work, and wire to help me relax at home, but I still know the truth when I see it, Phillip. Unfortunately for you, you can't say the same. Because the truth is as elusive as what motivates each one of us, as grey as the world is. To a man who can see only the high contrasts of black and white, truth is something that he will always be blinded to."

"If you truly believe that I—"

"Let me make you a wager, Phillip. I believe that our esteemed employer will get rid of me. I thought to further my position, but instead I have merely proven myself untrustworthy. I see that now. He will think, a man who betrays his partner, what else will he betray? But you—he knows you did what you did for altruistic reasons. A man such as you can be controlled. Easily manipulated. They have but to point you in the direction they wish you to take—in this case to rid them of the threat that the Co-Op presents to them. You are useful. This is a truth, *neh?*"

"What is your point?"

"If he kills me, you'll know I was right—that I speak the truth. If he doesn't, then I will turn my life around and follow your way."

"If you're so certain Takahata will have you killed," Yip said, "why do you remain here?"

Huan smiled wearily. "If I had anywhere to go but down into the squats, I would be long gone. But there is no place left to me, Phillip. Do we have a wager?"

"It's a fool's wager."

"Perhaps—but do we have one?"

"*Hai.*"

"Then go."

Yip didn't move.

"What is it?" Huan asked. "Are you afraid I will throw myself from the roof simply to win our wager?"

"Those drugs . . ."

"Will make me do or say anything." Huan laughed. "You *are* innocent, Phillip. Please go."

Yip hesitated a moment longer, then rose smoothly to his feet. He looked down at the man he'd thought his friend, a man he'd thought he knew, and realized that there was more truth in Huan's accusations than he'd like to believe. If, after all these years, he didn't know Huan at all, of what else was he unaware?

"*Ja mata,*" he said.

"*Mata,*" Huan replied.

Yip walked away, through the *torii* where he disturbed the gulls once more, and across the roof. Stone rattled underfoot, then he was back inside the cubicle again. The door of the cubicle slid shut behind him as he stabbed the elevator's control board with a stiff finger.

Huan listened to the hum of the elevator as it took Yip away, then another faint sound caught his attention and he turned to look at the far side of the roof. A black shape slipped over its edge to glide soundlessly towards the shrine. An augmented yak in ninja black.

So soon, Huan thought.

A thousand regrets flooded his mind. Fear made his pulse drum so fast it was difficult to distinguish the spaces between the beats. It took all his will to close his eyes and try to meditate. Though he had lived a dishonourable life, he meant to die well. Perhaps his death would open Yip's eyes. Perhaps it would not be entirely meaningless. For no matter what he'd told Yip, Huan still loved him. It was his love for Yip that made his betrayal so foul. He almost welcomed the death Takahata had sent him.

He could feel the assassin's presence draw close until the black-clad figure was directly in front of him. He opened his eyes. A katana glinted in the yak's hand, the sword blade silver in the vague light cast from the sky.

Domo arigato, Takahata-san, Huan thought. You do this *gaijin* great honour.

Through the slits of his face scarf, the assassin's eyes glittered with the same silver fire as his katana blade. His gaze met Huan's, the metal contact lenses accentuating his dispassion.

"You win, Phillip," Huan said.

The soft-spoken words and Huan's immobility gave the yak a moment's pause. Then he stepped forward, blade descending in an arc.

"*Korozu zo!*" the assassin cried as his blade bit into Huan's neck.

Huan's head tumbled from his shoulders. He had a final view of his own body, blood fountaining from its headless neck, before the abyss swallowed him.

The assassin wiped his blade on the corpse's kimono, then withdrew from the rooftop the same way he'd come, his katana returned to its lacquered wooden sheath on his back, the *nekade* cat-claw grips on his hands giving him purchase on the weather-roughened stone sides of the building.

Seven

~ 1 ~

Gahzee woke with the lightening sky that passed for dawn in the Outer Lands.

"Hey, Waubun," he said to the dawn, standing at the open door to look out at the empty street. "I miss Mishomis's clean light."

Turning from the depressing sight, he made himself a gruel of oats and dried fruit, then broke camp quickly. With his gear loaded on his bike, he pedaled off through the deserted ruins in the direction where he'd seen the flashes of light the previous night. He made good time here. This close to the Megaplex, the scavengers had been at work for years salvaging the metal hulks of the abandoned vehicles that had choked so many of the streets earlier in his journey.

A klick or so from where he'd spent the night—it was difficult judging distances in these street canyons between the buildings—the coyote rejoined him. Nanabozho was carrying a dead rabbit and when Gahzee brought his bike to a halt, the coyote laid it at his feet.

"My brother is a good hunter," Gahzee said.

He reached out to pet the coyote, but Nanabozho backed quickly away. Gahzee shrugged. He made quick work of dressing the kill, then hung the carcass from his handlebars and started off again.

Not much later, when he went to make a turn down one street to skirt a pile of rubble from a collapsed wall, the coyote yipped sharply to get his attention. Gahzee paused, then circled around the rubble on its far side where the coyote was waiting for him. He let Nanabozho take the lead. By following the coyote he was brought to the source of last night's mysterious light flashes.

He had stepped onto a Stalker's Wheel as soon as he'd woken that morning so that when Nanabozho suddenly froze, Gahzee brought his bike to a quiet halt. Every sense alert, he leaned the bike against a wall and crept forward to crouch beside the coyote. From that vantage point, he could see a three-wheeled scooter that he recognized as one of the principal means of private transportation in the Megaplexes.

His moccasined feet were absolutely soundless as he moved to a new position. From this one he could see the first body. It lay near the doorway of a building, flies gathered like a black mask on the dried blood that lay thick on its face and torso.

Crossing the street, he crept closer. The bulk of the building in front of which the corpse lay was now between him and the body. He rounded the corner cautiously. Gliding alongside the building, he paused a half-dozen paces from the corpse and listened. Nothing. Except for the buzz of the insects, the day was still.

He waited a full two minutes, then completed the distance between himself and the corpse. Without pausing, he slipped into the building, hugging the inner wall, and moved a few quick paces along its length before pausing to listen again. Still nothing. Nothing alive at any rate.

There were more bodies inside, all clustered around the doorway. Two more men and the smaller shape of a woman who appeared to be wearing warpaint. From his studies of the Megaplexes and their surrounding squats, he realized that what she wore was more permanent than warpaint—striped messenger's tattoos. There was another three-wheeled scooter inside the building.

What do we have here? he thought as he moved closer to the bodies. A falling out? An attack of one party upon another? Reading the signs, he settled on the latter. The woman and largest man had been set upon by the two wearing kevlar overcoats.

He picked up an auto-pistol and studied it for a moment. Safety-coded with smart circuitry. No use to him. The others would be the same. Setting it aside, he rolled over the nearest man. Tugging off the overcoat, he stripped the corpse to its waist. When he saw the tattoos covering the entire back and upper arms, he realized that the two attackers were yakuza. That made it easier to choose sides to sympathize with. There was a great deal of information on the criminal yakuza in the Enclave library files.

Going from that corpse to the woman's, he reached out to touch the tattoos on her cheek. It was when his fingertips touched her skin that he realized with a shock that she was still alive. A quick study of her body showed that she was bruised, but otherwise unhurt.

He sat back on his heels and considered for a long moment. Did he wish to get involved? Closing his eyes, he could hear his teacher Manitouwaub giving a lesson as though the old *medé* were standing beside him, rather than a hundred or more klicks away.

To stalk well, one must be able to heal well. To dream well, one must be capable of true complete awareness when awake. As a medé *we have no choice. Either one always heeds the medicine, or one never does. We are never parts of a Wheel—we are the whole Wheel.*

So there was no choice. Simply being here, he was already involved.

He left the woman where she lay for the moment while he dragged the corpses outside and out of the way into the next building. After a few moments of playing with the scooter's various controls, he started the machine up and brought it inside the building, parking it beside its mate. He gathered all the weapons and the woman's com-link, and hid them behind some rubble. Then he fetched his own bike.

He started a small, almost smokeless fire on one side of the building, where what little smoke there was could escape through a window, and set to boiling water. Thrusting a stick through the rabbit, he started its roasting, then went back to the woman, stepping onto a Healer's Wheel.

He unrolled his bedroll and carefully carried her to it. Stripping her, he brought the boiling water from the fire and used it to heat poultices and make pastes from the various healing powders he carried in his pack. He rubbed the paste onto her bruises—the worst were on the small of her back, her right arm, and around her neck—covered them with the crushed leaves of Joe Pye weeds, then wrapped the wounds with strips of cloth soaked in a solution of herbs and dogbane.

When he was done he covered her with a blanket and went back to the fire. Nanabozho came into the building and settled near the woman. Gahzee turned the spitted rabbit, this time collecting its juices in a small metal bowl to which he added more herbs along with dried vegetables and mushrooms to make a thin broth. He set both the broth and half the rabbit beside the fire to keep them warm and returned to the woman's side. Squatting on his haunches, he chewed on rabbit meat and waited for her to wake.

~2~

Utter dislocation greeted Lisa when she first opened her eyes. Someone was pounding on a steel drum inside her head. She had flares of pain in her back and right arm when she tried to move. Her throat felt thick, as though someone had stuffed it with rags. Then her vision came into focus and she was sure she'd dreamed herself into an action vid as the helpless captive of a Claver.

Because that's what he was, she realized, this man with his coppery skin sitting on his haunches beside her.

He had a flat, open face that was almost round, twin black braids, the hair greasier near the scalp, hanging on either side of it. His jacket and trousers looked like genuine leather, the shirt real cotton. He had a beaded belt, more beadwork on the jacket, a leather bag hanging from the belt, leather moccasins. He was as big as a squats strongarm, but another kind of power hung about him—something she couldn't put her finger on, but it wasn't just physical.

His eyes were a deep dark brown—liquid pools that sucked her in as she met their gaze. When he smiled down at her, his entire face became animated, but it was the humour in his eyes that tugged an answering smile from her. Never mind the pain. never mind that she was only dreaming that he'd captured her.

She started to sit up, winced at the sudden pain in her lower back, and then realized that she was naked under the blanket.

"You must take care not to attempt any quick movements," the Claver said. His accent was funny. He spoke patois, but it came out sounding formal—like a Plex baby new to slumming in the squats.

"Are you . . . for real?" she asked.

He nodded and then that smile returned to his features, but this time Lisa didn't give one back. Her head was throbbing again. And she was starting to remember. The yaks. Donnybrook turning in the doorway, his face shot off. . . .

"Oh shit . . ." she began, tears welling in her eyes. First Kay, and now Donnybrook.

"The man in the vest—he was your companion?"

Lisa nodded, not trusting herself to speak. The movement made her headache worse.

"I will see to it that he is properly interred then," the Claver said. "But first I want you to take some broth."

Even through the blur of her unshed tears, Lisa could see that this Claver could move. He was quick and smooth, not a wasted motion. He returned with a small metal bowl from which came the most astonishingly good smells. Lisa's stomach was in knots and she had absolutely no appetite. Still he helped her sit up, tucking the blanket in around her like a towel after a shower. When he placed the bowl in her hands, her palms protected from the hot metal sides by padded cloth, her mouth began to water.

"Please," the Claver said. "Drink it. It will help you heal more quickly; make you strong."

What if there was something in it? Lisa thought. But if he'd wanted to hurt her, he wouldn't have gone through the trouble of bandaging her wounds—would he? Still, what was a Claver doing here, so close to the Plex? She'd never heard of such a thing. Unless . . . And then she knew. He was after the same thing Goro and everybody else was—the Claver chip that the chinas had taken from her.

"This is an old bruise?" he asked, pointing to her cheek.

"Yeah. Bunch of chinas jumped me."

"I see. They are not of your tribe?"

Lisa shook her head. She immediately regretted the movement as it made the headache throb more sharply between her temples. She sipped at the broth.

"What is your symbol?" He frowned, unhappy with the word. "Your patron animal?"

"You mean totem?"

He smiled. "Yes."

"We don't have 'em."

"Then how is it that you know—"

"What you're talking about? Gimme a break. I watch the vids."

She paused after sipping at the broth some more. Her headache was receding and the other pains weren't so prominent any longer. She was feeling almost perky, she realized. The hole inside her that Kay had filled, the despair she'd been feeling over Donnybrook's death . . . everything had taken on a distant quality.

"What's in this?" she demanded.

"Herbs. Roasted rabbit drippings. Dried vegetables."

"I'm feeling a little buzzy."

"That would be the mushrooms—a form of psilocybin that our *medé* have genetically altered so that it serves as a form of natural painkiller, rather than a hallucinogen. You shouldn't worry as it is non-addictive."

"Yeah," Lisa said, "but what about the way it's making me float away from everything that's real? I don't like pain. I don't like hurting for lost friends. But I don't like being cut off from what's real by some buzz. I'm not ready to party just now."

"I apologize," the Claver said. "I realize that you would wish to grieve for a comrade—especially one who suffered a Stalking Death—but my concern was for the pain that your wounds would be causing you."

"No shit? Then how come I'm still hurting?"

"Believe me, without the mushroom's medicine, you would be feeling a great deal more pain."

Lisa tried glaring at him, but the floating feeling made it hard to concentrate on anything negative. And it was hard not to trust that guileless face.

"Screw it," she said, and finished the broth in one long swallow.

"Do you wish more?"

Lisa shook her head. This time the headache hardly made its presence known.

"What's your name?" she asked.

"I am Gahzee Animiki-Waewidum of the Turtle totem. My people are the Anishnabeg."

"That's some mouthful. What does it mean?" In the vids all the Clavers had names like Running Bear, or Moon Over Dark Water, so she was curious about how true that was.

"My name means Swift Speaks With Thunder," he said, translating it into patois.

"And what about that Anishna-whatever?"

"We are the Spontaneous People."

"Come again?"

"Sky Woman gave us life, but unlike all else that is, we were made from nothing; our substances came not from rock, or fire, or water, or wind. And we were given spirits—

though not the same spirits as the mysteries. The mysteries receive visions; the People must quest for them."

"Right."

"I'm sorry. I did not mean to bore you."

" 'Sokay. I'm just finding it hard to concentrate. My name's—" she hesitated, "—Maki Ota."

The Claver regarded her for a long moment, the pupils of his dark eyes expanding. "That name," he said finally, "suits more what you were wearing than what you are."

Lisa shrugged. "What can I say? It's all I've got."

Gahzee took the bowl from her hand. "You should rest," he said, gently pressing her back down onto the bedding. "I will see to the interring of your friend while you sleep."

Lisa tried to connect with the sorrow she knew was inside her, but the drug in the broth washed over her with a wave of blurriness. Before she knew it, the comforting dark had taken hold of her again.

~ 3 ~

Fumiko Hirose was still at home that morning when the call came. She sat down in front of her com-link and switched it to receive.

"Goro-san," she said, startled. "I hadn't—"

"I was monitoring your conversation with the drone last night," the *oyabun* said without any preliminary discussion, "and am most displeased."

"*Gomenasai*. But—"

"It seems to me you play a very dangerous game, Fumiko. Did I not specifically request you to nurture a friendship with him?"

Hirose was thinking quickly. *"Hai,"* she said. "But, Goro-san, he is a man, and a man likes to think he is in control. And he already suspects my interest in him. It is for this reason that I have approached the matter in a more circular fashion. Yip cannot be taken by a frontal attack. As in *go*, one must make many apparently unrelated moves, until the moment comes when one's opponent is snared all unknowingly and there is no escape."

Goro's face studied her from the screen. "So this warning of our interest in him that you gave him—it was all a part of your plan to snare him?"

"*Hai*. Yip is no fool. His first thought on my contacting him was that you had sent me."

Goro nodded slowly. "Yes. I saw that. Continue as you see best then, Fumiko, only consider: I am only pleased with results, *neh?*"

"*Hai.*"

"*Ja mata.*"

The screen went blank before she could reply.

Hirose leaned back in the chair and wiped a thin bead of perspiration from her brow. She would have to be careful. And she would have to call Phillip again. But she would give him a little time. It was still early morning. She would wait until noon for him to call before she tried again.

As it turned out, she didn't have to wait until then.

~ 4 ~

If he kills me, you'll know I was right—that I speak the truth.

Yip sat in his office cubicle, staring at the news-vid on his desktop display, Huan's words ringing in his head. Minute by minute, it seemed, his familiar world was dissolving away from underfoot.

"SECURITY OFFICER SLAIN—INVESTIGATION LAUNCHED," the headline read. The Ho Anzen spokesman quoted in the report would make no statement except that an investigation was pending.

Yip read the article through for a third time. With Huan's death, he had lost his foothold in a normal world. There is no black and white, Huan had said. Only grey. Greyness that lies like a fog over everything. In such a world, how was a man to separate the good from the evil? Whom could he trust?

When his section head entered his cubicle, Yip gave him only a perfunctory nod.

"This is a terrible loss." Aoki said.

His features were solemn. Yip schooled his own to betray nothing of what he felt. If Huan was to be believed, here was one of those responsible for his death. It was difficult to accept. His section head. The company's owner. Who else was involved in this conspiracy?

If he kills me . . .

The grey fog fell thickly across Yip's sight.

. . . you'll know I was right.

He felt cut adrift from all he had ever believed. *Giri.* Duty. Responsibility. He no longer knew what to believe.

"If you wish, I can arrange some time off," Aoki went on.

"I was there last night," Yip said slowly. "It must have happened just after I left."

Aoki's tone of voice shifted from sympathetic to business-like. "What did you see?"

Yip shook his head. "Nothing. Only a troubled friend."

"Troubled? What did he speak of?"

Because he was watching for it, Yip spied the betraying twitch under his section head's left eye.

"He was lonely," Yip said. It wasn't a lie. "He was afraid of growing old without a family."

Aoki nodded. "You must take some time off, Phillip. A day at least, *neh*?"

"Thank you, Aoki-san. I will do that."

"Huan Som will be cremated with full company honours. Shall I see to the arrangements?"

"You do Huan great honour," Yip said.

The grey fog was clearing. Already he was adjusting, learning to lie, the untruths spilling easily from between his lips.

Aoki hesitated, as though he had more to say, then gave a quick nod. *"Ja mata,"* he said.

Yip nodded in return. "*Mata.*"

He waited until his section head had left his cubicle, then read the article for a fourth time. He sighed and cleared the display. Having lost the wager, now it was he who must turn his life around and follow Huan's way.

Can I live with constant deception? he asked himself. Trusting no one?

Another's recent words came to him. Those that Fumiko Hirose had left him with last night. Goro's Dragon Lady.

In any relationship, a certain amount of faith is required of all parties concerned.

Hai. Or as Huan had put it, all people were good and bad, weak and strong. In some the mix leaned more to yin, in others more to yang, but the mix was there in all of them. A simple truth. One of which he'd not been unaware. But he had also believed that a person's actions—good or ill—reflected to which side they leaned. Now he saw that circumstance . . . the grey fog of the world . . . could make a good man do evil. Could make an evil man do good. Another truth—but not so simple.

He reached for his com-link and punched out the numbers that would connect him to Goro's Dragon Lady lawyer, not caring that because he made the call from his office, it would be duly logged and filed in the company's files.

Hirose seemed startled to see him—her features immediately clouding with concern. "Phillip, I . . ." She hesitated, then began again. "I only just heard the news. I'm so sorry."

"*Domo.*"

"Please believe me, we had no—"

He cut her off before she could complete her sentence. He already knew that Goro had nothing to do with Huan's death. What he didn't want was anyone else to know he knew that.

"Are you free this evening?" he asked quickly. "For dinner?"

Her dark eyes blinked with surprise. "Regretfully, no," she said. "I have a previous engagement—a reception at the Ojika Gallery."

Yip knew the place, though he'd never been inside. The Ojika Gallery was in the Tonda District and far too posh for his budget. He gave a curt nod.

"Another time then," he said.

"But I don't have an escort," Hirose said.

Yip regarded her for a long moment. Was this her way of getting back at him for last night? Bring the half-blood to a gathering of Nipponjin highbloods where he'd stand out like a squat rat and make a fool of himself? But he remembered.

A certain amount of faith is required.

"What time shall I pick you up?" he asked.

Hirose's smile was so warm that he could almost feel the temperature of his display screen rising. "After work," she said, "*Ja mata,* Phillip. I'm glad you called."

"*Mata,*" he said as they both cut the connection.

He was glad, too. There was no question but that he was attracted to her, yet he also wished to observe her. To learn how such a master of the art navigated through the grey fog of the world with such success.

I am changing, Huan, he thought as he left his cubicle. But the cost of this learning has been far too dear, *neh?*

Eight

~ 1 ~

Three generations past, the Okados were one of Trenton Megaplex's primary yakuza clans. Their fall from power was in part premeditated by their then-*oyabun* Ishidi Okado, in part brought about by Chomei Goro who was attempting to consolidate the yakuza into one clan at that time. As Goro worked for a takeover of the yakuza underworld in Trenton, Ishidi was moving his own Okado Clan into legitimate business. When his yakuza realized that the new business was not merely a front, more than half defected to the growing Goro Clan.

Ishidi's plan had its roots in the mid-twentieth century. The original yakuza in medieval times were outlaw gamblers and outcasts. Their code of an honour among thieves sprang from Japan's peasant lower classes and was necessary for survival in those times, since it prevented them from killing each other with impunity, and gave them a core of human dignity. The Samurai Code was a Code of divine duty; the Yakuza Code was a code of personal duty.

The Yakuza Code was a rough mix of Confucian ethics

and Zen self-discipline. It demanded courtesy and honesty in all conduct—from eating to gambling, from being a house guest to being an assassin, and expressly forbade any violation of a man's social obligations and debts. Although the early yakuza were hardened homeless outlaws, living on the fringe of Japan's feudal society, they assisted the lower classes from which they'd come, often protecting them from the samurai of their lords.

In the mid-twentieth century, however, the yakuza formed bureaucratic syndicates which purged their ferocity of all possible sympathies. Adapting the Yakuza Code to those times, they continued to plunder and blackmail the rich, but also ended their traditional protection of the poor.

Some very few *oyabun* maintained the original spirit of the Yakuza Code. They tried to move into legitimate businesses, but were blocked by both their followers as well as the other clan *oyabun* who wished to see no change in their current levels of power. Periodically then, over the generations, some few *oyabun* would make the attempt again, though few succeeded like Ishidi, and more retained their status in the yakuza community.

These renegade clans became fair game, but because they knew the ways of their brothers so well, they were better equipped to deal with their attacks. Those yakuza that remained with Ishidi grew in power as he did, buying shares of small companies until they had enough clout to have their own people sitting on Inizi/Bell Northern's board of directors.

By the time Chomei Goro handed over the consolidated Goro clan to his son Shigehero, two generations of Okados had served as chairmen of the IBN board. The current chairman was Kenzo Okado, president of Usaijin Motors, a major shareholder of IBN, and the grandson of Ishidi Okado.

He had an office in the IBN building in the Jimu District and lived in the penthouse of the same building. A slender man with stern features, he bore the current assault on IBN with a public image of stoic restraint. His private face was one of despair, however, and more than once he half-seriously wished that his grandfather hadn't been so quick to trade the solid backbone of power of a yakuza clan for that of the legitimate business world. Some augmented yaks were exactly what he needed at a time like this.

He could hire security officers, but they would only protect. Industrial spies were just that—capable of stealing secrets, not lives. Neither had the clean efficiency of an *oyabun* sending out a man to bring him back the heads of his principal foes: Shigehero Goro, whose clan members were slowly eating away at Okado's control; the presidents of Shiken Sciences and Exxon Technics who were taking the legal route through the courts; the faceless leaders behind the Jones Co-Op.

IBN and its affiliates were under assault from every side and there was little Okado could legally do to stop any of them. It was for that reason that he waited now in his penthouse office for a spokesman from the Ho Fung Triad with his personal aide Muato Kamo. His aide was a compact, round-faced an in his late forties—a full decade older than Okado.

"My grandfather would roll over in his grave," Okado said. He took a sip from his second whiskey of the day though it was still before noon.

His aide made no comment. They'd been through it all too often before. There were only two options that they could undertake to save IBN from being swallowed by the Goro Clan, or letting the other corporations or the Co-Op eat away at its majority of Megaplex holdings. The first was that they could throw in with one of the Triads, but that was unthinkable. Bad enough to have any dealings with them—but to let them gain a foothold in the principal Nipponjin holdings? Never. Their other option was what they were now attempting—to buy stolen Claver technology.

With new high tech product on the market—particularly product that had its source in the mysterious *dojin no* Enclaves—they could recoup their position in the marketplace, thereby acquiring enough time to deal with all their problems. Liquid assets were the commodity they needed.

Judges were far more partial to helping a company that could make such help worth their while in untraceable funds. And credits could buy upscaled protection from the yaks' continuing attacks as well. Hard currency in place of data-based power in the Megaplex's central computers.

"We have no choice," his aide said.

"Hai."

Kamo frowned as Okado finished his whiskey in one long gulp and went to pour another. Before he could voice a carefully phrased protest, there was a rap at the door. A younger aide stepped inside.

"Chien Foo is here," she said.

Kamo glanced at Okado. "Send him in," he said at his employer's quick nod.

The Triad representative was dressed in an immaculate red and gold bodysuit. His black hair was cropped short, his eyes hidden behind dark glasses which he didn't remove when he entered. When the aide closed the door behind her, he gave a short bow to the two men waiting in the room.

"Tsao, ni hao ma?" Foo said in Mandarin by way of greeting. "Huen Ho Fung sends to you his regards."

Okado put his empty glass down on the bar and Kamo rose, both men returning Foo's greeting.

"Please return our regards to the esteemed Huen Ho Fung," Kamo said, also in Mandarin.

A thin smile touched Foo's lips. *"Hsieh—hsieh,"* he said. Thank you. Formalities over, he took a chair that commanded a view out the window. "To business?"

The two Nipponjin joined him by the window.

"You have the Claver chip?" Kamo asked.

"Shih-ti," Foo replied affirmatively. "But there has been a slight change in price, *ma?*"

"What kind of a change?" Okado asked.

"Ho Fung desires a certain . . . presence in your firm," Foo said. "Some shares as well as the previously agreed-upon credits."

Okado shook his head. "Impossible. The shareholders will not accept a non-Nipponjin buying into the company."

"Wo men tung." We understand. "For this reason Ho Fung has acquired a Nipponjin who will accept the shares on our behalf—in name only, *ma?*"

Okado and his aide exchanged glances. Was it worth it? At this point they really had no choice.

"We must have time to discuss this," Kamo said. "Shall we meet tomorrow?"

"Hen hau," Foo said. Very well. "But if you please, thus far we have kept very quiet about the goods that we have acquired for you. You must understand that there are others who would be interested in them as well, *ma?*"

"The new price requires new considerations," Kamo said.

Foo shrugged. *"Yang-yang hen kuei."* Everything's expensive. He stood up. "Until tomorrow, gentlemen."

Okado felt as though his last hopes were leaving the room with the Triad representative. When the door shut behind Foo, he slumped in his chair.

"What do we do now?" His voice was weary, the question almost rhetorical.

Kamo leaned forward. "We proceed as before."

"But to give them shares . . ."

"Not them," Kamo said. "We give them to their Nipponjin front man. *We* are not responsible for what he does with them."

Okado stared out the window. He could see his own reflection, vaguely present in the glass. The reflection looked to him like his grandfather's face—frowning at him.

"I must think on this some more," he said.

Kamo gave him a sympathetic nod. *"Hai.* I will see that your agenda is kept free for the day."

"Domo."

Kamo rose to leave. He hesitated at the door as Okado went over to the bar and poured a double shot of whiskey into a glass. Okado turned to look at him, the strain all too apparent in his drawn features. Kamo gave a quick short bow.

"Ja mata," he said softly, and left the room.

~ 2 ~

In Shigehero Goro's office on the other side of the Jimu District, Goro's second-in-command Yamamoto Ishimine shifted uncomfortably before his *oyabun's* impassive features. Only the dark glare in Goro's eyes betrayed his impatience.

The office was spartanly furnished. Goro sat behind a broad wooden desk that held his computer terminal. Ishimine sat on one of the two chairs in front of the desk. The only other furnishing was a table, across the room from the window, on which a matched pair of antique swords were displayed. Both blades had black lacquered scabbards and were mounted horizontally on a black lacquered rack with red and gold filigree, the shorter wakizashi above the longer katana. The polished lacquer gleamed in the soft light thrown from the window.

"What puzzles me," Goro said, "is that there has not been one word of rumor as to the whereabouts of the Claver chip."

"Which means that the messenger *must* have it," Ishimine said, "and is too frightened to market it. We will find her."

"I smell something else brewing, *neh*?"

"*Domo*, but—"

"One squat messenger does not kill—how many of our men now?"

"Three, Goro-san."

"Three!"

Ishimine sensibly said nothing.

"We still have the ship," Goro went on after a moment, "and our techs can take it apart, but all the software was on that one chip—everything that ran it. Without it we are faced with years of trial and error before we can claim even the smallest success. In the meantime, whoever has that chip will always be ahead of us."

This time he looked at his second-in-command, obviously expecting a response.

"Hai, so desu," Ishimine said. Yes, that's right.

"I am not pleased."

"Hai."

"You will bring me a member of one of the tongs, I think," Goro said. "I believe it is time for me to personally question one of them."

When Goro waved a hand in dismissal, Ishimine immediately rose from his seat and hurried from the room. Goro settled back in his chair and looked at his swords. He could sense that something ran deeply through the Megaplex and surrounding squats—the possibility of a new shift in power. It could be the tongs, or the triads. It could be the Co-Op. But whatever it was, he would not allow it to root itself too deeply.

Rising from his desk, he walked to the table that held his swords and ran his fingers across the smooth lacquered wood. His eyes grew distant.

There was only room for one power and that was the Goro Clan. But something was stalking him, something that did not understand that in this Megaplex—unlike the others—there could be no balance of power. There was only room for the Goro Clan.

"I am not pleased at all," he said to the empty room.

Dreamtime

Under Nanabozho's curious gaze, Gahzee stripped the yaks of all their clothing and gear before burying them in a shallow grave. To Maki Ota's companion he gave full burial rites, folding the big man's arms on his chest and facing him westward towards Epanggishimuk—Man's Last Destiny, the Land of Souls—before raising a cairn over him. He offered smoke to the grandfathers, then sat cross-legged beside the grave to meditate.

After a time he loosened his medicine bag from his belt. He took his spirit bell out and rolled it back and forth across his palm, letting its fey jingle speak to the four quarters. When his mind had grown quiet, he brought out his dreaming crystal. Interlacing his fingers, he shaped the Dreamer's hand sign—index and little fingers protruding at straight angles from the curved backs of the center four fingers, the dreaming crystal clasped between his palms.

Fire finger, water finger; spirit and motion. Stalker sides

of a Dream Wheel, for he was determined to stalk and hold a waking vision-dream.

He closed his eyes.

The Kachina-hey brought Mandamin to him.

They stood high on top of one of the abandoned buildings in the TOPQ corridor, looking out across the wounded land. Mandamin had the broad features of the People, but his skin was a burnished gold, his hair the yellow of maize, his loincloth the green of young corn. His eyes were the dark of an Enclave night when Grandmother Moon walked in shadow —black eyes, touched with glinting specks like stars.

"Do you remember the first time I came to you?" he asked Gahzee.

The *medé* nodded, though he had never met this *manitou* before. He understood that Mandamin spoke of his first visit to the People.

It was in the long ago.

Upon her deathbed, the grandmother of a young man named Zhowmin foretold the coming of a stranger. "When he comes," she told him, "you must do what he says."

Not long after her death, a stranger did arrive in the village. He was a tall, broad-shouldered man with surly features and an irritable manner who demanded to know if there were any good men in the village. After consulting with each other, the village elders sent for Zhowmin and presented him to the stranger.

Because they were of the same totem and he was thus bound to treat him as a brother, Zhowmin took the stranger into his own lodge. There they ate, and they smoked, and then Zhowmin asked the stranger why he had come.

"My name is Mandamin," the stranger told him, which meant Food of Wonder, from *manda* meaning wonder and *meen* meaning seed or berry. "The *manitou* have sent me," he went on to explain, "to test the worth of you and your people. As the most fitting test of your inner strength is through battle, so we will fight, you and I, to prove your merit. If you win, you live; but if you lose, you will die."

Zhowmin, who truly was a good man, shook his head. "I have no need to prove myself to you or any man."

Mandamin sighed. "If you won't fight, then I must take your cowardice as defeat. You will die and I will be forced to return to the *manitou* to tell them that there is not a single good man among the People."

It didn't matter to Zhowmin that his own courage or worth were in doubt, but he was angered that the overall worth of the People was questioned. And then he remembered what his grandmother had said when she foretold the coming of the stranger. *You must do what he says.* Partly from anger, partly through obedience, Zhowmin rose to his feet.

"I will fight you," he said.

They went into the forest that night and after selecting a clearing, they stripped to the waist and fought. But they were so evenly matched that by the time morning came, neither had gained the upper hand. They fell exhausted to the ground to regain their breath. Finally, bruised and bleeding from many wounds, they returned to Zhowmin's lodge to rest.

When they awakened it was evening once more. They ate a meal and shared smoke as though nothing had come between them, then returned to the clearing and fought again. Once more they fought until dawn, returning to Zhowmin's lodge with the morning light.

Not until the third night did Zhowmin gain the upper hand. Though both were weak, he managed to knock Mandamin to the ground. Before the stranger could rise, Zhowmin was upon him and had snapped his neck. Exhausted, Zhowmin knelt beside the body and wept for the stranger's pointless death.

In sorrow, he picked up Mandamin's body and buried it beside that of his grandmother, giving it all honour. When he went to the village *medé*, the medicine man counseled him to look after the stranger's grave as he did his grandmother's, and this Zhowmin did. Each day he went to the grave, bringing offerings and prayers of thanks and sorrow.

Then one evening in late spring, Zhowmin noticed a strange plant growing from the very center of Mandamin's grave—a plant that neither he nor the village *medé* could recognize, for all their knowledge of flora. As spring gave way to summer, the plant grew. By the end of the summer it was as tall as a man—a slender plant, crowned by a tuft of hair.

When the *medé* examined the new plant, he opened the wrappings about its seed and ate one yellow kernel to determine if the plant was good or evil. Upon swallowing the kernel, he turned to Zhowmin and said, "Be glad, for you have done the People a great service. You have not killed Mandamin; by demonstrating your worth, and thereby the worth of the People, you have given him life in a new form."

In such a way did the People receive corn from the *manitou*.

Remembering all of that, Gahzee said, "I have no wish to fight you, Mandamin."

Mandamin smiled. "I have not come to test your worth," he said. "I have come to instruct you. As once I brought a thing of great value to the People, now I bring you something new again. As once Zhowmin proved his worth through his obedience and strength, so now will you become a harbinger of that which is new through your own obedience."

Gehzee sighed. In the Dreamtime, there was no question but that he must listen to what the Kachina-hey had sent him.

"What must I do?" he asked.

"Follow me."

Spreading his arms wide, Mandamin threw himself from the rooftop. As soon as his feet left the solid footing of the building, he changed into a gold-feathered raven and flew off, towards the west. Gahzee hesitated. He looked down at the rubble-strewn street some ten stories below him.

Obedience.

He spread his arms, still looking down.

His teachers had warned him often enough: Stalking Death can find you in the Dreamtime as easy as in any other place. Easier, perhaps. For the Dreamtime was the crack between the worlds, between the waking world and the inner realms of the *manitou*, and Stalking Death walked the Dreamtime as surely as did the Kachina-hey.

Mandamin was a golden speck in the distance now.

Obedience.

Hey, Gahzee thought. I am here to learn, am I not?

He cast himself out from the building. For one heart-stopping moment he plummeted towards the ground, then his body exploded with pain as it twisted into a new shape, arms and legs shrinking in towards his body, fingers spreading to become wings, feathers sprouting from every pore. And then he was airborne, black wings cutting the air as he sped after Mandamin.

The *manitou* led him a long way across the Outer Lands, over acres of abandoned streets and buildings, until they finally rode a down draft and descended in a wide looping spiral to enter a city square that was sheltered in the shadow of four blocks of tall skyscraping buildings. They perched on a lamppost that was rusted and pocked from acid rains. Gahzee looked around the square.

Amidst the rubble, animals were gathered. Coyotes and rats, a striped-faced badger and hares, gulls and crows. Small creatures and large creatures. Birds such as robins and jays that Gahzee hadn't seen since leaving the Enclave. Beasts such as otter, beaver, and a bear. All gathered, discoursing in their own tongue—a language Gahzee could almost, but not quite, understand.

He meant to ask, what is this place, why have these beasts gathered here, but all that came from the new shape of his mouth was a raven's cry.

This is a council, Mandamin replied, his words echoing in Gahzee's mind. *A gathering of the elders of the animal and bird people.*

What do they discuss?

The unhappy lands.

Gahzee regarded them all again through the strange gaze of his bird shape that gave him a wide vision on either side of him, but left him blind to what was directly in front.

Why have you brought me here? he asked.

To show you how enemies can gather in council for their overall good. If the hare and wolf can sit together in council, could not men put aside their differences to do the same?

I understand, Gahzee replied. *But you have brought this vision to the wrong man. I'm not placed high in any council—the Enclaves are closed to me now. This is a matter for chiefs.*

Or Twisted Hairs.

I am not a Twisted Hair.

No. But you could be.

A haze fell across Gahzee's vision. The council of the animals and birds was washed away by a thick grey mist. He lost all sense of body and then—

—he opened his eyes beside the grave of Maki Ota's companion. He disengaged his fingers from their Dreamer's hand shape, catching his dreaming crystal in one palm. He rolled it on his palm, then returned it to his *skibdagan*. Pulling the strings of the medicine bag closed, he returned it to his belt and slowly stood.

He was alone by the grave. Even Nanabozho who had accompanied him there earlier was gone.

"I am not a Twisted Hair," he said, "and I don't even know how to begin the journey to become one."

Somewhere in the distance, out of his sight, a raven cried. Unlike his visit to the council of animals and birds in the Dreamtime, this time Gahzee thought he could understand that cry.

If you would only open your eyes, the raven seemed to be saying, *you would know that your journey has already begun.*

Nine

~ 1 ~

"Hi."

Gahzee turned to find his patient standing in the doorway of the building where he'd buried the yaks and her companion, looking in at him. She was dressed in her imitation leather pants once more, with a white blouse of some synthetic material tucked into its waist, and yellow boots on her feet. Under her left arm was an empty shoulder holster for one of the auto-pistols he had hidden while she was sleeping. The red tattooing on her face still reminded him of the paint the People wore when they went on a vision-quest or to war.

Though she still appeared somewhat worn from her ordeal, he realized, now that he could see her in the daylight, that she was quite attractive—even by the standards of the People. She was perhaps too thin for some braves, but she had an indefinable quality that shone in her eyes from which true beauty spoke.

"Hey, Maki," he said. "How are you feeling?"

"Better'n I should. That's some magic mushroom you've got there."

She kept her tone light, gaze studiously avoiding the graves and cairn, but the strain was still apparent. Gahzee moved to join her outside.

"What's your dog's name?" she asked.

"Dog . . . ?"

"The one with the funny eyes—he *is* your dog, isn't he? I saw you sitting in there—meditating, I guess—so I waited out here throwing a stick for him till you were done."

Gahzee blinked, certain she joking, then he looked to see where she was pointing. Nanabozho sat a few yards away, head cocked to one side, tongue lolling. There was a well chewed stick at his feet.

"He's a coyote," Gahzee said. "He started following me when I left the Enclave. I call him Nanabozho."

"You should just call him Bozo—he's a real fool."

Are we speaking of the same animal? Gahzee wondered. He was sure that Nanabozho was grinning at him.

"Coyote has always been somewhat of a trickster," he said aloud.

Maki hoisted herself up onto a piece of fallen masonry and sat there dangling her legs, kicking her heels against the stonework. "What's it like in the Enclaves?" she asked.

"Everything the Outer Lands is not. The air is clean. There are forests and fields—everything is green. It's different in some of the others—such as the Nez Ch'ii or Wadi Enclaves where their deserts have a different form of beauty—but that's what it's like in the Kwarthas Enclave where I lived."

"So why'd you leave?"

"I have a . . . task to perform."

"Uh-huh," she said, when he paused and didn't go on. "What kind of a task?"

Gahzee thought of his experiences in the Dreamtime since leaving the Enclave. "It seems to change, the longer I am in these lands."

"So're you going to the Plex?"

"In its general vicinity, at any rate—why?"

"I might know someone who can help you find what you're looking for. 'Course it'll cost you."

"How would you know what I am looking for?"

She shrugged. "I get around."

She was probably a very capable young woman on her own familiar terrain, Gahzee thought, but he guessed that nine-tenths of her present attitude was bravado. He understood why she was putting on this front—alone in these wastes with what she assumed was an enemy of her people—but to put aside her grief as she had to continue the brave face she was putting forward would only hurt her in the long run.

"Your fallen companion," he asked in a gentle voice. "What was his name?"

Her lower lip trembled, a crack showing in the walls of her bravado. "D-donnybrook."

He reached out a hand to her. "You should bid him farewell on his final journey."

"I . . ."

Gahzee helped her down from her perch and led her inside to where he'd built a tall cairn over her friend's body. She leaned on one of his arms and he could feel her trembling increase as they approached the cairn. She went down on her knees beside the stones and leaned against them.

"It . . . it's my fault he died," she said in a low voice.

"There is no blame when Stalking Death chooses a victim," Gahzee said. "Let your guilt go—it does not belong with you and only holds your friend back."

"You . . . you don't understand . . ."

Her bravado was rapidly crumbling now. Gahzee sat on his haunches beside her and laid an arm across her shoulders.

"Death is sorrow for the living," he said, "not for the dead. They are merely stepping onto another Wheel and that Wheel turns for them once more." When she turned her tearstained face toward him, he added, "These are not merely empty words of comfort, Maki; they are truth. I have seen that Wheel in the Dreamtime and it is not an evil place. There is no death—only a change of worlds."

"For . . . for your people, maybe . . ."

Gahzee shook his head. "For all people," he said and he was surprised himself, for though he had never considered it to be so, he knew it to be true. "The terms men use to describe such things change from tribe to tribe, from people to people, but not the truths. Sing to your friend—teach him the words that will speed him on his journey."

"But I . . . I don't know . . . them . . ."

So Gahzee sang them for her, in the patois of the squats so that both she and her friend would understand them:

I do not fear death
My time has come
I will walk the Path of Souls
Back to whence I came

While she repeated them, Gahzee rolled a cigarette. When it was lit, they offered its smoke to the four cardinal points, and lastly to Nanibush who ruled in the west. Nanibush who called the souls of the dead home and set them on their new Wheels when they were ready to walk the path with heart once more. It might be in this world, it might be in another, but all spirits walked the Wheel again. Then he left her alone by the cairn, so that the grief she freed from her heart might be private, and waited for her outside.

Nanabozho was gone when he stepped outside the building, but the stick Maki had been throwing for him still lay in the dirt. Thoughtfully, Gahzee picked it up and ran a finger along the toothmarks.

Hey, brother, he wondered. And who in truth are you?

~ 2 ~

"Guess I'm not so tough after all, am I, Donnybrook?" Lisa said softly to his cairn.

The flow of her tears had eased now. She wiped her nose on her sleeve. Inside, the loss didn't ache so much anymore—that was the Claver's doing. It was just words. Stepping onto Wheels and changing worlds. But Gahzee's quiet assurances, his steady presence; and the simple ceremony of smoke and song had made her believe those words all the same. Maybe it was just because she wanted to, but somehow it seemed very possible that Kay and Donnybrook had gone on to a better place—what could be worse than the squats or the badlands? It was better to think they'd gone on, to believe Gahzee, than to accept what Donnybrook had told her.

I figure it's all shit. The lights go out and you hit the dark road. . . .

That was too hard to bear.

She'd wanted to put up a strong front to the Claver, hadn't wanted to trust him at all, but he'd undermined her attempts with his gentle manner and she found herself feeling glad that he had. Though there was no good rational reason that she should, she *did* feel free of her guilt. She wasn't going to forget. The sorrow was still there. But the raw pain of her grief, and her red anger aimed at the yaks, had both been tempered by an odd, displacing sense of peace.

She wasn't ready to give up her personal vendetta against the Goro Clan, but it was now possible to put it back into perspective again. Help the Co-Op—*that'd* take them down. And as for the Claver . . .

She didn't understand her reaction to him at all. In the very short time she'd been with him she felt she could trust him as she'd been able to trust few others. Kay. Her grandmother who'd raised her after her parents had died. Donnybrook and the Ragman. Eddie Ch'a—though she hadn't seen him for a couple of months. Not since he'd taken up junkwalking.

That didn't add up to a whole lot—not even in a lifetime as short as her own.

So what was it? Some kind of magic in his voice and manner? In his mushrooms and his smoke?

It didn't seem right. She'd grown up seeing the Clavers on the vids—treacherous *dojin no*, dirty redskins, puking Clavers. They were always the bad guys. And not just bad, they were evil. It was a racial characteristic that, according to history, would never change. The Clavers hated anyone who didn't have their own pure blood. They were supposed to be worse than the Nipponjin in that way.

They'd destroyed the world and then retreated into their Enclaves, leaving the rest of humanity to scrabble out a living as best they could. They kept a steady surveillance from their orbiting satellites and space stations to make sure that no one would develop technology to match their own. Anyone who did, they just burned them down with lasers from one of their space stations. It was the Clavers who were to blame for every ill.

She compared all of that against the way Gahzee had taken care of her this morning. The tenderness of his manner. The caring he showed for Donnybrook. None of those were the actions of an evil man. She might not be as tough as she liked to let on she was, but she sure as shit wasn't naive. You didn't grow up in the squats and stay innocent. She *knew*. What she saw in the Claver was what was there.

So what about all the stories? She thought of the Ragman talking about the Co-Op's bad rep. Plex propaganda, he'd said. Was it the same deal with the Clavers? The assholes who ran the Kaisha sure weren't going to take the fall for the way things were themselves—not if there was a scapegoat handy.

She had to talk to Gahzee.

And trust him?

What if she got burned?

Again her thoughts went back to his helping her, the care he'd shown with Donnybrook, the gentle touch on her shoulders, the quiet belief in his voice as he spoke of other worlds and Wheels.

"Shit," she said, running a hand along the stones of Donnybrook's cairn. "I don't know what to do."

It was a long time later that she finally rose from her place beside the cairn and went outside. She found the Claver sitting by the door of the building where she and Donnybrook had taken shelter last night. He was scraping clean rabbit skins. Bozo lay on the other side of the door, head lifting, ears pricked up, mismatched eyes watching her cross the square.

"I made some tea," Gahzee said, looking up at her approach. "It's inside by the fire and should still be warm."

Lisa slouched on the ground in front of him and hooked her elbow on a piece of fallen stone.

"We've got to talk," she said. "And no bullshit. I've got to know what you're doing here, what you want with me, what your people really want."

"What I am doing here is my own business," he said. Amusement touched his features, taking the sting from his words. "As for you—I never wanted anything from you, Maki Ota. I found you by chance, nothing more, and merely stopped to help a fellow traveller in need. And as for what my people want, I'm not sure I really understand the question."

Lisa sighed. No bullshit, she thought. Right. Everything he said was perfectly reasonable, but he obviously wasn't ready to open up to her. And she wasn't ready to open up to him yet either.

"Why did you guys do it?" she asked. "Why did you disappear into your Enclaves and leave the world the way it is?"

Gahzee set aside the skin he was working on. "How much do you know of the history of the tribes?" he asked.

Lisa shrugged. "Just what I've seen on the vids."

"We did not do this to our Mother Earth," he said. Picking up a handful of dry dirt he let it sift through his fingers. "Your people did this. Before any of you came to this continent, all the land was the way it is now in the Enclaves.

For centuries we lived in harmony with the land, sharing its bounty with the beasts and birds.

"It's true that we had wars with other tribes, but they were battles fought with honour—a natural part of the world's working that sees that only the true of heart survive. We harmed none but ourselves in those wars. We never destroyed the land.

"We took from it only what was needed, and we gave back to it as much as we took. Our Walk blessed the land and its children, beast and bird. Our drums and sacred smoke spoke to the *manitou*—the mysteries—weaving a harmony between the Wheels that are and the Wheels of the Great Mystery. Living in such a manner is what we call the path with heart.

"Your people came, and no sooner did you arrive, than you began a systematic rape of the land. You butchered the buffalo. You fought the tribes—not in honourable battle, but genocidally. You bound the land with roads and railways and concrete and steel wastelands you called cities. You fouled the air. You created weapons that could destroy vast tracts of land in a single flash of nuclear fire. Those of us that you let live were relegated to reserves. We were taken from our native lands and placed on lands that your people had no use for. But if oil was discovered, or gold, or timber, or anything you might use, the treaties were ignored, and we were displaced once more.

"We lived in abject poverty. Many of our people—especially our young—committed suicide. Others became alcoholic. Both were symptoms of a deeper malaise—dispossession and depression, the characteristics of all cultures suffering poverty.

"Then in the late twentieth century a Lakota man named Daniel Hollow Horn acquired a great deal of monetary wealth which he used to help the tribes. Our young went to universities and their studies became the foundation of our freedom. We won our lands back in the world courts. We created the Enclaves and later our space stations. We were finally free, but the world itself grew no better.

"While we struggled to regain our harmony with the *manitou* and Mother Earth, your people continued to rape her. Continued your dishonourable wars. Continued to destroy everything you could. *That* is why we withdrew into our Enclaves—to ensure that this time we kept our freedom. That some part of the world remains as it was meant to be."

The Claver paused. His features, which had grown stern as he spoke, softened now and he smiled.

"I'm sorry," he said. "You asked a simple question and I replied with a lecture."

" 'Sokay," Lisa said. "I wanted to know. I never heard about any of that stuff before.

"The history of most cultures tends to be kept in such a way that they themselves are always thrown into a positive light."

"I guess. But why do you still stay in your Enclaves? Why don't you share what you have now so that everyone can have a better life?"

"Because your people never changed."

"We just want to get by," Lisa said, thinking of her own life in the squats, thinking of her friends.

"And what of those who are in the positions of power?"

Like the Goro Clan, Lisa thought. Like the guys who ran the Kaisha—the big corporations.

"I guess I understand."

"That's not to say that we live in utopias," Gahzee went on. "It's true our lands are green. Our homes are no longer primitive tents and lodges. Our technologies are as concerned with the clean disposal of wastes as they are with advances. We have cities, integrated with their environment, but we also keep our old traditions. Each man and woman remains close to the *manitou* and Mother Earth—though some make a lifetime dedication to such efforts. Those we call *medé*.

"But we are still human. We have crimes and the need for tribunals. In our councils there are those who argue that we must finish what your people have begun—cleanse the world of you and all your works so that we may lead the world onto a new Wheel. There are others who argue that we must share what we have with those less fortunate beyond the Enclaves.

"In some respects, we have done that—but so far we have only shared our knowledge with those who hold similar beliefs to our own. Other tribes who maintain their traditions, who care for their world as they might a brother or sister—or a mother. There are few such left in the Outer Lands."

"Is that what you're doing now?" Lisa asked. "Scouting for people you can help?"

Gahzee shook his head.

Lisa took a deep breath, then slowly let it out. "It's the Claver flyer that went down—right?"

Gahzee's eyes narrowed. "How did you know about that?"

"There were rumors. Then there was this package—the one that's supposed to have the systems chip from the flyer—that's been floating around the squats. Everybody's after it."

"Your people have the chip?"

Lisa shook her head. "First of all, we're not all the same people—you gotta understand that. A rat in the squats has got about as much in common with people in the Plex as your version of history does with theirs. Then in the Plex itself, everybody's after each other. The Kaisha, the triads, the yaks, the Jones Co-Op. It's the same deal in the squats. You've got the rats, the chinas, the tongs . . .

"I don't know who's got the chip. I was delivering it and got robbed for my trouble. I didn't know what it was until all of a sudden I had yaks and you-name-its crawling up my ass looking for either it or a piece of my skin. You see—"

Here it was, Lisa realized. Time to play or fold. Did she trust him or not? If everything he'd told her was true . . .

She met his gaze, trying to read something in his eyes that wasn't there. *She* had to make the choice, take the chance. That was something nobody could hand her. There came a point when you had to either give a little trust, or let it all go. She'd said no bullshit—right?

"Maki," he began.

Lisa sighed. "First of all," she said, "my name's not Maki Ota. That's just a name the Ragman came up with to go with my swagger girl gear. My real name's Lisa Bone."

"It suits you far better."

"Yeah, whatever. Anyway, let me take you back to square one, okay?"

When he nodded, she began to relate the events of the past few days, laying it all out for him in the same straightforward manner he'd used to tell her about how the Enclaves came to be.

"That flyer must not fall into anyone's hands," Gahzee said when she was done.

"Looks to me like it already has," Lisa replied.

Gahzee rubbed at his face. "This is worse than we suspected."

"So you *are* after the chip, aren't you?"

"The chip, the flyer . . . and information as to what has become of the Maniwaki Enclave."

"What do you mean, what's become of the Enclave?"

"We've lost all contact with it. Satellite photos show that its barrier is still intact, but we can't get a clear shot of what's going on inside. We've sent two flyers out to it now. Neither have ever returned. What the elders fear most is the possibility that our tech has fallen into enemy hands."

"Well, now you know at least half of the story," Lisa said. "The Goro Clan's got one of those flyers."

Gahzee nodded. "He shouldn't have been able to retrieve the chip that ran the flyer. They're made to self-destruct in a situation such as this."

"Well, you know tech," Lisa said, "if it *can* break down, it will. At least that's the way it usually goes in the squats."

"You said earlier—before this talk we've had—that you knew someone who could help me find what I was looking for."

"Yeah. The Ragman."

"You spoke of a cost . . . ?"

Lisa met his gaze. "It won't be from me—not now. But the Ragman'll want something."

"Will you take me to him?"

"Sure. But we'll have to go in at night. If somebody spots you in the squats, we'll have yaks and drones all over our asses." She looked over to the doorway of the building. "Maybe we can dress you up in one of those kevlar overcoats and pass you off as a yak. You're big—but so are a lot of them."

"I would be very grateful."

"Hey, we're on the same side, aren't we? We both want a piece of Shigehero Goro."

"He has something we both want," Gahzee amended.

"Whatever."

"You should let me replace your poultices. Are you starting to get stiff?"

Lisa nodded. "A little. 'Specially my back."

He reached out a hand toward her cheek, but didn't quite touch the skin. "I have something that will help this heal more quickly as well."

Out in the daylight now, and feeling more herself, Lisa took a good look at him.

"You're not in all that great shape yourself. Have you been in a fight lately?"

Gahzee nodded. "With some *windigo*."

"Winda-who?"

"A band of Outlanders—they were flesh eaters. We call them *windigo*."

"The people out here are really cannibals?"

"I've only had limited contact with them, but so it would seem."

Laying his knife down on the half-cleaned rabbit skin, he rose smoothly to his feet and led the way back inside the building. She followed him in and lay down on the bedding so that he could replace the poultice on her back. It felt kind of funny having his hands on her. Stranger's hands. But they were gentle.

"What's this path with heart you were talking about?" she asked.

"It's the Walk of the People. A harmonizing to bring all things to Beauty."

"You guys are big on good looks?"

She couldn't see his smile, but she could feel it.

"I speak of inner Beauty," he said. "We have many different terms for such intangibles, but the one I prefer comes from one of the other tribes—*quaheystamaha*. That means 'you dance in my heart.' That is something one can feel for a place of great beauty, in the love one holds for another, in the mystery that binds us to the *manitou*."

Lisa didn't say anything. She closed her eyes while he replaced the bandage over the new poultice. Turning around, she sat up, pulling up her sleeve so that he could replace the one on her arm. But before he could begin, she laid a hand on his arm.

"Can you teach me that stuff?" she said. "You know, the path with heart and the quahey-whatever?"

"Why would you want to learn?"

She shrugged. "I dunno." But then she smiled. "No, that's not true. It . . . it's got meaning, I guess. That's the best way of putting it. And I'd like to be a part of that. Things don't mean a whole lot in the squats and I don't want to be one of that people that doesn't care about . . . the Beauty."

He held her gaze for a long moment, then glanced towards the doorway where Bozo was sitting.

"A tribe of three," he said softly to the coyote.

"Say what?" she asked.

His gaze returned to her. "I would be honoured to teach you what I can," he said.

~3~

The opening at the Ojika Gallery was in honour of a new showing of Kimitake Mitsui's work. His three-dimensional art celebrated a return to the old *asobi* style of work—sculptural puzzles, visual puns, and geometric paradoxes of the Fukuda School that took its inspiration from the twentieth–century Kamikitazawa master, Shigeo Fukuda. They ranged from sculptures no larger than one's hand—such as "Elemental," which when viewed from one side showed a woman rising from a crouched position, but when turned one hundred and eighty degrees, became a clenched fist—to an entire room of red and white tiles that proved, only when one slowly ascended the stairs on the side of the room to the second level and looked down, to be an illustration from the *Kojiki*, showing Urashima rescuing the Dragon King's daughter while she was still in the shape of a tortoise.

Yip's favorite was a small black and white statue of the trickster Tanuki. Viewed one way it was a black badger, from another angle it became a white teakettle such as the one that, according to the old folktale, Tanuki was capable of transforming himself into. The price was merely five thousand credits.

"Are you enjoying yourself?" Hirose asked.

Yip thought: Rubbing elbows with the Megaplex's Nipponjin elite, viewing such masterpieces of art, on his arm the most beautiful woman in the room—was there any question?

"Very much," he replied. "This is all marvelous."

"We should meet the artist," Hirose said. "He considers his work a part of a twofold Zen process—it is a transmission not dependent on words or phrases as much as a direct transmission from mind to mind. He says, you should not rely on what is written about art; you should take your vision directly from the mind of the artist into your own mind. Do not interpret—sympathize. The vision that can be explained in words is banal."

"And yet you use words to explain the process of appreciation," Yip said with a smile.

Hirose replied with an eloquent shrug.

Yip nodded. "*Domo.*"

"Have you seen enough?" Hirose asked.

"Can one ever see enough of such work?"

"I thought perhaps you might be hungry—or did you eat before we met?"

Yip shook his head.

"If you would like, I have the makings of a simple dinner at my home. Shumai and noodles. Fresh octopus . . ."

"Fresh?"

"Goro has it sent in," Hirose said, then she hesitated, obviously uncomfortable.

"Fumiko," Yip began.

"My friends call me Miko."

"*Hai.* Miko. I am trying hard to follow your advice, but when I look at what you are, and what I am, and consider us together, my ability to keep faith falters . . ."

The spectre of Shigehero Goro lay between them. Yip glanced at the nearest of Mitsui's statues and thought, the same object viewed from different perspectives . . . were people really any different? Hirose caught his glance.

"*Dozo,*" she said, "Please. Let tonight belong to us."

He met her gaze for a long moment, then inclined his head slightly. "I would bc honoured to have dinner at your home," he said.

It was after the meal, while they lay together still entangled in each other's arms on the round bed in Hirose's *apato*, that the spectre of Goro rose between them again. It was Hirose who spoke of him, breaking her earlier request of Yip. She ran a delicate finger along his chest, then sat up, breasts bare as the sheets fell away. She drew her legs up to her chest and faced Yip.

"Goro told me to nurture a relationship with you," she said.

Yip sat up slowly. He began to reach for her, then let his hand fall to the futon. "Why?" he asked softly.

She shrugged. "He believes you will be of some use to him. Not today perhaps, or next week, but at some time. Shigehero Goro is a man who looks far into the future."

"Do you . . . do this often?"

Yip kept the regret from his voice but he couldn't stop the tightening in his chest. It *had* been too good to be true—as common sense had told him. Lies in a grey world.

"No," she said softly.

"Why have you told me this? Why now?"

Her smile was sad. "I didn't lie to you, Phillip. I do like you. I would have spoken of this sooner, but I was being selfish. I wanted one evening with you—uncluttered by Goro's presence, by your work, or my work. And now, with that evening behind us, I find I like you better still, and would have no more lies between us."

Yip regarded her steadily. Was this yet another facet she was presenting, another role to be played out? Pretending she sympathized with him, admitting to the orders that Goro had given her, merely to draw him deeper into her snare?

"What you are telling me," he said. "It makes trust difficult."

"I know. I will understand if you leave now."

Again he thought of Mitsui's art—the clever sculptures that changed, depending on the viewer's perspective. Looking at her now as she faced him, he saw a beautiful woman, untouched by blemishes. But he remembered when she first disrobed, the silky cloth falling from her skin to pool on the floor about her feet, and there on her back, from the nape of her neck to just above the swell of her buttocks, was the ornate rococo design of a yakuza-styled tattoo. A red and green Chinese dragon swam through a gleaming blue ocean, its menacing head drawn back on her right shoulder blade, spitting red and golden flames across to her left.

Depending from which side one viewed her, she was a

woman, more beautiful than most, but still much the same as any other he might meet in the Megaplex, or she was a yakuza Dragon Lady, geisha-trained and potentially deadly.

"If I asked you to stand by me against Goro," he asked, "what would be your reply?"

Surprise touched her features. Her eyes darkened as she thought, but her gaze never left his.

"I . . . I don't know," she said finally.

"Hai," Yip said. "That, at least, is an honest reply."

The question was plain in her eyes, but he merely drew her toward him. As they lay down on the futon once more, his hand moved over her breasts, then down the flat expanse of her stomach to cup the soft triangle of her pubic hair. From this position, he could no longer see the yakuza-styled tattoo.

"If I leave, Miko," he breathed softly into her ear, "it will only be because you have sent me away."

She covered his hand with her own. "Then you will have to wait a very long time," she whispered.

After that, they had no more breath for words, no more interest in Shigehero Goro or yakuza. Only in each other.

Ten

~1~

The Ragman was holding court in the part of the squats Market that lay closest to the badlands. This was where the junkwalkers sold their salvaged goods, everything from machine parts and scrap metal to computer components and electrical gear in various stages of disrepair. Most of the latter a Plex tech wouldn't even consider looking at, little say using, but in the hands of a squats tech wizard like the Ragman, the most worthless-looking bits of wiring and outmoded chips were the heart and soul of the amazing computer wares that he jury-rigged in his workshop.

He sat beside a wheelbarrel already half-filled with newly acquired gear, haggling with the junkwalkers, while his strongarm stood behind him, arms folded across his enormous chest. J.D.'s presence kept the junkwalkers honest.

"This is crap," the Ragman was telling Jaenie Lash. He tossed the tangled nests of wiring back at her. "It's all corroded, darling—worn right through in parts. Can't you do any better?"

"It's the best you're gonna find, Ragman. You been out in the badlands lately?"

Jaenie was a small compact woman, dressed in baggy overalls, scuffed boots, and a worn synth leather jacket a size too big. She kept her hair dyed orange and cropped short, top and sides, letting it hang down in a long braid in back. She carried her gear in a pack that had to weigh seventy pounds, but she could lift it without any strain. At either hip was a sheathed foot-long knife.

"If I was walking the badlands, darling," the Ragman asked her, "then why would I be looking at this crap you're dragging around?"

"I'm just telling ya—times are hard."

And didn't he know that? the Ragman thought to himself. He took in the gaunt look of her and sighed.

"Times are always hard," he said. He picked up the wiring again. "Aw, shit. I'll give you a half-dozen credits for the lot—just find me something sweet next time."

The gratitude in her eyes embarrassed him.

"Thanks, Ragman. I—"

He laid a finger across her lips. "You owe me first crack at your next big find, darling—then we're square. Okay?"

"You got it."

The Ragman counted out the credits and handed them over, giving Jaenie a wink and a grin as she left, then he turned to the next junkwalker.

"Hey, Eddie. Watcha got for me today?"

By the time he was finished with his business, the day was failing. With J.D. pushing the wheelbarrel, the Ragman returned to his workshop behind the Ch'ing-jen Fan. There he found one of the Co-Op's undercover toms waiting for him.

Sun Hang was a wiry teenager, half china, half who-knew-what. He wore his black hair in an approximation of the Ragman's dreadlock Mohawk, but it was too fine to knot in the same snakelike braids, falling in a wave to one side of his head unless he tied it back. Like a lot of the chinas, his jacket had an ornate design embroidered on its back in bright day-glo thread. His had the Chinese ideographs for *ni deh*—fuck you.

"You got some news for us, Jack?" the Ragman asked as he settled in behind his desk.

Sun Hang glanced back at J.D., then took the padded crate in front of the desk and drew it up closer. "Nothing on Donnybrook or the swagger girl he was strongarming, but I heard that three yaks got themselves lost—looking for Lisa Bone. They were leaning heavy on the chinas, and then Goro pulled in a couple to question himself, and they ain't been back on the streets yet, *tung ma*?"

"Yeah, All too well." The Ragman frowned. "You got to run them down, Jack. The girl's name is Maki Ota. Goro gets his hands on either her or Donnybrook and we're looking at some real grief."

"*Shih-ti,*" Sun Hang said with a quick nod.

"So whatcha waiting for?"

Sun Hang jumped to his feet. "I'm gone," he said.

Kowtowing with great exaggeration, a mocking grin on his lips, he slipped out of the room. The last thing the Ragman saw before the door closed behind the departing tom were the ideographs emblazoned on the boy's jacket.

"Yeah, fuck you, too," the Ragman said, a grin tugging at his own lips. But then he frowned again. "What do you think, J.D.?" he asked. "Is Goro gonna send some of his clowns to see us? I'm trying to keep business as usual, but sooner or later he's gonna come looking for the Ragman to find what he lost. He's gonna know, like everybody knows, that if it's tech, it could end up here."

"I an'. I's gonna eat dem yaks, dey come in here," J.D. told him.

"I'm wondering if we might not be smarter to find ourselves a little hidey-hole," the Ragman said.

He was just thinking aloud, a habit he'd gotten into when he was alone with his strongarm. Not that J.D. understood half of what he heard. The radiation had seen to that. Nobody knew how long he'd been out frying in the badlands before the Ragman picked him up, but what he lacked in brains, he more than made up for in brawn and loyalty, and the Ragman liked to feel as though he was talking to someone.

"Thing is, we go into hiding and then nobody's gonna be able to find us—not our own people, not Lisa and Donnybrook. I don't know . . ." But then he had it. "J.D. I want you to run down Jaenie—tell her I need someone to run me a message."

It was simple. He'd hole up and leave Jaenie to watch the place from outside. If the right person came along, she'd show them to where he was waiting. If it was yaks, she'd just do a quick disappearing act herself.

"Who's gonna eat dem yaks if I an' I's gone?"

The Ragman blinked, then he lifted a Steeljack from under his desk and thumbed off the safety. "Me and 'jack, J.D. Get a move on now."

The big man moved quick and soft for all his bulk. He was out the door and halfway across the bar beyond it before the door swung shut behind him. The Ragman scratched a cheek and stared at the door, willing Lisa and Donnybrook to step through it. Three yaks gone, huh? Maybe Donnybrook had taken them out, but maybe they had him and Lisa up against the wall somewhere.

In the pit of his stomach, the Ragman had a bad feeling about how things were going and it just wouldn't go away. He kept the muzzle of the Steeljack pointed at the door, and then leaned his head on the desk, propped up by his free arm.

Interesting times, he thought, remembering the old Chinese curse. Nothing ever seemed simple anymore. Maybe things only got simple when you were dead. That being the case, he was happy to keep on living in interesting times. At least it meant he was still alive.

~ 2 ~

In an interrogation room hidden in the back of one of the Goro Clan's warehouses, Shigehero Goro stepped back from the body hanging on the wall. There was blood on the blade of his razor-sharp *aikutchi*—the small hiltless dagger that he liked to use for such work. The woman hanging by wires that were strung to meathooks embedded in the walls had died under that blade—just as the other china had done before her. Both of them had told him whatever they knew, but it wasn't enough.

He already knew that the triads were interested in the missing Claver chip. That the tongs were using their own men and hired chinas to search the squats the same as his own *kobun* were. That the Co-Op's toms were everywhere, also looking. What he wanted was some hard facts.

Goro plucked a shirt from the heap of clothes that they'd stripped from the chinas and used it to clean the *aikutchi*. He dropped the bloodied cloth on the floor and sheathed the blade.

He was not yet prepared to launch a full frontal attack upon either the triads or the tongs. There was no profit in such a war. But there were other avenues of inquiry that he could still pursue.

"Torogano," he said softly.

"Hai."

A grey-clad yak stepped smartly forward from the line of six *kobun* who had watched their *oyabun* question the prisoners. His silver contacts gleamed in the bright lights of the interrogation room.

Goro regarded him with pleasure. Torogano carried a Steeljack in a shoulder holster, but he also carried a *wakizashi*—the shorter of the paired swords known collectively as *daisho*. Goro allowed his men to carry whatever weapons they felt comfortable with, but in his heart he was still a traditional yakuza, and a true yakuza lived by his sword.

"Bring me the one who calls himself the Ragman," Goro said.

"Hai."

Torogano signaled to one of the other yaks who gave Goro a quick nod, then left with Torogano. Goro thrust his sheathed *aikutchi* into his belt. He glanced back at the two dead chinas.

"Dump them," he said to his remaining *kobun*. *"Ugokuna zo!"* Get a move on it.

Ignoring them as they went about their business, he unrolled a straw mat on the far side of the room and sat down upon it to meditate.

Eleven

~ 1 ~

Lisa sat on a folded blanket, her hands on her knees, her knees drawn up to her chin. The firelight gleamed on her striped messenger's tattoos and her eyes were bright with interest. On the other side of the small fire, sitting cross-legged on one of the dead yaks' overcoats, Gahzee was talking. The thin tendrils of smoke given off by the fire were drawn out the door into the dusk where acid rain was hissing on the pavement. Bozo lay a few yards away from them, inside the building, his head pillowed on his crossed paws, blue eye watching Lisa, brown eye watching Gahzee.

"Everything fits onto a Wheel," Gahzee was explaining.

"You mean, like everything repeats itself? History rolling in cycles?"

"Not exactly, although there is a Wheel of history. But to the People, the opposite of present is not past, but absent."

"So you guys don't get into what's already gone down, or worry about what's coming up? Sounds like living in the squats. We just try to make it through the day."

"It's not that the past has lost its importance, nor that the future should be ignored," Gahzee said. "Nor is it that the present is so difficult that one has no time to expend on anything but survival. It is that what is here and now is most important, because *we* are here and now. Everything else is absent."

This was getting spacey, Lisa thought. Now. Here. Put 'em together and you get nowhere. Kinda like Zen. You only hit satori when you weren't looking for it.

"Tell me about the Wheels," she said.

He drew a circle in the dirt, with a cross inside it. "I will show you the Wheel that explains the Twenty Count," he said. "They are the numerical tones that make up Kitche Manitou—the Great Mystery.

"Grandfather Sun rises here in the east—" he wrote the number one at the place the right arm of the cross touched the rim of the circle, "—giving the wörd its basic illumination as he moves west to marry Grandmother Earth." Now he wrote the number two where the left side of the cross met the circle. "She is the intuitive go-within power. They make love in the west and move together."

He wrote the number three where the bottom of the cross touched the circle. "Their first born are the plants that live here in the south. Their song is 'give it away and know you are a part of everything,' and so they give us food and oxygen. The second born are the animals in the north—" he wrote the number four where the top of the cross met the circle, "—who realize resonance with all that is. They are happy to be themselves.

"Third born are all sacred humans, and they live here, in the center." He wrote the number five at the joining of the cross's two lines, then looked up at her. "And those are the first five Counts of the Great Mystery."

"Why do you say sacred humans?" Lisa asked.

"Sky Woman," Gahzee began, then he smiled. "Mother Earth is also known as Grandmother Moon—Nokomis, the Sky Woman."

"She's a grandmother and a mother?"

"Is that so odd? When the mother's child has a child, what does the mother become?"

"Okay. You were talking about sacred humans."

"Sky Woman created the People to Walk the path with heart. We are here to bless the land and its children with our care. We speak with drum voices and sacred smoke to the *manitou* and weave a harmony between the Wheels that are and the Wheels of the Otherworld where the *manitou* dwell. When the People Walk the path with heart, they are fulfilling their sacred duty."

It all made a certain amount of sense, though Lisa couldn't help but think that these sacred people hadn't been doing such a shit-hot job or else why was the world the armpit it was? But she didn't speak that thought.

"What are the other Counts?" she asked instead.

Gahzee wrote a six between the one and three, placing it southeast on the Wheel. "This is the place of our ancestors." Seven in the southwest portion. "This is the place of sacred dreams." Eight in the northwest. "Here is where the records of all that has passed are kept—what some call karma, others the Book of Life." Nine in the northeast. "This is the place that balances the male and female sides of each of us—a place of movement." Above the five in the center of the Wheel, he wrote the number ten. "And this is the place of sacred intellect."

He looked up at her again. "Are you with me still?"

"Yeah. I guess."

"It takes time to understand the relationships between the various parts of any Wheel. Let me finish this one and we will explore them."

"Sure," Lisa said. How does he remember all this stuff? she wondered. She was finding it confusing, but at the same time it spoke to something in her.

"The eleventh Count is placed here, beside the first. It is the place of the enlightenment of the collective unconscious. Its placement relates to Grandfather Sun who provides basic illumination. Beside the second, here in the west, is the twelfth—the collective memory of all humans, which is also the first movement of life."

"Because the moon remembers for them?" Lisa asked.

Gahzee nodded. "Because Mother Earth never forgets. The thirteenth Count is the spiritual essence of all plants and its place is here in the south, where the plants dwell. This is the second movement of life, known as White Buffalo Woman. The fourteenth Count is the third movement of life, and it lives with the animals in the north. Its name is Sweet Medicine, but it is also called 'Death is an Ally.' The fifteenth Count is that of the universal mind, and it dwells in the center with the sacred humans and intellect."

"What do you mean by 'Death is an Ally'?" Lisa wanted to know.

"One should not fear death, but think of it as a friend."

Lisa's face clouded. Think of it as a friend? What about when it took your friends away?

"Easy to say," she said.

"Not with true intent," Gahzee replied.

"I suppose."

"Let me give you the final Counts. Each tribe has its own names for them, but I will teach you those that the Twisted Hairs use."

"Twisted Hairs?"

"They are a council of elders, of *medé*—shaman—who belong to all tribes and no tribe. Their name comes from their method of teaching—a braiding of knowledges from all the tribes.

"The sixteenth Count is placed here in the southeast. They are the Achaloda-hey—the sacred avatars who represent the last movement of life. Next are the Kachina-hey, the dream teachers, who dwell here in the southwest. In the northwest are the Chulamahda-hey, the magic teachers, who hold the Book of Life in trust. In the northeast are the Hokkshideh-hey, the enlightened ones—what you might call the great Bhuddas. And here in the center, is the twentieth Count—Wakantanka, whom my people name Kitche Manitou."

"What does the 'hey' mean in those names?" Lisa asked.

"It comes from the Lakota word *heyoka* which means *manitou* or spirit. The Iroquois use *orenda* . . . Many words with one meaning."

Lisa looked down at the finished Wheel that he'd drawn in the dirt:

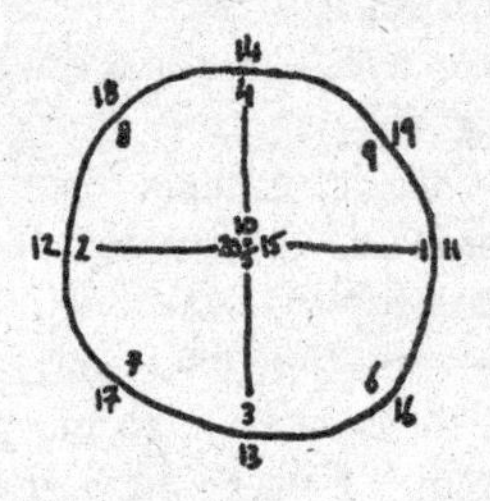

"This last one—Wakantanka," she said, pointing to the number twenty. "Isn't that what all the Counts are supposed to be—just parts of the Great Spirit?"

Gahzee nodded. "Collectively, the Twenty Count is the Great Spirit, but it still has a place on the Wheel. You see its placement? It shares the center with the sacred humans, intellect and the universal mind—again, all parts of the same thing."

"It's confusing."

"Then let me show you a simpler Wheel—one that compares man's studies with the Wheel of nature." He made another circle in the dirt. "In the center we have a catalyst that compares to man's math and language. North, we have wind and science. East, we have fire and media communication—writing and art. South, we have water and music. West, we have earth and magic."

"Magic? You guys believe in magic?"

"Magic works by will, focus, and intent. If you truly wish something, and can focus on it to the exclusion of all else and concentrate on attaining it, then it will come to you. So, yes, I believe in magic, though it is but a convenient term for something far more complex than what you appear to perceive. When I take you into the Dreamtime, you will understand better."

He smiled, then went on. "Everything fits on a Wheel, just as everything one does is a Walk. The trick is to understand which Wheel you are on and use that knowledge to continue to Walk the path with heart. It can be as simple or as complex as you wish it to be."

Lisa rubbed at her eyes. "I think I'm hitting overload," she said.

Gahzee nodded. "We have talked enough of this for one day. It's time we prepared to visit this Ragman of yours."

"Okay. Just let me copy down these Wheels."

She took out the com-link that Gahzee had returned to her and switched it to its internal memory mode that could hold a limited amount of data—enough for notes and the like. Outside, the rain had let up again.

Gahzee rose smoothly to his feet. "Do that—but don't work too hard at remembering. The Wheel of the Twenty Count lies in your subconscious now. As we move on to further lessons, it will rise to the fore of your thoughts when needed, and you will understand it and its relationship to every other Wheel you find yourself on."

"Where are you going?" Lisa asked.

"I wish to look over the terrain from the roof."

"Yeah," Lisa said as she bent back over her com-link. "Take a good long look for some more yaks. We don't need their grief."

~ 2 ~

Was it to be this simple—doing the work of a Twisted Hair? Gahzee wondered as he made his way to the roof. He was still young and the Twisted Hairs were all so old, but the lesson he was teaching Lisa was no different from the lessons he himself had learned. Perhaps this was how one began the Walk to become an elder. You took the Walk of a teacher and accepted the responsibility of guiding another into the mysteries.

Simple and complex, he thought. All at once.

The Twisted Hairs taught that any human could learn the Walk and understand the Wheels. The reason that the knowledge wasn't passed on to those who weren't born of the People, before the People had withdrawn into their Enclaves, was simply because few of them had ever professed an interest before. Unless it was to study the quaint customs of a primitive people. Unless it was to catalogue and list every nuance of a Walk and store it away in some book or museum where it became merely a dry shell of what it once had been.

Those who weren't of the People always seemed to find it easier to take than to give.

Could that change?

A tribe of three.

A squat rat learning her Walk—what would be her totem? Would she even have one? A coyote with mismatched eyes, partly tame, it seemed, and all trickster. And a scout of the People that the Kachina-hey were leading onto a new Walk.

They seemed as mismatched as Nanabozho's eyes.

On the rooftop, Gahzee looked across the dull smudge of the sky. He missed his home with a sudden ache so sharp that his breath caught in his throat. Never to see the blue again. Grandfather Sun hidden from sight. Nokomis and her stars, gone as well. No more the clean rain that the *animiki* brought.

He forced air into his lungs, let it out in a long slow sigh. This is my Walk now, he told himself. Make do.

Reaching up, he pressed the control of the biochip comlink implant behind his left ear, sending out a signal that was bounced off an Enclave satellite, back to Kwarthas. A moment later, the response came—a tinny voice that resonated against the bone of his skull and was relayed through his ear to his brain's auditory center so that he could understand it.

"We are receiving, *animkwan.*" Distorted as the voice was, Gahzee still recognized it."

"Hey, Manitouwaub," he said aloud, so that the implant could pick up his voice from its resonance in his own ear and pass it along on its signal beam. Speaking quickly in the language of the People, he passed on the information he had gotten from Lisa and how he meant to recover the stolen chip from the downed flyer.

"Proceed as you see best," came the reply. "And be careful, brother."

Gahzee wanted to ask his mentor about the visions he had seen in the Dreamtime, about the Kachina-hey advising him to become a Twisted Hair, and his teaching Lisa a Walk, but there was no time. The transmission had to be brief or else the Megaplex's security might get a fix on him. He reached up and touched the implant's control once more and his head filled with silence.

He stood for a long time staring out over the abandoned city, then finally went back down where he put on the yak gear over his own, and started up one of the Usaijin scooters. Lisa sat behind him, arms wrapped around his waist and giving him directions, as he pointed the machine toward the squats outside of the Trenton Megaplex. He kept their pace slow, to let Nanabozho keep up with them, but all too soon the lights of the Plex still seemed to grow bright and tall before them.

~ 3 ~

Yip couldn't sleep. He lay awake, long after their lovemaking, listening to Miko's quiet breathing beside him, watching the play of the shadows in an unfamiliar room, the sounds of an unfamiliar *apato* all about him. After awhile he slipped quietly from the bed. Naked, his bare feet cool on Miko's hardwood floor, he ran through the Thirteen Postures of his T'ai Chi Ch'uan.

He breathed slowly and evenly, allowing his *ch'i*— his

breath—to sink calmly through his body and permeate his bones, while his *shen*— his spirit—was gathered internally. His movements were slow; his entire body grew light and agile. Now his *i*—his mind—and his *ch'i* were king, his bones and muscles the court. The deliberate motion of his body as it moved gracefully across the hardwood floor was a picture of contained power, harnessed in beauty.

When he was done, he sank slowly to the floor, buttocks on the hard wood, legs assuming a half-lotus while his thoughts floated with a sense of peace through the once-tangled corridors of his mind. When he finally opened his eyes, it was to find Miko sitting up on the futon, regarding him.

"Now I know what I saw in you when you first entered my office," she said. She touched a closed fist to her chest. "It was your *ki* shining out at me." She used the Nipponjin term for *ch'i* which, while it meant breath, could also mean energy.

"Domo."

She smiled. "When I was younger, I studied Taoism, for I was curious about the fact that Tao cannot be defined. It cannot be conveyed by either words or silence. When I watched you just now, I saw that same mystery shine from, not just your eyes, but from your whole body."

"My father was disappointed that I chose T'ai Chi over his own Kung Fu," Yip said. "He thought it not manly enough, though it utilizes many of the same movements."

"And your mother?"

"She was pleased."

"Because she was soft?"

Yip shook his head, seeing the trap that she was laying out for him by the gleam in her eyes. "Because she understood that one who studies T'ai Chi, also studies Kung Fu, though the reverse is not necessarily true. Defense/attack . . . yin/yang. They are but parts of the *Yung Ch'uan*—the bubbling well inside us from which our energy springs. To be complete, a man needs inner peace as well as outer strength."

"I knew I should have introduced you to Mitsui earlier this evening—you speak the same language."

Thinking of Mitsui's sculptures, Yip nodded. There were two halves to every whole—a simple concept that appeared over and over in Mitsui's art, but also in life itself. Like the two sides of Huan Som—one his friend, the other a betrayer. . . .

Miko rose from the futon and slipped into a dark green kimono. *"O sake-wa?"* she asked.

"Dozo."

He took a quick shower while she fetched the rice wine. Afterwards, he joined her where she sat on a cushion by the window overlooking the inner Megaplex streets. They sipped sake and shared a long silence that Miko finally broke.

"You spoke not a word when you saw my tattoo," she said. "Why was that?"

Yip shrugged. "It was not important."

"Most men can speak of nothing else—a woman with a yakuza tattoo. It's a seven-week wonder for them. Now I will tell you what I never told them. I was born into a yakuza family, you see, to a father who wanted only the son that my mother never gave him. So he trained me in that absent son's place. Long hours in the *dojo*, and then when I turned fifteen, I received the tattoo."

"Do you still practice your father's craft?"

"Every day."

"You seem very much the lady for all your warrior's training."

"*Hai.* But that came later. My father died and I added to my study of weapons with a study of law, but the yakuza knew of me and Shigehero Goro decided he had use for a woman yakuza who was also a lawyer. I had no choice but to do as he bid me."

Yip wanted to know why, but he waited for her to tell him rather than ask.

"He threatened my mother—such a simple thing really. He could have threatened me, but it would not have mattered. My father saw to that. I could be as stoic as any of the *oyabun*'s yaks. But with my mother in danger . . ." She shrugged eloquently. "So at Goro's bidding, I embarked upon a third career—that of the geisha."

Yip filled their small clay glasses with more sake.

"But now . . ." Miko sighed. "You asked me, if I would stand with you against Goro if you asked me to."

"The question is no longer important."

"To me it is. My mother is five years dead now, yet still I do Goro's bidding. Where is my father's stoic warrior? Where the lawyer I became on my own, the lawyer with her cunning and strength? I ask myself tonight, why do I still do Goro's bidding, and I realize that it is because I have learned to be afraid for myself now. That is what he has done to me, and for that I can never forgive him."

"*Sa,*" Yip said softly. "Being afraid is nothing to be ashamed of. We are all afraid of one thing or another."

"Do you fear Goro?"

"*Hai.*"

"Yet still you would stand against him."

"*Hai.*"

"Then I will answer your question so: I will borrow of your strength and stand against him with you—but only when you ask me to. Until then, I will do his bidding, for I cannot stand against him on my own."

Yip reached across the small table between them and cupped her chin. Drawing her face towards him, he kissed her gently.

"I would never ask you to stand alone against him," he said.

Miko smiled and rose from her cushion. Letting her kimono fall to the floor, she walked back toward the bedroom. For a long moment Yip stared at the tattoo on her back, then he finished his sake and followed the dragon to where its mistress would take him.

Twelve

~ 1 ~

The Ragman was always careful about who he killed. So when he heard footsteps in the hall outside his workshop, he aimed his Steeljack at the doorway, but waited as the door opened until he cold see the metallic gleam of the yak's contact lenses, the flat grey of his kevlar overcoat; and the black Steeljack in his hand, before he fired.

The fléchette hit the yak between those silver contacts and blew out the back of his head, but the Ragman wasn't watching. He knew he'd hit whatever he'd aimed at. He was already on the move, shifting to a new position, getting ready for the next yak to be coming through the door with his augmented reflexes jacked up to full power.

Instead there was only silence.

C'mon, girls, the Ragman thought. Don't insult me. You gotta have sent more than one little *kobun* to take in the Ragman.

He crouched in the corner of his workshop, under a table laden with wiring and dismantled computer guts, Steeljack steady in his hand, aimed at the doorway.

Nothing.

Why do I get such a bad feeling about this? he wondered as he crabwalked from under the table and slowly straightened to a standing position, gaze never leaving the door.

~2~

The minute Torogano died, Senjyaku Bannai's augmented reflexes took over. His first instinct was to move in and cut down Torogano's killer, but he wasn't being paid to take the initiative. Let others think for themselves. If they were successful, they reaped the reward. But if they failed, they dared the *oyabun*'s wrath. Bannai liked having all of his fingers and preferred to do his gambling at the Flower Card tables.

He withdrew back down the corridor and around the first corner, moving silently in a blur of speed. Unclipping his com-link from his belt, he spoke quickly into it to make his report.

"*Matte zo,*" came the brusque reply. Hold your position.

"*Hai.*"

Reinforcements were on the way.

Bannai returned the com-link to his belt. Steeljack in hand, he edged forward down the corridor, taking up a position at the corner where he could see the door to the workshop. Torogano's body lay sprawled on the floor, his blood splattered all over the doorjamb and walls.

There was no sound in the room beyond the corpse.

Bannai frowned. They had checked for a rear exit before making their frontal assault. What was the Ragman doing in there? Had Torogano managed to get off a shot before he'd died? He ran through the incident in his mind. *Iie.* There'd been only one shot. Then what—

A footstep in the corridor behind him made him turn. With a yak's fluid speed, Bannai brought up his Steeljack to take down the giant black man who, as he realized that he'd been discovered, bellowed an inarticulate string of sounds and charged the yak.

Bannai fired.

~ 3 ~

Fang Wo was the barman of the Ch'ing-jen Fan, behind which the Ragman had his office. He was playing with his com-link during an idle moment, looking for a better bootlegged Plex transmit than the Kinzoku trans that his old com-link kept picking up. The *deh* box needed an overhaul, bad. He was sick to death of Metaldrone. All it did was give him buzz-fatigue between his ears, and he didn't need that on this job. He got enough just listening to drunks and wireheads.

He nodded to J.D., who walked by with a junkwalker in tow—nice ass on the kid, he thought—and wondered if J.D. knew that a couple of yaks had gone back to the Ragman's office ahead of him. The Ragman was always busy, which was why Wo had been trying to fix his com-link by himself the past few nights, instead of taking it in back. He adjusted his earphones, twiddling the com-link's dials some more, then froze as he accidentally tapped into a personal transmission.

Yaks. Coming here in force?

He tore off the earphones and went running for the manager.

Three minutes later, armed chinas and tongs were deployed around the building and upon its roof, waiting for the yakuza assault.

~ 4 ~

J.D. wasn't much good at explaining, Jaenie Lash thought—not so much because he wanted to sound mysterious like so many pretenders did, but just because he had a hard time communicating. But if the Ragman wanted to see her, Jaenie'd be there. Like a lot of rats in the squats, she felt she owed the Ragman more than she could ever repay.

The Ch'ing-jen Fan was an assault on her senses as J.D. led her past the doorman and into the club. Vids blaring at full volume, customers dancing or burning up wire in a corner, smoke so thick you could cut it with your hand. They passed the barman who was playing with his com-link—how's he hear anything over all this shit? she wondered—then they were going back to the Ragman's office and all hell broke loose.

She saw the yak crouched on the floor, turning so fast he was a blur, Steeljack aimed at them. J.D. just roared and charged, but Jaenie dropped to the floor and crawled as fast as she could back out into the club. She was fast, but the yak's fléchette caught J.D. full in the chest before she could get away, the small explosion splattering her and the walls with blood.

Then she was in the club. She stood up, the blood smeared on her face and clothes, trying to scream out a warning above the roar of the music. It took her only a moment to see that she didn't have to.

The whole club looked like it was preparing for war. Chinas and tongs with knives, swords, Steeljacks and one-shot spot-welded pistols. When the yak behind her stepped out of the door, he sprouted three throwing knives from his chest while a fléchette from someone's Steeljack taking off the side of his face before he even got to fire one shot.

The music died as its plug got pulled. Jaenie heard some wireheads start to moan at the far side of the club. She took out her own knives, one in either hand.

"Here they come!" she heard someone cry.

She didn't know what was going on, and wasn't sure she cared, but so long as she was here . . . She thought of the Ragman. If she had to stand by somebody, she'd be standing by him before she would the tongs or chinas. With everyone's attention on the front of the club, she stepped over the dead yak and started back down the corridor to the Ragman's office.

As she went, the first sounds of the squat defenders attacking the incoming yaks followed her down the hall.

~ 5 ~

As soon as the Fax Vid broadcasted their initial report of the riot in the squats, Tomiji Takahata opened a conference link with all the department heads of Ho Anzen Securities.

"I want our men down there in full riot gear—*ima!*" he ordered. Now.

"But Takahata-san," Aoki protested. "The riot is in the squats. Our franchise doesn't cover—"

"This is a direct order."

"Hai," the other security heads immediately said.

"Our responsibility doesn't—" Aoki tried.

"Include the squats?" Takahata said. *"Hai.* But what better time to rid ourselves of some yaks, *neh?* Besides, our men could use the practice."

Protesting was useless, Aoki realized. Obediently, he gave a brisk *Hai* himself, then cut the connection. Before he put in a call to his own men, he tried to call Goro, only the lines were all engaged. He hesitated a long moment further, then sent out the order to those under his command.

Within minutes, black armour-suited security officers, laser rifles in hand connected to computer backpacks, were converging on the riot in the squats.

It was going to be a bloodbath, Aoki realized, and Goro was not going to be pleased. Outfitted in his own armour, laser rifle slung from his shoulder, he tried again to get through to the *oyabun* as he rode down in an open-bedded Ho Anzen land cruiser, but the connection couldn't be made.

~ 6 ~

The klaxon whine of his com-link's alarm circuits brought Yip out of bed and scrambling for his clothes before he was even fully awake. He killed the alarm on his com-link and listened gravely to the orders he was given, sleep dropping away as the import of what he was being told sank in.

"Phillip, what is it?" Miko asked from the bed. Her eyes still appeared half-asleep, her dark hair mussed.

"A riot in the squats—yaks attacking a club."

"Yaks?" Miko sat up, suddenly awake now herself. "That's impossible."

Yip shrugged and began to put on his clothes. "I only know what I've been told."

Miko reached over to a side table and used the remote control unit there to turn on her vid. She switched stations until she was tuned into the Fax Vid report. Their cameramen were already on the scene of what looked like a full-blown war from an action vid. Chinas and tongs warred with yaks. She and Yip had tuned in just in time to see the arrival of the first Ho Anzen security officers who indiscriminately sprayed laser fire at either side.

"Chiksho," she murmured and turned to Yip. "Why is Ho Anzen getting involved? The squats aren't included in their franchise."

Yip was wondering that himself. "Apparently Goro hasn't got friends at the very top of the company yet," he said. "Takahata must be using this as an excuse to hunt down a few yaks. Dealing with them in a situation such as this allows for a far cheaper and more conclusive solution to them than one can gain in the courts, *neh?* To attack Goro's men in the city like this, couldn't be justified, but in the squats . . . Who cares what happens in the squats?"

He started for the door.

"Phillip—be careful. Come back to me."

Yip paused, hand on the door. *"Hai,"* he said. Then he left to join the madness in the squats.

~ 7 ~

The Ragman almost shot Jaenie as she came through the door.

"What the hell's going on out there, darling?" he asked.

"Everybody's gone crazy. Yaks attacking the club, chinas and tongs attacking the yaks. We've gotta get out of here, Ragman."

"Only one way out," he said and pointed back the way she'd come.

"Then we gotta hide."

The Ragman took a moment to think, then he nodded. "Up on the roof," he said. You get cornered, you take to the high ground.

He led the way out into the corridor, coming to an abrupt halt when he saw J.D.'s corpse sprawled on the floor. J.D.'s Steeljack was still holstered. He'd gone after an armed, augmented yak bare-handed.

"If Jah's dead," the Ragman said softly. "Maybe you'll find him now, Jack."

He knelt on the floor beside the body and put his hand on J.D.'s face, gently closing the eyes. His chest was tight, throat feeling swollen.

"Ragman—we gotta move."

When he turned back to look at her, Jaenie almost didn't recognize him. Gone were the easy smiling features, the laughing eyes. The Ragman's face was a stiff mask, the eyes hard and cold.

"They just declared war," he said. There was ice in his voice.

"Ragman . . . ?"

"I'm coming, darling."

He rose from the body and continued to lead the way onto the roof. We'll hide, he thought. We'll get away any way we can. But I'm coming back for you, Goro. You don't know it yet, but as of when your boy shot down J.D., you became a walking dead man. Believe me, Goro, 'cause the Ragman don't tell lies.

Thirteen

~ 1 ~

Gahzee had seen satellite photos of the squats in the Enclave, but photos alone could never have prepared him for what they were actually like. The smell was the worst, hitting him from blocks away with a mixture of rot, human wastes, and the acid sting of the fouled air. The buildings were in worse repair than those out in the badlands, tottering concrete and metal structures that leaned against each other for support. There was garbage and litter in the streets, feral dogs darting away from the stabbing light of the Usaijin's headbeam.

The *medé* worried about Nanabozho when he saw the dogs, but when he looked for his brother, the coyote was already gone.

Moving on a Stalker's Wheel, Gahzee's gaze pierced the darkness to catch glimpses of movement in the buildings, quick head and shoulder shots before the occupants ducked out of sight. They were frightened of the threat that he and Lisa appeared to present—he in his stolen yak clothes, she in the mask and feathered headdress of a swagger girl. An unlikely pair to be speeding through the squats. The rats who lived here wanted nothing to do with them.

It was noisier than he'd expected as well. In the distance he could see a flare of lights that could only come from conflagrations and laser fire. It sounded like a full-scale battle. They got within blocks of the disturbance, then just as he was bringing the three-wheeler to a halt to take stock of the situation, Lisa hit him between the shoulders.

"Pull over!" she cried.

Cutting the Usaijin's quiet engine, Gahzee peered off between the buildings. In the distance he could see lines of figures advancing on each other. Poorly equipped rats, dozens of yaks, Megaplex security officers looking like giant black bugs in their full riot gear—all involved in a violent melee.

"What—" he began.

"Shit!" Lisa cut him off. "That's where we were going. Something's gone wrong."

"The Ragman . . . ?"

"The building they're all fighting around's where he keeps his workshop and office. Shit."

Gahzee started up the Usaijin again. "Let's work our way in closer."

But as he pulled away again, Lisa suddenly gripped his shoulder. He slowed the three-wheeler, his own gaze locking on the china running down the street toward them, momentarily caught in the Usaijin's headbeam.

"That's one of the guys that jumped me!" Lisa cried.

The china darted into the nearest alleyway. Before Gahzee could stop her, Lisa had jumped off the slow-moving machine. She stumbled in the refuse, caught her balance, and was after him. Gahzee brought the Usaijin around in a tight circle, slowing down even more to avoid the debris in the street. By the time he reached the mouth of the alley and pointed his headbeam down it, there was no sign of either Lisa or the china.

He looked back to where the china had come from. The riot was little more than a short block away. He fed the

Usaijin some fuel and started down the alley, but before it swallowed him, a security officer had spotted him. The black-armoured drone brought up his laser, computer circuits locking on the target.

The blast of the laser hit the back right wheel of the Usaijin, spinning the vehicle out of control. Gahzee fought the spin, but then the fuel tank that was under the machine, between the two rear wheels, exploded. He was thrown into the air, hitting the nearest building with the full length of his body, before sliding down into a mound of trash.

He lay unmoving. Further down the alley, what remained of the uncontrolled Usaijin smashed into another wall. Flaming fuel rained on the debris in the alley, setting it all a-flame.

The security officer jogged down the street to finish off his target, but a couple of yaks jumped him before he was halfway to the alley. He brought the laser rifle around. The yaks were too close. One was armed with a katana that bit through his armour. He never had a chance to fire another shot. The sword opened his chest and he fell to the street, his intestines heaving from his body like a spill of ghastly streamers.

Stripping off the laser rifle and backpack, the two yaks withdrew from the street with their booty. Behind them, the security officer died, his eyes clouding behind the protective mask of his helmet. Further away from the riot, the fire spread in the alleyway, eating up the inflammable debris with a greedy hunger as it darted for Gahzee.

The *medé* never stirred. Unconscious, he remained unaware of his danger.

~ 2 ~

Lisa wasn't sure what had possessed her to jump off the moving Usaijin, but there was no time to puzzle it out. A pile of garbage broke her fall, sending up a cloud of stench that was so strong even her mask couldn't filter it all. Regaining her balance, she went running down the alley after the china, not even waiting for Gahzee to follow.

The alley took a turn to the left when it reached the end of the building and stopped in a dead end at a battered fence. The china was almost at the top by the time she'd halved the distance between them. She dragged the Steeljack from its holster under her jacket.

"Wei!" she cried in Mandarin. *"Tang i tang!"* Wait up there.

"Ni deh!" he called back. Fuck you.

"Fuck yourself," she muttered and fired the Steeljack.

Unfamiliar with the weapon, she didn't come close to hitting him, but the impact of the fléchette as it exploded against the wall was enough to make him lose his grip and come tumbling down. Before he could recover, Lisa was on him, sitting on his chest, the Steeljack pointed at his head.

"Shih-mo hsin-wen," she said conversationally. What's happening?"

When he started to struggle, she pushed the muzzle of the Steeljack right up against his temple.

"I might not be such a shit-hot shot, pal, but I don't think even I can miss at this range, *ma*?"

He was scared to death, Lisa saw, and it wasn't just because she had the auto-pistol to his head. He couldn't have recognized her, because she was still wearing the swagger girl mask. So what was his problem?

"I want the package you stole from me," she told him.

"Wo pu tung." I don't understand.

She pulled the mask off. The stink of the squats hit her like a blow. "See this face, asshole? Do you remember me now?"

His eyes widened, taking in her striped messenger's tattoos, recognizing her for who she was, but the fear that had gripped him began to lessen.

"Where's your yak?" he asked.

So that was it. He was scared of the Goro Clan.

"I've got the 'jack, so you'd better—"

There was the sound of gunfire—closer than ever—

followed by an explosion that roared down the alley like a clap of thunder. Worrying about Gahzee now, Lisa pressed the gun harder against the china's temple.

"I haven't got the time to shit with you. Tell me what you did with the package and you can walk outta this alley in one piece. Otherwise your friends'll be picking pieces of your head out of the bricks for the next twenty years—*tung ma*?"

Can I do it? she wondered. Just shoot him down in cold blood? Not likely, but she realized that it didn't matter. Just so long as *he* believed she could.

"Shih-ti," he said.

"That's a good start. Now gimme some names."

"We delivered the package to Chien Foo."

The name only rang a faint bell. "That doesn't mean anything to me. Try a little harder."

"He's Huen Ho Fung's lieutenant."

Oh, shit, she thought. She hadn't recognized the name, but she knew the man by sight. He was *San Ho Hui*—part of the Triple Union Societies known as the triads. Next to Ho Fung himself, Chien Foo was the highest member of the local Ho Fung Triad. You never saw Ho Fung in the squats, but Foo was always around. The triads supposedly dated back to the reign of Yung Cheng in the eighteenth century. They'd started as a political movement to oust the Manchu dynasty, but evolved into organizations not a whole lot different from the yaks—except they were primarily made up of Chinese. And *they* had her package?

"If you're shitting me . . ."

"Hey, we made a bad move—okay? Hitting a messenger and all. The money was just too good. But now I'm making good."

Watching him, Lisa wondered if she could believe him. And where was Gahzee? The *medé* should've been here by now. He probably had some kind of lie-detecting Wheel he could've used on this guy. Now she had to decide whether to trust him or not on her own. The Ho Fung Triad? It sounded about right. The tongs wouldn't have the balls, and the chinas were interested in turf, not tech.

Lisa got off him slowly, Steeljack never wavering in her hand. When she was far enough back, she made a motion with the weapons that made the china jump nervously.

"Up you go," she said. "Get outta here."

The china wasn't prepared to argue. He went up the fence like it was a ladder and was gone in moments. Steeljack still in her hand, Lisa ran back the way she'd come. When she started to round the corner, she came face to face with a wall of flames that singed her eyebrows and the feathers of her headdress.

She backed around the corner once more, spotted a door. The lock wouldn't give, so she shot it out, then ran through the building to the street where she'd left Gahzee. All she saw now was a dead Plex drone in his black armour, lying sprawled in the middle of the street with his guts spilling all around him. Looking at him, she wanted to throw up.

Turning away from the corpse, she bolted for the alleyway and her worst fears were realized. She saw parts of the Usaijin and realized that it had taken a hit. And Gahzee? Clouds of smoke billowed from the mouth of the alley. She stepped closer, coughing until she got her mask back on. Though the air was still bad through its filters, it was at least breathable. Then she moved in.

She spotted Gahzee straightaway, lying just inside the mouth of the alley, the flames licking close to him, the smoke starting to settle down around him. Without taking the time to find out if he was alive or dead, she grabbed him by his heels and started to drag him out. When she reached the street, she made a careful survey, but there wasn't much action. Most of the fighting was still down around the Ch'ing-jen Fan. It seemed to be dying down. There were a few figures moving on the street, but no one seemed to take much notice of one swagger girl dragging a yak.

She wrestled Gahzee up the stairs of a building across the street and inside, then collapsed in the doorway. She stared out across at the fire for long moments, catching her breath, before she had the strength to return to Gahzee's side.

He lay as she'd left him, half-propped up against the wall, head lolling on his chest. Even in the poor light, his ruddy skin looked washed out. You'd better not be dead, she thought fiercely, surprised at the vehemence of her feelings. Opening his overcoat, she took off her mask and laid her ear against his chest.

He was breathing. Faintly. His heartbeat almost nonexistent.

She laid him on the floor and cocked back his head. Pinching his nostrils, she blew a breath into his body, gave it a moment to come out, breathed in again. His skin tasted like a mixture of salt and soot. In. Wait. In again.

Suddenly he gasped and began to choke. She rolled him over on his side, slapping his back, wondering what the hell she was really doing. Just because she'd seen it on the vids, didn't mean it'd really work.

He coughed, a deep wracking sound.

"Oh, shit, don't go and die on me," she told him, still slapping his back.

But then he was trying to sit up. She helped him lean back up against the wall. He tried to talk, but his throat was raspy from the smoke, his voice a croak. His eyes were only open to slits, not really seeing her.

"Kinda different from your sacred smoke, huh?"

He coughed again, spitting up phlegm. She wiped his mouth on the sleeve of her jacket.

"Guess the only thing that kept you alive was you were lying so low, the smoke didn't have a chance to settle down to where you were."

"Sec—security off . . ." Another cough wracked him.

"The drone's dead. Looked like someone knifed him. That wasn't you?"

Gahzee shook his head.

"Are you gonna be all right?"

He nodded slowly. "J-just need . . . time . . ."

Lisa sat on her heels, her face level with his. "Look, the

Usaijin's had it and I'm not up to dragging you around, so I'm going for some help. You just hang in here. Stay real quiet and don't move. I'll be back, quick as I can."

"Wh-here . . . ?"

"I'm gonna try and find the Ragman."

He reached out and weakly caught her arm as she began to rise. Gently Lisa disengaged his fingers.

"Don't worry. I'll be back. I'm not gonna abandon you here. I owe you one—remember? If anyone can help us, it'll be the Ragman. And if you're worrying about your chip, I know who's got it: the Ho Fung Triad. You just take it easy."

"B-be . . . careful . . ."

Lisa nodded. *"Ja mata."*

She stood up and looked down at him. Shit, he didn't look good at all. Then she put her mask back on and slipped out the door, heading for the Ch'ing-jen Fan. At least things seemed to be settling down. There were still drones patrolling the area in their black bug suits, but the yaks were gone. So were most of the chinas and tongs. She just hoped none of the bodies that the drones were dragging out in front of the Ch'ing-jen Fan was the Ragman's.

~ 3 ~

By the time Yip reached the Ho Anzen headquarters, most of his fellow officers were already gone. Suiting up in his riot gear and signing out one of the Jiszuki three-wheelers that the security franchise preferred above the Usaijin, he sped out of the Megaplex and into the squats. The scene he found waiting for him outside the Ch'ing-jen Fan was a riot that could have been lifted straight from a war-vid by the Indochinese director Daongam.

It was a three-sided pitched battle between squats residents, yaks, and the Ho Anzen security force. Laser beams hissed and crackled through the air, indiscriminately cutting down chinas and tongs armed with only knives and sticks as well as yaks with tech gear to match the security forces' weaponry. Smoke filled the already rancid air. Buildings smoldered. Disabled three-wheelers and one land cruiser sparked and burned. Bodies were strewn everywhere.

What had started it? How had it gotten so out of control?

He brought up his Jiszuki to one of the control areas and cut the engine. Climbing into the cab of the land cruiser to get his orders, he nodded brusquely to his security head, Aoki, who was punching out a number on the cruiser's com-link. Glancing idly at Aoki's fingers, Yip realized that the number didn't begin with the 353 code that Ho Anzen used, so he filed it away for future reference.

"Calling reinforcements?" he asked.

"You're late," Aoki merely said.

"I was off duty and nowhere near headquarters."

Aoki gave him a considering look. "Well, you're here now, *neh?*" He disengaged the com-link and motioned towards the door. "Let's go in and clean out a couple of those buildings."

"Hai."

They left a com man in charge of the cruiser, with two backup officers. Aoki led the way to the nearest building, spraying the doorway and windows with rapid-fire blasts from his laser. Yip followed his security head at a trot, finding motion awkward in the riot gear. He'd better plan on getting some more training time in on the suit as soon as he had a chance, he thought.

When they entered the structure, a pair of chinas made a break for the rear entrance at the far side of the building's foyer. Yip's computer link automatically brought them in closer with magnified infrared vision. He saw that all they had was a knife each. He held his fire. Might as well let them go. They were out of the picture now.

Aoki cut them down before they got away, then turned to face Yip.

"Getting soft-hearted?" he demanded.

It was impossible to read Aoki's features behind the flat mask of darkened glass that made up the front of his helmet.

Through the cheap speaker in Yip's own helmet, the security head's voice came through tinny and sharp.

"What?" he said.

"Letting the pukers go—have you lost your taste for your work?"

Yip's eyes narrowed invisibly behind his own helmet's glass. Aoki was enjoying this. As he'd enjoyed having Huan killed? It would be so easy, Yip realized, to simply lift his laser-rifle's muzzle and cut Aoki down.

"I asked you a question, Yip."

Outside, the battle was winding down. Yip stared at Aoki. I'm always doing what's right, he thought. Following the rules. You're the black and white man, Huan had told him. And now Huan was dead. While this . . . worm still lived.

That was wrong.

But killing Aoki would be wrong as well.

If the world was grey, if you had to balance one wrong against the other, which was more wrong?

"Yip—" Aoki began.

Then he saw something in his subordinate's stance, in the way Yip held his weapon. Aoki brought his own laser-rifle up in a defensive move, but Yip had already made his decision. His laser-rifle swept up in an arc, trigger thumbed to full blast, cutting Aoki in two. Aoki's weapon got off one blast that went wild, bringing down a part of the ceiling on the far side of the wide foyer, then he tumbled in a heap.

"For Huan," Yip said softly. "Now I'm a grey man too, Aoki-san. Just like you, *neh*?"

Shouldering his rifle, he bent down and removed the security head's computer pack and weapons to take back to the cruiser. They couldn't be allowed to fall into squats hands. As for Aoki himself . . . the body could be retrieved later.

Outside, the violence had been reduced to the odd sniping. The yaks were mostly gone, except for their dead. Chinas and tongs were fleeing now as well. The black-suited security officers moved in to clean up.

Standing there, Yip tried to feel some emotion for what he'd done—sorrow, anger, pain. There was nothing. Not for Aoki. Not anymore. The slate with his name on it was wiped clean inside Yip—all except for that number Aoki had been trying to reach in the cruiser.

The destruction that lay before him made Yip angry. He still felt sorrow for Huan—that was an ache that might never stop hurting. But he felt nothing for the security head's death, or the fact that it had come by his hand.

I've changed, he realized wearily. Truly a grey man now. In love with the enemy's Dragon Lady. Killing my own superior. Truly grey. Truly changed.

It wasn't until he started across the street that the first reactions to what he had done began to set in. Bile rose in his throat and he paused, shivering, trying to keep the vomit down. He swallowed the bitter taste with a quick convulsive motion of his throat. Took steadying breaths. Squared his shoulders. Started walking again.

He wasn't so certain that this change he was undergoing was for the better. Wasn't sure at all. But like a gambler at the Flower Cards table, he couldn't rise from his cushion now. He was in the game until its end. Wherever that might take him.

Deeper into the greyness of the world until what he became was so changed from what he thought himself to be, that the one would not be able to recognize the other?

He wasn't sure he wanted to know the answer to that.

Fourteen

~1~

The Ragman had bolt holes all through the squats. It was through talking to him that Lisa had planned out her own extensive escape route from the squat she'd shared with Kaoru—over the rooftops and down through another building. But for all his bolt holes and safe squats, the Ragman had never prepared for the madness that they were caught up in right now. They were in the middle of a small-scale war and—face it, Jack—there just weren't any safe squats. Nowhere to bolt.

When he and Jaenie reached the roof, a tong turned with a bootlegged Steeljack in his fist, aiming it at them.

"Tang i tang!" the Ragman cried. Hold on. "Watch where you're pointing that thing, Jack!"

But the tong had already recognized him and was turning back to the fight. A moment later a drone's laser beam caught the tong in the throat, and he fell in a welter of blood, head almost severed from his neck.

Jaenie bent over and threw up.

Crouching low, the Ragman made his way to the waist-high wall that encircled the building and looked down. So much firepower. He ducked back out of sight and returned to Jaenie's side. She was just starting to recover from losing the contents of her stomach. He laid an arm over her shoulder.

"Sorry to get you into this, darling," he said.

Giving her shoulder a squeeze, he let go. He took the knife out of her left hand and sheathed it, picked up the one that had fallen from her right and sheathed it as well.

"We're gonna stay low—wait for things to die down a bit—and then we're going over."

"O-over . . . ?"

The Ragman pointed to the building on their right. There was a three meter gap between the buildings.

"A quick hop and then we'll scurry outta here like the rats we are. When those drones get up here, we'll be—" he snapped his fingers, "—long gone."

Jaenie sat up straighter and looked at the distance between the buildings Her face grew paler. "It's too wide . . ."

"Just looks that way, darling. We'll make it."

"Why can't we just—"

"Stay? You want to hang around and wait for the drones to bust up your pretty little ass?"

With his own Plex connections, he knew there was going to be a load of trouble when this was all over. Those drones down there knew it too. They had a chance to kick some ass right now. Tomorrow they'd pay for it—there'd be suspensions and all kinds of shit to pay for all the equipment that was getting trashed tonight—but right now they were having too good a time cutting down rats. They sure as hell weren't gonna be arresting nobody. Convicted felons just got dumped in the squats. That wasn't much of a threat to a rat who was already stuck here.

"They really hate us, don't they?" Jaenie said.

"Let's just say that we remind them of what they mighta been with the wrong turn of the cards—you know?"

"I don't know if I can make it, Ragman."

He shook his head. "'Course you can, darling. You're

tough, aren'tcha? Out in the badlands, junkwalking on your own."

Jaenie kept her face studiously turned from that of the dead china. "I just never seen this shit for real, Ragman. That's all."

"Yeah, well I ain't seen its like for a long time myself."

It seemed to be getting quieter. He looked around the rooftops, and saw that the pair of them were the only live bodies up here. He chanced another quick glance down to the street. The drones were moving in.

"Showtime, darling."

"I can't do it, Ragman."

"You gotta—plain and simple. Now are you going first, or do you want me to go and show you how it's done?"

"You go."

The Ragman gave her a long hard look. "You're not gonna play quitter on me, now are you, darling?"

She shook her head.

"Okay."

He crept over the side of the building, checking the streets, clearing some rubble that he might slip on. It was dark on the other roof, but he'd been over there before. He hadn't been smart enough to leave himself a nice soft futon for the landing, but he knew it was relatively clear.

He came back to where Jaenie was waiting and gave her a broad wink. "Don't punk out on me, darling."

"I won't."

He took a run and launched himself over the gap, hitting the other roof in a roll that he didn't stop quite in time. He came up hard against a pile of refuse, but stood up quickly, not wanting Jaenie to start getting colder feet by seeing him all shook up. It took him a moment to catch his breath, then he waved her over.

"C'mon, darling!" he called in a low whisper.

She stood hesitating for a long moment, then gathering her courage, she took the run and jumped. No problem, the Ragman thought as he got ready to break her fall. She's gonna make it easy as—

A drone's laser beam caught her in mid-leap, right between the buildings. The Ragman reached for her, but it was already too late. The shot had blown a hole in her chest and all he could do was watch her plummet. He turned his head before she hit the ground.

"Bastards!" he screamed down at the drones. He stood up on the wall. "You fucking, puke-faced bastards. I'm gonna kill every fucking one of you. You hear me? YOU HEAR ME?"

Twin laser beams seared the air on either side of him, and he dropped out of sight. As the drones continued to fire at him, he huddled behind the cover of the roof's low wall, shaking with anger, then slowly he began to crawl to the other side of the building.

Get away, he told himself. Get away and you live to kill them later. Hang around and all you do is die yourself.

Halfway across the roof, he got to his feet and ran for the far side of the building, launching himself across the alley between buildings, landing in a sprawl. He lay there for a long moment, watching the dirty smudge of the sky. When he closed his eyes, he saw Jaenie falling again. J.D. lying in the hallway outside his workshop. The china on the roof, almost beheaded.

Yaks and drones. Wasn't a whole shit lot of difference between them, was there? Give somebody a little power and right away they're shit king of the hill.

"Fuckers," he muttered as he got to his feet.

He pushed some rubble away from the roof's door and squeezed himself through the narrow gap he'd made, then headed down the stairs into the bowels of the building. He took out his Steeljack. Maybe they'd come here looking for him, maybe not. They were slow movers in their bug gear. They might just not bother trying to chase him down. But if they came, he'd be ready.

When he got to street level, he peered out a window. Nothing coming. Then he heard the scrape of a footstep behind him. He turned, finger already squeezing the 'jack's trigger, but the shadowed figure he was aiming at threw itself to one side.

"Ragman!" it cried. "Are you nuts?"

He was already tracking the figure, ready to fire again, when the voice registered. He kept the 'jack pointed at her.

"That you, Lisa?"

"Yeah. You want to point that thing somewhere else?"

The Ragman looked down at the weapon in his hand, then slowly lowered his arm "How'd you find me?"

"I saw you go crazy up on the roof. What the hell's going on around here?"

"Guess we were trying to start ourselves another world war—waiting for 'em to get the nukes out again, darling. You know what it's like. It was a dull night."

"You don't sound right, Ragman."

He closed his eyes and dead faces swam in his vision. "Guess I don't feel right, darling."

"Was . . . was there someone with you up on the roof? I wasn't really paying attention till I heard you screaming, but I thought I saw the drones catch someone in their beams."

"Jaenie Lash," the Ragman said.

"Aw, shit."

"Lotta good people dead, darling."

Lisa nodded. "Let's get outta here. I need your help, Ragman."

He laughed. "You came at a bad time."

"I'm serious. I've got a Claver and I gotta get him outta here."

"A Claver?"

"Big as life, Ragman."

"You're not just shitting me?"

A Claver? the Ragman thought. Here in the squats? Just what the hell *was* going on?

"Are you coming?" Lisa asked.

"Wouldn't miss it for the world, darling."

Already he was figuring on how he could use a real Enclaver's presence to their own advantage. Who needed a chip, when you had the real thing?

~ 2 ~

While the final cleanup continued in the squats, Tomiji Takahata called a meeting of all the Ho Anzen section heads in the corporation headquarters in the Megaplex. Yip was surprised when orders arrived for his own attendance, but he dutifully signed his Juszuki back in, cleaned up the locker area, and joined the section heads in the conference room.

Takahata was furious. Never mind that he himself had been the one to give the orders to bring out the riot gear and attack the yaks. He sat behind a computer display, company losses in men and equipment in stark relief on the screen before him, and glared down the length of the table. For forty-five minutes he harangued his staff. They were a disgrace to their uniforms. New training schedules were to be implemented immediately. Company heads and officers were to be docked pay for the equipment losses.

"The head count for squat dwellers was high," he concluded, "but—" he glanced back at the screen, "—apparently only fifteen yakuza bodies have been recovered. Yet *we* sustained losses of twenty-three men with another seventeen incapacitated for weeks—in one case months—due to their injuries. I will repeat this only one more time: There is no great skill to killing rats. They are not the problem here. The Goro Clan is our problem, *neh*? We had an opportunity to legally decimate their ranks, yet through your blundering we have set ourselves back—not the yakuza.

"I will not tolerate such incompetence in future. Do I make myself clear?"

A sharp chorus of *Hais* rose in response around the table.

"That will be all," Takahata said. As Yip rose to leave with the other heads, he added, "Yip-san, *matte zo*."

Yip remained in place, face expressionless. Takahata must know that he'd killed Aoki. His mind worked furiously, but he could find no reasonable explanation that the Ho Anzen owner might accept.

"Aoki-san was killed by a yakuza?" Takahata asked when the others were gone.

"*Hai, so desu,*" Yip replied. Yes, that's right.

Takahata slowly shook his head. "We should have had them tonight." His hands made fists on the table. "We could have dealt that *neijin* Goro such a blow . . ."

Yip remained silent, waiting. Takahata's face was flushed, eyes clouded with anger. Finally he let his fists unclench. He looked at Yip.

"Your partner—Huan Som. He came to us with a tale of your treachery, *neh*?"

Yip found a look of surprise to put on his face. "I was not aware—"

"Oh, yes. He came to us with a tale of you selling secrets to the yakuza. But Aoki-san spoke in your defense, and it appears he was correct, for not only did you deal with the DMC problem, efficiently and quickly, but it appears that it was Som himself who was dealing with the yakuza and subsequently had a falling out with them."

Yip studied his employer, looking for the lie in his words, but Takahata's features appeared free of guile. Still, that meant nothing. Old as he was, he would have had years of practice playing the grey man. But it made Yip wonder. What if Aoki had been working on his own . . . ?

Takahata sighed. "I need good men, Yip, and they are hard to find. *Sa*, I admit that due to your mixed blood, I have seen fit to pass you over for promotion more than once, but I believe now that your mother's Nipponjin blood runs stronger in you than your father's Chinese, and I mean to rectify any past slights. In Aoki's memory, you will be your section's new head."

This was madness, Yip thought. "Takahata-san," he said aloud. "I am honoured . . ."

"You will continue to concentrate on the Jones Co-Op for the present. Speak to Genda-san in the morning. He will see to it that your systems are transferred to Aoki's computer.

His office is now yours. If you have any problems, feel free to contact me directly, *neh?*"

"*Domo arigato,*" Yip said. Thank you very much.

Takahata waved a hand. "You may go now, Yip-san."

Numbly, Yip rose and gave his employer a quick nod, then retreated from the conference room, thoughts spinning. Was it this simple, playing the grey man? Did the benefits accrue so quickly? He felt sick as he walked down the long hall to his own cubicle. Standing in the doorway, he stared at its confines.

It was no longer his. He could move into Aoki's larger office tonight if he wished. The benefit of murder. Position paid for with another's blood.

Turning quickly, he left the building and walked out into the night. Was it possible that Takahata had nothing to do with Huan's death? Then he remembered the number he'd seen Aoki punching in during the riot.

He stopped at the first public com-link he came to. Clearing the screen so that it would accept video, but not broadcast it, he dug out a hard credit and inserted it, then punched in the same number. When Shigehero Goro's features appeared on the screen, he cut the connection and stepped quickly away from the booth.

Again, the yaks. And Aoki had been their man in Ho Anzen.

His thoughts turned to Miko. His *asobi* woman. A living Mitsui sculpture. Her appearance shifting, depending on one's perspective. On the one hand, a woman he could love. On the other, a Dragon Lady with her yakuza tattoo. Did her loyalties shift as easily.

A certain amount of faith is required. . . .

He had thoughts of returning to Miko's *apato*, but now he turned his footsteps homeward instead. He needed to think.

There was an incoming call blinking on his *apato*'s com-link when he got home. He hesitated in answering it—knowing it must be Miko. Standing indecisively in front of the screen, he finally sighed and punched the connection open. When the screen came to life it wasn't Miko's features that regarded him, but those of the *oyabun* of the Goro Clan.

"Mushi-mushi," Yip said. "To what do I owe this dubious pleasure, Goro-san?" He kept his tone, if not his words, polite.

The *oyabun* frowned, but recovered smoothly. Be careful, Yip told himself. This man is a coiled snake, ready to strike. Keeping his hands out of Goro's view, he surreptitiously switched the link to a record mode.

"Be so kind as to not record this conversation," Goro told him.

Of course, Yip realized. He would have surveillance gear on his system. He switched the recorder off.

"As you wish," he said.

"There was some trouble in the squats this evening," Goro said. "Most unfortunate, *neh?*"

"Especially for you," Yip replied, "considering the death of Kimitake Aoki."

"So you know."

"Hai."

"Aoki-san's most unfortunate death leaves an opening in my organization."

"I don't wear tattoos well," Yip said.

This time Goro made no effort to hide his frown. "I made you," he said. "Don't ever pretend to yourself that it was any different. My influence brought you up from the ranks. And what I make, I can break, *neh?*"

Yip regarded the screen in silence for a long moment. Here was the real cause behind Huan's death, behind Miko's enslavement, behind ninety-nine percent of the Megaplex's troubles. And he was supposed to join him? Is that what a grey man would do?

"I will think about your kind offer," Yip said.

Then he cut the connection. The incoming light immediately blinked again, but he ignored it. He stood in the middle of his living room and stripped, leaving his clothes where they fell. He began the Thirteen Postures of his T'ai

Chi Ch'uan. Once. Then again, until the sweat glistened in every pore and finally his mind was still.

He showered, then fetched himself a plastican of Tombo beer and stood in front of the living room window to drink it. Still naked. Skin clean now, tingling in the recycled air of his *apato*.

That's right, he said to himself. Find peace through meditation, then drown that peace in alcohol. *Hai*, you are a wise man, are you not?

Downing the Tombo, he went to get another.

Dreamtime

Smoke.

That was all he could breathe. All he could smell. Not the sacred smoke of the *manitou*, but roiling dark clouds with an acrid chemical taint.

And there was sound.

Not the drums that spoke to the grandfather thunders. Nor the sounds of the battle in the squats. This was a mechanical sound. Engines roaring. Pistons thumping. Ungreased gears squealing. A deafening cacophony.

He opened his eyes.

Crouched before him was an elder. His skin was dark, grey braids framing a lean weathered face, so lined that it appeared to be made of parchment, crumpled, then smoothed out once more for reuse. He wore grey cotton trousers, a bandolier of intricate beadwork across his bare chest, scuffed leather moccasins.

He was neither Anishnabeg nor a member of any tribe Gahzee knew.

His *skibdagan* hung from his belt, fat with medicine bundles. For a headdress, he wore the skin of a coyote, the animal's head on his own like a cap, the pelt falling down past his shoulders, to his back. Keeping the coyote pelt in place on his head was a wide-brimmed black hat, worn so that the coyote's head appeared to peer out from beneath it. Under the brim of the hat and the coyote's head, the elder's left eye was blue, his right brown.

"N-nanabozho . . . ?"

Gahzee's voice was dry, the words came out as a croak. The roar of the pounding of machinery stole them away with its wash of sound.

Does your every trick have but the one name? the elder replied.

His lips never moved, but Gahzee heard him all the same.

What is this place? he asked, thinking the words rather than trying to speak them.

Dreamtime.

It was so hard to think, with the roar of the engines, the crash of the machines.

I have never seen such a Dreamtime, he replied.

The elder grinned. *Hey, Gahzee. And are you so wise? Has your Walk taken you everywhere, and you still so young?*

These machines . . . ?

The elder replied with his own question. *The workings of the world?*

Gahzee shook his head. *I don't think so.*

Come with me, the elder said.

He stood smoothly, not a stiff joint in his ancient frame, and set off briskly, taking a path through the pounding machines. Gahzee followed, looking left and right. The machinery appeared to serve no purpose beyond its noise, the foul fumes it released into the air, the ceaseless motion. Their roar deafened him.

The elder led him out of the vast building into a flat square. All around stood buildings similar to the one they had just quit, manufacturing nothing but noise, pouring filth into the air from their smokestacks. In the center of the square was a lodge made of deerskins tied to birch poles.

Sitting cross-legged in the lodge was a curious being, hairless and white, smooth-skinned, fat body round as a ball of jelly, with a smaller ball of a head attached to the torso without the benefit of a neck. The being wore not a stitch of clothing. His penis, long and fat like a white snake, lay across his ankles. His eyes were black, like two daubs of tar dropped onto that jelly face, his nose flat, his mouth a slit.

Beside him was a war club. Hanging from the leather thongs that kept the deerskins in place were many severed hands, some mummified and dry, others rotting and covered with flies. In the dirt in front of the lodge was a flat wooden dish upon which stood four carved figures.

He is the Great Gambler, the elder explained to Gahzee. *And in his dish you see the four ages of man.*

"Hey, Whiskey Jack," the Great Gambler said. "Have you come to try your luck? You don't think I'm so good anymore?"

He began to laugh, a horrible sound like fingernails on glass, and his white jelly body shivered like pudding.

Gahzee regarded his companion. Whiskey Jack, was it? That was a white man's name, but it was phonetically similar to a name in the tongue of the People—Wee-sa-kay-jac. It meant Bitter Spirit and belonged to a trickster *manitou.*

"All these hands you see," the Great Gambler went on, waving to his collection, "belonged to those who came to gamble. They all thought they could win, thought they had nothing to lose. But I don't gamble except with those who gamble their lives. I keep their scalps and ears and hands and give what's left to the *windigo*. And their spirits—" he grinned, confident, the flesh of his face and torso moist like a poisonous mushroom, "—I feed to the darkness.

"Do you still want to play the game of the four ages of man with me, Whiskey Jack?"

"Tell us the rules," Whiskey Jack said. He looked at Gahzee and gave him a wink.

"Here are the four figures in this dish," the Great Gambler said, picking up the wooden dish. "One for each age of man. I'll shake the dish four times, and if they remain standing each time, then I'm the winner. If they fall, then I lose."

Fat sausage fingers tipped the figures over so that Gahzee and his companion could see that they were loose in the dish.

"I'll play," Whiskey Jack said. "But it's the custom where I come from that the one who's challenged has the last play."

The Great Gambler nodded his agreement, fat flesh moving across his torso in waves at the movement. Taking the first play, he stood up the figures once more, then struck the ground with the dish. The four figures remained standing. He repeated this two more times and each time the four figures representing the four ages of man remained standing in their wooden dish.

He's cheating, Gahzee said. *He must be.*

Whiskey Jack winked again. *Of course he is.*

But if the figures remain standing a fourth time, he'll win. He'll kill you.

And not just me, Whiskey Jack replied, *but you as well and all of the People. Our spirits will go into the darkness and the* windigo *will feast on our flesh—all except for those parts the Great Gambler keeps for himself.*

This is madness. Why are you gambling?

Whiskey Jack turned to look at him. *Because it's that kind of Dreamtime, grandson.*

At that moment, he sounded exactly like the squat rat, Lisa Bone. Gahzee wondered if he'd stepped from a Dream Wheel into a hallucination. The gambler, the elder, their surroundings, this dish game—they were all the makings of a peyote vision gone mad.

The Great Gambler brought the dish down a fourth and final time. Gahzee tensed. The sound of the machinery from the surrounding buildings was suddenly very loud, twinning the accelerating jump of his own pulse. The dish hit the ground and the figures remained standing. But then Whiskey Jack whistled through his teeth and a wind sprang up, blowing the four figures down.

They fell into the darkness of the dish. The Great Gambler shivered. His rotund shape seemed to grow brittle, pieces of it flaking off as he turned his black-eyed gaze to the elder.

"I win," Whiskey Jack said. "Now it's my turn." He took the dish and righted the figures, then handed it to Gahzee. "You will play for me."

Gahzee took the dish with shaking hands. The figures trembled, ready to fall at the slightest motion. He brought the dish down. When it hit the ground, the dish shattered. He held only a piece of it in his hand. The broken shards lay spilled across the ground, but the four figures remained standing.

Oh, very good, Whiskey Jack said. *You've broken the past, grandson.*

The Great Gambler was no more than a dried gourd now. Cracks ran up and down his fat brittle body. He split open, the two halves of his body shattering when they hit the ground. A stink of old decay rose to clog Gahzee's nostrils. Slowly he lay the last shard of the dish upon the ground.

I don't understand, he said.

It's simple, Whiskey Jack told him. *You must take your Walk into the future that you have made, upon the broken pieces of the past.*

But there is no past, Gahzee said, repeating the lessons that the Twisted Hairs taught. *Only now.*

And the path with heart? Whiskey Jack asked. *Does it follow only one route?*

Gahzee shook his head. *All deeds are Walks.*

And all men?

Can be sacred humans? Gahzee tried.

Whiskey Jack grinned. Above his brow, under the brim of his hat, the coyote headdress appeared to be grinning too.

Exactly, the elder said.

He took a step back. When Gahzee moved to follow him,

he heard Whiskey Jack whistle through his teeth again. This time the wind blew clouds of roiling smoke between them.

Gahzee choked and coughed. His head ached to the rhythm of the pounding machinery. He waved the smoke away from his face until he could see once more. He found himself standing on a wide open plain. Alone. The elder was gone. As were the lodge and the fragments of the wooden dish and the Great Gambler. The buildings housing the machinery.

All that remained was the pounding between his temples. The thick taste of smoke in his lungs.

He fell to his knees, then laid his head upon the ground, the dirt pressing against his cheek. Closing his eyes, he let the pain take him away.

Fifteen

~1~

At the commencement of business hours, Chien Foo arrived promptly at Okado's office in the IBN building in the Jimu District. Okado's secretary showed him into the office where Okado and his aide Muato Kamo were waiting. Okado stood by the window, turning only slightly at the Ho Fung representative's entrance. Once he saw who it was, he looked out the window once more.

Kamo stood behind the desk. Without preamble, he placed a briefcase on its glass surface.

"The full amount," he said. "In hard credits—as specified." Laying an envelope on top of the briefcase, he added, "And these are the IBN shares."

Chien Foo's eyes widened slightly, then he smiled. "What a pleasure it is doing business with you, gentlemen."

As he reached under his jacket, Kamo stiffened, but all Foo brought out was a small package, wrapped in rice paper. Crossing the office, he laid it down on the desk.

"This belongs to you now, *ma*?" he said.

While Kamo unwrapped the package, Foo cast a quick gaze over the documents, then opened the briefcase.

"Count it, if you want," Kamo said.

"But we trust you," Foo said, once he saw the briefcase was full of hard credits. He laid the envelope on top of them and snapped the hasps shut. "And besides—we know where to find you, *ma*?"

Kamo regarded him silently for a long moment, then returned to his task. From out of the rice paper he drew a small computer chip. He walked over to the computer on a side table, entered the chip, and called it up on the screen. A gridwork of interconnecting lines appeared there.

"This is coded," Kamo said.

Foo shrugged eloquently. "But we offered you only the chip. You must decode it yourself. Surely, in a company this large, you would have the facilities to do so?"

Kamo nodded.

"As shareholders," Foo said, "we will be most interested in your results."

Okado finally turned from the window. "You may go now," he said. "Our business appears to be concluded."

Foo smiled thinly. "Of course. Gentlemen—*tsai chien*." Good-bye.

As the door closed behind the triad representative, Okado joined his aide at the computer. "Is it genuine?"

Kamo had been testing the code in a cautious fashion so that the chip wouldn't shut itself down. "I believe so."

"And the men—they are waiting for Foo?"

"*Hai.*"

"And they will make it appear to be a yak assassination?"

Kamo frowned slightly, but he nodded again. "This must be taken down to the labs," he said.

"Then do so," Okado said.

When his aide had left the room, Okado returned to look out the window once more. His grandfather would not be pleased with how he had undertaken to solve this problem, but his other ancestors . . . those who had came before Ishidi Okado and his schemes of legitimacy . . .

Okado looked not so much at the view from the window as at his own reflection upon its glass.

Those yakuza warriors. He did not think that they would find fault with what he was doing.

~ 2 ~

The Trenton VHST tubecraft station was three stories below the Megaplex's streets. The Very High Speed Transit vehicles connected the various Megaplexes of the TOPQ corridor, moving at speeds of 22,500 klicks per hour through airless tunnels. The tubecrafts had the appearance of streamlined subway cars without wheels, riding on, and driven by, electromagnetic waves. Superconducting cables produced the powerful opposing magnetic fields, so that the vehicles floated in the middle of the tube, air being suctioned from the tunnels to reduce friction.

The system was operated by CanNational, a consortium of corporations with offices in every Megaplex. To defray the initial building and operating costs, the tunnels included pipelines, power lines, laser and microwave communication channels, and a slower railroad freight system. The various tubecraft stations were open to anyone with the credits to use the system—citizen or squat dweller—with maintenance and policing provided by CanNational's own cleanup and security forces. The Megaplexes had no jurisdiction in either its stations or freightyards.

The tubecrafts ran west-east in the morning, east-west in the evening. On the morning following the riot in Trenton's squats, the *oyabun* of the Goro Clan and three of his *kobun* were waiting in the docking area. The incoming tubecraft had just entered the airlocks that preceded its actual entrance into the station. None of the yaks carried weapons—CN screening procedures were simply too strict to make the attempt worthwhile.

As the doors of the tubecraft hissed open, Goro and his men waited to one side while the wave of commuters and travellers went by, stepping forward as an older Japanese man appeared in the doorway. He moved slowly, hair grey, features lined and worn, but his eyes were bright and missed nothing. He wore a light grey bodysuit with a loose pale jacket overtop. Flanking him on either side were two tall, broad-shouldered men in kevlar overcoats.

Approaching him, Goro assumed the yakuza introductory position—left hand on his left knee, right hand extended palm up, gaze turned upward to the older man.

"I am Goro Shigehero of Trenton," he said in yakuza dialect, "*oyabun* of the Goro Clan."

The old man waited a heartbeat, then assumed the same position. "I am Tano Kishi of Toronto," he replied. "The *Oyabun* of *oyabuns*."

Goro waited for Tano to straighten before doing so himself. "I hope your journey was pleasant, Tano-san."

"*Hai, domo.*" He looked about the station. "We have business to discuss . . .?"

"*Hai.* If you will come with us?"

Goro guested Tano in his *tatami* room, seating the senior *oyabun* in the position of *tokonoma*—the place of honour—where his geisha had set a modest arrangement of leaves and flowers taken from the greenhouse that Goro maintained on the roof of his building. Though it was still midmorning, they ate first before discussing business. The geishas brought out a series of colourful dishes, placing them on the lacquered table with fluid grace. There was sliced nashi, kiku leaves, tempura, sushi, sake, tsukemono, and steamed rice.

The two men ate alone, although their bodyguards sat on cushions behind them. Not until the final tea was served did Tano delicately wipe his lips with a cloth napkin and nod to his host.

"*Domo domo,*" he said with a smile. "It is a pleasure to spend time with a man who understands the importance of custom."

Goro nodded. "You honour my home, Tano-san."

Tano set the napkin aside. "You had some . . . difficulties last night?"

"*Hai.* We were bringing in a man for questioning, when the tongs went crazy and attacked us. We sent in more men, but then the drones decided the situation would make good practice for their men—they have so much battle gear, and little opportunity to use it."

Goro's voice was bitter as he spoke.

"You lost men." It was not a question.

"*Hai.* Good men. And for nothing."

"The man you sought—he knew something of the chip?"

"We believe so."

"*Hai.*"

"Is it possible that the tongs are protecting him for that reason?"

Goro shook his head. "Possible, but not likely. It was a misunderstanding, *neh*?"

"A costly one."

"*Hai.*"

For a long moment Tano said nothing. He watched the geishas as they cleared the table, smiling at their trim figures and graceful movements. They flirted with him—as Goro had instructed them to—and he appeared pleased by their attention. When the last dish was removed, Tano sighed.

"We are running out of time, Shigehero. The Clavers will send more flyers soon—perhaps even a fully armed force. We must be inside the Maniwaki Enclave before they do so."

Goro nodded. It was the senior *oyabun* who had initially conceived the plan of breaching one of the Enclaves. Maniwaki Enclave was chosen because it was the only one along the TOPQ corridor that sent out robot work drones to mine the land outside the Enclave. Yak scientists had developed a time-released spore. Sealed in a spray that bound its molecules in a dormant state, a young *kobun* had given his life in spraying it on one of the robot drones.

The spray dried clear, without gloss, and was resistant to

all standard decontaminating procedures, dissolving automatically after forty-eight hours to release the lethal spores into the Enclave's controlled atmosphere. Seventy-two hours later, when it had completely permeated the Enclave, the spore became active. It was fatal only to humans and killed within thirty-eight seconds.

To the best of their knowledge, everything had gone according to plan. Broadcasts from the Maniwaki Enclave had ceased. Although the codes used in the Enclave broadcasts had yet to be broken—they changed every thirty seconds in a random pattern that the best Megaplex computer had yet to crack—they could be measured. Maniwaki Enclave was dead on the airwaves. The spore had done its work. Unfortunately, the postulated systems shutdown that was to have let the yaks inside had never occurred.

And then the Kwarthas Enclave began to send up flyers to investigate.

The first one had been downed by the Eisai Clan in Ottawa, but had been completely destroyed in the ensuing crash. Goro's own *kobun* had shot down the second flyer a hundred klicks north of the Megaplex. The pilot was dead, and the flyer unusable, but the chip that contained a wealth of Claver tech in its encoded circuits had been salvaged. Once they broke its code, they would be able to breach the Enclaves' protective barriers.

But the secret of the chip's existence had leaked out. Wary of an attack by the triads or tongs on an armed escort, Goro had thought he was being clever in using an unobtrusive squat messenger service in transporting the chip to the yak labs, only someone had been more clever still. Either the messenger had stolen the chip and was still planning on selling it, or it was in a tong or triad lab at the moment, its secrets being pried from it . . . if its built-in safeguards hadn't already destroyed it through careless attempts to break its codes.

"Considering last night's losses," Goro said, "I should have used an armed escort to transport it. At least we would still have it, *neh*?"

Tano shrugged. "It seemed the wisest course at the time. What we must consider now is what we will do next."

"I am of a mind," Goro said grimly, "to take all my men and simply sweep through the squats."

"*Iie,*" Tano said. "*Tonde mo nai.*" I forbid it.

"*Hai.* But—"

A discreet knock at the wooden sliding door interrupted him. Frowning, he nodded to a bodyguard who ushered in one of Goro's *kobun.*

"What is it?" Goro demanded.

"*Gomenasai,* Goro-san. But we have a problem. A high-ranking Ho Fung representative was just slain in the Jimu District. The drones say it's a yakuza-styled killing and they wish to speak to you."

Goro and the senior *oyabun* exchanged puzzled glances.

"What do you know of this?" Tano asked.

"Nothing." Goro turned to the messenger. "Tell them I am in a meeting. I will speak to them shortly."

"*Gomenasai,* Goro-san, but they demand to see you immediately. Considering the events of last night, I believe they have no time for patience."

"No," Goro said. "What they want is our blood." His face was a flat mask as he raised his bulk from the table and glanced at Tano. "Your pardon, Tano-san, but I must attend to this."

The senior *oyabun* arose as well. "I will come with you, Shigehero. I have some influence that might prove beneficial."

"*Domo,*" Goro murmured.

He stood back to allow Tano to proceed him through the door. "Call Hirose," he told one of the bodyguards. "I want her here immediately."

The bodyguard nodded briskly. "*Hai,* Goro-san."

Still frowning, Goro followed Tano out into the hall.

Sixteen

~1~

Gahzee experienced a sense of vertigo when he regained consciousness. For a long moment he lay staring up at a vast ceiling, trying to understand where he was. There was no sound. The air, such as it was, smelled cleaner than that of the squats. So this place was neither that strange city of factories from the Dreamtime nor the squats.

He turned his head slowly and realized that this was the building where he'd first found Lisa. He tried to sit up and his every muscle and bone ached at the small movement. A drumming started up between his temples—all the *animiki* sounding their voices at once. Slowly he lowered himself back down on—his own bedding? He touched the finely woven blanket, recognizing the weave. Maudji-Geezhigquae's work. His aunt.

Something moved in the corner of his vision and he turned to see Lisa approaching him, a bowl in her hand. Beyond her, by the fire, Nanabozho lay, watching him. Lisa crouched down in front of him, the position she assumed reminding him of his first view of Whiskey Jack in the Dreamtime.

"Hey, Lisa," he said, his voice still a croak.

"Hey, yourself. How're you feeling?"

"I've felt better."

"Try some of this."

She helped him sit up, then held the bowl to his lips. Weak broth went down his throat, tasting like nectar.

"Bozo brought in a rabbit," Lisa said, "so I thought I'd do you the favour back—you know, play nurse and all that?"

"How did we return to this place?"

"I had some help. Tracked down the Ragman. He killed a drone and stole the sucker's Jiszuki to bring us all back. It's not a mean machine or anything—not like a Usaijin; it doesn't handle so shit-hot outta the Plex—but it did the job okay."

Gahzee swallowed more of the broth. Already the thunder in his head was lessening, but his body still ached. Every joint stiff. Every muscle bruised. The broth made him feel a little stronger.

"Where is the . . . Ragman now?"

Lisa shrugged. She set the empty bowl down beside her knee. "Out and about. He's checking things out. But he'll be back. He's got a hard-on for the yaks and drones now, so if we're out to hurt them, then he's in. You want some more of this stuff?"

She indicated the bowl. Gahzee nodded. "Please. It's very good."

"Yeah? I didn't want to mess around with your stuff, so it hasn't got anything in it but bits of rabbit and a few greens I scrounged."

"You can find green growth in this wasteland?"

"Well, it's just rootweed. It's kinda yellowy green, but yeah, I know where to find it. Living in the squats, you gotta know how to scrounge, and sometimes that don't mean begging at a fan's backdoor."

"A fan?"

"You know—restaurant. *Ni hui shuo Kuo-yu ma?*" Can't

you speak Mandarin? At Gahzee's puzzled expression, she gave him a grin. "Guess not. How's your Nipponjin?"

"That I can speak," he replied in classical Japanese.

"Ooo—aren't we formal?"

"Do I speak incorrectly?"

"Nah. Just kinda highbrow. You'd never come off as a native, Gaz. Course the way you look, no one's gonna be making that mistake anyway—right?"

Gahzee just blinked and looked at her. The flow of her words never ceased to amaze him. Her patois was nothing like he'd learned in the Enclave. Compared to the loose tumble of her speech, his own phrasing sounded tight and constrictive to his ears. And Gaz? Like Nanabozho, he appeared to have gained a new name.

"Hang in there," Lisa said. "You look like you're gonna fade out on me again and I'm sick to death of lying around here with no one to talk to. Lemme get you some more of this soup. It'll either kill you or perk you up."

"Could you bring my pack as well?"

"Sure thing."

She bustled off, returning first with another bowl of broth that Gahzee felt strong enough to drink on his own. While he finished it, she fetched his pack and dragged it over.

"Whatcha got in here—rocks?"

Gahzee smiled as he sorted through his collection of dried herbs. He had Lisa boil a decoction of mushroom powder and the dried scrapings of flesh taken from the middle of a rattlesnake.

"You going tripping?" Lisa asked.

Gahzee shook his head. "A different kind of mushroom."

"What's this other shit?"

"Dried rattlesnake."

Lisa pulled a face, but went ahead and did what he'd asked. After drinking the decoction, Gahzee felt much stronger, but his body still ached with every movement. With Lisa's help, he built up the fire and heated stones. In a corner of the room, they made a small sweat lodge using scrap wood that Lisa gathered on the second floor of the building for the framework and Gahzee's deerskin groundsheets for the sides.

"What's this for?" Lisa asked.

"Sweat lodge. Pain is a Wheel as well. I want to move to a healthier one. One of the best methods is to purify the body by sweating the pain from it."

"So what do you do?"

"When the stones are hot enough, we'll place them in the lodge, then pour water over them." He looked at their handiwork. "The lodge is big enough for two," he added as he stripped down to a loincloth.

"I dunno," Lisa said.

Gahzee shrugged. "Suit yourself."

But once the stones were hot and in place and Gahzee was entering the lodge, carrying a watersack, she hovered nearby, obviously interested, despite herself.

"Is this, like, part of a Walk?" she asked.

Gahzee nodded.

She looked at him for a long moment, then sighed. "Aw, shit. I said I wanted to learn . . ."

Turning her back on him, she took off everything except for her shirt which, freed from her leather trousers, hung halfway down her thighs. Barefoot and shivering, not from any chill, Gahzee realized, but from embarrassment, she followed him into the lodge. She gasped when Gahzee poured water onto the stones, clouds of steam rising up to wreath them.

"That's hot!"

"It's supposed to be," Gahzee said. "Or you won't sweat."

He poured on more water until the lodge was so steamy and hot that it was hard to breathe. He leaned back against the wall, eyes closed, feeling the pain escape as the sweat beaded in his pores. When he opened them again, it was to find Lisa looking back at him. She turned away when she caught his glance, but then looked back again with a nervous smile.

Her shirt was soaked and almost transparent, clinging to her like a second skin. Her nipples were hard and dark against the fabric. Her skin was so white she appeared like a ghost. The striped messenger's tattoos on her face gave her features odd shadows. Her dark hair lay flat against her scalp.

Gahzee had liked her right from the first, but he'd never really considered her as a woman—simply a companion. But now he sensed a magnetic attraction that crackled in the air between them, drawing him to her. And her to him? Between his legs his penis hardened and lifted against his loose loincloth.

Now was not a good time, he thought.

He hoisted the watersack again, pouring more water on the stones. New clouds of steam arose around them.

"The *medé* of the People," he said, as much to take his mind off of Lisa's closeness and his body's reaction to her as to instruct her, "perform a dance called 'eluding the *manitou*' for their ritual purifications. Negik, the Otter, was the first patron of the Midewein Society and the path of the dance that the *medé* perform twins the route that Negik took to elude the evil *manitou* who sought to destroy the medicine that he was giving to the Midewein. By performing this dance, we purge the ceremonies of evil.

"But 'eluding the *manitou*' has symbolic meaning as well. It exposes life as a hard conflict of ethical forces allowing us to see the path with heart for what it is: a Walk that becomes not only a refuge against evil and defeat, but a Walk that moves against that evil so that Beauty is retained in the world."

"Not a whole lot of beauty left now," Lisa said. Her voice came spectrelike from the steam.

"We spoke of this before," Gahzee said. "Of inner Beauty and *quaheystamaha*."

" 'You dance in my heart,' " Lisa said softly. "You said it can be something you feel for a place, or for a person. You figure a squat rat could get to be like that?"

"How do you feel now?"

The steam was clearing and again Gahzee could make her out—the bright eyes gleaming, the cloth clinging to her breasts and belly, accentuating her sensuality, rather than hiding it.

"I feel . . . good," she said. "Sorta light-headed, but clean. All-the-way-inside kinda clean."

"Would that not be a manner of Beauty?"

There was a long moment of silence.

"So I guess you're saying I could," she said finally.

"I'm saying you already are—you only have to learn to touch it, to find out were it rests inside you, and then keep the channels open."

"That's what I want to learn," Lisa said.

When they finally left the sweat lodge, it was all unplanned, but they moved as though they had choreographed the moment. Their hands met and joined. They crossed the room and lay down on Gahzee's bedding, neither one nor the other leading, but moving as one. The wet shirt and loincloth were laid aside and they explored each other's bodies with hands and tongues, licking the salty glisten of sweat, following the contours of two such dissimilar shapes that could so comfortably fit together and merge as one.

"I think I like this sweat lodge business," Lisa murmured later, curled up against Gahzee, his arm lying across her back, a comfortable weight.

Gahzee lifted his head so that he could look into her features. Even with her tattooing, she appeared different. Younger. More vulnerable. But stronger too. The tough edge that was so much a part of her had softened from their lovemaking, but had not disappeared. It still remained in her eyes, in the quiet strength of her body where it lay against him.

"This is, I think," he said as he laid back down, "a case of the teacher learning from the student."

"Is that good or bad?" Lisa asked.

"It's good. Very good."

Sighing contentedly, she snuggled closer. Gahzee looked over her shoulder to where Nanabozho still lay, watching them with what appeared to be a grin. The *medé* wasn't sure how wise it was for the relationship between teacher and student to have changed as it had, but he found that he didn't care.

We are our own tribe now, he thought to himself. Like Twisted Hairs, we must find our own methods of braiding knowledge.

And already she danced in his heart.

~ 2 ~

When the Ragman returned, Lisa was just painting on the last of the rainbow design she wore on her eyelids. She leaned in close to a little square of mirror propped up on a stone, chewing on her lower lip as she concentrated on getting lines straight.

She felt wonderfully languid and at peace with herself. The trauma of the past couple of days felt distant—not quite real somehow. Like it had happened a long time ago. The opposite of present was absent. Present was her new lover. For the time being, all the craziness was absent.

Though she was anything but a virgin, making love with Gahzee had been so different from doing it with previous partners that it was like a first time. Not the awkward gropings she remembered of her real first time—on a beat-up futon in the back of a warehouse with a messenger half again as old as she was herself—but a real first time that left her understanding monogamy and all that vid crap where people did crazy things just because they were in love.

It never made sense before. But glancing at Gahzee, she knew she just wanted to be with him. Learn about Walks and Wheels and all that shit, sure, but more importantly *be* with him. All the prop that the Plex vids fed out about Clavers was just washed away now.

But what if he dumped her? Went back to his Enclave, got hooked up with some pureblood Claver girl?

He looked up under her intense scrutiny and smiled.

Nah, she thought. Besides, he couldn't go back.

When they heard a three-wheeler pull up outside, Gahzee rose from where he'd been fletching arrows and melted into the shadows. Bozo was already gone. Lisa didn't move. She recognized the sound of the motor. Drone mechs never bothered too much with serious maintenance. The engine she heard had the same knock in it that it had had when the Ragman drove it away earlier.

She finished the last swath of rainbow on her left eyelid as the Ragman filled the doorway, then put away her paints and mirror.

"You're looking cheerful," the Ragman growled. He glanced at the empty bedding. "Where's the Claver?"

"His name's Gahzee," Lisa said.

The Ragman caught the protective tone in her voice. His eyes narrowed thoughtfully.

"I don't care what his name is—we got business to discuss."

Gahzee appeared suddenly from the shadows and nodded to the Ragman. Lisa smiled as the Ragman started.

"You move like a spook, Jack," he said. "Don't know's as I like that."

"My People are quiet walkers," Gahzee said. He took in the Ragman's bulk, his strange mohawk of dreadlocks. "What is your tribe?"

The Ragman stared at him for a long moment. "The fucked-over tribe, Jack."

"Gahzee."

"There's only two kinds of people in the world besides the Ragman—darlings and Jacks. The darlings like a hug, while the Jacks walk around with their dicks in hand when they ain't got a Steeljack to make 'em feel big. I don't figure you for a darling, Jack."

"Don't mind him, Gaz," Lisa said. "They call him the Ragman 'cause he likes to rag people."

"I got serious problems, darling," the Ragman said, turning to her, "and what I don't got time for is screwing around."

When she saw the pain in his eyes, absent suddenly didn't have any meaning and the past was very real. All the pain came back in a rush. The Ragman had lost friends, too. He was hurting—just like she was.

"I'm sorry," she said. "I was just . . . just starting to feel a little real again, I guess. I wasn't thinking . . ."

The Ragman's hard gaze softened. "That's okay, darling. We all got to cope the best way we can. Some people try to put the hurt aside. Me, I ride the pain 'til I can fuck the bastards over." He hunched down by the fire. "Whatcha got to eat?"

"Rabbit."

She and Gahzee joined him by the fire, drinking tea while the Ragman ate and filled them in.

"Everything's gone to shit in the squats," he said. "You think we had it bad before, well, you ain't seen nothing. Drones gathered up their own dead to take 'em back into the Plex and burned everybody else. Fucking stink's enough to make you puke. People are lying real quiet and low—but only on the surface. Chinas and tongs are gearing up for war. Yaks took out Chien Foo this morning—the Jack that had your chip," he explained to Gahzee, "so we got the triads gearing up for shit too.

"Meanwhile, the drones got a sudden hard-on for the yaks—no prize for guessing why after last night—and they want whoever took down Foo, or they're gonna dismantle the Goro Clan."

"It'll be a bloodbath," Lisa said.

"Tell me something I don't already know. But we can use all this shit to our advantage." He looked at Gahzee again. "Which is more important to you—the flyer or the chip?"

"The chip."

"Yeah, I figured that. So here's what we're gonna do. I'm gonna do you a favour and blow up your flyer—I like the idea of sticking it to Goro like that—but then we're gonna get serious. I'm putting together a strike force of bullyboys and we're gonna start a problem with the yaks—right in the Plex. I figure we can get things going real fine and then the drones'll step in to keep their fucking peace and finish the job for us."

"What about the chip?" Gahzee asked.

"Well, now I figure that's your problem, Jack. I can use the Co-Op's connections to get you and Lisa into the Plex, but after that you're on your own. You can try and face down Ho Fung's boys, but I'll tell you, he ain't got the resources to handle anything like your chip. I'm betting he's already moved it."

"To who?"

The Ragman shrugged. "I'm only guessing, but word has it that Chien Foo's been seen in the IBN building more'n once in the last little while. Considering that IBN's going down the tubes and it needs all the help it can get, I'm betting they bought that chip. Or they were planning to, but the yaks offed Foo before he had a chance to move the fucking thing.

"So that's your choices. The Ho Fung Triad—I'd put them third. The yaks—they get a big second. My bet's on IBN."

"What makes you so sure?" Gahzee asked.

"Weren't you listening, Jack? I've already laid out a shitload of reasons, but if you want some more, how's this—according to today's market listings, IBN transferred some of its shares to one Ichiro Owada."

"So?" Lisa asked.

"So Owada's a Nip front man for Ho Fung, darling—do I gotta spell it out any clearer? Something big's going down between him and IBN, because it sure as shit'd have to be big for IBN to cough up some shares to a china."

He looked from Lisa to Gahzee. "So if you want that chip back, Jack, you gotta go play Kozo Goh on the headman of IBN."

"Kozo Goh?"

"You know," Lisa said. "This samurai detective who's always busting heads and stuff on the vids—or don't you get them in the Claves?"

Gahzee shook his head. "But I understand the reference now."

"So you're going after IBN?" the Ragman asked.

Gahzee glanced at Lisa, then nodded.

"Okay. Yak gear's out for you, Jack, but I think I can fix you up with the right kind of swash that a swagger girl'd put on her strongarm if she was taking him back into the Plex. You still got your ID, darling?"

Lisa nodded.

"Shouldn't be a whole lot a problem then. I'll lay out your route in—you can figure your own way out. Place is gonna be in such an uproar by that point, there'd be no point in me mapping anything out for you."

"What about you, Ragman?" Lisa asked. "How're you getting in?"

"Oh, I got no problems along that route, darling. I've been in and out of the Plex for years now. Got my Co-Op connections—who the fuck do you think's been running that show?"

"Lisa said there would be a price for your help," Gahzee said.

The Ragman frowned. "Well now, I won't shit you—normally there would be. But I've got my own scores to settle right now. We all get outta this thing in one piece, I'll be coming to you for something then."

"For what kind of something?" Gahzee pressed.

"Fucked if I know, Jack. We'll work something out. Don't you worry. The Ragman's not a greedy man." He glanced at their remaining yak Usaijin. "That thing run?"

"Yeah."

"Okay, darling. Then I'm outta here. Comes on to getting dark, you shake your asses down to the junkwalkers' yard, other side of the Market. I'll have some ID for your boyfriend here, and your route all worked out."

Lisa found herself blushing and shot a quick look to Gahzee, but the *medé* simply smiled at her. Something quick and warm seemed to reach out from him to touch an answering echo deep inside her. Remembering her earlier worry, she found herself smiling back. No way he was gonna run out on her.

"Okay, Ragman," she said. "We'll be there."

"Thank you," Gahzee said, rising with the Ragman.

"Just fuck 'em over good once you get inside," the Ragman said. "It's time they got a little of their own back." He started for the door, then suddenly caught sight of Bozo lying in the shadows. "What the fuck—"

"His name's Nanabozho," Lisa said with a grin.

"I don't care if his name's Sugar, just keep that sucker away from me, darling. I hate dogs."

"He's not a dog—he's a coyote." She glanced at Gahzee. "A trickster."

"He gives me the fucking creeps with those eyes a' his," the Ragman said. "You figure on bringing him along with you tonight?"

"He goes where he wishes," Gazhee said.

"Well, I ain't got any ID for him—just so's you understand."

"We'll see ya tonight," Lisa told him.

As they stood in the doorway, watching him leave, Gahzee laid his arm around Lisa's shoulders. For the moment, there was only the present again, all else absent, leaving with the Ragman on his stolen Jiszuki. She leaned against Gahzee, happy at the contact.

"Want to help me make up the bed?" she asked.

"Make it up, or mess it up?" Gahzee asked.

Lisa shrugged. "Whatever. Just so long as we're doing it together."

But she was already unbuttoning his shirt.

~ 3 ~

Yip met Miko for lunch in a small *kissaten* in the Baidai District. She wore a pale rose dress that showed off her long legs and her mane of black hair hung loose. Watching the hostess lead her to his booth, Yip thought that she didn't appear nearly so formidable as she did on the court vids or when he'd first met her in her office. But he couldn't forget the yakuza tattoo on her back—invisible to the *kissaten*'s other patrons, but very much present for him.

"You never came back last night," she said as she was seated across from him. "I was worried."

"I had to think."

"I see."

The sudden frost in her voice woke a chill up Yip's spine. "*Gomen,*" he said quickly. "Not about you—about us, but . . ."

How could he tell her that last night he had killed his own section head and subsequently been given Aoki's position. That Aoki had been in Goro's employ and was demanding that Yip fill that position as well? That every time he looked at her, thought about her, her tattoo was there to remind him of the yaks?

"Goro called me last night," he said finally. "He wants me to work for him."

The coldness in Miko's eyes immediately turned to worry. "What did you say?"

"What could I say? I told him I would think about it."

"And his response?"

"I didn't give him time to make one—I simply hung up."

Miko reached across the table and took his hand. "You are playing a dangerous game, Phillip."

Yip thought of Huan. Of the riot in the squats last night.

"It's no game," he said.

"*Hai.* And it gets worse. Have you heard of the triad lieutenant who was slain in the Jimu District this morning—supposedly a yak assassination?"

Yip nodded. "Chien Foo. We have witnesses who will swear to it that it was yaks who killed him."

"I've spent all morning dealing with Ho Anzen's prosecutors and Goro. The want the man who killed Foo, or they want Goro. But he didn't do it."

"How do you know this?"

"He told me."

"And you believe him?"

Miko sighed. "This will be hard for you to understand, Phillip, but in his own way, Goro is an honourable man. He does not lie—not to his *kobun*. Not to me."

"Then who killed Foo?"

"Someone who wishes to implicate the Goro Clan. Goro believes it was done by Ho Anzen officers disguised as yaks."

"Impossible!"

"And how do you know that?"

It was Yip's turn to sigh. "I don't."

Miko nodded. "It is because you yourself would not condone such an action that you find it unacceptable that another officer might have."

I would not? Yip thought bleakly. He studied Miko's features. He was more drawn to her today than ever—by the memory of her body, by her clever wit, by everything that made her who she was. Tattoo notwithstanding, how could he do anything but trust her? If she failed that trust, he realized, there was simply no point in going on.

"I killed a man last night," he said.

A puzzled look touched Miko's features.

"Not in the riot—or at least not a rioter."

He explained, in quick clipped sentences, just what he had done. When he was finished, he waited. Was that disappointment he saw in her features? Had she only cared for him because she saw him as a moral man in a world faded grey?

"Aoki deserved to die," she said softly. "But it must have been hard for you, Phillip."

"I don't know who I am anymore."

"I do. You are a faithful man who believes in justice. You could do no less than what you did. Aoki was yakuza."

"I know."

"With his rank in Ho Anzen as well as the Goro Clan, he

would never have paid for all the wrongs he had done." Her fingers tightened around his own. "Oh, what will we do, Phillip? What is to become of us?"

It took Yip a moment to realize exactly what she was saying. Not you. But we. Commitment. He lifted his gaze to meet hers and slowly shook his head.

"I don't know, Miko."

The waitress approached their booth just then and they ordered their lunch. When the waitress left, Miko leaned towards Yip.

"I have other news," she said. "There is something important taking place, but at this point I have not been able to discover just what. All I know is that Kishi Tano is in Trenton, doing business with Goro."

"The *oyabun* of *oyabuns*?"

"*Hai.* They were in conference when this business with Foo came up, and he was present at the meeting with Ho Anzen's prosecutors. He was very displeased that his influence was ignored."

Yip thought of the Claver chip that Goro had lost. "I begin to see a pattern in all of this," he said. He explained what he meant.

"I know of the chip," Miko said. "Goro speaks of little else. A squat messenger was either robbed of it, or stole it for herself."

"Claver technology represents a great deal of power to whoever decodes that chip."

Miko nodded. "As I said, Goro has been most disturbed by its disappearance."

"It might also explain a great deal of what is going on. If the triads, tongs and Goro are all scrambling to acquire that chip . . . then last night may have been only a taste of what is to come. The violence could well spread into the Megaplex itself."

"Foo's death could be the beginning."

"I will have to look into this," Yip said.

* * *

Yip saw Miko off in a private cab before he set out for the office. As he moved away from the front of the *kissaten* heading for the nearest Okuda Line subway station, a small man in a grey business bodysuit approached him.

"Phillip Yip?" he asked.

Yip nodded.

"There is a call for you, Yip-san." The man pointed to a public com-link on the corner.

"You've made some mistake," Yip began, but the man shook his head.

"Goro-san will be most displeased if you do not speak with him immediately."

Goro-san. Goro-san. Yip half-wished that it had been Goro in front of his laser last night rather than Aoki.

He could ignore the call, but he knew it was going to be important. And seeing that the *oyabun* had traced him so easily to his luncheon engagement, who knew what he might do next if Yip didn't speak to him. If Goro was to use Miko as a bargaining tool against him . . . Yip didn't even want to think about that.

The screen was blank, but as soon as Yip acknowledged the call, Goro's familiar voice came through the speaker. The screen remained blank.

"I want Ho Anzen to leave me in peace—let them hound someone else."

"I doubt that there is anything that I could—"

"You will see to this," Goro said, breaking in, "or you will learn firsthand what it means to displease me. Am I making myself clear?"

"Very clear. But—"

"Then see to it."

The connection was cut off. Yip stood staring at the blank screen, the buzz of an empty line filling the booth until he slowly reached over and punched the button that turned the speaker off. He looked around for the man who had called him into the booth, but the small figure in the business grey had vanished.

Stepping from the booth, Yip eschewed the Okuda Line subway in favour of walking back to his office. He needed time to think. Not to make a decision. He already knew what his answer to Goro would be. What he had to do was consider some way that he and Miko could survive the *oyabun*'s wrath when Goro realized that Yip was not, and would never be, his man.

Seventeen

~1~

Shoji Aoto.

The Ragman hadn't thought of his old systems *sensei* in years. But waiting for his strongarms to show up for the raid, he found himself remembering the wizened little Japanese computer wizard. The Ragman flexed his long fingers. Aoto's fingers had been tiny—more like little filaments that could squeeze into just about anywhere. And there wasn't a thing about systems that he didn't know. Or that he couldn't figure out.

Aoto had owned Denshin Systems, a small Plex corporation trying to buck the big gun Kaisha. Unfortunately, Denshin Systems never quite made it. But it wasn't for want of trying. Aoto used to haunt the junkwalkers' yard in the squats Market, even heading out into the Badlands himself, looking for lost tech that he could use to give Denshin a better foot in the competitive Plex marketplace.

But for all Aoto's wizardry, Denshin never quite had the capital to become solvent. There was always money owed, Combank knocking on the door. It would have been completely swallowed by one of the larger Kaisha if Aoto hadn't left his shares to the Ragman when he died.

Denshin Systems became the basis of the Jones Co-Op—named after Desmond Jones, better known as the Ragman.

It was going on twenty-five years since that young junkwalking Ragman—just a punk like any other squat rat—stepped in and saved Aoto's ass. Aoto'd gotten in a little too deep, carrying one shitload of hard credits for a big tech buy, when a gang of chinas backed him up in an alley. They were looking for some quick cash, happy to be cutting themselves a little bit of Nip ass in the bargain.

The Ragman still didn't know why he'd stepped in with a couple of his friends and broke it up, didn't know why he hadn't just taken the Nip's credits himself, once he saw what Aoto was carrying. But he hadn't. He took to looking for the good stuff that he knew Aoto'd buy, found himself trailing along with the little *sensei*, picking up bits and pieces of tech until it got to the point that when something got broken in the squats, they'd take it to the Ragman to get fixed.

Once Aoto recognized the apt pupil he had in the whip-thin black junkwalker, he began to train the Ragman in earnest.

We had us some good years, the Ragman thought, remembering. Because they didn't share just a love for computers; they had the same social politics as well.

It was Aoto'd who first talked about a Co-Op, but he was never solvent enough to get it off the ground. That took the Ragman's smarts. When Aoto died and the Ragman got those shares, he parlayed them into what he had now—he was the man to see in the squats, and slowly but surely, he was taking on the Plex corporations as well. Hell, there wasn't a Plex president that slept well at nights for worrying about who the Co-Op'd target next.

Someday it was all gonna belong to the people—that was the Ragman's dream. Fuck the Kaisha. Fuck the clowns in their fancy towers. Rats were gonna get in on the action too. And maybe he was just some jive-ass squats rat, chasing after a dream, but fuck that too. At least what he was doing had meaning.

That was the big lesson that Aoto had taught him. It was no good just playing with the tech, fixing old shit, working up some new angles. You had to use the tech as a tool to make a difference. Just like the Clavers did. Come the big business invasion from Japan and China, it was the blacks that got the shaft again. Only this time the whites went down with them. All they were good for was to scrabble out a living in the squats with the other rats. Chinas too lazy to make it in the Plexes. The criminals that lost their citizenships and got tossed out.

Well, fuck it. We're all people too.

"You got a nail up yore ass or something, Ragman?"

The Ragman blinked to see that the last of his bullyboys had showed up. Fifteen men. A couple were chinas—big mothers, broad-shouldered and mean-looking. Three whites. The rest were his own. Dark skin glistening, woolly hair cut short around their scalps, or hanging in dreadlocks, bodysuits and kevlar vests all in primary colours.

The one talking was an old friend from the Ragman's junk-walking days—Sly Bobbie Rye.

"What's your problem, Jack?" the Ragman asked him.

Sly Bobbie held his hands out in front of him and let them shake. "Whoa, man. Lookit me tremble. Old Ragman's got a big frown for me and I'm just all fucked-up."

A chorus of laughter rose up that the Ragman joined. When it died down, he looked around at them. Including his own stolen Jiszuki, they had twelve three-wheelers between them. Doubling up, that'd be enough to get them where they wanted to go.

"Here's the deal, girls," he said. "What we got right now's a cakewalk—a dry run out to where some yaks are guarding a Claver flyer. We're gonna ride on out to them, blow up their toy, and leave 'em for the dogs."

"So what's the real gig?" one of the chinas asked. Jimmy Poon.

The Ragman explained briefly.

Linton Zadie, another of the blacks, shook his head. "Oh, man. Take on the yaks on their own turf? You been burning wire, Ragman? Are yore brains all fried?"

"It's a kamikaze run, girls. That's all I can say. But the deal's this: whichever of you fuckers is tough enough to make it, you got yourself a citizenship."

"Ain't nobody gonna let a bunch of brothers keep their citizenships," Sly Bobbie said.

"And once we got our asses in there," Linton added, "who the fuck'd give us a job anyway?"

The Ragman was sitting on a rock. Pulling out a bag, he spilled ID cards on the stone surface beside him.

"Here's your citizenships, if you want 'em," he said. "And I'll tell you right now, girls, every one's the real thing. And you want a job—the Ragman'll give you one."

"Who're you jiving?" Linton said. "You got no jobs for us in the Plex."

Jimmy Poon nodded. "Why would ya be living in the squats if you did?"

"I'm the Jones Co-Op, girls," the Ragman said. "I got digs everywhere—in the squats and in the Plex. Only reason I don't stay in the Plex is they got no good pussy." That got a laugh. "And I got me a social conscience."

"You the head man?" Linton demanded. "You been setting your toms on us rats?"

"That's Plex prop talking in you, Jack. You all know the Ragman. When'd he ever fuck one of you over? When'd he ever let one a' you down?"

Sly Bobbie nodded slowly. "Makes a kinda twisted sense. I remember Des Jones."

The Ragman grinned. "Sure you do. Here's a brother made good. So what about the rest a' you girls? You want to take the chance? Lose your ass, fighting the good fight, but maybe making good? When was the last time any of you dumb fucks had an offer half so good?"

"You got one a them cards with my name on it?" Sly Bobbie asked.

The Ragman went through them. When he found Sly Bobbie's, he tossed it over.

"Motherfucker," Sly Bobbie said, checking out his picture. "Will you look at that handsome brother? Where'd you get that picture, Ragman?"

"VD clinic—where'd you think, Jack?"

"Well, you can count this brother in."

The other strongarms had a good look at Sly Bobbie's ID, then one by one they signed up to get their own.

"Wasting this flyer's not gonna be no big deal," the Ragman said, "but I'll tell you again, hitting the yaks could be a suicide run."

"I'm tired of yaks walking around like they're fucking kings," Jimmy Poon said. "It's time we kicked their asses, *tung ma?*"

"Well, let's get rolling, girls," the Ragman said. "We got a hundred klicks ahead of us and another hundred back and I gotta meet some friends at the junkwalkers' yard come nightfall."

"You got some pretty tech hardware for us, Ragman?" Sly Bobbie asked.

"Yeah," Linton said. "Like some smart laser-rifles?"

"I got better than that, Jack. I got rocket launchers that pack eight pounds of smart missile with each fucking shot."

The strongarms grinned at each other.

"This is gonna be fun," Jimmy Poon said.

I just hope most of us live to laugh about it, the Ragman thought as he started up his Jiszuki and led the way out.

~ 2 ~

The IBN systems labs were in the basement of the IBN building, two floors underground. In a controlled clean-air environment, banks of computers, capacitors, storage systems, printers, and displays lined the walls. Techs sat at various operating consoles, running programs. Every screen showed the same gridwork of interconnecting lines of the Claver chip's encoding.

"We have to work with the utmost caution," Izumi Sho, the head tech, was explaining to Okado and his aide, Kamo. "One false move and everything on that chip could be destroyed."

"How long will it take?" Okado asked.

Sho shrugged. He was a portly man, broad-faced, eyes set close above a flat nose. "At least a week."

"We need that data immediately," Okado said.

"You don't know what you're asking," Sho protested. "The Clavers don't think like us, *neh?* We have yet to break their broadcast codes. Something like this chip is infinitely more complex."

"Are you making any progress?" Okado asked.

"The process we are using is not measurable in such terms. First we attempt to build a similar code, so that we can understand its scope. Then, once we begin work on the actual chip, we must move in infinitesimal steps to assure that we don't trigger a self-destruct mechanism within the code. Your pardon, Okado-san, but it could take a very long time."

Okado looked at Kamo. "Does any other company have a tech that can do better? Someone whose contract we can buy out?"

His aide shrugged and glanced at Sho.

"*Sa,*" the head tech said. See here. "What you want is a wizard—a systems *sensei*—not a common tech."

"I want whatever it will take. Where can I find such a 'wizard'?"

"The best Trenton had was Shoji Aoto—but he has been dead for many years."

"And among the living?" Okado said, his patience wearing thin.

"A man who signs his work 'Spook'."

"Spook?" Okado said. "What kind of a name is Spook?"

"A code name, I believe," Kamo said.

Sho nodded. "There are in-system bulletin boards where

the various techs can speak to each other, or leave messages. New processes are discussed—only unclassified material, of course. Everyone utilizes a code name when online."

"Then leave a message for this Spook," Okado ordered. "Whatever his contract with any other firm, tell him we'll double it."

"*Hai.*" Sho nodded brusquely.

Okado sighed. "I don't question the abilities of either yourself or your men, Sho-sán. We are simply in a situation where we are rapidly running out of time."

For if the yakuza should ever discover where their Claver chip was . . . if the Ho Fung Triad realized that it wasn't yaks, but IBN's men that had killed Foo . . .

Okado didn't want to think about any of it. He just wanted that data. Wanted it on-line where it could be used to boost IBN's flagging reputation once more. By the time either Ho Fung or Goro realized what had become of the chip and who had killed Foo, IBN would be in such a strong position that it couldn't be touched.

"We have always been extremely proud of the work you do in the IBN labs," Okado added. "Now please—contact this Spook and have him working on this problem as soon as possible. Naturally he will answer to you."

"*Hai,*" Sho replied. This time his quick nod was respectful.

~ 3 ~

It took Yip an hour, sitting in Aoki's office—now his office—idly playing with his terminal that he'd connected to Aoki's system, before he knew what to do.

The answer lay in the squats. In the Ch'ing-jen Fan.

Last night's riot had been sparked by Goro's yaks converging on the club. They were looking for something. Or someone. Now it would be up to him to find out what it was.

The answer had to be there.

He left the Ho Anzen headquarters with a squad of officers—the promotion was convenient for some things—and took them down to where the Ch'ing-jen Fan stood on the Strip. Small groups of chinas and rats glared sullenly on the street corners, watching them. There was movement in windows as they passed by—heads ducking out of sight.

While Yip had allowed his men riot gear, he wore none himself. The smells of the squats stung his nostrils. The stink of the funeral pyre was still strong in the air. The outside of the Ch'ing-jen Fan was scarred from laser fire—black streaks of burnt stone, crisscrossing in a webwork that made the building even uglier than it already was.

The doorman had a shotgun on his lap, but he made no move to stop Yip and the two officers he took inside. Yip left four more out front, another pair at the rear of the building, the remainder of the squad taking up positions nearby with clear lines of fire. Inside, there were only a few wireheads plugged into their fiberdiscs and some tongs gambling with Flower Cards at a long table. A Metaldrone vid played at low volume on the screens, filling the air with a low buzz, overriding the sounds from the bank of *pachinko* machines.

Yip crossed the club to where a solitary barman was conversing with a geisha in a shimmery bodysilver that left her breasts and genitalia bare.

"I wish to speak to your manager," Yip said.

The barman shook his head. "He's not in."

Yip drew his Steeljack and laid it on the bartop, his hand still on its grip, muzzle pointed in the general vicinity of the barman's torso. On either side of him, his officers flicked their laser-rifles off safety. Heads lifted through the room, bodies tensing. At the Flower Card table, hands reached under kimonos and jackets.

"Perhaps you could find him, *ma?*" Yip asked.

The barman nervously licked his lips. "I . . . I'll see what I can do."

It took only moments for the barman to return with his

tong manager in tow. He was a muscular man, a head taller than Yip, bare-chested, skin gleaming with sweat. Obviously he had been working out.

Yip reholstered his Steeljack. His officers put their laser-rifles back onto safety. At the Flower Card table, the interrupted game commenced once more.

"You are?" Yip asked.

"Ron Yeh. You got no right busting in here."

"My pardon, Yeh-sen. My name is Phillip Yip; I am with Ho Anzen Securities."

He offered Yeh his hand. The manager took it without thinking, then narrowed his eyes as they shook.

"My reason for disturbing you today is that I'm investigation the unfortunate incident which took place here last night."

"This is the squats, drone. You got no jurisdiction here."

"Very true. And yet—would you care to have a repetition of last night's disaster?"

"You threatening me?"

Yip shook his head. "Hardly, Yeh-san. I am here in hopes of avoiding such problems in the future. While it's true that I have no jurisdiction in the squats, by the same token, many of our citizens come to the Strip for the purpose of entertainment. I'm sure your own establishment caters to more than a few. When the possibility of such violence exists, with the potential harm to citizens, I must make it my business to investigate—even beyond what is normally considered my jurisdiction."

Yeh nodded, bored. "What do ya want to know?"

"What did the yaks want with your club?"

"Fang here," Yeh said, jerking a thumb towards the barman, "said they came looking for the Ragman."

Of course, Yip thought. The Ragman. Even in the Plex they knew of him. A computer wizard who was capable of working magic with any system. A true *sensei*.

More pieces were beginning to fall into place. The missing Claver chip. This Ragman. Either he had acquired the chip and Goro wanted it back, or Goro was using the Ragman to break the Claver code. Perhaps they'd had a falling out . . .

"Is the Ragman here?" Yip asked.

Yeh glanced at the barman.

"Nah," Fang Wo said. "He's been in a coupla times since last night, but I ain't seen him for awhile."

"I would like to see his office," Yip said.

Yeh laughed. "*Ni deh*, drone." Fuck you.

"Very well." Yip turned to the officer on his right. "Contact headquarters. I want a fully amoured contingent sent down here immediately. Put the men on full alert."

"Hang on!" Yeh cried, before the order could be sent. "What the fuck do you think you're doing?"

"I have no jurisdiction here, yet in the squats, superior force rules, *tung ma*. So I'm arranging for the required superior force. Of course, we could avoid all of this if you would merely allow me to see the Ragman's offices . . . ?"

Yeh sighed, obviously not wanting another riot. "Down the hall there," he said, pointing across the room, "take the turn and it's the door at the end."

Before Yip could thank him, the manager turned away and left the club through the door behind the bar through which he'd initially come. The door slammed behind him.

"You," Yip said to one officer, "remain here."

The other he set guarding the hallway itself. Then with his men deployed, he set off down the hall.

On first entering the Ragman's office, all he could do was stand and gape. The chaos of wiring, machines, and computer parts left him with a sense of hopeless dismay that only increased as he started to poke through things. Finally he turned his attention to the desk. The drawers were filled with chips, circuitry, and more wiring—a baffling nest of parts. He looked at the terminal.

It was manually operated, like his own. He called up the Ragman's system. When the gridlines of its encoding appeared on the screen, he settled down to work on it. Twenty minutes of trial and error later he had it broken, but he felt no sense of satisfaction. If there was anything important in this system, he would never have been able to break in this easily. Not when dealing with a *sensei* like the Ragman. Still, as long as he was inside . . .

He spent a half-hour reviewing numerous files, then finally sat back in the chair. While there was nothing in here that wasn't readily available in the Plex systems—market reports, bulletin boards, news service clips, and the like—there *was* one continuing thread. The Jones Co-Op. Everything in the files led back to the Ragman's interest in it.

Well, that wasn't so unusual, Yip thought. It was common knowledge that the Co-Op was making Plex material available in the squats. Obviously they needed a squats front man.

Leaving the system on screen, he went back to a physical search of the office. It was another twenty-five minutes before he found the small plastipack stuck to the back of one of the desk's drawers. Inside was a full set of Plex ID for one Desmond Jones. The ID photo showed an Oriental man. But the Ragman was supposed to be a black. Was he another Mitsui sculpture—living a double life, half in the squats, half in the Plex?

He shuffled through some more of the ID. Jones had an *apato* in the Baidai District. A penthouse in the Exxon Building.

Going to the computer, he called up a list of businesses in the Exxon Building, stopping the scroll of the screen at one that caught his eye. Denshin Systems. He flipped through the ID packet again. There it was. A Denshin Systems company ID card. But it didn't give Jones's position in the company.

Yip used the computer to run down Denshin's holdings, stopping the screen when a name leapt out at him. The Co-Op. Denshin Systems was its major shareholder and Denshin was entirely owned by Desmond Jones. Desmond Jones—the Jones Co-Op.

As though he were caught up in a moment of satori, Yip simply stared at the screen for long silent minutes. For all intents and purposes, the Ragman *was* the Jones Co-Op.

One of the Co-Op's main targets was the Goro Clan's growing stranglehold on the Plex economy.

It was perfect. If he could connect with the Ragman . . .

He cleared the screen and began to work the keyboard. "MESSAGE FROM PHILLIP YIP, SECTION HEAD, HO ANZEN SECURITIES," he typed, "TO DESMOND JONES, A.K.A. THE RAGMAN. **URGENT** THAT WE SPEAK **PRIVATELY**. CONCERNS GORO CLAN. CAN PROVE NO DUPLICITY UPON MY PART SHOULD SUCH REFERENCE BE NEEDED. PLEASE CONTACT ME ***IMMEDIATELY***."

Miko, he thought as he left the Ragman's office. We might still have a chance to survive.

Behind him, a red light on the Ragman's computer flashed on and off, indicating that it held a message.

~ 4 ~

The attack on the yaks guarding the Claver flyer proved to be just the cakewalk that the Ragman had promised it would be. There was only one sentry watching from the height of a dilapidated warehouse. Jimmy Poon's cousin Huai Jen Pa spotted him, taking the yak out with Linton Zadie.

On the approach the Ragman divided their small force into four groups, hitting the yaks from each cardinal point of the compass. Each group was armed with a rocket launcher and two smart missiles—homing projectiles with tiny built-in circuitry that locked the missile in on its target. After the explosions that followed the first round of missiles, there was nothing left of the flyer or the yaks guarding it—just a wall of flame that swallowed the pieces whole.

"Mo*ther*," Sly Bobbie murmured. "I ain't never seen that kind of firepower before." He turned to the Ragman. "That what we're using on Goro's headquarters?"

"I wish, Jack. But there's no way we'd get 'em into the Plex."

Sly Bobbie looked back at the conflagration. "Too bad, man," he said wistfully.

Once the flames died down, they drove in closer to reconnoiter.

"Where'd you get this shit?" Jimmy Poon asked, patting the length of the rocket launcher he was holding.

"Scrounged the launchers," the Ragman said, "but I built the SMs myself."

"No shit? In that little place you got in back of Yeh's?"

The Ragman shook his head. "Built 'em in the Denshin labs and smuggled 'em out in sections." He turned over a piece of hot metal with his boot. "Looks like we're finished here, girls. Let's head for home."

"Wish we could've saved a couple of those yak three-wheelers," Jimmy's cousin said glumly. He was one of those riding double.

By the time they got back to the squats it was late afternoon. The Ragman set up a meet with his bullyboys—same time as he was getting together with Lisa and her Claver—then headed for his homeground. The Ch'ing-jen Fan's manager stopped him as he was crossing the main floor of the club.

"You had visitors, Ragman," Ron Yeh told him.

"What kind a' visitors?"

"Drones. We don't need anymore of this shit, Ragman. One more time and you're outta here."

"They were in my office?"

"Yeah, yeah. You hear what I'm telling you?"

The Ragman regarded him coldly. "Who do you think pays your salary, Jack?"

"Huh?"

"Forget it."

Leaving Yeh standing at the bar, scratching his head, the Ragman made for his office. Despite the usual mess and disorganized jumble, he knew immediately that someone had been going through his shit.

"You don't need it, Yeh?" he said softly. "What the fuck makes you think I need it?"

He laid the cloth-wrapped bundle of launchers and missiles by the door and went around to his desk. His Desmond Jones ID was lying scattered on top of it. Fuck, now they knew. He glanced nervously around the small room. So what were they waiting for? Then he noticed the message light blinking on his computer.

He sat down and called the message up, then leaned back, arms behind his head after he'd read it through. Phillip Yip, was it? Wanted to cut a deal with this brother?

The name sounded familiar. He had his system do a quick search and it came up with the Fax Vid story about Co-Op terrorists shutting down a DMC. That deal still smelled like Goro to the Ragman. Yip was the investigating officer. And now he was a section head, was he?

The Ragman reread the message.

No duplicity on my part.

He had to admit he was curious. Like for starters, how was Yip going to prove he could be trusted?

Concerns Goro Clan.

Didn't everything these days?

Speak privately.

Right. What else? But if this Yip had managed to track him down, then he had to have enough smarts to know that the Ragman was no dumbass squats rat that he could take for a ride.

He cleared the screen and idly began to scan the on-line bulletin boards of the Plex while he thought. He stopped the screen when a message caught his eye. "SPOOK. HIGH-PAYING PUZZLE GIG UP FOR GRABS. INTERESTED? RIDER."

The Ragman had made it his business to track down the identities behind the code names that appeared on the bulletin boards. It was a hobby of his that sometimes paid off. Like now.

Rider. He was the tight-assed Nipponjin who headed up IBN's systems labs; by all accounts, big on formality and

Keisando—the Way of the Computer. But get him on-line under his code name Rider and he loosened up like a drunk squats geisha handing out free favours.

So IBN wanted Spook did they? The fact that they wanted a systems *sensei* confirmed his guess that they had the Claver chip. Things were beginning to heat up, no question about it.

Yip and IBN. He didn't know what the drone's game was, but it was worth checking into. As for IBN . . . well he'd always had a hankering to check out their labs. . . .

He punched up information on his com-link and got the number for Ho Anzen Securities. Keeping his outgoing vidscreen blank, he put a call through to Yip. The face that appeared on his screen rang no bells.

"I got your message," he said.

"I'm afraid you have the wrong connection," Yip replied. "Who were you attempting to reach?"

"Don't fuck around with me, Jack."

But then he saw that Yip had pulled his computer display screen around so that he could see it. He copied the displayed *apato* address onto his own screen.

"Do you realize who you are speaking to?" Yip was saying.

As he spoke, he added a time under the address that the Ragman copied as well.

"Look for me," the Ragman said and cut the connection.

He called up the Megaplex directory and had it find exactly where the *apato* was and who it belonged to. The name was familiar, but not at all what he'd expected. Fumiko Hirose. Goro's lawyer.

"What kinda games are you playing with me, Jack?" he asked softly.

The set-up was about as subtle as a junkwalker's sledgehammer, and that was wrong. Whatever else Goro was, he wasn't stupid. And he wasn't about to underestimate anybody either. So why did Goro think the Ragman was gonna fall for this shit?

Because, he realized, Goro probably knew the Ragman's biggest failing: his curiosity.

He checked the hour and saw it was time to go meet Lisa and her Claver.

Let's do this nice and orderly, he told himself as he left his office. We get Lisa and the Claver in. We check out the "high-paying puzzle gig" at IBN. And then, with his bully-boys in tow, he'd pay a visit to Phillip Yip and Goro's lawyer.

It was shaping up to be an interesting night.

Dreamtime

They had fallen asleep in each other's arms, on the bedding in the deserted building where Gahzee had first found Lisa. When he opened his eyes, they were lying on green grass, the sky blue above them, the air so clean it hurt his lungs. Lisa stirred beside him, then sat up, blinking. She stared around herself with wide-eyed wonder.

"Where . . . where are we?"

"Dreamtime," Gahzee said.

In the Enclave it took ritual to cross over to Dreamtime. But ever since he'd left the Enclave, the borders between the Third World, the world of men, and Dreamtime had grown so thin that he never knew when he'd cross over. And Lisa's presence here with him now—what did that mean?

"Is it . . . real?" Lisa asked.

"Depends on how you define real. It's here and now. We're experiencing it. It's not a part of the three-dimensional world in which we usually find ourselves, but it's certainly very much present—don't you think?"

Lisa nodded. "I've never seen shit like this before—only on the vids, and then it's all synth anyway, right?"

She didn't wait for him to answer. She stood up and stretched, then did a slow happy pirouette. Gahzee leaned on one elbow, content to simply take in her trim figure, the stretch of her skin across her ribs, the firm bounce of her breasts. She rubbed her feet on the grass.

"It feels so weird." She turned to look at him. "Is this what the Claves are like?"

Gahzee nodded.

"How could you ever have left 'em?"

He stared to answer, to speak of the duty a *medé* had to his People, but she cocked her head suddenly.

"What's that?"

Now Gahzee heard it as well. "Drums," he said. "Sacred drums speaking to the *animiki*—the grandfather thunders." He rose to his feet, as naked as his companion. "Come," he added, taking her hand. "Let's see whose hands are speaking."

Lisa held back. "I dunno. It's kinda spooky."

"Don't be afraid. This is the realm of the Kachina-hey—the dream teachers. There's nothing to fear."

But then he remembered Whiskey Jack, gambling with the Great Gambler. No danger? If Whiskey Jack hadn't won the game . . .

"Whatcha thinking about?" Lisa asked.

"Old dreams. Come. We'll go carefully."

Still reluctant, she let him lead her in the direction of the drumming. Leaving the meadow, they cntered a forest of tall old pines. The wind sighed in the upper boughs. Sunbeams descended in a cathedral effect through openings high above. Under their bare feet, the needle carpet was spongy and soft.

"Now I understand what you meant about a place having Beauty," Lisa said at his side. "I've never been anywhere so wonderful before. It's like . . . I dunno. Makes you wonder how anybody could ever let it all get fucked up—the way things are now, you know?"

"Thoughtlessness," Gahzee replied softly. "Men lost respect for their Mother. They abandoned her. Most never even realized their mistake in doing so. They went on to make more war, to spoil the very earth itself."

"What are they like—these Kachina-hey?"

Gahzee thought for a moment. "Mysterious," he said finally. "Like the *manitou*, but like men too. Like the Twisted Hairs, only they couch their wisdoms in riddles and tricks, while the Twisted Hairs instruct more clearly."

"So why're they like that?"

Gahzee shrugged. "Because they are Kachina-hey."

The ground was rising underfoot, broken now by huge granite outcrops. Where the sunlight touched the stone, mica flickered and gleamed. Lisa touched the bright flaky metal with her fingers, her face shining with wonder. The trees began to clear and suddenly they were on the brow of a cliff. Below them was a valley. The drumming rose from it, and looking down, they could finally see the drummers.

They were clustered in a group, the brightness of their beaded bandoliers and feathered headdresses a riotous splash of colour against the deeper green of the meadow grass and forest. Long lines of dancers wove intricate patterns, stamping their feet to the solemn rhythm of the drums. Chanting rose up above the rumbling beat.

Lisa suddenly gripped his arm. "Those people . . ." she began.

But Gahzee had already seen. "Dead men," he said.

And not just men. There were women and children. Elders and babes so young they were still carried in cradle boards upon the backs of their parents. All dead. A dance of the dead.

Their flesh was the ghostly white of death. They were parodies of living people. Stalking Death had walked among them.

"Gahzee . . . I'm scared."

The dancers were turning their faces upward, looking to the top of the cliff where they stood. Gahzee could see the dark hollows of their eyes, the gaunt cheeks. Their chanting grew more plaintive. Deep sorrows ran through the rhythm of the drums.

"Gahzee . . ."

He looked to where the drummers played in a circle. In the center stood a banner that the breeze unfurled in lazy flaps. Gahzee recognized the symbols upon it, the tribes they represented.

"Maniwaki Enclave," he said. "Dead . . . all of them dead."

Lisa's fingers were still tight on his arm. He turned to face the forest.

"Why are you showing me this?" he cried. "Is this the present, or has it yet to occur?"

The only sound was that of the ghostly drums and the chanting that came up from the valley below them.

"Answer me!" Gahzee cried.

"I don't want to be here anymore," Lisa said. "Take us back."

I never brought us here, he wanted to say to her, but he merely nodded.

They entered the forest, but it was changed now. No longer peaceful. No longer a place of beauty. Shadows moved in their peripheral vision. A sense of foreboding lay over the gloom, settling inside them. The sound of the drumming and the chants followed them, the volume undiminished for all the steps they took away from the valley.

When they reached the meadow where they had arrived, the sky was overcast, thick with dark clouds. Thunder rumbled. Beskinekkwam, the thunder that comes with a sharp crack and sets fire to trees and lodges. The downpour came and they remained under the boughs at the forest's edge, watching the sheets of rain cross the meadow. Beskinekkwam cracked loudly in the sky directly above.

"Why are we here?" Lisa asked. "What are we supposed to learn from this?"

"It's a vision," Gahzee said, his voice flat. "The Kachinahey are showing us what's become of Maniwaki Enclave."

"Those . . . those dead people back there . . . ?"

Gahzee nodded. He reached out his hand and gently closed her eyes, then held her against him.

"We've seen enough," he said to the rain and the forest.

He spoke not to Lisa, but to the Kachina-hey.

Thunder cracked. The rain still fell in sheets. The drumming and chants of the dead never diminished.

Gahzee closed his eyes as well.

"Enough," he said again, softly now.

Vertigo came upon him and then he was opening his eyes and the vast ceiling of the building where they took shelter was above him. Lisa lay wide-eyed and frightened beside him.

"Believe me," he said. "It's not always so."

But he had to wonder. If the People of Maniwaki Enclave were all dead, if somehow the Outlanders had found a way to breach the Enclave's barriers, then was anyone safe anymore? Would Mother Earth's last defenses fail and the People die, their flesh turned to dust, that dust cast to the wind? No more the sacred Walks. No more the path with heart. Only desolation to remain?

And the Dreamtime. Would it then reflect only death and dying too with no one but the Kachina-hey to walk its visions?

At this moment, with the memory of that drumming still sounding in his ears, it all seemed very possible.

He held Lisa more tightly.

Eighteen

~1~

Shigehero Goro sat in the *seiza* position in the middle of his *dojo*—on his knees in calm repose. The great bulk of his body was clothed in padded black canvas sweatpants and a kimono-styled jacket. Today he worked with a *bokken*—a wooden practice sword. His right hand rested on his right knee. His left clasped the *bokken* just above where, if the wooden sword had been a katana, the hilt and blade would meet.

Four of his *kobun* approached from the rear, straw sandals silent on the hardwood that covered the *dojo*'s floors. Three wielded the wooden practice swords. The fourth had a *naginata*. The halbard had a curved end for cutting and stabbing, while the butt of the weapon was used as a staff.

Goro sat with his eyes closed. Through the sharpness of his *ki* he knew the position of every man in the room—from his four attackers, to the lieutenant who sat on his haunches by the door, watching the practice session. This awareness was so natural for Goro—almost second nature—that he was contemplating his parting speech with Kishi Tano rather than the imminent attack.

"The security force here needs to be taught a lesson in manners," Tano had said. "I am most sorry that my influence has been of no help to you, Shigehero."

In truth, Goro knew, Tano was embarrassed. Ho Anzen had made him lose face.

"I will see that it is done," he had said.

Tano touched his arm. "I know you will. You are one of the last true yakuza, Shigehero Goro—a source of great pride to this old man."

"You honour me."

"As you honour the Yakuza Code. I will do what I can upon my return to Toronto where my influence is undiminished by such *neijin*, but we must move quickly. We have made a great investment in this attempt to acquire the Claver holding. If we fail, there are those who will whisper that Kishi Tano is too old a man now to rule the clans."

"Tell me their names," Goro said.

Tano smiled. "I welcome your loyalty, Shigehero, but such a course is not necessary at this time. Find that stolen chip—that must be our first priority."

Goro gave a quick nod of acceptance. "I will do so," he said. "If I fail, I will rip my belly open and die."

"That will not be necessary," Tano said, "for you will not fail, *neh?*"

The curved end of the *naginata* came whistling for Goro's head, but he was no longer there. He rose and drew his *bokken* in one smooth movement. The wooden sword deflected the blow of the *naginata*—had it been a katana, the sword's blade would have broken under the impact. With the same motion, Goro turned slightly, reversed his grip on the *bokken* and drove its point into the stomach of the nearest of the swordsmen. The man dropped to the floor, gagging.

The other two swordsmen came in from either side, but

Goro, despite his bulk, moved like liquid. A sweeping blow downed the one on his right. He spun lightly, *bokken* rising to catch the downward blow of the man on his left. They strained for one moment, faces close, the wooden swords grinding against each other, then Goro's superior strength won over.

He gave a push, throwing the swordsman off balance, then brought the sword down on his assailant's shoulder. If the *kobun* hadn't been wearing chest armor of black lacquered bamboo and rawhide, the blow would have broken bones. A second blow knocked the man to the floor. Goro's *bokken* spun in his hand. He faced the last man's attack, catching the descending sweep of the *naginata* and deflecting the blow. Turning his back to the man, he stabbed the *bokken* behind him, under his arm. The end of the wooden sword caught the man in his solar plexus and he dropped to the floor.

All in all, the attack and Goro's defense took less than thirty seconds. Goro stood alone in the center of the *dojo*, his *kobun* lying scattered about him. They breathed heavily, but shielded their pain behind expressionless masks as they rose slowly to their feet to bow to their *oyabun*. Goro was breathing normally and had yet to break a sweat. He replaced the *bokken* in his belt, handling it as though it were a katana, and accepted their bows with a quick nod. Then his *ki* sensed someone at the door.

"Shirato," he said to the lieutenant by the door.

The lieutenant rose quickly and opened the door. Yamamoto Ishimine entered the *dojo*.

"Yip has left the Ho Anzen complex," he reported. "He has made no attempt to help us."

Goro frowned. The drones had given him an ultimatum—produce Foo's assassins by tomorrow morning, or face arrest himself. Yip was supposed to defuse that ultimatum.

"The men are standing by," Ishimine added.

"Send two to kill him," Goro said. "But make sure they are accompanied by one of the Ho Anzen officers in our employ. And be certain that there is no question but that it was a yakuza assassination."

"Hai."

If Ho Anzen wanted war, Goro thought as Ishimine left to implement his orders, then war the Goro Clan would give them.

~ 2 ~

Miko lay languorously on her bed, breasts taut, hands and feet reaching for headboard and endboard in a delicious stretch. Satisfaction lay warm inside her, spreading from a heat in her belly to tingle every nerve end. There was no comparison between Phillip and her previous lovers. They had come to her looking for conquest—especially when they saw the Dragon tattoo upon her back; Phillip thought first of her.

She turned on her side and nibbled his shoulder. "So what is this mysterious plan of yours that we couldn't speak of earlier?"

"Regrets?" Yip asked, stroking the long length of her body, fingertips trailing from shoulder to the side of her knee.

"*Baka,*" she whispered—fool—and bit his shoulder.

He continued to stroke her, the gentle hand moving up between her thighs. She caught it with her own, entwined their fingers.

"Oh, no," she said. "This time I won't let you off so easily. Tell me."

Yip smiled. "I have an appointment with the head of Denshin Systems—Desmond Jones—who also owns controlling stock in the Jones Co-Op and lives in the squats where he calls himself the Ragman."

Miko sat up, leaning her weight on one elbow. "Why?"

"Because he's our only hope against Goro. Think for a moment, my Dragon Lady lawyer. Not even IBN or Ho Anzen have waged so successful a war against the yaks. If we ally ourselves with him, we might survive."

"And live in the squats?"

"We could move to another Plex."

Miko leaned forward and kissed him. "So long as it would be with you."

Yip returned the kiss with ardor, but Miko stayed his hands again.

"Why should he trust us?" she asked. "You belong to Ho Anzen and I belong to Goro."

Yip shook his head. "We belong to ourselves. That is the trouble with the Plex. Corporate heads, yaks, Ho Anzen officers—these are the people who appear on Fax Vid. Their intrigues and schemes are what run the Plex, but what of those we never hear of? All the citizens who wish merely to live their lives, who become fodder in these wars? They are the ones I want to protect and help. The people like you and I, *kawaii*."

"Darling yourself," she said with a smile, but she was listening intently.

"We are not Goro, or Okado, or Takahata," Yip went on. "What does it matter to us who runs the Plex, so long as we may lead peaceful and fulfilling lives?"

"I agree," Miko said, "but that is only a pipe dream. There will always be the Goros and Okados to run the world, simply *because* men such as you have no interest in power. Do you understand? To reach for power—one already has a flaw in one's character. There has never been an altruistic politician or corporate head, and there never will be one, because the men who could become such have no desire for power. Their lives are fulfilled without it. And those who seek it are already corrupt."

"You think it impossible?" Yip asked.

Miko sighed. She pushed a pillow to the headboard and sat up, leaning against it.

"What you seek is a benevolent dictator," she said. "One who cares more for his people than himself. Nothing else could succeed. But 'benevolent dictator' is a contradiction of terms. Political systems don't work, Phillip."

"If the people ruled . . ."

"There would be chaos—until a strong enough man arose and took the power to rule them. And he would be, or become, corrupt. I'm sorry, Phillip. In my heart I believe as you do, but one has only to view the history vids to see that such a state has never succeeded. To think otherwise is naïve. It is the people themselves who must change, not the system. And it must be *all* the people, or it has no hope of success."

"You paint a bleak picture."

"We are a bleak people—the human race. We have the potential for greatness within us. We are capable of great beauty and good. Yet we are also capable of the most despicable evils, *neh?*"

She was quiet for a long moment, then added, "Perhaps the Clavers have found what you seek. Who knows what goes on behind their barriers? At least history shows that after great hardship—poverty, alcoholism, and suicides—they united to create their common goal. But history also shows that before the coming of the Europeans, many of their tribes were a cruel people. They had strengths within their tribes, but little compassion for any who did not belong.

"So now they have one great tribe, made up of all their smaller ones, but they still have no compassion for strangers, or why would they remain hidden in their Enclaves and leave the world to suffer on as it does?"

"Perhaps they do not wish to repeat their earlier defeat."

"A people of great heart would take the chance," Miko said.

"Would you?" Yip asked.

Her eyes grew troubled. "*Gomen,*" she said. "I don't know."

"I would try," he said. He drew her back down on the futon beside him.

"That is why I love you."

Again Yip's hands began to move upon her body, but this time the entrance buzzer of her *apato* building interrupted them.

"Shall we ignore it?" she asked.

Yip sighed and shook his head. "It might be our expected guest." He glanced at the time. "If so, he is early."

Too lazy to leave the bed, Miko thumbed on the speaker system beside her. It had no vid screen.

"*Hai?*" she said.

"*Gomenasai*, Hirose-san," came an unfamiliar voice. "Please forgive me. I am looking for Phillip Yip."

"Who is speaking?"

"I am Kudo Goseki, a security officer for Ho Anzen. I have an information chip from Takahata-san for Section Head Yip."

Miko left the switch on receive while she turned to Yip. "Do you know him?"

Yip shook his head. "Have him leave it—we'll go down for it later."

"You may leave it in my box," she said into the speaker. "The slot is to the right of the door."

"*Gomenasai*, Hirose-san, but Takahata-san expressly ordered me to deliver it to Section Head Yip in person. I require his thumbprint as confirmation of the delivery."

Miko turned to Yip, eyebrows raised. Yip swung his feet to the floor and put on a kimono.

"The joys of being a section head," he said. "I think Takahata spies on us to find the most inconvenient times to make such deliveries. Send him up, Miko. It will take but a moment."

Miko pushed the buzzer to let the officer in. Tying the belt of his kimono, Yip went into the outer room to wait. Miko pursed her lips, then put on a kimono herself. An unexplainable tension had stolen her warmth, knotting her stomach. She went to the doorway where she could see the front door, but not be readily seen herself.

When the buzzer for the *apato* door sounded, Yip undid the bolt and slid the door open. Miko thought her tension would ease when she saw the familiar dark green uniform, but instead it grew sharper.

"*Gomenasai*, Yip-san," the officer said. His gaze drifted

to where Miko stood. "I'm sorry to have disturbed your evening."

He stepped into the *apato*. From his pocket he took a small box with a sensor on its lid that, due to it programming, would only open through contact with Yip's thumbprint.

It was as Yip was placing his thumb against the sensor that Miko suddenly realized what had sharpened her tension. The officer. She had seen him before. Working out with Goro's *kobun* in the *dojo*.

"Yip!" she cried.

Too late. A pair of yaks suddenly filled the doorway. Yip backpedaled into the *apato* to give himself room to maneuver. The yaks drew katanas from under their overcoats.

"This does not concern you!" one of them warned Miko.

His companion's katana rose up for the first cutting blow. Yip had dropped into a defensive position, but unarmed he could be no match for two sword-wielding yaks with their augmented reflexes.

Miko grabbed the closest thing she could find—in the hands of a trained fighter such as herself, anything could be a weapon. In this case, what her fingers found was a fan that had been lying on the table beside the bedroom door. She snapped it open. The edges of the lacquered rice paper were as sharp as a knife's blade.

The Ho Anzen officer was drawing his Steeljack, pointing it in her direction; the two yaks converging on Yip. Her *ki* was sharp, aware of everything in the room. She cried out, a wordless shout, and moved so quickly across the room that the fan cut through the officer's throat before he had finished drawing his weapon. Blood sprayed in her face, on the walls, but she was already turning to face the yaks.

She was just in time to see the katanas cut Yip down. Then her gaze went red and she attacked the yaks.

~ 3 ~

Lisa sat on a slab of stone, legs dangling, her swagger girl gear on the rock beside her, and watched Gahzee prepare to leave. He had stripped down to a black loincloth. Pulling a jar of white clay from his pack, he smeared his face and limbs with it, then painted his hair parting white as well. He drew white leggings from the pack and put them on. Next he put on his ghost shirt to cover his chest; it too was beaded and quilled in a black and white pattern. His medicine belt hung on the right side of his belt, a three-and-a-half-decimeter blade hung on the left.

Lisa looked at the knife. "How come you never brought any high tech gear outta the Clave when you left?"

"For the same reason I have to recover the chip and see that the flyer is destroyed," he replied. "We can't let any of our tech fall into Outlanders's hands where they could duplicate it and use it against us."

He crouched beside the fire and taking ashes, added black streaks over his nose and eyes.

"You look like a ghost."

"Tonight I must be a ghost," he said. "The ghost shirt will protect me from harm in battle. It will call to the spirits of my ancestors, that they may find me more readily."

"It's all kinda spooky," Lisa said.

Neither of them mentioned the Dreamtime they had shared, but it lay there between them all the same.

"White and black are wolf colours," Gahzee explained. "White for the north and winter, when the wolves rule the forest; black for the west and Stalking Death."

"I thought you said your totem was the turtle."

"It is. But Makinak is a Medicine totem of messages, of communication. Tonight we go to hunt, so I must call upon his brother Myeengun, to help me stalk as a wolf would."

"I thought Stalking Death was an enemy."

When he turned his face to her, Lisa shivered. In the fading light, he looked too much like a creature from a monster vid. No longer quite human.

"Tonight I *am* Stalking Death," he said.

Lisa swallowed drily. "Maybe Makinak's my totem too," she said, trying to keep her tone light. "You know, 'cause I'm a messenger? Or can I have a totem? I mean, I'm not like one of the People or anything . . ."

"I have come to believe since I left the Enclave," Gahzee said, "that there is but one People and we are all a part of that tribe."

Lisa kept twisting her fingers where they lay on her lap. He'd been so solemn . . . so stern, ever since they'd come back from the Dreamtime. She'd thought she was getting to know him, but right now he was more of a stranger than he'd ever been. He was so distant. Whenever he spoke, it sounded more like he was reading some prepared text from an instructional disc.

"I know what we're doing is . . . important to you, and to the People," she said. "I just wonder what . . . I mean, what about you and me?"

The ghost face seemed to soften for a moment. "*Quaheystamaha,*" he said.

"Really?"

"Never doubt it."

"I'm not trying to be pushy or anything," Lisa said. "It's just . . . well, if we don't make it back . . ."

Gahzee crossed the room to where she sat and crouched in front of her, head just above the level of her knees. He had to tilt his head to look her in the face.

"I'm sorry, Lisa. Usually when the People prepare for battle, there is a ceremony to see them off. War Dances. Sacred smoke. Hands speaking to the *animiki* through the voices of our drums. It helps us to concentrate on the difficult task at hand—to focus all of our attention upon it, that we may do our best and prevail." He paused and gave her a questioning look. "I'm not familiar with your customs. Are they different?"

"Well, yeah. Sorta. Rats don't really go to war. If there's a fight, it just happens all of a sudden, you now?"

"I see. I didn't mean to make you feel ignored today . . ."

"It wasn't that," Lisa said quickly. "I knew you were getting ready—stepping onto some kinda Wheel. I just . . . I dunno. I just wanted to know how you felt in case . . . well, something happens to us tonight and we don't . . . you know, come back."

"You're scared?"

She nodded.

"I am too."

Her eyes widened. But before she could speak, he lifted a finger and placed it against her lips.

"*Quaheystamaha,*" he said again, then he rose to his feet. Taking a coil of rope that lay by his pack, he wrapped it around his waist. "It's time to meet the Ragman," he added.

Lisa stood up beside him. "Me too," she said, as she adjusted the way her Steeljack was digging into her armpit. "You know—*quaheystamaha.*"

A brief smile touched Gahzee's ghost face, then he turned to where Nanabozho was sitting by the Usaijin.

"Hey, brother," he said. "Do you hunt tonight as well?"

The coyote stood up and padded to the door where he turned and cocked his head as if to say, Are you coming? His blue eye studied them.

Lisa laughed to look at him. "Sometimes it's just like he knows what we're saying, isn't it?"

Gahzee nodded. "I think he's a Kachina-hey," he said. "This is only the shape he wears in the Third World."

Lisa gave the coyote a hard look, but he turned and disappeared out into the gathering dusk. Gahzee started the Usaijin and then they were off as well, heading for their rendezvous with the Ragman. Lisa held Gahzee's bow and the half-dozen arrows he'd finished making earlier in the day. Her other arm was around Gahzee's waist, holding tighter then the ride required.

~ 4 ~

Even with his augmented reflexes, the closest yak turned too slowly. Miko was pure fluid motion as she closed the distance between them. The fan licked out and half-severed his wrist from his arm. She caught his katana in her left hand as it fell from suddenly numbed fingers. The fan licked out a second time, darting for the yak's throat. It cut through the flesh, but she was no longer looking at him. The sword in her left hand rose to meet the descending blade of the second yak's katana.

She deflected his blow. Sparks flew as the blades screeched against each other. She stepped back, two quick paces. The fan dropped from her right hand. She gripped the hilt of the katana with both hands and assumed a ready position. Standing perfectly motionless, she waited. Her kimono had slipped slightly on one shoulder, revealing a part of her tattoo.

The yak's eyes widened slightly at that, then he streaked towards her. He was fast, as he should be with his augmented reflexes, but Miko's movement was a blur. She sidestepped, her katana descending. The first blow severed the yak's sword hand from his wrist. The upstroke that followed, removed the left hand. Then she drove the blade into the center of his chest, the tempered steel skewering him.

They were face to face for a long moment, until she jerked the blade free and he collapsed to the floor.

Miko's sword arm lowered until the bloody tip of the katana touched the floor. She breathed slowly, eyes slightly glazed. She let the katana fall. The rug was crimson with blood. Her face, her hair, her kimono and body were splattered with it. Slowly she sank down beside Yip, sitting on her haunches.

She put a trembling hand to the side of his throat.

Dead.

She lowered her head and kissed his cooling lips, then straightened once more.

Dead.

She closed his eyes and touched his wound with a light butterfly touch, bringing her fingers to her lips. The blood was salty against her tongue.

Dead.

She rose slowly to her feet and crossed the room to where a lacquered wooden trunk stood below the window. Sweeping the ornaments from its lid, she opened it and withdrew a set of *daisho* in worn wooden sheaths. She brought the shorter *wakizashi* back to Yip's body and sat upon her haunches once more.

Her kimono fell free with a shrug of her shoulders. The short sword came out of its sheath with a click, followed by the sound of tempered metal drawn against wood. She held the *wakizashi* by its hilt with both hands, reversed so that the blade was turned inward, its true edge touching her belly.

"Forgive me, Phillip," she said softly, "but how can I live without you?"

Female *seppuku* had its own rituals. A woman would first kneel in *seiza*, then tie a string for her obi tight around her knees so that when she died she would fall over in a tidy, elegant bunch. She stabbed the heart, not the stomach.

But while Miko was a woman, she was yakuza as well. As much tied to the ancient codes through the teachings of her father, as Goro was through the heritage that his father had passed on to him. There was no honour in this *seppuku*, for she had forsworn honour long ago when she let Goro rule her life. Had she moved against him sooner, had she denied him, Phillip would not lie dead here in her *apato*.

Goro.

Heat burned between her temples at the thought of the *oyabun* of the Goro clan. A read haze touched her sight.

She slowed her breathing until she was calm once more, her *ki* sharp and aware of everything. The dead men. The sharp metal against her skin.

Her mind cleared of the rage. The cool fire of her *sei*, her calm, filled her. Her mind became like water, freed of the four sicknesses: surprise, fear, doubt, and indecisiveness.

Goro.

Her gaze settled on Yip's dead features.

"I will kill him for you, Phillip," she said.

But there was still *giri* owed to Phillip Yip. A debt incurred that Goro's death alone would not atone for.

The *wakizashi* went back into its sheath, the hilt locking with a sharp snick. She returned to the wooden chest, bringing a smaller knife and two handkerchiefs—one cotton, one silk—back to where Yip's body lay. She lay the handkerchiefs aside and drew the knife from its wooden sheath.

Giri. Obligation.

A yakuza would die for his *oyabun* if he had failed him. A yakuza would die for a wrong incurred against a brother-in-arms. Or he could offer *yubitsume*—the ritual removal of the little finger.

Miko took a deep breath, then placed her left fist on the floor, the little finger extended. Sticking the point of the blade beside the first joint, she quickly pushed the knife down. The sharp crack of the bone as the knife sliced through it was loud in the silent room. The cleanly severed finger lay on the floor.

The pain was a sharp fire that raced up her arm, screaming up her nerve until it touched the cool flame of her *sei*. Face white, with her left hand dripping blood onto her thighs, Miko picked up the cotton handkerchief. Wrapping it around her bleeding hand, she clenched the cloth into a fist. With her right hand she wrapped the severed finger in the silk handkerchief, carefully folding each corner of the cloth over it. Blood stained the white silk in a pattern like a flower opening its petals.

Bowing deeply, forehead against the floor, she pushed the red and white offering across the floor to Yip's corpse.

"Please accept this token of my apology," she said.

She held her bow for long moments, not expecting a response, expecting nothing. Then slowly she straightened once more, both hands in her lap in the formal position, her back perfectly straight, gaze rigid.

She let her *ki* taste the pain of her hand—

Remember, remember.

—until the pain was part of her *sei*, her calm, then she slowly rose to her feet and went into the toilet to properly bandage her hand.

This pain is yours, Phillip, she thought as she worked. I will use it when I face Goro so that a part of you shall share in his defeat.

~ 5 ~

"Oh, man," the Ragman said, looking at Gahzee, "I can't get you in looking like that, Jack."

There was quite a crowd gathered at the junkwalkers' yard in the squats Market. Jimmy Poon and his cousin Huai Jen Pa. Sly Bobbie Rye, Linton Zadie, and the Ragman's eleven other bullyboys. Matching them in number was an equal amount of squats rats and chinas dressed as swagger girls. Nobody carried weapons. The Ragman had those waiting for them at his Plex digs.

Bringing the number to thirty-three was Lisa and her Claver, looking like he'd just stepped out of a war party from a *dojin no* vid. The Ragman didn't count the Claver's dog with its weird eyes, but he kept an eye on it while it was skulking around the discarded scrap metal that bordered the yard.

The Ragman took Gahzee and Lisa aside.

"See, this is the deal," he went on. "I was taking you and Lisa through with me, leaving a message with the drones that I was having a squats-style party in my Plex digs. Bunch a my guests were picking out themselves some strongarms and'd be bringing 'em through the checkpoint over the next coupla hours. So we'd get down to our own business, then head back to my digs where the girls'd be waiting for us. Then we hit Goro's. Real simple, Jack—you following me?"

Gahzee nodded.

"Trouble is, the drones won't be letting you through looking like some *dojin no*."

"That is exactly what I am."

"I know that, you know that—looking the way you do, now we all know that. But that ain't the point. I got to get you *in*."

"You and Lisa can go in through the checkpoint. I'll meet you inside."

The Ragman rubbed his face. "I don't have time for this shit, Jack. I want you to go clean that crap offa your face while I scrounge up some gear for you to wear." He looked down at Gahzee's bow and arrows Lisa was still carrying. "And get ridda that shit, would ya, darling? What're you planning to do—go up against a laser-rifle with some handmade toys?"

Gahzee took the weapons from her. At her worried look, he gave her a quick smile, then lowered his head, and kissed her. He turned back to the Ragman.

"Do what you must to get inside," he said. "I will meet you in there."

"Fuck that, Jack. You ain't—"

But Gahzee was turning away from him again. Three quick steps, and the Claver was gone. As though he'd never been present. The Ragman looked for Gahzee's dog, but it wasn't around anymore either.

"Your boyfriend operating on a half load or something, darling?" he asked Lisa.

He could see the worry in her eyes, but she immediately stood up for the Claver.

"He's on a Stalker's Wheel," she said. "Don't worry about him."

"Stalker's Wheel. Right. Whatever the fuck that means."

"Tonight he's Stalking Death. That means—"

"Never mind. I don't wanna know. Let's just get this

show on the road before the Claver fucks it up for all of us."

He returned to the others, Lisa trailing along behind him.

"Me and Lisa are going in on foot, so that leaves a couple more wheels free. You girls can figure out who's going to get 'em. Remember the deal. Remember the address for my digs. The drones are gonna rag you some, girls, but let 'em."

"We gotta take their shit?" Sly Bobbie asked.

"You're not gonna have any problem getting through, Jack—they just like to have some fun with big squats strongarms who can't do diddly 'cause they're on the wrong turf. So behave, girls. Got that?"

"What about on the way out?" Linton Zadie asked. "Can we cut us some drone ass then?"

"Anyone who makes it outta Goro's can do what they damn well please," the Ragman said. "But you might think about this—you'll be citizens, living in the Plex. I'll give you jobs. You can set yourselves up real fine. You want to fuck that up by cutting a few drones?"

Jimmy Poon fingered his Plex ID. "These things . . . ?" he began.

"Don't let no drone see them when you're going in," the Ragman told him. "Going in you're strongarms—hired to escort a bunch a swagger girls to a squats-style party. And anybody that's carrying a 'jack, a knife, *anything*—dump it before the checkpoint. I got everything you need inside."

"But we don't hafta leave when we're finished with Goro, right?" Linton said. He was looking at his own ID card. "With these we can just stay in the Plex."

"You got it, Jack." The Ragman looked around at them, grinning. "Anyone else got any more lamebrained questions? No? Okay, girls. Then this is it. I'll see ya at my digs." He took Lisa's hand. "Showtime, darling. You and me—we're the opening act. You nervous?"

"Yeah."

"Well, put a good swagger in your ass when we're going

through the checkpoint, so's they don't see how you're feeling."

Knowing her mind was on her dumbass Claver, who just had to play things his own way, no matter how it fucked everything up, the Ragman continued to tease her as they headed for the Plex checkpoint, trying to get her to loosen up.

"You're not putting much feedback into my jokes, darling," he said after awhile.

"I don't feel like laughing."

The Ragman sighed, thinking of what lay ahead. "Yeah. Guess I know what you mean."

Lisa paused, tugging on his hand so that he had to stop with her. "I don't really know what I'm doing here, Ragman," she said. "I'm not like your bullyboys. Trouble comes, I usually want to run."

"Shit, darling. Who was it took out two yaks on her own?"

"That was dumb luck."

"Maybe. You want out?"

She shook her head. "All I gotta do is think about Kay and Donnybrook and I know I'm in. And Gahzee's in there now." Sure he is, the Ragman thought. "I'm just afraid of fucking up."

"That's something everybody's afraid of, darling. You got no inside line on it."

"But—"

The Ragman started walking again, pulling her along.

"You're gonna do just fine, darling. Trust the Ragman. When's he steered you wrong before?"

"Hitting Goro's a kamikaze run," Lisa said.

"Well, yeah. There's that."

The checkpoint was coming up and they didn't talk anymore. The Ragman led them into an alleyway where he stripped off his baggy clothes and stuffed them into a sack that he pushed under some refuse. Under the now-discarded clothes, he'd been wearing a conservative grey bodysuit. From its back pocket, he pulled a biomask. The synthskin fit against his face like a second skin, lightening the dark ebony of his features, pulling his eyes into narrow slits. Gloves of the same material changed his hands.

Lisa watched him, comprehension dawning on her. "So that's how you get in and out the way you do. That stuff costs a frigging fortune."

"I got a frigging fortune, darling. Might as well use it for something, right?"

"I guess."

He unrolled a rainjacket then and put it on, pulling up the hood until it fit snugly around his head, leaving just his face bare. He could tell by the look on Lisa's face that she could hardly recognize him.

"Ready, darling?"

She nodded.

The gate was down across the checkpoint, but because they were on foot, they went directly to the guardhouse. Inside the small building, their retina, voice, and thumb prints all matched the information stored on the Ho Anzen computers. The weapons check came up clean, since Lisa's Steeljack was duly registered.

"Making an early night of it, Jones-san?" the drone asked as he waved them through.

"Hai," the Ragman replied. He spoke flawless Japanese without a trace of a patois accent. Glancing at Lisa, he gave the drone a broad wink. "Homegrown is still the best—even when one must visit the slums to find it."

The drone grinned. "Have a good time, Jones-san."

"Oh, I will. I'm throwing a party tonight—squats-style, *neh?* The girls are out looking for strongarms now and should be coming through over the next few hours."

"I'll keep an eye out for them. Do you have a list of their names?"

"Hai."

The Ragman called up the names on his com-link and the drone transferred them onto his own screen.

"If you are free this evening . . . ?" the Ragman added.

"*Gomenasai*, Jones-san," the drone said with obvious regret. "I work all night."

"Another time, then."

The drone nodded. "I would be honoured."

The Ragman returned his nod. *"Ja mata."*

"Mata."

Once they were out on the Plex streets, the Ragman turned to Lisa. "What did I tell ya? Piece a cake."

Lisa shook her head in admiration. "Where to now?"

When she started to look around them, the Ragman knew she wasn't just taking in the sights of her first visit to the Plex. She was looking for her Claver.

"Best bet's to head straight for IBN, darling. If your Claver makes it in, then I guess he's good enough to find us. Meanwhile, we might as well see if we can't lift that chip."

"You got some smartass plan for that too?" Lisa asked.

The Ragman grinned and patted his pocket. "Right here, darling. See, it's all in the way you play the game. You give the fools what they think they're looking for, while you pick up the cash and run. Just a—"

"Piece a cake."

"You got it, darling."

Nineteen

~1~

They stepped like two ghosts through the squats streets, Gahzee and the coyote, walking a Stalker's Wheel. They moved only in the shadows, working their way towards the Megaplex, to all intents and purposes, invisible. Nanabozho appeared to be just another squats dog, running feral—who would give him a second glance? The *medé*, on his Stalker's Wheel, was merely a silent shape, cloaked by the darkness, his personality submerged so that there was no sense of a human presence where he walked, no reason for anyone to look in his direction.

They stepped over rats, sleeping under blankets of refuse or passed out in alleyways. When they reached the strip, they took to the back lanes that ran behind the clubs until they finally reached the border of the Megaplex.

There was no checkpoint here. The sides of the building facing the squats were devoid of windows or doors. Seven-meter-high walls blocked the streets between the buildings. Crouching under one wall, Gahzee waited until his hunter's sense told him that the security officer on the other side of the wall was moving on to the next street.

Unwinding the rope from around his waist, he tied it to the V-shaped piece of metal he'd taken from one of the scrap heaps in the junkwalkers' yard, then tossed it up. The makeshift hook caught on the inside lip of the wall. Holding the rope taut, Gahzee glanced at his companion.

"Hey, brother," he said. "This is where we part."

He stuck his moccasins in the front of his belt, the arrows in back. The bow went over his head and shoulder. Climbing up the rope, his bare toes helped him move more quickly as they found small ridges in the brickwork to propel him upward. Just as he neared the top, a grey blur passed him, Nanabozho, running up the wall like a cougar . . . like an ape. He reached the top first. He mismatched eyes looked down at Gahzee as the *medé* completed the last few meters.

Gahzee crouched on the top of the wall, hunter's sense seeking out the guard, his gaze trained on the coyote.

"What are you?" he asked softly.

The animal made no reply. It turned like a cat on the wall and ran towards one of the buildings. When it was just a few meters away, it jumped down toward a window ledge, to another, then was on the ground. A slight chill rode up Gahzee's spine. This was no ordinary beast. What did it want with him?

He would get no answer sitting up here.

He drew up the rope, changed the placement of the hook so that it hung from the wall's outer lip now, and let the rope fall down on the inside. In moments he stood on the ground himself. He shook the rope until it came free, catching the hook before it could hit the ground. Untying the hook, he left it in the shadows where the rightmost building touched the wall and returned the rope to his waist.

And now?

He replaced his moccasins. Taking two arrows from his belt, he put one in place on the bow, string slack, the second arrow between his teeth. He looked at Nanabozho. The coyote, seeing that he had Gahzee's attention, began to trot down the street.

Gahzee hesitated for a moment.

He thought of the wall, the impossible grey blur of the coyote as it scaled its height. His Stalker's Wheel sensed a change in the air. *Manitou* were stirring tonight. Kachina-hey stepping from the Fourth World into the Third. What concern did they have with the affairs of one Anishnabeg *medé*?

There was only one way to find out.

Moccasins silent on the pavement, he followed Nanabozho deeper into the Megaplex.

~ 2 ~

Miko dressed herself for agility and speed. She wore dark stretch pants and soft-soled shoes. Binding white gauze bandages around her abdomen, she made them as tight as she could without cutting off her breath. If stabbed in the stomach, the bandages would prevent her entrails from spilling out, letting her fight on for precious moments longer. She continued to wrap the bandages, up around her breasts now, to keep them flat against her chest. Overtop she donned a tight sleeveless shirt, covering the tattoo on her back. Her hair she cropped short so that it wouldn't get in her way.

Be like a katana when you go into battle, her father had told her in training. Walk sleek as tempered steel, with no protrusion save the true edge of your *ki*.

Katana.

She knelt before the lacquered wooden chest that had held her swords. It was transferred now into a *tokonoma*, a position of honour. Below the scroll pinned to the wall behind the chest, on a black lacquered rack, were her *daisho*. The dark wood of their scabbards was unvarnished. They looked like a pair of short, slightly curved staves or walking sticks.

Kneeling in the formal sitting position, she gazed at the scabbards, meditating on the history of the paired blades that they hid from sight. She let that history fill her, ridding her mind of all else until her *ki* burned cold inside her, tempering her, purifying her, until she was worthy of the pure steel of the blades.

Failure only occurred when the swordbearer failed the Sword. The Sword never failed its bearer.

She continued to meditate until only one thing remained in her heart.

Giri.

Debt and duty.

She reached out and lifted the long scabbard from its rack. Jerking out the safety collar, she slowly exposed one meter of pure steel. The katana's *ki* rushed up her arm to join her own. The razor-sharp edge was a dark blue sheen set against the pure silver of the blade's flat surface. It was a perfect blade, centuries old, that had been in the Hirose family for generations.

Giri.

Using her thumb for a guide, she returned the blade to its scabbard. It locked with a snick. Bowing low to the *tokonoma*, she rose to her feet and thrust the scabbard in her belt. From a closet she took a raincoat that covered her from neck to ankles. She looked in the mirror. The scabbard protruded, pushing the cloth away from her leg. Removing it from her belt, she held it under the coat with one hand, keeping the coat closed with another.

Again she looked in the mirror. It would do.

She found a hat to match the coat and hide the short stubble of her newly shorn hair, then slowly turned to look upon Yip's corpse a final time.

Giri, she repeated to herself as a new rush of pain arose in her. But she found she could not go.

She walked to his side, knelt on her haunches, scabbard across her knees, gripped in both hands.

"No more *ja mata* for us," she said. She bent and kissed his now-cold lips. "*Sayonara,*" she added softly. It was what you said to someone you did not expect to see again for a long time. If you ever saw them again.

Her knuckles whitened as her fingers tightened on the scabbard. Tears lay waiting behind her eyes, but she could not set them free. Not yet. The pain of her missing finger helped to steady her. It sharpened her *ki*. Kept the cool fire of her *sei* banked with calm intent.

Giri.

Abruptly she rose, and left the *apato*. The door remained open behind her. It didn't matter.

Giri.

She wouldn't be returning.

~ 3 ~

After a circuitous route that finally took them into the Jimu District, the Ragman stopped across the street from a seventeen-story building that pointed skyward, like a tall finger jutting up from the fist made by the shorter structures on the block. The entire front of the ground floor was dark opaque glass. Large windows of the same glass dotted the side of the building in a checkerboardlike pattern.

From where they stood, they could see private security guards patrolling the lobby. There'd be others, lots of others, the Ragman thought, throughout the building. Could be a problem—except they had an invite. Or at least Spook did.

"This is it," he said, turning to Lisa. "IBN headquarters. Giving the finger to the world."

Lisa had grown increasingly silent on the journey, and not just because the wonder of being inside the Plex had left her speechless. The Ragman touched her arm.

"What's the matter, darling?"

"I'm worried. About Gahzee."

The Ragman sighed. "I gotta level with you, Lisa. I don't think he's gonna be joining us."

Fire flashed in her eyes. "If you've done someth—"

"Now hold on there. Before you start cranking up the decibels on your old friend the Ragman, you just stop and think a minute. Think about that checkpoint we went through, about how you don't get into the Plex unless you go through one. Now how's some Claver who don't know shit about—"

He broke off as Lisa's eyes widened, gaze fixed on something over his shoulder. He turned, reaching for the 'jack he wasn't carrying, then let his hand fall slowly back to his side. Standing there in the alleyway was Lisa's Claver, big as life and twice as spooky-looking, all black and white. Like a ghost.

"Now how the fuck did you . . . ?" the Ragman began.

He voice trailed off as he caught sight of the Claver's dog. There's no way he could've got the dog in through a checkpoint or over the wall. Ghosts.

"Did I what?" Gahzee asked.

"Nah," the Ragman said. "I don't even want to know."

Lisa ran to the Claver and they embraced briefly. Holding his hand, she walked with him back to the Ragman's side. Coupla frigging lovebirds, the Ragman thought. It's like we're on a little honeymoon.

"Is this the building?" Gahzee asked.

The Ragman nodded. "And this part of the gig we do *my* way, we got that understood, Jack?"

"You're in charge . . . Jack."

"You bet your ass I am," the Ragman growled, but he gave the Claver a grin.

"How do we get in?"

"Getting in's not gonna be a big problem. They're expecting me, remember? Least, they're expecting Spook. What do you know about Claver tech? You work the machines back home at all?"

Gahzee nodded.

"See, the thing is, I need to know the code that's locking up that chip. I got a match for it—" he pulled a computer chip from his pocket, "—here, that I'm gonna switch for the real thing, but I need to know the code."

"I can't give you that."

"Listen, Jack. They're gonna be sitting right on my ass, watching me work on that thing. I got to break the code on it, or they're gonna know something's up. But once I got it open, I can pop the chip, and jimmy in my own. This thing's filled up with enough weird shit to keep 'em puzzling it out for months. Now do you want your chip back or not?"

The Claver didn't trust him. That was okay. The way the guy moved around with that dog of his, the Ragman didn't trust the Claver either, even if he *was* Lisa's boyfriend.

"Time's wasting," he said. "I got other calls to make tonight."

Gahzee sighed. "It's based on a Wheel," he said finally.

Great, the Ragman thought. Here we go with the Wheel shit again, but he listened carefully as the Claver explained.

"That's good," the Ragman said when Gahzee finished. "I like that. Changes constantly like it's an AI—almost organic. No frigging wonder nobody's cracked it yet. Okay, I got to make a call. Anybody got any change?" He grinned at their blank looks. "That's okay, I got a few hard credits—no way I'm using my card so they can track me down."

He pulled a fake mustache out of a pocket and affixed it to his upper lip. A pair of infrared shades came next.

"You want to change your look," he said as he put them on, "you gotta keep it simple. Not like you, Jack, walking around like a Kabuki clown with all that whiteface on. Now you folks just wait for me here."

He walked down the block to a public com-link. Inserting his credits, he punched up the number of the IBN systems lab. When Izumi Sho's face came up on the screen, the Ragman smiled.

"*Moshi,* Rider."

The IBN head systems tech looked confused. "*Gomenasai,* but I—"

"Did you not request Spook for a 'high-paying puzzle'?"

"*Hai.*"

"*Sa*, I am in a booth just outside your building—on the way to a costume party with two good friends—but I believe I have time to see to your problem. Do you have some place for them to wait while I work?"

"This is most unorthodox . . . ah . . . Spook-san. The job I have is high-paying, *hai*, but it will require a great investiture of your time, *neh?*"

"Perhaps you should let me be the judge of that, Sho-san."

"*Hai.* I . . . *Gomenasai*, Spook-san. One moment, if you please."

Conferring with the boss, the Ragman thought as Sho turned away from the screen. Sho was back on screen in moments.

"*Domo,* Spook-san. Thank you for your patience. If you will come to the building we will meet you in the lobby."

Gotcha, the Ragman thought. He cut the connection and went to collect Lisa and the Claver.

"The dog stays," he began, but then he saw it wasn't around anymore anyway. Right. Ghost dog. He cleared his throat. "We get inside, I do all the talking. You just play the part of a coupla dumb Plex babies—got it?"

Sho didn't meet them alone. Accompanying him were Kenzo Okado and Muato Kamo, the chairman of IBN and his head monkey. The big guns. The Ragman's own companions received puzzled glances from the three. A circle of IBN's private security officers stood all around them, hands on the grips of their Steeljacks.

"*Gomenasai*, Spook-san," Sho said, "but we will need to run a security check on you and your friends."

The Ragman shook his head. "No security checks, no IDs. I will come in and deal with your problem and then I will leave. My friends will wait here in the lobby—I do hope you have some place comfortable for them to rest. As you have undoubtedly called upon me as a last resort—your own techs being unequal to the task—the charge will be 100,000 credits. Hard credits."

"Impossible!" Sho began, but Okado waved him to silence.

"That is not unreasonable," he said. "Only how do we know you are who you say you are?"

The Ragman smiled. "Faith?"

"That will not be sufficient," Okado said.

The Ragman looked at Sho. "One year ago. You were looking for a bypass smart circuit for your Hayai drives. You came on-line with the question and I provided you with the answer: quickslip trans based on biowires. The conversation was, I believe, a private one, *neh?*"

She turned to his employer. "He is Spook."

Okado nodded. "If you will come with us."

"One moment," the Ragman said. He looked at the Claver. "Kazuki-san, give the officers your weapons. And Lisa, your Steeljack."

When they were handed over, the Ragman smiled at Okado. "To show you that we have no ill intentions. Now perhaps you will provide some refreshments for my friends while I work."

Okado nodded to Kamo who led Gahzee and Lisa to the reception area of the lobby. The Ragman followed Okado and Sho down to the IBN systems labs.

The Ragman paused in the middle of the lab, staring at the bewildering gridwork displayed on the various monitors. Mother, if the Claver hadn't let him in on it he'd be spending weeks down here trying to break into this thing.

"I will need a private monitor with a manual operating console," he said to Sho. "Be sure to in-line some recording gear so that I will not have to waste time explaining what it is that I have done when the job is completed."

And so that it'd make it just that much easier for the chip he had in his pocket to do a burn-out number on the recorder. Ain't tech wonderful, he thought.

While techs were bustling to set things up, he transferred the swap chip from his pocket to his sleeve, fitting it under his wristband.

"What exactly are we dealing with here?" he asked Okado as Sho had a pair of techs set up a monitor and console to fit his needs.

"I am afraid that is classified," Okado replied. "Sho has told me that you will not require such information to break the code that locks it."

The Ragman shrugged and glanced around at the hardware. "Interesting system."

Sho returned to where they were standing. "We have been working on it all day," he explained, "but every time we begin to pry free a piece of the grid, the entire formation changes. It acts like a biosystem, rather than a tech one."

"May I see the chip?"

Sho looked first to Okado, fetching it when the IBN head nodded.

"I don't recognize the registration markings," the Ragman said as he turned it over in his hands.

"That, too, is classified," Okado said.

"I see. Do you have a work area prepared for me now?"

The Ragman sat down at the console. He inserted the chip then called up the gridwork on his monitor. Okado, Sho, and a number of the other techs gathered to watch. The Ragman turned to look at them.

"I find it difficult to concentrate with so many of you hovering over my shoulder," he said. "Everything I do will be recorded. Sho may remain, of course, but I would appreciate it if you would allow me the space to breathe."

Okado regarded him for a long moment, then nodded. He and the techs backed off, while Sho drew up a chair.

Give 'em a show, the Ragman thought.

He sat rigid in his own chair, back straight, hands on his lap, eyes closed. After a few moments of faking some quiet meditation, he began to shape the *kuji no in* with his fingers, a series of nine hand movements drawn from the Mikkyo sect of Buddhism that were part of a magical technique to focus the mind through a concrete series of ritual gestures. When he completed the secret tenth movement, he heard the gasps and whispers arising from the techs that stood with Okado.

"Sensai."

"Keisando."

Beside him, Sho nodded solemnly.

Eat it up, girls, the Ragman thought.

He played the meditation bit out for a few quiet moments longer, then opened his eyes and began to work the keyboard. Sho leaned closer, gaze alternating from the monitor to the dance of the Ragman's fingers on the console.

I ought to take up vid work, the Ragman thought as he pretended to work on the code. I'm a born actor.

He stayed at the console for the better part of twenty minutes, then he closed down the system he was working on. He turned to Sho.

"Which is your mainline system?"

"This way," Sho replied.

The Ragman popped the Claver chip from the system, palmed it as he was handing it to Sho, dropping the swap chip in the head tech's palm.

"Have a tech hook up the record to the mainline," the Ragman said, "and then we'll have a look at what we've got."

When the chip was inserted, the monitors flared with a blur of strobing gridlines in a burst that lasted thirty seconds, then the screens cleared and the menu came up. It was still in code.

Read that, suckers, the Ragman thought, and I'll eat the frigging chip.

"It's still encoded," Okado said.

The Ragman nodded. "But the locks are broken. Your techs should have no trouble breaking this."

Again he heard murmurs of *sensei* and *Keisando*. The Way of the Computer. Right. But not for you girls.

"Sho?" Okado asked.

"He is correct, Okado-san. The difficult work is done. We should have this deciphered by morning. It will require the use of all the company's systems, but—"

"Do it," Okado said.

"That will be 100,000 credits," the Ragman told him.

Even Okado had respect for him in his eyes. "It will be waiting for you in the lobby."

Out on the street, the three headed for the nearest Okuda Line station to take the sub to their next stop—the meeting with Phillip Yip. The Ragman grinned to himself, hefting the briefcase that Okado's aide had presented to him when they reached the lobby. Always nice to make a few credits on the side.

"What did you *do* in there, Ragman?" Lisa asked.

"Just gave 'em what they wanted, darling. Always leave the customer satisfied."

"You gave them Gahzee's chip?"

"Nah." He dropped the chip from his sleeve into his palm and tossed it to the Claver. "I just left 'em with what they thought they wanted. It was just the sweetest scam in a long history of sweet scams, darling."

"How long do we have before they find out what you did?" Gahzee asked.

"Well, the recording they made of what I was doing should burn out in about another half-hour. But if they spend their time trying to crack the code on the chip I left—and we're talking random crap here, Jack—we've got until morning at the latest. But you see—the real sweetness in this deal is they got no way of tracking us down. All they got's a name—Spook. That ain't gonna take 'em far."

"I've never been on a sub before," Lisa said as they reached the station.

"You're gonna enjoy it, darling." The Ragman looked around. "Don't see your dog, Jack, but it's just as well. Couldn't ride the sub anyway."

"He can find his own way around," Gahzee said.

He paused at the top of the stairs leading down into the station. The Ragman looked at him.

"You still with us, Jack?"

"What do you mean?"

"Well, you got what you wanted."

The Claver looked from him to Lisa. "That's true," he said.

He dropped the chip on the street and ground it under his heel. With what he was wearing, the Ragman thought, that's *got* to have hurt.

"You seem disappointed," Gahzee said.

The Ragman looked down at the ruined chip. "Yeah, well I hate to see good tech go to waste."

But I'm one up on you all the same, Jack, he thought, 'cause I got the way to break your Claver codes right up here in my head and one thing the Ragman's real good at, and that's remembering.

"You still didn't answer my question," he added aloud.

The Claver shot another glance at Lisa. "You've helped us," he said. "Now we will return the favour."

"What did you think, Ragman?" Lisa asked. "That we were gonna take the goods and run?"

"What the hell do I know, darling?" The Ragman asked, then he gave them another wide, toothy grin. "Let's go meet ourselves a drone."

He led the way down to the sub station.

~ 4 ~

The streets of the Plex were dark and no longer seemed familiar. Miko cut through their shadowed lengths like a katana cutting through flesh. Above her the fouled sky roiled with clouds, threatening rain, but she continued to travel by foot. Each step served to imprint her task deeper in her mind, sharpening her *ki*.

Giri.

Debt and duty.

Giri.

The word rhythmed inside her like a heartbeat. Her missing finger throbbed in time. Memories of Phillip ran through her thoughts, entwined with the heartbeat.

If I asked you to stand by me against Goro, he had asked her, *what would be your reply?*

I was a fool, she thought. But their relationship had grown too quickly for her. A long life without him, a few days with him. How could he have become so precious so soon?

If I leave, Miko, it will only be because you have sent me away.

I would not send you away, Phillip. I could never have sent you away.

The sweet languor of lying next to him after making love. *Regrets?* he had asked.

Never.

The steel of Goro's yaks cutting him down in her *apato*.

She had not sent him away—Goro had taken him.

You were my father's *oyabun*, Goro, she thought, and you thought you were mine as well, but tonight you will truly understand where my loyalties have always lain.

Michi, the road of obligation, had to be earned. The old yakuza knew that. They had a Code. But Goro only remembered the parts of the Code that suited him.

Giri.

The heartbeat drummed her duty inside her. The palm of the hand that gripped the katana under her raincoat remained dry. Her *ki* made her aware of every small movement in the buildings that enclosed the street upon which she strode. She could sense a distant spark in the Plex now—Goro's *ki*. It was a pinprick of fire that drew her across the cityscape. Her lips shaped a cold smile, but otherwise her features remained expressionless. She concentrated on her *sei*, wore her calmness like a cloak.

Can you sense me coming, *oyabun*?

Giri.

My name is death.

~ 5 ~

"Stalking Death walks this city tonight," Gahzee said.

They had reached the front door of Fumiko Hirose's *apato*, but the *medé* turned away, looking down the street.

Following his gaze, Lisa didn't see anything. Then she caught movement from the corner of her eye and saw Nanabozho appear from the mouth of an alleyway across the street. The coyote sat on the pavement, watching them.

"Are you talking about Bozo?" she asked.

Gahzee glanced at the coyote and shook his head. "Out there," he said, with a motion of his hand that took up half the city. "Someone walks a Stalker's Wheel."

"Another Claver?" the Ragman asked.

"No. The . . . intent is similar to that of the People when they hunt, but not the same."

The Ragman caught sight of the coyote then. "What's the deal with the dog, Jack? I mean, with our taking the sub, there's no way it coulda kept up with us, so how'd it know to meet us here?"

"He is a *manitou*—a mystery."

"You're telling me. It's starting to give me the creeps."

"He means Bozo's like a teacher," Lisa said. "From the—" she glanced at Gahzee, "—uh, Fourth World, right? One of the Kachina-hey?"

"I don't need this shit," the Ragman said, turning back to the door.

He took a thin band of metal from the pocket of his jacket and inserted it into the computerized lock, popping its cover. Studying the circuitry inside, he connected a couple of wires attached to the back of his com-link to the wiring in the lock and punched in a number. The front door hissed open.

"I thought we were expected," Gahzee said as the Ragman closed up the lock again.

"I kinda like to make my own entrance, Jack—just in case it's a set-up. You coming?"

Lisa and Gahzee followed him inside. Before the door slid shut again, Nanabozho slipped in with them.

"Aw, Jack. We don't need your dog on our ass."

"Then send him away."

"He's okay," Lisa said quickly. "Let's just go."

She didn't like the tension between the two men. New

friend, old friend. Why couldn't they get along better? Probably because they were both used to doing things their own way, she decided.

She followed them into the elevator. As the car shot up, she held back a little gasp. Everything was so weird in the Plex. Without the Ragman to help them, she knew they wouldn't have gotten much further than the checkpoint. Of course, Gahzee and Bozo had found their way in without IDs. . . .

But the Ragman was fast on his feet. In the sub, while it was all Lisa could do but grab the edge of the seat and try not to freak out too badly as the rocking car sped through its dark tunnel, the Ragman started talking to the other passengers, inviting them to the costume party they were going to, giving them the address. She wondered if anybody would take him up on the invite, and if they did, where they'd end up, because the Ragman wasn't about to hand out invites to his own squat. Not with his bullyboys waiting for him there, getting all geared up for the attack on the Goro Clan.

The elevator came to a stop, the doors sliding open. Lisa leaned against the wall for a moment until her stomach caught up with the rest of her, then stepped out to join the others in the hall. The Ragman started down towards the left, but Gahzee blocked him with his arm.

"There is something wrong in the air," he said. "Stalking Death has been here."

"Yeah, I'm getting the creeps myself," the Ragman said, "but I want to see this through."

Pushing away Gahzee's arm, he headed off down the hall. Gahzee notched an arrow and fell in step with him. Lisa took a deep breath, then she drew her Steeljack and followed the pair. The coyote brought up the rear.

When they reached the *apato*, the door was half-open. The smell of blood filled the air. The Ragman glanced at Gahzee.

"No one is inside," the *medé* said. "No one alive."

They entered the *apato*. When she caught sight of the

corpses, Lisa thought she was going to be sick. She leaned weakly against the doorjamb, Steeljack hanging down at her side, and tried to push back her nausea.

"Ninja work," the Ragman said as he went from corpse to corpse. "See this?" He picked up a bloody fan from the floor. "Nothing but paper, right? But it cut the throats of two of these fuckers all the same. That's a ninja trick—they use whatever's at hand to get the job done."

Gahzee moved to Yip's corpse. "These two yaks killed this one," he said. "The others were slain by Stalking Death."

"That's Yip," the Ragman said as he joined Gahzee. "A coupla yaks, drone lying there by the door. What the fuck's going on here?"

"An assassination?"

"Looks like. Yaks and drones working together? It don't figure. And where's the lawyer lady who owns this squat?"

Gahzee crossed the room to where a sword stood on the lid of a chest. He recognized it for what it was, including the scroll. Only the short sword was on the stand.

"She did this," he said, turning back to the Ragman. "The woman who lives here. She killed these men, then took her long sword and left. It is her spirit I sense that has merged with Stalking Death."

"We're talking about Goro's lawyer," the Ragman said. "But then again, if she was in with Yip, setting up a meet with the Co-Op . . . Maybe she's turned on him."

"What's this?" Gahzee asked.

He knelt by Yip's corpse and pointed to a small folded handkerchief, stained with blood. The Ragman hunched down beside him and carefully opened it up. Watching from the door, Lisa lost her battle with her stomach. She turned and threw up when she saw the severed finger lying in the center of the white silk. It was small. A woman's finger.

"*Yubitsume,*" the Ragman said.

"What is that?"

"The ritual removal of the little finger. Yaks use it to earn back their honour. If whoever you owe the debt to doesn't accept it, the guy handing it out commits *seppuku*—ritual suicide. It's considered really bad form not to accept it."

"It appears that the woman was offering her finger to this dead man—Yip."

"Uh-huh. And that means I can figure out where she's gone—after Goro."

"I didn't realize that there were women in the ranks of the yakuza," Gahzee said.

"Neither did I, Jack. Lemme think about this for a moment. Maybe there's something here we can use."

Gahzee left him by the corpse and joined Lisa. He took her Steeljack from her hand and replaced it in its holster, then put his arm around her shoulders and led her deeper into the *apato*, looking for a washroom. When he found it, he sat Lisa down on the closed toilet seat and removed her swagger girl mask. Dampening a cloth, he used it to wipe her face and brow. On the floor by their feet, he spied another bloody handkerchief. He kicked it back behind the toilet with one foot.

"Will you be all right?" he asked, going down on one knee to bring his face level with hers.

Lisa nodded slowly. "And I . . . I thought things were weird in the squats," she tried to joke.

Her face was very pale—almost as pale as the white clay Gahzee wore. Her legs felt all rubbery. When she thought of the corpses in the other room . . .

"I don't think I'm cut out for this," she said. "I'm way outta my league."

"It's nothing to be ashamed of," Gahzee told her. "We were put on this earth to care for our brothers and sisters—not kill them. Be proud. You have a pure heart."

If she wasn't feeling so rotten, Lisa would have laughed. "I'm not pure, Gaz. I've done a lot of shit I'm not proud of."

"But you feel regret for those mistakes, don't you?"

"Well, yeah. Most of them."

"That is the difference between the pure-hearted and the evil. The latter has no regrets. They do not even consider what they do to be wrong."

"I guess."

"Rest here for a few moments until we are done in the other room. I'll come and get you when we are ready to leave."

"Okay."

She didn't want him to go. She wanted to be babied, to be held, and told that what had happened to those men out there wasn't going to happen to her, but she let him go. If what they had between them was going to work, she had to stand as tall as he did. She didn't want him to feel that he always had to be taking care of her. She wanted him to accept her as an equal.

Be proud. You have a pure heart.

There'd still be room to be comforted. It just had to wait, that was all.

She looked up suddenly, feeling a new presence in the room, and saw the coyote standing in the doorway, watching her with his mismatched eyes.

"How ya doing, Bozo?" she asked softly. "Is that your real name, or do they call you something else in the Dreamtime?"

She reached out a hand, and Nanabozho stepped closer, allowing her to run her fingers through his thick rough fur. He looked up, blue eye's gaze fixed on hers. A sense of strangeness spread through Lisa as she looked into that eye, a feeling of dislocation. The walls of the small washroom appeared to expand in endless directions on all sides. Her eyes fluttered shut, her head sagged, chin touching her chest.

Consciousness slipped away.

Dreamtime

She opened her eyes to find herself on top of a small mesa, surrounded by desert on three sides, the emptiness stretching off for as far as she could see, with mountains to the north. The mesa was round, its edges enclosed by a ring of rock slabs that appeared to have been purposely arranged in the pattern they made. She stood in their center. The mesa top was absolutely flat, tufted with short growths of vegetation that she didn't recognize; the soil appeared to be badly leached. The sides of the mesa fell steeply away, a drop of hundreds of meters. Above her the sky was a desert blue—absolute, not a cloud. The sun was so bright it hurt her eyes.

Dreamtime.

It was the exact opposite of the lush forestland and meadow that she'd visited with Gahzee, but she knew that this place had to be in the Dreamtime all the same.

I don't want to be here, she thought. Not alone. Not without Gahzee. I don't want to see any more dead people dancing.

She walked slowly to the edge facing the mountains,

stopping in her tracks when she saw a small figure bent over in the dirt. A boy, peering over the steep drop, precariously balanced between a rock slab and the cliff face. Her hand rose to her mouth.

He's going to fall.

His limbs and torso were a dark brown. His head seemed strange, viewed from the back—grey hair on a young boy, the head the wrong shape, somehow. When he turned to look at her, her throat went dry. The boy had a coyote's head, eyes the same mismatched colours of Nanabozho's.

A mask, she thought. It had to be a mask, like her swagger girl's mask, but she knew it wasn't.

Dreamtime.

Things weren't real here. Anything could happen.

I don't want to be here, she thought again. What if I never get back?

The coyote-headed boy rose quickly from where he'd been kneeling, tottered, stopped his fall with a hand on the rock slab, and stepped around it to face her. His feet, knees, and hands were dusted with the grey dirt. Cocking his head, he looked at her the way Bozo did, tongue lolling.

"What . . . what are you?" she asked.

He made no reply.

Kachina-hey. That's who lived in the Dreamtime. The Ka-china-hey and the dancing dead. Oh, Gahzee. Get me outta here.

"What's your name?" she tried.

We don't have names in this place. The People name us, but we have no need for such. We know who we are.

His lips never moved—his voice echoing in her head. Lisa swallowed drily. The dust seemed to have lodged a rock in her throat.

"I . . . I'd like to go home," she said.

The coyote-boy ignored what she said. *Look,* he said, pointing towards the mountains. *What do you see?*

"See? I . . ."

Who the fuck *cares*? she thought, but she looked and saw only the mountains.

There were four main peaks. She started to turn back to her bizarre companion, but movement on the sides of the mountains caught her eye. She stepped closer to a rock slab, giving the coyote-boy a wide berth. The distant mountains came into a sudden sharp focus.

On the side of the first peak, there were infants crawling —hundreds of babies—all trying to reach the top. Of the ones that began the journey, only half seemed to make it to the top. Some hardly started their journey before they collapsed. Others continued on, before they stopped moving and went no further.

When she looked at the second mountain, she saw much the same thing, except the babies had grown up now. They ranged in age from toddlers to young boys and girls, eleven or twelve. Where the travellers on the first hill were quiet, the boys and girls on the second were full of energy. They played games as they ran up the mountainside, racing, wrestling, hunting. The range of their moods was a broad spectrum compared to the mountainside of babies, but there were deaths here as well. The survivors seldom stopped to help those hurt. When they did it was to run back for only a moment, then race on again.

On the third mountain, the children had grown older, but they went up the hill with the same constant pace. There were few games there, and little laughter. Men and women began to walk together, though there were still those who walked alone. And they still died on their journey with the same indifference on the part of the survivors.

On the fourth mountainside, ancient women and old men clambered laboriously upward, stumbling and gasping as they climbed the steep slope. In the end, most crumpled to the ground to move no more. While they lived they looked back, shouting encouragement to the stragglers, but they didn't wait either. Some very few made it to the top. There was a heat haze there, a shimmer that those few survivors disappeared into.

Lisa blinked sweat out of her eyes and suddenly the mountains were distant again. She looked at her companion.

Those are the Four Hills of Life, he said. *The Four Ages of Man. Look.*

The mountains were gone. In their place stood four immense carved figures. An enormous hand came down from the sky and plucked the figures off of the earth, one by one, storing them in a wooden dish. The figure that the hand belonged to was so big it seemed to fill the sky. Lisa huddled against the rock slab, afraid to even breathe. The figure's immense shadow covered the mesa top, the sudden shade giving her a chill. Then the figure slowly stepped away, the ground rumbling and shaking under its tread. The shadow pulled away to follow, and there was the sun once more, blinding and bright.

Gone now, the coyote-boy said. *Into the game.*

Lisa sank slowly to the dirt and drew her knees up to her chin. She stared at her companion.

"I . . . I don't understand."

It's part of a Wheel, he explained. *Are you ready to die?*

She shook her head. "I dunno. I don't *want* to die."

If you're not ready to die, then how can you live?

"Look, Kachina-hey-san or whoever you are, just . . . just let me get outta here, okay?"

You know Coyote, he said conversationally, ignoring her again. *They say he made the world, brought fire into it, played a lot of tricks. But one day the Great Mystery came down out of the sky, looking like an Old Man, and he took Coyote away. Old Man left word with the People, told them that he'd send them messages by way of the little mysteries, who'd share his knowledge with the People through vision-quests.*

"But you won't see me and you won't see Coyote again," Old Man told them, "not until the Earth Woman is real old. Then we'll come back, because there'll be need of a change. Coyote'll come first, so you'll know that I'm coming, and when I come, I'll be bringing all the spirits of all the dead with me. There won't be death anymore and there won't be dying. Earth Woman'll go back to her first shape and live with her children, and everything's going to be fine again."

So now what do you think of that?

"Are . . . are you Nanabozho?" Lisa asked.

The Bozo she knew was a coyote. He'd come back. Did that mean everything was going to be all right?

We've already talked about names, the coyote-boy said. *Don't you ever* listen, *Stripe-faced Girl?*

"I don't understand."

It means everybody's waiting for Coyote to come back, but Coyote's here— he tapped his chest, *—already. You go tell Swift Speaks With Thunder that. Tell him to find a Coyote Wheel, hey? He's been shown the visions—tell him it's time to stop thinking so much; time to do.*

"But—" Lisa started to say, only her vision began to swim.

She felt herself falling, off the mesa top, into a black hole, then suddenly she was back in the *apato*'s small washroom, head between her knees, weak with vertigo. She sat up, and the polished fixtures swam all around her. When they settled down, she found herself looking at Nanabozho, still sitting there on the floor in front of her, watching her with his blue eye.

"I'll tell him," she said. "Okay? Is that what you want?"

The coyote merely looked at her, tongue lolling.

Twenty

~ 1 ~

Gahzee could sense spirits stirring. *Manitou* speaking, close at hand. He stood at the window of the *apato*, looking out into the night. Though he strained to understand them, he could only hear the soft presence of their voices, not the content of what they said.

The Ragman stood beside him, also watching the night, speaking from time to time. But it was merely thoughts spoken aloud that he voiced, they required no answer. Gahzee didn't listen.

Finally the Ragman straightened.

"I don't like it," he said. "I wanted to spark a firefight between the yaks and the drones and let them fight things out, but I'm guessing now that the best move we can make is to take the same route Yip's lawyer friend did—sneak in ninja-style. There's no telling how close Goro's working with the drones."

Gahzee turned to look at him. "What will Goro's death really accomplish?"

"Everything, Jack. See, things have gotten way outta

hand now. I'm in too deep. What happened at the Ch'ing-jen Fan last night. Hitting the flyer this afternoon. Ripping off the chip tonight. He's gonna see my hand all over it. I gotta hit him, before he hits me. We're talking plain survival now—never mind what he owes me."

"I understand."

" 'Sides, we get in there, Jack, what do you wanna bet I can plug into his system and find out what happened to that Enclave of yours for you?"

"You can do that?"

"We get in and I get the time, I can do it, Jack. I'll bet that's making you think twice now—right?"

"It changes nothing," Gahzee said. "We were already committed to helping you."

"Gahzee . . . ?"

Both men turned from the window to see Lisa standing at the sliding panel that led to the washroom. Her features were still strained, but Gahzee sensed it was more than a simple continuation of her earlier shock.

He remembered. *Manitou* speaking.

He crossed the room in a few quick strides.

"Is something wrong?" he asked.

She shook her head and kept her eyes averted from the corpses. The Ragman slid open another panel which opened into the *apato*'s kitchen.

"In here," he said. He slid the panel shut behind them once they were all inside. "What's up, darling?"

Lisa turned to look at Gahzee. "I . . . I went into the Dreamtime."

Gahzee's eyes widened slightly, but he said nothing.

"Say what?" the Ragman asked.

Lisa told them what she had seen. "Do you understand what he meant, Gahzee?" she asked when she was done.

The *medé* nodded slowly. "Ever since I left the Enclave, the Kachina-hey have been tugging me into the Dreamtime—not because I seek a vision, but because they wish to converse. They want me to become a Twisted Hair—but not to teach the tribes. To teach all people."

"That's good, isn't it?" Lisa asked.

"Yes and no. Outside the Enclave, I realize that it is wrong to leave Mother Earth and her children to suffer so, while we live in comfort behind our barriers. But then I see events such as last night, and what we are embarking on this evening . . . We have nothing like this inside. We have some crime yes, but we have no wars. Not like here. You that we left behind are the descendants of those who let the world fall into its present state. I'm afraid, from what I've seen, that you haven't learned from the mistakes of your ancestors. Instead, you merely repeat them.

"To open the Enclaves, to share our knowledge with those beyond our barriers, I believe would be a grave mistake."

"Bullshit," the Ragman said.

Gahzee looked at him. "Then how are you so different?"

"What I'm doing, Jack—it's got meaning. I'm trying to leave the world a better place than it was when I found it. What the hell do you think the Co-Op's all about?"

"And of course it doesn't hurt that you have everything you could want personally while you're doing so?"

"Fuck you! What I want is a better life for everybody, Jack. Every squats rat, china, tong, black, white, you name it. But nobody's gonna hand it to me—I gotta take it, or things are just gonna go on the way they always have. Or get worse. Now maybe I ain't got goofy shit like Wheels and dog-headed space cadets pumping me up with the good talk, but, I'm. Doing. Something. You got that?"

Gahzee nodded.

"Maybe it could work," Lisa said. "People want something to believe in—something to give 'em hope. Lookit me."

"Yes. And look at your friend the Ragman. Can you see me teaching him or his friends the Wheels?"

The Ragman started to reach across the table for him, but Lisa pushed him back onto his cushion. She turned to Gahzee.

"Does everybody have to think the same, believe the same? Is that the only way the world can work?"

"No. But it helps if people have at least agreed to take care of the world and maintain a certain non-aggressive stance."

"That what you want before you'll share the good shit and help me, Jack?" the Ragman demanded. "You want me to back offa Goro and prove I can be non-fucking-aggressive? And who's gonna keep him off *my* ass? The Clavers gonna fly in some big guns to help this brother? You got some Wheel that you can spin and have everything work out all pretty and nice?"

Gahzee shook his head slowly. "No."

"Then let's quit fucking around," the Ragman said. He stood up from the table. "I'm gonna call the boys and get *my* wheel rolling. We're going in ninja-style and we'll fuck 'em up any way we can. Anybody got problems with that?"

When he left the room, Lisa reached out and took Gahzee's hand. "I'm sorry. I didn't mean to get things going like that."

"It isn't your fault. I think there's a kind of madness in this Outland air and it just makes people crazy. I feel a little crazy myself."

Lisa nodded. "That place . . . what happened to me with the boy with the coyote's head. I have to ask you again, was any of it real?"

Gahzee smiled wearily. "As real as we let the Fourth World be."

"I think you could do it," Lisa said. "I think you could teach rats and chinas to live a better life. I know Kay would've listened. People just need hope. Not the kinda hope that lets them see citizenship and slaving for the Kaisha as the only way outta the squats, but a hope for something that's *really* better."

"I don't know. Perhaps you're right. But it's not my decision to make. The council of elders would have to decide that in the various Enclaves and I doubt, no matter how eloquent an argument we might present, that they'd allow any

Outlanders within their barriers. Don't forget—*I* can't go back in either. If I was the one to carry the argument to them, they would probably think I was doing so for my own personal reasons."

Lisa sighed. "I guess we'll just have to make our own Enclave, then."

Gahzee looked at her. The recent messages from the Kachina-hey went whispering through his mind.

"What is it?" Lisa asked, seeing something change in his face behind the light mask of white clay and ash.

Before he could reply, the Ragman was back. "Okay—it's all set. Let's hit the road. Better get your dog, Jack. You trained him to take on yaks yet?"

But Nanabozho wasn't to be found anywhere in the *apato*. He'd vanished like smoke, even though they'd closed the front door while he was still in the washroom with Lisa.

"Aw, man," the Ragman said. "This just gives me the creeps. What kinda hoo-doo *is* that thing?"

Lisa couldn't resist teasing him. "Starting to believe a little, Ragman?"

"I tell you what, darling. Sly Bobbie and the guys are picking us up, so we're riding 'cross town. That dog shows up at Goro's, I'll give things a serious listen."

"You got a bet," Lisa said, sticking out her hand.

The Ragman shook his head. "I gotta be nuts. But I'll tell you something else, if he shows up like the coyote-headed Jack from your dreams, all bets are off, 'cause I'm gonna be outta there. I'll head out into the badlands on one of them Usaijins and just set up a squat wherever the fuel runs out. Now let's go."

~ 2 ~

Miko was too well known at the Goro Clan headquarters for her presence there ever to be questioned, whatever the time, day or night. The eyes of the guards in the lobby widened as they took in the bandaged left hand holding her raincoat losed—no *kobun* was unfamiliar with *yubitsume*, though, n a woman . . . ?—but they made no remark until the elevator doors had closed and she was on her way upstairs to Goro's penthouse.

Once inside, Miko leaned against the far side of the elevator, cheek pressed against the mirrored wall, breath condensing on the glass. Her left hand throbbed with pain.

Giri.

Her heartbeat continued its measured drumming.

Debt and duty.

She could sense the fire of Goro's *ki* burning in the building above her. Did he sense hers?

Giri.

When she reached the top floor and the elevator door hissed open, two *kobun* were waiting for her. One put his foot against the door to keep it from sliding shut. The other had a drawn Steeljack in his hand. Seeing who it was, they gave her quick nods and stepped aside.

"*Domo,*" she said. "Would you be so kind as to inform Goro-san that I will be awaiting his pleasure in his private *dojo*?"

Puzzled looks touched the faces of the *kobun*. They looked at the bandage on her hand.

"*Hai,*" one of them quickly. "I will tell him at once."

"*Domo.*"

She waited while he walked towards Goro's offices, then turned the other way, stopping at the doorway of the *dojo*. She slid the door open, flicked on a light, slid the door shut behind her.

Giri.

She walked to the far side of the room where she tossed away her hat and raincoat. Her hand was a steady ache of pain. Ignoring it, she used that hand to hold her scabbard, then slowly withdrew the katana. The scabbard joined her raincoat and hat on the floor.

Debt and duty.

She faced the doorway through which Goro would enter and assumed the ready position. Sword held in a two-handed grip, hilt level with her chin, blade pointing outward. Body turned slightly to one side, right foot pointing forward, left foot at a slight angle pointing to one side.

She held herself as rigid as the steel of her katana, but she was relaxed, her breathing steady and regular. Her *ki* burned inside her. Her *sei* cloaked her with calm. The spirit of the Sword filled her. She took strength from its *ki* and in the knowledge that she was fulfilling an obligation long overdue.

Giri.

Not just for Phillip, she realized, but for her mother too.

She held herself ready.

And waited.

~ 3 ~

"I don't like it," Gahzee said.

Lisa nodded. "Me neither. Who says they bring their prisoners in through the front door of the place, anyway?"

"Trust the Ragman, darling. Nobody travels this area at night unless they're connected, okay? And it's the only way in—least it is for us—so it's the chance we gotta take."

They were gathered in the mouth of an alleyway between two warehouses across from the building that housed the Goro Clan's headquarters. Besides the three of them, the Ragman's fifteen bullyboys were hiding in the shadows with them, along with four of the rats who'd been playing the role of swagger girls. There was no sign of Nanabozho.

The Ragman was looking like himself again, raggedy clothes, the dreadlock mohawk, ebony skin making him almost invisible in the darkness.

"I gotta admit," Sly Bobbie said, "I liked the first plan better. Lob a few of those sweet smart missiles of yours at the side of the building, when they come running out, we hit 'em, then fade back and let the drones take over."

"I'm telling you, Jack," the Ragman said, "the yaks got

ome kinda deal cooking with the drones. I don't even think he drones'd come."

"Last night—"

"I don't give a shit about last night. We're talking now, ack, and the Ragman says we run things his way. It's my how."

"I count five yaks in the lobby," Jimmy Poon said, joining them at the mouth of the alley.

He was dressed up in yak gear, along with his cousin Iuai Jen Pa and a rogue Nipponjin who just called himself Kikkawa. He looked the part so well in his yak gear that the Ragman was tempted to check his back for tattoos.

"And we gotta hit 'em all," the Ragman said, "before hey send in an alarm, or the deal's fucked. So are you eady, girls? Then let's go."

He put his hands behind his back and Jen Pa wrapped a ord loosely around them. When the Ragman gave the cords sharp tug to test them, they fell free. He nodded to Jen Pa o put them back in place. Jimmy Poon picked them up rom the ground and tossed them to his cousin.

The four squats girls and a half-dozen of the strongarms noved out. Some were taking positions on nearby buildings vith rocket launchers. Others were going to move in on the eadquarters from the side and back. Poon and his men put he Ragman on back of one of the stolen Usaijins, then the hree machines pulled out of the alley and approached the ront of the headquarters building. Those left behind—Gahzee, Lisa, and the remaining six strongarms—drew closer to the front of the alley to watch what happened.

To the Ragman's credit, everything went as smoothly as e'd promised. On the signal they were waiting for, Gahzee and the remaining strongarms set out from the alley at a run, heading for the yakuza building. Lisa followed behind them, heart in her throat.

What the hell am I doing here? she asked herself as she ran. Think of Kay. And Donnybrook. It helped. Thinking about them stirred the coals inside her, fanning them into flames, but it wasn't quite enough. She was still scared shitless. She'd seen too many dead people in the last couple of days. Somehow, she didn't think a few more were really gonna even the odds.

Then she was inside and it was too late for anything but staying on her toes. The grip of her Steeljack was sweaty in her hands. She forced herself to look at the dead yaks. They got what was coming to them, she told herself.

It still didn't seem right.

"We're going up, girls," the Ragman told the three strongarms in yak gear. "Anybody comes in through that door that you don't know, kill 'em. Things get too hot, you got a choice: Come up to the top floor, or get your asses outta here."

He was the last to squeeze into the elevator.

"Watch where you're putting your hand, asshole," someone muttered at the back.

Gahzee found Lisa's fingers and gave them a squeeze. She looked up gratefully.

"When those doors open," the Ragman said, "there's gonna be yaks sitting right in our faces. Linton, you and Fat Bo get up front here. If we can take 'em quiet with your knives, everything's gonna go so much smoother."

All Lisa could do was crane her neck up and stare at the floor lights as they lit up, one after the other. Then they reached the top floor.

"Showtime, girls," the Ragman whispered.

The doors began to open.

~ 4 ~

Goro came alone into the *dojo*. When he saw Miko at the far side of the room, assuming the ready stance, katana blade glittering in the light, he slowly slid the door shut behind him.

"What is this?" he asked softly.

"Giri."

The *oyabun* shook his head. "Your *michi* runs only along the paths that I dictate, Hirose-san. Put that blade away."

"You had Phillip Yip killed?"

"Hai, so desu." Yes, that's right.

"And my mother?"

"*Baka!* Are you . . . mad?"

But she could sense his *ki* flicker, disturbed by his momentary hesitation, and she knew he was lying.

"Pick up a sword," she told him.

"My *daisho* are in my office. If you will wait I—"

She shuffled a few steps closer as he moved toward the door, a swift sudden movement. Now her left foot was forward, her torso still turned to the right. The false edge of her katana lay upon her left forearm. Her right hand gripped the hilt, close to where it met the blade.

Goro appeared startled by the perfect execution of the stylized movement. She could sense him reading her *ki*, reassessing the danger she presented. His eyes, like those of his yaks in the lobby, widened slightly at the sight of the bandage on her left hand. He too was aware of its significance. The utter clam of her *sei* entranced him. She was in that pure moment of commitment to action—*shin*, the mind tranquil and not attached to anything.

"Giri," she said again.

"*Hai.* I see now."

"There are swords on the wall behind you. Choose one."

Goro shrugged his kimono from his shoulders, letting it fall behind him to the floor. He turned his back on her, obviously unconcerned at the broad target it presented. That she was here, facing him in combat instead of employing a subtler and safe method of assassination, would tell him that for honour's sake, she had to confront him in this manner. The lurid dragon tattoo on his back gleamed in the *dojo*'s overhead lights.

"May I ask why the sudden change of heart?" he said mildly as he chose a blade and turned from the wall.

"Yokeina osewa da." It's not your business.

"It seems very much my business, *neh?* You say *giri*, but

that duty is owed to me, your *oyabun*. *Giri* is not something you can change like a fashionable new dress."

She knew he was trying to goad her, so she made no reply. Her *sei* shielded her with calm. All her intent and will were focused on the moment, not on words. Nothing remained but the Sword. Her *ki*. Herself. And her opponent.

"Shigehero Goro," she said. "I will receive your death."

He assumed the ready stance.

"You will try," he said.

His voice was no longer mild, but hard now, like iron. The fire of his *ki* burned as cold as did Miko's own.

~5~

The corridor that the elevator doors slid open on was in the shape of a T, the elevator placed where the corridors met. There were four yaks straight ahead, none on either side. Linton and Fat Bo took out the two closest, but the other pair were further down the corridor, ready to sound the alarm. Augmented reflexes made their hands a blur as they reached for their Steeljacks. But then Gahzee was moving out of the elevator, walking his Stalker's Wheel.

He notched an arrow, drew the bowstring back—all in one smooth motion. He was so quick that his second arrow was already airborne by the time the first pierced its target's neck. The second drove through the yak's hand, whipping the limb away from his body. His weapon was flung from numbed fingers, skidding down the corridor. A third arrow took him in the right eye.

The Ragman looked at Gahzee with new respect. "Knew there was a reason I brought you along, Jack," he said.

Gahzee gave him a brief nod then went to retrieve his arrows. He had too few to spare any and knew the battle was only just begun. With their kevlar jackets, the yaks presented few target areas. It was likely he'd need every shot, and then some.

"Okay, girls," the Ragman called softly. "Sly Bobbie, you

nd Tembo guard the elevator. The rest of you, let's hit the ooms."

Gahzee stood quietly, his hunter's sense searching, then e turned to the left when he focused in on Stalking Death. Down there. At the far end of the corridor. Only there were ow two sparks, two humans walking a Stalker's Wheel. He otched an arrow, bowstring still slack, and set off down the eft branch of the corridor.

Behind him, Lisa hesitated for a moment, then trailed after him, her Steeljack still gripped in a sweaty palm. The *nedé* stopped in front of a door.

~ 6 ~

Goro nodded with satisfaction as he and Miko stalked each other in a slowly rotating circle across the hardwood floor. By her every motion, by the slow steady coolness of her *ki*, he knew that he finally had himself a true challenge.

"Your father trained you well," he said. "You honour him."

Miko made no reply.

Their blades met once, clanging, disengaged, and they assumed the ready stances once more. Both knew the other wielded a blade of perfect quality. Although Goro's family *daisho* were in his office, he would not allow a lesser blade to hang in his *dojo*.

Suddenly they exchanged several furious lightning-quick blows. Sparks flew and the sound of the blades clashing rang in the small *dojo* like the clang of bells. They backed away from each other again, continuing to circle, measuring each other's reflexes.

Goro studied his opponent. Her *ki* burned as strong and cold as ever, but her skin glistened with sweat. The *yubitsume* she had performed earlier in the evening had weakened her. Already blood was seeping through the bandage. But this was no samurai vid—it could be over in seconds. And it would take but a moment for her to kill him if he allowed her the opening.

As though aware of his thoughts, she gave him one. Goro lunged forward, katana flashing, the bladepoint cutting through her shirt and the bandages wrapped around her abdomen and breasts. New blood stained her. Goro's *ki* flared. She was circling back, eyes hard with concentration. He closed the distance between them. Then at the same time they both launched sudden full-power offensive blows.

Instantly they saw that the other's blow was fatal. They converted in mid-strike to defensive blows, swinging with all their strength. Their katanas met in a clash of sparks and a deafening clang, but Goro's strength was the superior. Miko's sword was torn from her hand and went sailing through the air. Out of reach.

They faced each other, two meters apart. Miko's eyes were narrowed, gauging the distance to her blade, her ability to reach it before Goro struck. They both knew it was hopeless. Sweat dripped into her eyes. Her hand bled. Her abdomen bled.

Goro smiled. "Now, Fumiko Hirose," he said, "I believe I will receive your life."

At that moment the door to the *dojo* slid open. Miko's back was to the door, but Goro faced it. His eyes widened at the sight that met his gaze, widened more when he realized what the intruder was.

Dojin no. Here. In his headquarters.

White clay and streaks of ash masked the intruder's features. He was an image of black and white. A ghost. But the weapon he held in his hand was no ghost's weapon. Behind the Claver stood a swagger girl, a Steeljack in her hand.

~7~

Gahzee stood in the doorway of the *dojo* and regarded the pair. The woman had her back to him. She had a bandage on one hand from which blood dripped to the hardwood.

She had no weapon. That lay on the floor same distance to her left. Facing her and him was an enormous fat man, katana upraised, prepared to deliver a killing blow to the woman. The fire in the fat man's spirit was a molten flame, hot and cold, all at once.

"Stalking Death," Gahzee said, more to himself. Both of them.

"Goro," Lisa murmured from behind them.

That settled Gahzee's target for him. He drew back the bowstring.

"Dojin no!" Goro spat. "Where is your honour? Facing a swordsman with such a weapon?"

"I don't have time for your games," Gahzee said.

"Honour is no ga—"

The first arrow took the *oyabun* in the throat. The woman glided to one side as Goro lunged forward, katana descending. Gahzee had his second arrow notched and ready to fly, but the woman had scooped up her fallen weapon. She turned, katana rising high above her head. The blood deepened in the bandages about her abdomen from the strain. Then she came forward, blade flashing, and the tempered steel bit through Goro's neck, decapitating him.

The head bounced free, across the hardwood, coming to rest on a *tatami* against one wall, eyes staring at them. The headless body spouted blood, then collapsed, the impact of its weight shaking the *dojo* floor.

In one fluid motion, the woman raised her blade back up, assuming a ready stance, and faced them.

"It was *giri*," she said. "For Phillip. For my mother."

And for yourself, too, Gahzee thought, his hunter's sense reading beyond her words. He nodded slowly.

"Fumiko Hirose?" he asked.

She frowned at his use of her name. *"Hai."*

"If that man was your enemy, then I believe we can be allies, if not friends."

"You are *dojin no*."

"And you are yakuza. Yet we have the same enemy and we have shared his death." Gahzee let his bowstring go slack. He brought the arrow away from it. "Put down your sword."

For a long moment the woman merely stared at him and Lisa, then she lowered her sword and sank slowly to her knees on the hardwood. She laid the bloody katana on the straw mat in front of her. The fire that Gahzee had sensed burning in her flickered, banking into a dull glow. Then she fell onto her side.

"See if you can find some fresh bandages, Lisa," Gahzee said as he laid down his weapon and approached the woman.

"Yeah. Sure."

Lisa turned and stepped into the hall and all hell broke loose. She ducked back into the *dojo*. In the sudden burst of 'jack-fire, only one target presented itself to her through the open door. She fired, once. Twice. The yak, who'd come out of a door midway between the *dojo* and the elevator, was still turning towards her. The third fléchette took him down.

Lisa leaned weakly against the doorjamb.

~ 8 ~

The Ragman didn't have Gahzee and Lisa's luck. The first two rooms he checked with Linton were empty. The third had four yaks, gambling at a low table. Both he and Linton opened fire, but a yak fléchette took out Linton. The Ragman shot the remaining two. He was too late. The sound of the exploding fléchettes was too loud in the quiet building. He heard doors opening, voices raised in alarm, and then he and his men were in the middle of a firefight.

By the time it was over and they'd cleaned out the last of them, there were only five of the Ragman's party left, not including Gahzee and Lisa. And nobody'd spotted Goro yet.

"If that fucker's not here," the Ragman muttered to Sly Bobbie, "we've had it."

Without their *oyabun* there could be enough confusion amongst the yaks for the Ragman still to get his people out of the headquarters. But if Goro was alive to coordinate a counter-strike, then everything would have been for nothing.

He holstered his Steeljack, then looked down the corridor to see Lisa cautiously emerging from a room at the far end.

"You guys okay, darling?" he called.

Lisa nodded. "We need bandages. Gahzee and Hirose killed Goro, but she's hurt."

Goro was dead?

"Maybe there is a god," the Ragman said. "Help her out, Sly Bobbie. I want to check out Goro's office. The rest of you, split up. Half stay here with the elevator—fuckers could come crawling up the shaft for all I know, the rest of you guard the stairs."

"What about the guys in the lobby?" Fat Bo asked. "If the alarm got out past this floor, they'll have yaks crawling all over their ass."

"I'll give 'em a call from Goro's office. Now c'mon, girl. Let's get some men on that stairwell."

~ 9 ~

Miko's wounds were not as bad as the amount of blood made them seem. Gahzee carried her out of the *dojo* into the first vacant room where he stitched closed the cut on her abdomen and bandaged it, then rebandaged the hand. He took powdered herbs and mushrooms from his medicine pouch and stirred them into the bowl of water that Lisa had heated up for him. With Lisa holding the bowl to Miko's lips, and Gahzee supporting her and rubbing her throat to make her swallow, they got most of it down.

He laid Miko back down on the futon, touched a hand to her brow. No fever.

"Not much else we can do," he said.

"She's gotta be something else," Lisa said, "taking on Goro, one on one like she did."

"She was on a Wheel," Gahzee said. "Stalking Death

rode inside her body. Will you stay with her? I want to speak to the Ragman."

Lisa nodded.

Gahzee held her face in his hands and kissed her. "Are you all right, Lisa?" he asked.

"Well . . . we're alive, right? And we did it."

"So far."

"Right. It's just . . . I dunno, Gaz."

"Too much death?"

She nodded again.

"It will pass."

"I mean, I think we did the right thing and everything, and I don't wanna come off sounding like a wimp, but I'm just not cut out for this shit. I guess I'm not as tough as I'd like to . . . you know, think I am."

"There's no shame in seeking peace—the path with heart, remember?"

"I guess."

He kissed her once more, then slowly rose and left the room.

~ 10 ~

"We're in deep shit," the Ragman said, bent over the computer console in Goro's office. "Lookit this."

Gahzee studied the monitor. A bleakness settled inside him.

"The vision was true," he said. "They are all dead in Maniwaki Enclave."

He read how the yakuza had accomplished it, pain growing inside him, spreading throughout his body in a physical reaction to the shock. At length it became impossible to read through the blur of his vision. He'd had friends there. So many of the People . . . all gone.

"It gets worse," the Ragman said. "Fucking yaks are all connected to each other, Jack. They got a head *oyabun*, sort of a chief of chiefs, tying all the clans together, running the whole show."

He looked up from the monitor. "You know what that means? They're taking over everything, Jack. Every Enclave, every Plex. With the tech they steal from you guys, they're gonna run the world."

Gahzee drew a deep, steadying breath and stepped back onto the Stalker's Wheel, putting aside his grief.

"Can you call up a map on the console?" he asked.

"What of?"

"Maniwaki Enclave—the land between it and this Plex."

"I'll see what I can do."

Goro appeared to prefer the old ways of doing things in more than just his *dojo*, Gahzee realized. His system was hooked up to both voice input and a manual keyboard. The Ragman's fingers danced on the keys, frowning as he worked. When the map finally appeared, it was specked with red dots in a circle around Maniwaki Enclave.

"What do those signify?" Gahzee asked.

The Ragman played some more with the keyboard, then looked up at the *medé*. "Yak camps," he said. "They're set up to blow away anything that gets near the Enclave."

"Can you condense and transfer this information into something I can send out over a broadcast?"

"Like an audio data-burst?"

Gahzee nodded. The Ragman did a quick inventory of Goro's equipment, then found the necessary recorder.

"Guess the yaks like sending their data in bursts, too," he said.

He made a copy of the files and transferred them all into the recorder which he handed to Gahzee.

"Goro's got a broadcasting unit here," he said. "Give me the coordinates you want, Jack, and I'll fire it up."

Gahzee hefted the recorder. "This will be sufficient. Thank you."

The Ragman regarded him for a long moment, then shrugged and went back to the files. Taking the recorder, Gahzee left the room and headed for the stairwell.

~ 11 ~

Alone under the starless sky, Gahzee stared at the smog cover that hovered over the city. It was not right that people—any people—should live in a place such as this. Closed in under those dead skies, dwelling in boxes stacked one upon the other. And in the squats . . .

Slowly he reached up and pressed the control of the biochip com-link implant behind his left ear.

"We are receiving, *animkwan*," came the prompt response. Gahzee didn't recognize the voice.

"Prepare to accept a data-burst," he said.

There was a moment's pause, then: "Prepared."

Gahzee flicked on the recorder. The data-burst came out in a sharp piercing signal that hurt his ears, but there was no other way for him to send it.

"Received."

"Please have a ship meet me at these coordinates tomorrow evening." He sent out two coordinates. "Elders should be aboard."

"Not possible, *animkwan*."

"They would be well advised to make the effort," Gahzee said. Then he cut the link. Until he opened it again, the Enclave could not communicate with him unless they met him at the coordinates he had given. What he had to say to them required that it be said face to face.

He returned to Goro's office.

~ 12 ~

"Finished talking to the spirits, or whatever it was that you were doing, Jack?" the Ragman asked him.

Gahzee nodded.

"Well, unless you can call 'em up to give us a hand, we got us an immediate problem."

"We don't call the *manitou*—they come to us."

"Yeah. Whatever. But talking about coming to us, Jack, we got us a whole building of pissed-off yaks underneath us. Somebody put a call out before we finished killing them all on this floor. The boys we had in the lobby are all dead. I've had everybody else draw back and hold their positions. They're waiting for my signal—no sense all of us dying."

"So we're trapped."

"You got it. And it just keeps getting worse. Right now all we've got is the local yaks to worry about. But I intercepted a call someone sent out to the other clans. Seeing's how they're all working together, come daybreak, I figure we'll have just about every yak the other clans can spare showing up here, crawling up our ass. So my question to you is, you got any bright ideas, Jack?"

Lisa chose that moment to come into the office. "Look who's back," she said.

Nanabozho stood by her legs. The Ragman looked at the coyote.

"Where the hell did he come from?" he asked.

"He just walked into the room where I was sitting with Hirose," Lisa said. "Are you ready to listen to Gahzee's teachings now?"

"Can you get him to magic us outta here?" the Ragman asked Gahzee.

The *medé* shrugged. "Why don't you ask him yourself?"

The Ragman gave him a glare, but at this point he was obviously ready to try anything. "What do you say, Jack?" he asked Nanabozho. "You gonna give us a helping . . . ah, paw?"

The coyote merely looked at him, head cocked.

"Aw, shit." The Ragman looked disgusted.

"Can you call up that map again?" Gahzee asked. When the Ragman did, he pointed out the coordinates that he'd sent to the Enclave. "We have to be there by tomorrow evening."

"Good luck, Jack."

"Why didn't you go back to your original plan?" Gahzee asked.

"Which original plan?"

"Call in the Plex's security force."

"I tell you, Jack. They gotta be tied in to the yaks."

"Considering our present situation," Gahzee said, "what have we got to lose?"

"Guess you got a point there, Jack." The Ragman pulled out his biomask and gloves. "Guess it's time for Desmond Jones to make another appearance. Drones'll listen to him a hell of a lot quicker than they will the Ragman."

He started to fit the mask on, then paused.

"Hey, lookit this," he said, pointing to the computer monitor which was still displaying the map he'd called up. One by one, the red dots signifying the yak camps were blinking off. He looked at Gahzee, a question in his eyes.

"It's the Enclaves' doing," Gahzee said.

The Ragman grinned. "All of a sudden I'm starting to feel lucky again, Jack."

Twenty-one

~ 1 ~

As soon as the security officer taking Jones-san's call realized the import of what he was hearing, he had a co-worker put in an immediate call to Takahata-san's private line. In his *apato*, Takahata was transferred to the in-coming call at headquarters.

"*Gomenasai*, Jones-san," he said. "I am Takahata Tomiji, the—"

"The honour is mine, Takahata-san," Jones broke in. "You are a most respected man of our community."

Takahata's momentary anger at being interrupted gave way under Jones' flattery. He studied the face on his screen. What was this man? Chinese? Korean? No matter. He was a citizen, an important man, president of Denshin Systems. And if what he said was true . . .

"My officer tells me that you are reporting the death of Shigehero Goro?"

"*Hai.* His men kidnapped me and some of my guests at a party I was giving. It appears he had a highly secret computer chip he wished me to decode for him and chose this most disagreeable manner in which to enlist my aid."

Kidnapped? Takahata thought. Better and better. He listened to Jones tell his story. Kidnapped by yakuza, he and his guests threatened with death if Jones himself did not cooperate. The timely intervention of Goro's lawyer, Fumiko Hirose who, when she saw that her employer was determined to follow through on his criminal course, aided the victims. The subsequent battle in the penthouse that included the death of Goro and his guards and the unfortunate destruction of the chip Goro had wished him to decode. How they were now trapped on the penthouse floor, merely a few of them left alive against Goro's enraged *kobun*.

"What you tell me, Jones-san, dismays me to no end. We have long sought the end of this criminal, but the legal process is very slow, *neh*? Rest assured that I will have a full contingent of officers on hand to rescue you and your companions from this unfortunate situation."

"*Domo*, Takahata-san. I am feeling most desperate."

"My men are already on their way."

Cutting the connection, Takahata sat back and rubbed his hands together.

"*Domo, domo,*" he said aloud. "*Domo arigato.*"

The monster was dead, his grip on the Megaplex broken.

~2~

Kishi Tano, *oyabun no oyabun*, sat in his Toronto office staring numbly at the display console of his computer. One by one, the camps of Goro and Eisai's *kobun* surrounding the stricken Maniwaki Enclave were being destroyed by the Clavers. Goro himself was dead. All they had worked for was in ruins. And all they had to show for their efforts was a small handful of assassins, trapped in the upper floor of the Goro Clan's headquarters.

Yonosuke Tahara, one of his lieutenants, stepped up to his desk and respectfully waited for his attention.

"Hai?"

"*Gomenasai*, Tano-san, but Ho Anzen Securities have
arshalled their men for an attack upon Goro-san's head-
uarters."

Tano sighed. The taste of ashes was bitter in his throat.
le was unused to failure. But it must be accepted.

"Send word to the clans—no *kobun* are to be dispatched
Trenton."

"Hai."

As Tahara returned to his seat to fill his orders, Tano
alled up the Goro Clan's headquarters. The face of
amamoto Ishimine, Goro's second-in-command, appeared
n his screen. A weak man, Tano thought and shook his
ead. That was Goro's failing. He was too strong. Rather
han delegating to his lieutenants, to allow them to grow in
trength with him, he took too much on himself. That was
vhy he had failed.

Ishimine waited for Tano to speak, sweat glistening on
is upper lip.

"Ho Anzen mounts an attack," Tano told him finally.
You will withdraw from your headquarters and scatter the
lan's *kobun*. On no account will you engage in further bat-
le. We have lost enough."

Ishimine swallowed. "*Gomenasai*, Tano-san, but what of
Goro's assassins? They are still alive, on the top floor . . ."

"You would kill them for your *oyabun*'s honor?" Tano
sked.

"Hai."

"Tonde mo nai." I forbid it.

"Hai."

Ishimine had trouble getting the word out. Tano sighed.
He took pity on the man.

"Ishimine-san," he said quietly. "A wise man knows
when to retreat so that he may fight again. We are not samurai. We do not follow the Bushido Code. We are yakuza.
I need you alive, Ishimine-san, you and those that remain of
your *kobun*. You are the new *oyabun* of Trenton. Shall I lose
you as well?"

Ishimine straightened with pride. There *is* strength in him, Tano thought. Hidden, perhaps, but he will learn to use it.

"You honour me, Tano-san," Ishimine said.

"*Hai.* Now, please, do as I say. *Sa*, it is not merely Ho Anzen we have to deal with this night, but the Clavers as well. This battle is already lost to us—so we need spend no more lives, *neh*? But we are yakuza. We will live to fight again. Now go. Contact me once matters have settled down."

"*Hai*, Tano-san. *Ja mata.*"

"*Mata,*" Tano said.

He broke off the com-link and stared at the dark screen for a long moment. Then he bowed his head.

I will miss you, Shigehero, he thought, most loyal of men. I will burn incense for you, for you belonged to one of the last of the old yakuza families, but I will not lose more than we have already lost in your name. Perhaps the future will allow us to avenge your death. Perhaps our descendants will. In the end, we will prevail. One day we will have it all.

One day.

Sayonara, Shigehero. Your journey is done.

~ 3 ~

"They are leaving," Gahzee said, an hour or so after the Ragman had made his call to the head of the Ho Anzen Securities.

"Who's leaving?"

"The yaks."

The Ragman gave him a long hard look. "How do you know that, Jack?"

"It concerns Wheels," Gahzee said. "Are you sure you want to hear about it?"

"You said you'd listen," Lisa said.

"Yeah, yeah. I know." The Ragman turned away and

alled up his men that were still watching the building from utside. When he got their report, he said, "Okay. Get outta here, girls. You done good." He looked back at Gahzee. "I lon't know about this shit, Jack."

"We can talk about it later. I have to leave now as well, before the security officers arrive. I don't exist in the Plex, emember?"

"You've been like a ghost all night. I like you better without your whiteface."

"Remember those coordinates I showed you earlier?"

"What about 'em?"

"Be there tomorrow evening. I think you will find it to be worth your while."

"I'll think about it, Jack."

Gahzee turned to Lisa. "Will you come with me?"

The Ragman laughed. "You kidding? She thought you'd never ask. Now get outta here."

They left by the stairwell, hand in hand, Nanabozho trailing at their heels. The Ragman looked at the coyote and slowly shook his head. Wheels, huh? Spirits talking. Mysteries.

Yeah, I'll be there, Jack. You can count on it.

Realtime

Somewhere behind the thick cloud covering, the sun was setting. Light leaked from the sky. Shadows grew long. Gahzee and Lisa shared a meal by a fire lit in the doorway of a long-abandoned warehouse. After the long ride north from the Plex, they'd spent most of the afternoon inside the warehouse, lying on their bedding—sleeping, making love, sleeping again. Now, with the night coming, they were waiting.

"Do you think they'll come?" Lisa asked.

"Who? The Ragman?"

"No. Your people. The elders."

"Someone will come."

Thunder rumbled in the sky, distant still.

"*Animiki,*" Lisa said.

Gahzee smiled and nodded. "Bodreudang."

"What's that mean?"

"Bodreudang is the approaching thunder—the People have names for all the grandfather thunders. We even have a name for that moment between seeing the lightning and hearing its thunder."

"What's that?"

"Svaha. A waiting for promises to be fulfilled."

"Like hope."

Gahzee nodded. He fed more wood to the fire. Outside the door, Nanabozho lay, his mismatched eyes gazing out into the gathering dark.

"I've spent my whole life in svaha," Lisa said. "Waiting for something better to come along. Hoping. It keeps you going in the squats, pretending things'll get better. But now . . ."

Her voice trailed off. Gahzee waited a moment, then asked, "And now?"

Lisa gave him a smile. "Things got better. It's weird. There's been so much going on these past few days, everything happening so fast, I feel like it's been a lifetime. I feel like I've known you forever."

"That's what happens when you walk in the Dreamtime with another—after that there comes a true closeness between you. It makes it hard to tell lies to each other."

"*Quaheystamaha,*" Lisa said, obviously enjoying the taste of the word and what it meant.

Gahzee nodded. He sensed movement in the night then and reached for his weapons. Nanabozho's ears pricked up, but he didn't move otherwise. Gahzee let his hand relax.

"Yo, the fire!"

The Ragman's voice was unmistakable. There was room in the doorway for him to ride his three-wheeler through. He was followed in by a number of other machines, driven by the survivors of last night's attack on the Goro Clan and some other faces that Gahzee didn't recognize.

Gahzee looked for and found the pale face of Fumiko Hirose amongst them. There was little expression in her features. She had suffered a great loss, he realized. He had only to imagine Stalking Death taking Lisa from him to understand how she felt. But she was strong of spirit. Gahzee hoped she would allow him to teach her of the Wheels. They would not replace her loss, but they could help her live with it.

"Well, we're here, Jack," the Ragman said, stepping up t the fire. He took off the gloves he was wearing and knel down, holding his hands out to the flames, though the nigh air wasn't cold. "So what's the deal? Kinda a long ways ou to be throwing a party."

Gahzee glanced to where Nanabozho lay. The coyote ha lifted his head to look skyward, then he rose to his feet an melted away into the darkness. Gahzee rose from the fire hearing the hum in the air. The silver shape of a large En-clave flyer slowly descended from the sky and landed ir front of the warehouse. The lights on its roof threw a pal glow all around the ship, scattering shadows.

"Not so much a party," Gahzee said. "More a council."

"Holy fuck," one of the Ragman's companions muttered.

Gahzee led them all outside where they stood in a rough half-circle facing the flyer as its doors hissed open. A ramp emerged from below the door and lowered to the ground. Using it, a number of figures in white, armoured, decam suits descended. A half-dozen of them carrying laser-rifles immediately took up positions on either side of the ship, facing Gahzee and his companions. The remaining four walked to where the *medé* stood.

Gahzee recognized each face that showed behind the glass covering of their decam suits' helmets. His mentor, Manitouwaub—Sees Like A Spirit. The Enclave Chief, Zhawano-Geezhig—Blue Sky. And two elders. Kitchi-Zaudee—Great Poplar. And Mino-Nodiniquae—Gentle Wind Woman.

"Thank you for coming," Gahzee said.

"You may thank Manitouwaub," Zhawano-Geezhig said. "It was he who convinced us that if you requested our presence, it was important enough for us to come."

"What is it that you wish of us?" Kitchi-Zaudee asked. "You have done the People a great service, but surely you do not expect to be allowed to return to the Enclave?"

Gahzee shook his head. He spoke instead of the Kachina-hey and what they had bid him to do in the Dreamtime. He told of the Outlanders he had met, of the strength he saw in them, of the possibilities they held to help the People return Mother Earth to how she was when she was young.

"We wish you luck," Mino-Nodiniquae said. "It is a difficult Walk that you are undertaking."

Zhawano-Geezhig nodded. "Yet why did this require our presence? Could you not have sent your intentions to us in broadcast?"

Gahzee took a breath, slowly let it out. He straightened his back and regarded the elders square in the eye.

"Maniwaki Enclave lies empty," he said. "I claim it for my new tribe."

"Impossible!" Kitchi-Zaudee cried.

Manitouwaub touched the elder's arm with his glove. "Let him speak."

"I mean to go among the Outlanders," Gahzee said, "and teach them the path with heart, but I must have some hope to offer them—hope for themselves, not merely for the coming generations. The Enclave will become a place of learning and rest, a home that we may return to while we travel the Outlands.

"This is what I believe the Kachina-hey have been instructing me to do."

Kitchi-Zaudee shook his head. "You merely want to regain what you yourself have lost. But you knew the sacrifice you would have to make before you left."

"Gahzee," Chief Zhawano-Geezhig said softly. "Perhaps your time amongst the Outlanders has blinded you. Yes, they are people, like us, but unlike us they left the world the way you see it now. Shall we give them the opportunity to do worse? To destroy the safety we have created for the tribes?"

"It is *we* who have left the world the way it is now," Gahzee said. "Others caused the destruction, but it is we who have turned our backs upon it. It is time for us to rejoin the world."

"It cannot be done," Mino-Nodiniquae said.

"And certainly we could not agree to it alone," Chief Zhawano-Geezhig added. "It would require a council of all the Chiefs and elders of all the tribes—and I can tell you now, Gahzee, that they will never agree."

"What a load of crap," the Ragman said. Gahzee had been speaking in patois, so the elders, perforce, had been speaking it as well.

Kitchi-Zaudee turned to him. "Be still, Outlander."

"Why should he?" Lisa demanded. "We got a right to speak."

"But we are not required to listen," the elder told her.

"It's not our fault things're the way they are!" Lisa cried. "We had nothing to do with it. Our ancestors fucked up—but all we've ever done is tried to survive in the mess they left us. Why the hell *shouldn't* we get a chance?"

"Because it is in your genes to repeat the same mistakes," Kitchi-Zaudee said, "over and over again. We monitor your broadcasts—your news reports. We watch from our satellites and see how you do nothing but squabble amongst yourselves in your slums."

"So it's all a lie then, huh?" Lisa said. "All that crap the Kachina-hey told me in the Dreamtime about how things could get better? You're just gonna sit around and wait for Coyote to come back and not lift a hand to help anybody but yourselves? Well, fuck you. Who needs your help."

"You tell 'em, darling," the Ragman said. "They're just a bunch of shitters. I figure our Jack Gahzee here's the exception, not the rule."

But the elders stood suddenly silent, staring at Lisa.

"You . . . have been to the Dreamtime?" Manitouwaub asked.

Lisa just looked at him. "What's it to you?"

"It's a lie," Kitchi-Zaudee said. "The Kachina-hey would never converse to Outlanders. It's unthinkable."

"She has been there twice," Gahzee said. He turned to Manitouwaub. "Can't you sense the heartglow of her Walk, grandfather? Her strength?"

Manitouwaub slowly nodded his head.

"It's a lie!" Kitchi-Zaudee insisted.

"No," Mino-Nodiniquae said. She took a step closer to

Lisa. "It is the truth—an astonishing revelation and one that we will have to study upon. But unfortunately, Gahzee, it changes nothing. Shall we spoil Maniwaki Enclave? You and all those who live here are contaminated by the Outlands. Shall we allow that creeping death into an Enclave? Shall we allow our knowledge to fall into the hands of those who know only war in their hearts?

"We see now that the Outlanders can learn the Wheels and Walk the path with heart, but it will take generations for them to learn the ways well. And the contamination will always be a part of them—locked into their genes."

"So we should merely turn our backs on them?"

"No. We must study new ways to help them. But the Enclave must belong to the People—untouched by the creeping death. This knowledge you have brought can change the way we perceive the Outlanders—it gives us hope that one day the earth shall regain her former glory—but it cannot change our decision."

"It changes mine," Manitouwaub said.

Slowly he raised his hands and removed his helmet. He dropped it on the ground where it rolled to Gahzee's feet. One by one he undid the decam suit's fastenings until it too lay on the ground. Unencumbered by it, he stepped close to Gahzee and embraced him.

"I have missed you, grandson," he said.

Gahzee welcomed the embrace. "And I, you."

"Madness," Kitchi-Zaudee muttered.

"No," Manitouwaub said. "If my grandson has the courage to teach the Outlanders, then how can I not help him?"

"Your grandson strives desperately to regain what he has lost," Kitchi-Zaudee said. "His motives are less than altruistic. What we should—"

"These girls are fucked," the Ragman broke in. He looked disdainfully at the remaining three elders and their guards. "Why don't you get the hell outta here? We don't need your shit."

Suddenly, the sound of drums spoke from out in the night. For a long moment no one spoke, then one by one they turned to look out past the Enclave flyer to the source of the sound. From the shadows beyond the light cast by the flyer, figures approached, seven in all, three women and four men. Two of them carried the drums, slung from their shoulders, fingers speaking against the taut skin.

They were old, but they wore their age with power. There was medicine in their every step, strength in their carriage. Their eyes were so bright they almost appeared to glow. Four were of the People, though their facial features proclaimed that each was of a different tribe. One was a tall black man, his skin as dark as the Ragman's, his face bearing the ritual scars of the Masai. Another was a Maori woman, a thin figure with large brown eyes. The last was a Soyot, a small dark man, wizened like a dried apple.

"Who the fuck are they?" the Ragman muttered.

Lisa took Gahzee's hand. "The Kachina-hey?" she guessed.

Gahzee shook his head. "They are Twisted Hairs."

Thunder rumbled in the sky—closer now than it had been.

"Spirits are talking," one of the Twisted Hairs said. He had the flat broad features of the Anishnabeg, a powerful frame of a body, unbent with age. His grey braids hung to his waist. "They say, 'Gahzee needs a home for his new tribe.' "

"This is not your concern," Kitchi-Zaudee said. "You are the spiritual guides of the People—not their political leaders."

The Twisted Hair grinned. "Hey now, Kitchi-Zaudee. And what are the People without their spirit? What are their poli-ticks? Shall we ignore the spiritual growth of a new tribe of People?"

The elder had no reply.

"Heh," the Maori woman said to him. "Do you think you know better than the *kehua*, little brother?"

The word she used meant ghost in the Maori tongue, but no one misunderstood her meaning. Thunder rumbled again. Spirits talking.

"What will be the medicine of the People," the Anishnabeg Twisted Hair asked, "if they no longer pay heed to the wisdom of the *manitou*?"

"The councils of the other Enclaves will protest," Chief Zhawano-Geezhig said in an uncertain voice.

The Twisted Hairs laughed and they all began to speak at once.

"Protest what?"

"Wisdom?"

"The turn of the seasons?"

"The Wheels of life?"

"The advice of the Twenty Count?"

"Peace?"

"Beauty?"

"The *manitou* have spoken," the Anishnabeg Twisted Hair said. "Through us. Through our little brother. Will you deny their wisdom?"

Zhawano-Geezhig and Mino-Nodiniquae bowed their heads, ashamed. Chief Zhawano-Geezhig unclipped a control unit from his belt and silently handed it to Gahzee. With it Gahzee could now open the barrier that enclosed Maniwaki Enclave.

"Does this mean we all gotta learn about these frigging Wheels?" the Ragman muttered.

Gahzee could tell he was joking, but the Masai Twisted Hair gave the Ragman a mild look that spoke volumes. "Is it so wrong to seek a harmony between your brothers and sisters, and your mother the earth?"

The Ragman gave him a toothy grin back. "Hell, no, Jack. I'm just itching for a spin."

It was just starting to sink in. Everything he'd worked for was coming through. He turned to look at squats rats and chinas who'd accompanied him.

"We're going home, girls," he said.

"It is a hard task that the *manitou* have set you, little brother," the Anishnabeg Twisted Hair said to Gahzee, "but we will help you as we can."

Another Twisted Hair, one with the features of a Hopi,

added, "Begin small. Too much, too soon, makes for a weak foundation."

Good humour ran infectiously through the group. Two of the Enclave guards, both *medé* as well as warriors, removed their decam suits and came to join Manitouwaub. The Ragman slapped Gahzee on the back and bent down to give Lisa a kiss. Lisa held on to Gahzee's hands, happy, but a little scared. The steady pressure of his fingers around her own helped comfort her.

Only Kitchi-Zaudee saw no reason to rejoice. What was, should remain. The tribes had reached out a hand to strangers before, in long generations past, only to have their hands cut from them. Why should they risk the long years of enslavement again?

"You should name your tribe's new home Despair," he said, "for that is what you will bring to the People."

"No," Gahzee said, looking at Lisa.

"We'll call it Svaha," she said, "to remind us of all the time we waited and hoped."

The Twisted Hairs smiled. The two drummers tapped their palms against the skins of their instruments. The Anishnabeg Twisted Hair took out a spirit pipe, lighting it from a coal he kept in a small clay jar. He drew the sacred smoke in, released it to the sky, then let the pipe begin the journey from hand to hand.

From the shadows beyond the flyer's lights, the high-pitched *yip-yip-yip* cry of a coyote arose.

Thunder rumbled, almost directly overhead.

Spirits talking.